Emperor of Thorns

Ace Books by Mark Lawrence

PRINCE OF THORNS

KING OF THORNS

EMPEROR OF THORNS

Emperor of Thorns

BOOK THREE OF
THE BROKEN EMPIRE

MARK LAWRENCE

ACE BOOKS, NEW YORK

THE BERKLEY PUBLISHING GROUP
Published by the Penguin Group
Penguin Group (USA) Inc.
375 Hudson Street, New York, New York 10014, USA

USA I Canada I UK I Ireland I Australia I New Zealand I India I South Africa I China

Penguin Books Ltd., Registered Offices: 80 Strand, London WC2R 0RL, England
For more information about the Penguin Group, visit penguin.com.

Ace Books are published by The Berkley Publishing Group.
ACE and the "A" design are trademarks of Penguin Group (USA) Inc.

Library of Congress Cataloging-in-Publication Data

Lawrence, Mark, 1966–
Emperor of thorns / Mark Lawrence. — First edition.
pages cm. — (Broken empire ; bk. 3)
ISBN 978-0-425-25685-5 (Hardcover)
I. Title.
PS3612.A9484E47   2013
813'.6—dc23
2013004500

FIRST EDITION: August 2013

PRINTED IN THE UNITED STATES OF AMERICA

10 9 8 7 6 5 4 3 2 1

Cover illustration by Jason Chan.
Cover design by Annette Fiore DeFex.
Cover hand lettering by Iskra Johnson.
Interior text design by Laura K. Corless.
Map © Andrew Ashton.

Dedicated to my son, Bryn

ACKNOWLEDGMENTS

I need to thank my reader, Helen Mazarakis, for reading this whole trilogy one chunk at a time over the course of many years and telling me what she thought.

Sharon Mack, who poked me into submitting my *Prince of Thorns* manuscript, deserves another shout-out. Thank you, Sharon.

The good folk at Ace Books have made this all happen and put the book in your hands. Special thanks to Ginjer Buchanan and Kat Sherbo.

And finally a round of applause for my agent, Ian Drury, for getting my work in front of people who were willing to take a chance on it, and for continuing to sell my books across the world. Gaia Banks and Virginia Ascione, working with Ian at Sheil Land Associates Ltd., have also exceeded all my hopes by getting Jorg's story into so many translations.

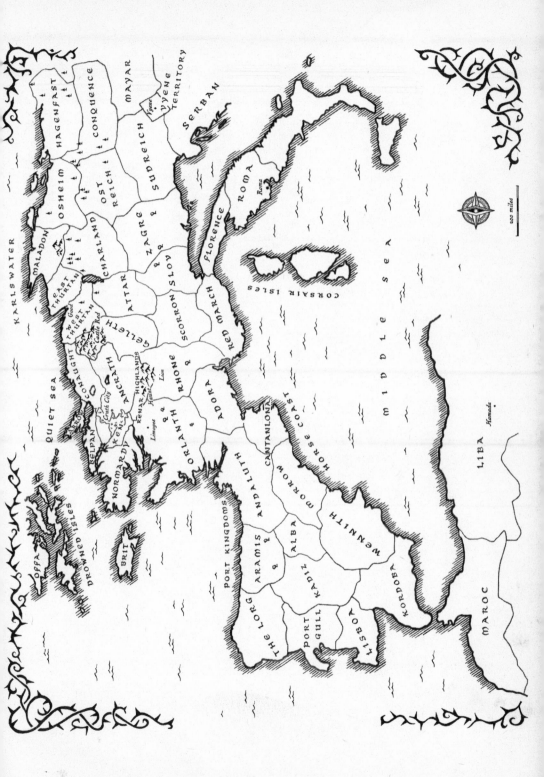

THE STORY SO FAR

For those of you who have had to wait a year for this book, I provide a brief synopsis of books one and two, so that your memories may be refreshed. Here I carry forward only what is of importance to the tale that follows.

i) Jorg's mother and brother, William, were killed when he was nine: he hung hidden in the thorns and witnessed it. His uncle sent the assassins.

ii) Jorg's father, Olidan, is not a nice man. He killed Jorg's dog when Jorg was six, and stabbed Jorg in the chest when he was fourteen.

iii) Jorg's father still rules in Ancrath, married now to Sareth. Sareth's sister Katherine is Jorg's step-aunt and something of an obsession for him.

iv) Jorg accidentally (though not guiltlessly) killed his baby step-brother Degran.

v) A man named Luntar put Jorg's memory of the incident in a box. Jorg has now recovered the memory.

vi) A number of magically gifted individuals work behind the many thrones of the Broken Empire, competing with each other and manipulating events to further their own control.

vii) We left Jorg still on his uncle's throne in Renar. The princes of Arrow lay dead, their army shattered and the six nations gathered under Orrin of Arrow's rule ripe for the picking.

viii) We left Jorg the day after his wedding to twelve-year-old Queen Miana.

ix) Jorg had sent men to recover his badly wounded chancellor, Coddin, from the mountainside.

x) Katherine's diary was found in the destruction outside the Haunt—whether she survived where her baggage train did not is unknown.

xi) Red Kent was badly burned in the fight.

xii) Jorg discovered there are ghosts of the Builders in the network of machines they left behind.

xiii) Jorg learned from one such ghost, Fexler Brews, that what he calls magic exists because the Builder scientists changed the way the world works. They made it possible for a person's will to affect matter and energy directly.

xiv) The gun Jorg used to conclude the siege on the Haunt was taken from Fexler Brews' suicide.

xv) The powers over necromancy and fire were burned out of Jorg when they nearly destroyed him at the finale of the battle for the Haunt.

xvi) The Dead King is a powerful individual who watches the living from the deadlands and has shown a particular interest in Jorg.

xvii) Chella, a necromancer, has become an agent of the Dead King.

xviii) Every four years the rulers of the hundred fragments of empire convene in the capital Vyene for Congression—a truce period during which they vote for a new emperor. In the hundred years since the death of the last steward no candidate has managed to secure the necessary majority.

xix) In the earlier thread "Four Years Earlier" we left Jorg at his grandfather's castle on the Horse Coast. The mathmagician Qalasadi had escaped after failing to poison the nobles. The Builder-ghost Fexler had given Jorg the view-ring that offers interactive views of the world from satellites and other optical resources.

PROLOGUE

Kai stood before the old-stone, a single rough block set upright in the days when men knew nothing but wood and rock and hunting. Or perhaps they knew more than that, for they had set the old-stone in a place of seeing. A point where veils thinned and lifted and secrets might be learned or told. A place where the heavens stood a little lower, such that the sky-sworn might touch them more easily.

The local men called the promontory "the Finger," which Kai supposed was apt if dull. And if it were a finger then the old-stone stood on the knuckle. Here the finger lay sixty yards across and at the edges fell a similar distance to meet the marsh in a series of steep and rocky steps.

Kai took a deep breath and let the cold air fill his lungs, let the dampness infect him, slowed his heart, and listened for the high, sad voice of the old-stone, less of a sound than a memory of sound. His vision lifted from him with just a whisper of pain. The point of Kai's perception vaulted skyward, leaving his flesh beside the monolith. He watched now from a bright valley between two tumbling banks of cloud, watched himself as a dot upon the Finger, and the promontory itself a mere sliver of land reaching out into the vastness of the Reed Sea. At this distance the River Rill became a ribbon of silver running to the Lake of Glass.

Kai flew higher. The ground fell away, growing more abstract with each beat of his mind-born wings. The mists swirled, and the clouds held him again in their cool embrace.

Is this what death is like? A cold whiteness, for ever and ever amen?

Kai resisted the cloud's pull and found the sun again. The sky-sworn could so easily lose themselves in the vastness of the heavens. Many did, leaving flesh to die and haunting the empty spaces above. A core of selfishness bound Kai to his existence. He knew himself well enough to admit that. An old strand of greed, an inability to let go. Failings of a kind perhaps, but here an asset that would keep him whole.

He flew above the soft brilliance of the clouds, weaving his path amongst their turrets and towers. A seris broke the pillowed alabaster, ghost-faint even to the eye of Kai's mind, its sinuous form plunging in and out of sight, a hundred feet long and thicker than a man. Kai called to it. The cloud-snake coiled on itself; describing lazy circles as it drew ever closer.

"Old friend." Kai hailed it. As many as a hundred seris swarmed amid the thunderheads when the land-breaker storms came, but each seris knew what every seris knew, so to Kai's mind there was only one. Perhaps the seris were remnants of sky-sworn who had forgotten themselves, forgotten all that they were to dance among the clouds. Or maybe they had always been, requiring no birth and knowing no death.

The seris fixed Kai with the cold blue glow of its eye-pits. He felt the chill of its mind-touch, slow and curious. "Still the woman?"

"Always the woman." Kai watched the light on the clouds. Architectural clouds, just ready for God's hand to shape, ready to be cathedrals, towers, monsters . . . It amused him that the seris thought he always brought the same girl to the Finger.

Maybe seris think there's just one man, one woman, and lots of bodies.

The seris moved around Kai in a corkscrew, as if he were there in person, cocooning him in its coils. "You would have one shadow?"

Kai smiled. The seris thought of human love as clouds coming together, sometimes brushing one to another, sometimes building to a storm, sometimes lost one in the other—casting one shadow.

"Yes, to have one shadow." Kai surprised himself with the heat in his voice. He wanted what the seris had. Not just a roll in the heather. Not this time.

"Make it." The voice of the seris spoke beneath his skin, though he had left that far below.

"Make it happen? It isn't that easy."

"You do not want?" The seris rippled. Kai knew it for laughter.

"Oh, I want." *She just has to walk in the room and I'm on fire. The scent of her! I close my eyes and I'm in the Gardens of Bethda.*

"A storm comes." Sorrow tinged the seris's voice.

Kai puzzled. He'd seen no sign of a storm brewing.

"They rise," the seris said.

"The dead?" Kai asked, the old fear creeping over him.

"Worse." One word, too much meaning.

"Lichkin?" Kai stared, he could see nothing. *Lichkin only come in the dark.*

"They rise," the seris said.

"How many?" *Don't let it be all seven! Please.*

"Many. Like the rain." The seris left. The mist from which it wove its body drifted formless. Kai had never seen a seris fall apart like that. "Make one shadow." The voice hung in the air.

Kai's vision arrowed toward the ground. He dived for the Finger. Sula stood at the fingertip, on the very edge, a white dot, growing swiftly. Sight slammed into body, hard enough to make him fall to his knees. He scrambled up, disoriented for a moment, then tore off toward Sula. He reached her in less than a minute, and bent double before her, heaving in his breath.

"You were a long time." Sula turned at his approach. "I thought you'd forgotten about me, Kai Summerson."

"Forgive me, my lady?" he gasped, and grinned, her beauty pushing away his panic. It seemed silly now. From on high he'd seen nothing to worry him.

Sula's pout became a smile, the sun reached down to light her face, and for a moment Kai forgot about the seris's warning. *Lichkin travel at night.* He took her hands and she came to him. She smelled of flowers. The softness of her breasts against his chest made his heart skip. For a moment he could see only her eyes and lips. The fingers of one hand locked with hers, the other ran along her throat, feeling the pulsing heat of her.

"You shouldn't stand so close to the edge," he said, though she stole his breath. Just a yard behind her the tip of the Finger crumbled away into two hundred feet of cliffs, stepping sharply down into the surrounding marsh.

"You sound like Daddy." Sula cocked her head and leaned into him. "You know, he even told me not to go with you today? That Kai Summerson is low-born trash, he said. He wanted me to stay cooped up in Morltown while he did his business deals."

"What?" Kai let go of Sula's hands. "You said he agreed."

Sula giggled and put on a gruff voice. "I'll not have my daughter gallivanting with a Guardian captain!" She laughed and returned to her normal tones. "Did you know, he thinks you have a 'reputation'?"

Kai did have a reputation, and a man like Merik Wineland could make things very difficult for him.

"Look, Sula, we'd better go. There may be trouble coming."

The tight little lines of a frown marred Sula's perfect brow. "Trouble coming?"

"I had an ulterior motive for bringing you here," Kai said.

Sula grinned where other girls might blush.

"Not that," Kai said. "Well, that too, but I was scheduled to check the area. Observe the marsh."

"I've been watching from the cliff while you were gone. There's nothing down there!" Sula turned from him and gestured to the green infinity of the mire. Then she saw it. "What's that?"

Across the Reed Sea a mist was rising. It ran in white streams, spreading from the east, blood-tinged by the setting sun.

"They're coming." Kai struggled to speak. He found his voice and tried a confident smile. It felt like a grimace. "Sula, we have to move fast. I need to report to Fort Aral. I'll get you over the Mextens and leave you at Redrocks. You'll be safe there. A wagon will get you to Morltown."

The darts flew with a noise like somebody blowing out candles, a series of short sudden breaths. Three clustered just below Sula's right armpit. Three thin black darts, stark against the whiteness of her dress. Kai felt the sting in his neck, like the bite of horseflies.

The mire ghouls swarmed over the tip of the Finger, grey and spider-like, swift and silent. Kai ripped his short sword from its scabbard. It felt heavier than lead. The numbness was in his fingers already and the sword fell from his clumsy grasp.

A storm's coming.

1

I failed my brother. I hung in the thorns and let him die and the world has been wrong since that night. I failed him, and though I've let many brothers die since, that first pain has not diminished. The best part of me still hangs there, on those thorns. Life can tear away what's vital to a man, hook it from him, one scrap at a time, leaving him empty-handed and beggared by the years. Every man has his thorns, not of him, but in him, deep as bones. The scars of the briar mark me, a calligraphy of violence, a message blood-writ, requiring a lifetime to translate.

The Gilden Guard always arrive on my birthday. They came for me when I turned sixteen, they came to my father and to my uncle the day I reached twelve. I rode with the brothers at that time and we saw the guard troop headed for Ancrath along the Great West Road. When I turned eight I saw them first-hand, clattering through the gates of the Tall Castle on their white stallions. Will and I had watched in awe.

Today I watched them with Miana at my side. Queen Miana. They came clattering through a different set of gates into a different castle, but the effect was much the same, a golden tide. I wondered if the Haunt would hold them all.

"Captain Harran!" I called down. "Good of you to come. Will you have an ale?" I waved toward the trestle tables set out before him. I'd had our thrones brought onto the balcony so we could watch the arrival.

Harran swung himself from the saddle, dazzling in his fire-gilt steel. Behind him guardsmen continued to pour into the courtyard. Hundreds of them. Seven troops of fifty to be exact. One troop for each of my lands. When they had come four years before, I warranted just a single troop, but Harran had been leading it then as now.

"My thanks, King Jorg," he called up. "But we must ride before noon. The roads to Vyene are worse than expected. We will be hard pushed to reach the Gate by Congression."

"Surely you won't rush a king from his birthday celebrations just for Congression?" I sipped my ale and held the goblet aloft. "I claim my twentieth year today, you know."

Harran made an apologetic shrug and turned to review his troops. More than two hundred were already crowded in. I would be impressed if he managed to file the whole contingent of three hundred and fifty into the Haunt. Even after extension during the reconstruction, the front courtyard wasn't what one would call capacious.

I leaned toward Miana and placed a hand on her fat belly. "He's worried if I don't go there might be another hung vote."

She smiled at that. The last vote that was even close to a decision had been at the second Congression—the thirty-third wasn't likely to be any nearer to setting an emperor on the throne than the previous thirty.

Makin came through the gates at the rear of the guard column with a dozen or so of my knights, having escorted Harran through the Highlands. A purely symbolic escort since none in their right mind, and few even in their wrong mind, would get in the way of a Gilden Guard troop, let alone seven massed together.

"So, Miana, you can see why I have to leave you, even if my son is about to fight his way out into the world." I felt him kick under my hand. Miana shifted in her throne. "I can't really say no to seven troops."

"One of those troops is for Lord Kennick, you know," she said.

"Who?" I asked it only to tease her.

"Sometimes I think you regret turning Makin into my lord of Kennick." She gave me that quick scowl of hers.

"I think he regrets it too. He can't have spent more than a month there in the last two years. He's had the good furniture from the Baron's Hall moved to his rooms here."

We fell silent, watching the guard marshal their numbers within the tight confines of the courtyard. Their discipline put all other troops to shame. Even Grandfather's Horse Coast cavalry looked a rabble next to the Gilden Guard. I had once marvelled at the quality of Orrin of Arrow's travel guard, but these men stood a class apart. Not one of the hundreds didn't gleam in the sun, the gilt on their armour showing no sign of dirt or wear. The last emperor had deep pockets and his personal guard continued to dip into them close on two centuries after his death.

"I should go down." I made to get up, but didn't. I liked the comfort. Three weeks' hard riding held little appeal.

"You should." Miana chewed on a pepper. Her tastes had veered from one extreme to another in past months. Of late she'd returned to the scalding flavours of her homeland on the Horse Coast. It made her kisses quite an adventure. "I should give you your present first though."

I raised a brow at that and tapped her belly. "He's cooked and ready?"

Miana flicked my hand away and waved to a servant in the shadows of the hall. At times she still looked like the child who'd arrived to find the Haunt all but encircled, all but doomed. At a month shy of fifteen the most petite of serving girls still dwarfed her, but at least pregnancy had added some curves, filled her chest out, put some colour in her cheeks.

Hamlar came out with something under a silk cloth, long and thin, but not long enough for a sword. He offered it to me with a slight bow. He'd served my uncle for twenty years but had never shown me a sour glance since I put an end to his old employment. I twitched the cloth away.

"A stick? My dear, you shouldn't have." I pursed my lips at it. A nice enough stick it had to be said. I didn't recognize the wood.

Hamlar set the stick on the table between the thrones and departed.

"It's a rod," Miana said. "Lignum Vitae, hard, and heavy enough to sink in water."

"A stick that could drown me . . ."

She waved again and Hamlar returned with a large tome from my library held before him, opened to a page marked with an ivory spacer.

"It says there that the Lord of Orlanth won the hereditary right to bear his rod of office at the Congressional." She set a finger to the appropriate passage.

I picked the rod up with renewed interest. It felt like an iron bar in my hand. As King of the Highlands, Arrow, Belpan, Conaught, Normardy, and Orlanth, not to mention overlord of Kennick, it seemed that I now held royal charter to carry a wooden stick where all others must walk unarmed. And thanks to my pixie-faced, rosy-cheeked little queen, my stick would be an iron-wood rod that could brain a man in a pot-helm.

"Thank you," I said. I've never been one for affection or sentiment, but I liked to think we understood each other well enough for her to know when something pleased me.

I gave the rod an experimental swish and found myself sufficient inspiration to leave my throne. "I'll look in on Coddin on the way down."

Coddin's nurses had anticipated me. The door to his chambers stood open, the window shutters wide, musk sticks lit. Even so, the stench of his wound hung in the air. Soon it would be two years since the arrow struck him and still the wound festered and gaped beneath the physician's dressings.

"Jorg." He waved to me from his bed, made up by the window and raised so he too could see the guard arrive.

"Coddin." The old sense of unfocused guilt folded around me.

"Did you say goodbye to her?"

"Miana? Of course. Well . . ."

"She's going to have your child, Jorg. Alone. Whilst you're off riding."

"She'll hardly be alone. She has no end of maids and ladies-in-waiting. Damned if I know their names or recognize half of them. Seems to be a new one every day."

"You played your part in this, Jorg. She will know you're absent when the time comes and it will be harder on her. You should at least make a proper goodbye."

Only Coddin could lecture me so.

"I said . . . thank you." I twirled my new stick into view. "A present."

"When you're done here go back up. Say the right things."

I gave the nod that means "perhaps." It seemed to be enough for him.

"I never tire of watching those boys at horse," he said, glancing once more at the gleaming ranks below.

"Practice makes perfect. They'd do better to practise war though. Being able to back a horse into a tight corner makes a pretty show but—"

"So enjoy the show!" He shook his head, tried to hide a grimace, then looked at me. "What can I do for you, my king?"

"As always," I said. "Advice."

"You hardly need it. I've never even seen Vyene, not even been close. I haven't got anything that will help you in the Holy City. Sharp wits and all that book learning should serve you well enough. You survived the last Congression, didn't you?"

I let that memory tug a bleak smile from me. "I've got some measure of cleverness perhaps, old man, but what I need from you is wisdom. I know you've had my library brought through this chamber one book at a time. The men bring you tales and rumour from all corners. Where do my interests lie in Vyene? Where shall I drop my seven votes?"

I stepped closer, across the bare stones. Coddin was ever the soldier: no rugs or rushes for him even as an invalid.

"You don't want to hear my wisdom, Jorg. If that's what it is." Coddin turned to the window again, the sun catching his age, and catching the lines that pain had etched into him.

"I had hoped you'd changed your mind," I said. There are hard paths and there are the hardest paths.

The stench of his wound came stronger now I stood close. Corruption is nibbling at our heels from the hour we're born. The stink of rot just reminds us where our feet are leading us, whichever direction they point in.

"Vote with your father. Be at peace with him."

Good medicines often taste foul, but some pills are too bitter to swallow. I paused to take the anger from my voice. "It's been nearly more than I can do not to march my armies into Ancrath and lay waste. If it's a struggle to keep from open war . . . how can there be peace?"

"You two are alike. Your father perhaps a touch colder, more stern and with less ambition, but you fell from the same tree and similar evils forged you."

Only Coddin could tell me I was my father's son and live. Only a man who had already died in my employ and lay rotting in my service still, out of duty, only such a man could speak that truth.

"I don't need him," I said.

"Didn't this ghost of yours, this Builder, tell you two Ancraths together would end the power of the hidden hands? Think, Jorg! Sageous set your uncle against you. Sageous wanted you and your brother in the ground. And failing that he drove a wedge between father and son. And what would end the power of men like Sageous, of the Silent Sister, Skilfar, and all their ilk? Peace! An emperor on the throne. A single voice of command. Two Ancraths! You think your father has been idle all this time, the years that grew you, and the years before? He may not have your arching ambition, but he is not without his own measure. King Olidan has influence in many courts. I won't say he has friends, but he commands loyalty, respect, and fear in equal measures. Olidan knows secrets."

"I know secrets." Many I did not wish to know.

"The Hundred will not follow the son whilst the father stands before them."

"Then I should destroy him."

"Your father took that path—it made you stronger."

"He faltered at the last." I looked at my hand, remembering how I had lifted it from my chest, dripping crimson. My blood, father's knife. "He faltered. I will not."

If it had been the dream-witch who drove a wedge between us then he had done his job well. It wasn't in me to forgive my father. I doubted it was in him to accept such forgiveness.

"The hidden hands might think two Ancraths will end their power. Me, I think one is enough. It was enough for Corion. Enough for Sageous. I will be enough for all of them if they seek to stop me. In any event, you know in what high esteem I hold prophecy."

Coddin sighed. "Harran is waiting for you. You have my advice. Carry it with you. It won't slow you down."

The captains of my armies, nobles from the Highlands, a dozen lords on petitioning visits from various corners of the seven kingdoms, and scores of hangers-on all waited for me in the entrance hall before the keep doors. The time when I could just slip away had . . . just slipped away. I acknowledged the throng with a raised hand.

"My lords, warriors of my house, I'm off to Congression. Be assured I will carry your interests there along with my own and present them with my usual blend of tact and diplomacy."

That raised a chuckle. I'd bled a lot of men dry to take my little corner of empire so I felt I should play out the game for my court, as long as it cost me nothing. And besides, their interests lay with mine, so I hardly lied.

I singled Captain Marten out amongst the crowd, tall and weathered, nothing of the farmer left in him. I gave no rank higher than captain but the man had led five thousand soldiers and more in my name.

"Keep her safe, Marten. Keep them both safe." I put a hand to his shoulder. Nothing else needed to be said.

I came into the courtyard flanked by two knights of my table, Sir Kent and Sir Riccard. The spring breeze couldn't carry the aroma of horse sweat away fast enough, and the herd of more than three hundred appeared to be doing their best to leave the place knee-deep in manure. I find that massed cavalry are always best viewed from a certain distance.

Makin eased his horse through the ranks to reach us. "Many happy returns, King Jorg!"

"We'll see," I said. It all felt a little too comfortable. Happy families with my tiny queen above. Birthday greetings and a golden escort down below. Too much soft living and peace can choke a man sure as any rope.

Makin raised an eyebrow but said nothing, his smile still in place.

"Your advisors are ready to ride, sire." Kent had taken to calling me sire and seemed happier that way.

"You should be taking wise heads not men-at-arms," Makin said.

"And who might you be bringing, Lord Makin?" I had decided to let him select the single advisor his vote entitled him to bring to Congression.

He pointed across the yard to a scrawny old man, pinch-faced, a red cloak lifting around him as the wind swirled. "Osser Gant. Chamberlain to the late Baron of Kennick. When I'm asked what my vote will cost, Osser's the man who will know what is and what isn't of worth to Kennick."

I had to smile at that. He might pretend it wasn't so, but part of old Makin wanted to play out his new role as one of the Hundred in grand style. Whether he would model his rule on my father's or that of the Prince of Arrow remained unclear.

"There's not much of Kennick that ain't marsh, and what the Ken Marshes need is timber. Stilts, so your muddy peasants' houses don't sink overnight. And you get that from me now. So don't let your man forget it."

Makin coughed as if some of that marsh had got into his chest. "So who exactly are you taking as advisors?"

It hadn't been a difficult choice. Coddin's final trip came when they carried him down from the mountain after the battle for the Haunt. He wouldn't travel again. I had grey heads aplenty at court, but none whose contents I valued. "You're looking at two of them." I nodded to Sirs Kent and Riccard. "Rike and Grumlow are waiting outside, Keppen and Gorgoth with them."

"Christ, Jorg! You can't bring Rike! This is the emperor's court we're talking about! And Gorgoth? He doesn't even like you."

I drew my sword, a smooth glittering motion, and hundreds of golden helms turned to follow its arc. I held the blade high, turning it this way and that to catch the sun. "I've been to Congression before, Makin. I know what games they play there. This year we're going to play a new game. Mine. And I'm bringing the right pieces."

2

Several hundred horsemen throw up a lot of dust. We left the Matteracks in a shroud of our own making, the Gilden Guard stretched out across half a mile of winding mountain path. Their gleam didn't survive long and we made a grey troop as we came to the plains.

Makin and I rode together along the convolutions of the track on which we once met the Prince of Arrow, headed for my gates. Makin looked older now, a little iron in the black, worry lines across his brow. On the road Makin had always seemed happy. Since we came to wealth and fortune and castles he had taken to worry.

"Will you miss her?" he asked. For an hour just the clip and clop of hooves on stony ground, and then from nowhere, "Will you miss her?"

"I don't know." I'd grown fond of my little queen. When she wanted to she could excite me, as most women could: my eye is not hard to please. But I didn't burn for her, didn't need to have her, to keep her in my sight. More than fondness, I liked her, respected her quick mind and ruthless undercurrents. But I didn't love her, not the irrational foolish love that can overwhelm a man, wash him away and strand him on unknown shores.

"You don't know?" he asked.

"We'll find out, won't we?" I said.

Makin shook his head.

"You're hardly the champion of true love, Lord Makin," I told him. In the six years since we came to the Haunt he had kept no woman with him, and if he had a mistress or even a favourite whore he had them well hidden.

He shrugged. "I lost myself on the road, Jorg. Those were black years for me. I'm not fit company for any woman I'd desire."

"What? And I am?" I turned in the saddle to watch him.

"You were young. A boy. Sin doesn't stick to a child's skin the way it clings to a man's."

My turn to shrug. He had seemed happier when murdering and robbing than he did thinking back on it in his vaulted halls. Perhaps he just needed something to worry about again, so he could stop worrying.

"She's a good woman, Jorg. And she's going to make you a father soon. Have you thought about that?"

"No," I said. "It had slipped my mind." In truth though it surfaced in my thoughts in each waking hour, and many dreaming ones. I couldn't find a way to grip the idea and it did indeed slip from me. I knew a squalling infant would soon appear, but what that would mean to me—what it was to be a father—I had no hold on. Coddin told me I would know how to feel. Instinct would tell me—something written in the blood. And perhaps it would come to me, like a sneeze arriving when pepper's in the air, but until it did I had no way of imagining it.

"Perhaps you'll be a good father," Makin said.

"No." Whether I somehow came to understand the process or not I would make a poor father. I had failed my brother and I would doubtless fail my son. Somehow the curse Olidan of Ancrath bestowed on me, and got most likely from his own sire, would infect any child of mine.

Makin pursed his lips but had the grace or the wisdom not to argue.

*　*　*

There's not much of the Renar Highlands that lies flat enough to grow crops on, but close to the border with Ancrath the land stops leaping and diving long enough for farming and for a city, of sorts. Hodd Town, my capital. I could see the stain of it on the horizon.

"We'll camp here," I said.

Makin leaned in his saddle to tell Sir Riccard, and he raised my colours on his lance.

"We could make Hodd Town," Makin said. "We'd be there an hour or so past sunset."

"Bad beds, grinning officials, and fleas." I swung out of Brath's saddle. "I'd rather sleep in a tent."

Gorgoth sat down. He let the guard work around him, tethering their horses, organizing their feed, setting up pavilions, each big enough for six men, with two ribbons streaming from the centre-point, the emperor's black and gold. Keppen and Grumlow threw their saddle-bags beside the leucrota and sat on them to play dice.

"We should at least pass through town tomorrow, Jorg." Makin tied off the feedbag on his mount's nose and turned back to me. "The people love to see the guard ride past. You can give them that at least?"

I shrugged. "It should be enough that I keep court in the High-lands. Do you think they've forgotten that I've a *palace* bigger than the whole of Hodd Town down in Arrow?"

Makin kept his eyes on mine. "Sometimes it seems you've forgot-ten it, Jorg."

I turned away and squatted to watch the dice roll. The ache in my thighs told me I'd been too long in the throne and the bed and the banquet hall. Makin had it right, I should travel my seven kingdoms, even if it were only to spend time on the road and keep its lessons sharp in my mind.

"Son of a bitch!" Keppen spat. All five of Grumlow's dice showed sixes. Keppen started to empty his coin pouch, spat again, and threw the whole lot down at Grumlow's feet. I shook my head. It seemed a waste of good fortune to buck such odds for a pouch of coin.

"Don't use up all your luck, Brother Grumlow. You might need it later." I stood again, biting back a curse at my legs.

I hadn't wanted to live in the palace Prince Orrin had built for Katherine. I spent a few weeks there after we had secured the allegiance of Arrow's surviving lords. The building reminded me of Orrin, austere but splendid, high arches, pillars of white stone, it could have been copied from the ruins of Macedon where Alexander grew to greatness. I rattled around in its many rooms with the brothers as my guards, and my captains planning the capture of Arrow's remaining conquests. The palace felt deserted despite a staff of hundreds, strangers all of them. In the end I'd been glad to ride out to secure Normardy, somehow a relief though it proved the bloodiest of that spring's campaigns.

If life in the Haunt had left me too soft for a day in the saddle then I was wise to avoid the luxury of that palace. Better the mountains than the plains, better the howl of the wind about snow-clad peaks than the foul air blowing off the Quiet Sea laden with the stench of the Drowned Isles. Besides, in Ancrath and in Renar the blood of my line ran thickest. I might not hunger for the warmth of family but in troubled times it's wiser to be surrounded by subjects who follow out of habit rather than out of new-found fear.

A gentle rain began to fall as the light faded. I pulled my cloak tighter and moved to one of the campfires.

"A tent for the king!" Sir Riccard shouted, catching the arm of a passing guardsman.

"A little wet won't hurt me," I told him. A good swordsman, Riccard, and brave, but rather too taken with his rank and with shouting.

Time spent around a fire, among the bustle of warriors, was more to my liking than watching the walls of a tent twitch and flap, and imagining what might lie behind them. I watched the guards organize their camp and let the aroma of the stew-pots tease my nose.

When you are a troop of more than three hundred, a small army by most reckonings, all the simple matters of the road require discipline. Latrine trenches must be dug, a watch organized on a defensible perimeter, horses taken to graze and water. Gone the easy ways that suited our band of brothers on the roads of my childhood. Scale changes everything.

A guard captain came with a chair for me, a piece of campaign furniture that would fold down again to a tight flat package with brass-bound corners to weather the knocks and bumps of travel. Captain Harran found me sat in it with a bowl of venison and potatoes in my lap, food from my own stores at the Haunt, no doubt. The guard expected to provision wherever they stopped—a kind of highway robbery legalized by the last echoes of empire.

"There's a priest wanting to see you," Harran said. I let him drop "King Jorg" into my expectant silence. The captains of the Gilden Guard hold the Hundred in mild contempt and are wont to laugh at our titles behind their oh-so-shiny helms.

"A priest? Or perhaps the Bishop of Hodd Town?" I asked. The Gilden Guard have little respect for the church of Roma either, a legacy of centuries punctuated by vicious squabbles between emperors and Popes. For the emperor's loyalists Vyene is the holy city and Roma an irrelevance.

"Yes, a bishop." Harran nodded.

"The silly hat gives them away," I said. "Sir Kent, if you could go and escort Father Gomst to our little circle of piety. I wouldn't want him coming to grief amongst the guard."

I sat back in my chair and swigged from a tankard of ale they'd brought me, sour stuff from the breweries of the Ost-Reich. Rike watched the fire, gnawing on a bone from his meal. Most men watch the flames as if seeking answers in the mystery of that bright dance. Rike just scowled. Gorgoth came across and elbowed a space close enough that the glow lit him. Like me he had a measure of understanding when he stared into the flames. The magic I'd borrowed from Gog burned out of me on the day we turned the men of Arrow from the Haunt—it was never truly mine. I think, though, that Gorgoth had wet his hands in what Gog swam through. Not fire-sworn like Gog, but with a touch of it running in his veins.

Grumlow alerted us to Bishop Gomst's approach, pointing out the mitre swaying above the heads of guardsmen lined up for the mess tent. We watched as he emerged, arriving in full regalia with his crook to lean on and a shuffle in his feet, though he had no more years on him than Keppen, who could run up a mountain before lunch if the need arose.

"Father Gomst," I said. I'd been calling him that since I could call him anything at all and saw no reason to change my ways just because he'd changed his hat.

"King Jorg." He bowed his head. The rain started to thicken.

"And what brings the Bishop of Hodd Town out on a damp night like this when he could be warming himself before the votive candles banked in his cathedral?" A sore point since the cathedral stood half built. I still poked at old Gomsty as if he were stuck in that cage we found him in years back on the lichway. My uncle had over-reached himself when he commissioned the cathedral project, a poorly judged plan conceived the same year my mother squeezed me into the world. Perhaps another bad decision. In any event, the money had run out. Cathedrals don't come cheap, not even in Hodd Town.

"I needed to speak with you, my king. Better here than in the city." Gomst stood with the rain dripping from the curls of his crook, bedraggled in his finery.

"Get the man a chair," I shouted. "You can't leave a man of God standing in the muck." Then in a lower voice, "Tell me, Father Gomst."

Gomst took his time to sit, adjusting his robes, the hems thick with mud. I expected him to come with a priest or two, a church boy to carry his train at least, but my bishop sat before me unattended, dark with rain, and looking older than his years.

"There was a time when the seas rose, King Jorg." He held his crook white-knuckled and stared at the other hand in his lap. Gomst never told stories. He scolded or he flattered, according to the cloth of his audience.

"The seas rise each day, Father Gomst," I said. "The moon draws on the deep waters as it draws on women's blood." I knew he spoke of the Flood, but tormenting him came too easy.

"There were untold years when the seas lay lower, when the Drowned Isles were one great land of Brettan, and the Never Lands fed an empire, before the Quiet Sea stole them. But the waters rose and a thousand cities drowned."

"And you think the oceans ready themselves for another bite?" I grinned and held a hand out to accept the rain. "Will it pour for forty days and nights?"

"Have you had a vision?" A question rasped from scorched lungs. Red Kent had come to squat beside Gomst's chair. Since surviving the inferno at the Haunt Sir Kent had got himself a bad case of religion.

"It seems I chose well when making court in the mountains," I said. "Perhaps the Highland will become the richest island kingdom in the new world."

Sir Riccard laughed at that. I seldom made a joke that didn't find an echo in him. Makin twisted a grin. I trusted that more.

"I speak of a different rising, a darker tide," Gomst said. He seemed determined to play the prophet. "Word comes from every convent, from Arrow, Belpan, Normardy, from the cold north and from the Port kingdoms. The most pious of the faith's nuns dream of it. Hermits leave their caves to speak of what the night brings them, icons bleed to testify the truth. The Dead King readies himself. Black ships wait at anchor. The graves empty."

"We have fought the dead before, and won." The rain felt cold now.

"The Dead King has overwhelmed the last of Brettan's lords, he holds all the Isles. He has a fleet waiting to sail. The holiest see a black tide coming." Gomst looked up now, meeting my eyes.

"Have you seen this, Gomst?" I asked him.

"I am not holy."

That convinced me, of his belief and fear at least. I knew Gomst for a rogue, a goat-bearded letch with an eye for his own comfort and a taste for grand but empty oratory. Honesty from him spoke more than from another man.

"You'll come to Congression with me. Set this news before the Hundred."

His eyes widened at that, rain stuttered from his lips. "I— I have no place there."

"You'll come as one of my advisors," I told him. "Sir Riccard will cede his place to you."

I stood, shaking the wet from my hair. "Damn this rain. Harran! Point me at my tent. Sir Kent, Riccard, see the bishop back to his church. I don't want any ghoul or ghost troubling him on his return."

Captain Harran had waited in the next fire circle and led me now to my pavilion, larger than the guards', hide floors within, strewn with black and gold cushions. Makin followed in behind me, coughing and shaking off the rain, my bodyguard, though a pavilion had been set for him as Baron of Kennick. I shrugged off my cloak and it landed with a splat, leaking water.

"Gomst sends us to bed with sweet dreams," I said, glancing around. A chest of provisions sat to my left and a commode had been placed on the opposite side. Silver lamps burning smokeless oil lit me to my bed, carved timber, four posted, assembled from pieces carried by a dozen different guards.

"I've no faith in dreams." Makin set his cloak aside and shook like a wet dog. "Or the bishop."

A chess set had been laid on a delicate table beside the bed, board of black and white marble, silver pieces, ruby-set or with emeralds to indicate the sides.

"The guard lay their tents grander than my rooms at the Haunt," I said.

Makin inclined his head. "I don't trust dreams," he repeated.

"The women of Hodd Town wear no blues." I started to unbuckle my breastplate. I could have had a boy to do it, but servants are a disease that leaves you crippled.

"You're an observer of fashion now?" Makin worked at his own armour, still dripping on the hides.

"Tin prices are four times what they stood at when I took my uncle's throne."

Makin grinned. "Have I missed a guest? You're speaking to somebody but it's not me?"

"That man of yours, Osser Gant? He would understand me." I let my armour lie where it fell. My eyes kept returning to the chessboard. They had set one for me on my last journey to Congression too. Every night. As if no one could pretend to the throne without being a player of the game.

"You've led me to the water, but I can't drink. Tell me plain, Jorg. I'm a simple man."

"Trade, Lord Makin." I pushed a pawn out experimentally. A ruby-eyed pawn, servant to the black queen. "We have no trade with the Isles, no tin, no woad, no Brettan nets, not those clever axes of theirs or those tough little sheep. We have no trade and black ships are seen off Conaught, sailing the Quiet Sea but never coming to port."

"There have been wars. The Brettan lords are always feuding." Makin shrugged.

"Chella spoke of the Dead King. I don't trust dreams but I trust the word of an enemy who thinks me wholly in their power. The marsh dead have kept my father's armies busy on his borders. We would have had our reckoning years back, father and me, if he were not so tied with holding on to what he has."

Makin nodded at that. "Kennick suffers too. All the men-at-arms who answer to me are set to keep the dead penned in the marshes. But an army of them? A king?"

"Chella was a queen to the army she raised in the Cantanlona."

"But ships? Invasions?"

"There are more things in heaven and earth, Makin, than are dreamt of in your philosophy." I sat on the bed and rotated the chessboard so the white queen and her army faced his way. "Make a move."

Makin had six victories before I set him to snuffing out the lamps. That he took his six to the floor and I took my single win to the luxury of a bed proved scant comfort. I fell asleep with the pieces flashing before my eyes, black squares, white, the twinkle of rubies and emeralds.

A storm came in the night, raging against the canvas. Tents are boasters, telling exaggerated tales of the weather they save you from. The sound was of a deluge fit to drown the kingdom and a wind that could scour the rocks from mountain slopes. Under a weather blanket, curled below a hedge, it might not have woken me, but beneath the great drum of the pavilion roof I lay staring into darkness.

Sometimes it's good to hear the rain, but not be wet, to know that the wind is howling but to feel no breath of it. I waited in that timeless comfortable dark and at last the scent of white musk rose, her arms folded about my chest, and she drew me down into dreams. There seemed an urgency to it tonight.

"Aunt Katherine." No doubt my lips twitched toward the words while I slept.

In the beginning Katherine sent me only nightmares, as if she counted herself my conscience and needed to torment me with my crimes. Time and again baby Degran died in my hands and I woke screaming, sweat-soaked, a danger to any who shared my bed. I spent nights roasting over the slow fire of Sareth's grief, shown from every angle by the arts her sister taught herself while married to the Prince of Arrow. Miana could not keep to my chambers and set herself a bed in the east tower.

Dream-sworn, I told myself. She's a dream-witch. Sageous's ilk.

But it didn't stop me wanting her. I painted Katherine's image across the dark storm of my imagination. She never showed herself and so I brought forth my first sight of her, that time-locked memory when we collided in the corridors of the Tall Castle.

Katherine showed me her loved ones—those I had killed. Sir Galen championing her through the bright days of her youth in Scorron, and her maid Hanna at a time when she looked less sour and offered a child-princess comfort in a loveless court. In dreaming, Katherine made me care about her cares, about her people, twisting me with the strange logic of the sleeping mind such that they seemed important, real, as real as the memories from before the thorns. And all of this in the too-bright light of the Gelleth sun, the flesh-stripping glare of that Builder Sun, always behind me, throwing my shadow like a black finger into the midst of their lives.

I let her arms draw me down through midnight. I had never fought her, though I felt I could, and I think perhaps she wanted me to. Even more than she wanted to show me the wrongs I had wrought, even more than she needed to make me feel it as she felt it, I think she needed me to fight her, to struggle against her spell, to close my dreaming eyes and try to escape. But I didn't. I told myself that I chose to face what I feared. That her torments would burn me clean of sentiment. But truly—I liked her arms around me, the feel of her close at hand, touching yet untouchable.

Whispers of light reached me through the starless night. Of late the dreams she drew me to were more confused, unfocused, as if she dreamed also. I would see her, or touch her, but never both. We would walk the Tall Castle, or the Palace of Arrow, her dresses flowing, silence binding us, the walls aging and crumbling as we passed. Or I would smell her, hold her, but be blind, or see only the graves of Perechaise.

Tonight though, the dream came cold and clear. Broken stone crunched beneath my shoes, the rain lashed me. I climbed a slope, bent against the gale. My fingers moved blind across natural rock, a wall rising before me. I knew every sensation but held no control as if I were a puppet and another kept the strings.

"What lesson is this, Katherine?"

She never spoke to me. Just as I never fought her—she never spoke. At first the dreams she wrought on me were all anger and revenge. Still they often carried that edge but I thought also that she experimented, trained her talent—as a swordsman crafts his technique and adds new strokes to his repertoire. These had been Sageous's skills and now that my aunt kept once more beneath Father's roof it might be she filled the heathen's role, though whether like him she spread a subtle web of influence and with touches turned the Hundred along Olidan Ancrath's paths, or indeed her own, I didn't know.

The storm fell away without warning and the wind died, though I heard it moaning behind me. A cave of some sort. I had passed through the narrow mouth of a cave. I crouched and swung the pack from my shoulder. Sure fingers found a flint and tinder. Within moments I lit the lantern fished from a pocket within the bag. I would have been proud of my work, but the hands that carried it out, the hands I held the flint in and struck flame with, were not mine. The lantern showed them to be pale, like flesh too long under water, and long-fingered. I have long fingers, but these were white spiders, crawling in the lantern's shadows.

I moved on, or rather the man whose skin I shared moved on and bore me with him. The lantern's glow reached out and found little to return it. My vision stayed where directed by the owner of the eyes I watched through—on the floor for the most part, natural rock smoothed by the passage of many feet. An occasional glance to the left and right showed waterfalls of frozen stone and unearthly galleries where stalagmites reached up to stalactites. And I knew where I walked. The Haunt's eastern sally port. The pale man had climbed the Runyard in the dark of the storm and entered the sally port through the concealed slot high on the Runyard's flank.

The man moved with confidence. Although many twists and

turns led off to dark unknowns it took no special skill to find the way, polished as it was by countless predecessors. The dream seemed accurate, drawing on my memories to make substance. A shiver ran through me, though not through the pale man. If Katherine strove for accuracy then soon a black hand would close around the intruder, reaching from the shadow, and pull him with inexorable strength and merciful speed into the gaping maw of a troll. I hoped not to feel those black teeth close in my flesh, but it seemed likely. Already their stink hung in my nose and his collar chafed my neck.

He walked his path and no hand came reaching. If I had been able to hold a breath I would have let it sigh through my teeth. For a while the dream had convinced me I was there, but no; Gorgoth's trolls guarded the subterranean paths to the Haunt and many more secret routes besides.

We came now through hand-hewn tunnels, gouged into the rock to join the Haunt to the natural caves. The man stopped, not far from the lowest of the Haunt's cellars. Ahead a clot of darkness swallowed the lantern light and gave nothing back. For long moments he held still, no motion in him, almost inhuman in his lack of twitch or tremor. When he advanced he moved on swift feet, the hilt of a knife cool in his grip though I couldn't see the blade. A single troll lay across the rough stone, sprawled out with its long limbs reaching. The beast's face nestled, hidden against the black knob of its shoulder. It might have been dead, but with careful observation the pale man and I saw the slow rise and fall of its back as breath came and went.

Without haste the man stepped around the sleeping troll, ducking where the tunnel's roof curved low, picking his way over black legs.

"A poor dream, Katherine." I spoke without needing his lips. "Trolls are made for war. It's written through them. This man's scent would have woken a dozen by now and set their mouths running with hunger."

My escort found the wooden door that gives onto the Haunt's

wine cellars. He worked the lock with heavy picks suited to such an old and solid mechanism. A drop of oil to take any squeak from the hinges and he pushed it open, stepping through without hesitation. I caught sight of his knife then, an assassin's tool, long and thin, its handle of turned white bone.

He emerged from the false front of the huge barrel that disguised the exit. Propped against a real barrel, opposite the false one and of nearly equal size, a guardsman in my colours sat, helm to one side, legs stretched in front of him, head forward in slumber. I crouched before him. I felt my haunches settle on my heels, I felt the strain in the muscles of my thighs, the coarseness of the guard's dirty blond hair as I pulled his head back. I knew him. The name fluttered behind my thoughts. Rodrick, a little fellow, younger than me, I once found him hiding in my tower when Arrow besieged the castle. My knife lay cold against his throat now, and still he didn't stir. I'd half a mind to open his neck just for being such a useless guard. Even so, it came as a shock when my hand slipped lower and drove the blade into his heart. That woke him! Rodrick watched me with hurt eyes, mouth twisting but silent, and he died. I waited. All trace of motion left the boy but still I waited. And then I pulled the knife free. Very little blood flowed. I wiped my blade clean on his tunic.

The pale man had black sleeves. I noticed that much before his gaze found the stairs and he went to them. He left his lantern beside Rodrick and his shadow led the way.

The man walked through the Haunt's corridors and halls as if he belonged there. The castle lay in darkness with only the occasional lamp set to light a corner or doorway. Shutters rattled, shaken by the wind, rainwater pooled below, driven past lintels and running over stone floors. It seemed my people huddled in their beds while the storm howled, for none of them wandered, no servant tending lamps, no dun-man for the night-soil, not a nursemaid or guardsman's har-lot slipping from the barracks . . . not a guardsman come to that.

At last, as the assassin reached the internal door to the east tower, we found a guard who hadn't abandoned his post. Sir Graeham, knight of my table, asleep on his feet, held upright by a combination of plate armour, a halberd, and the wall. Pale hands positioned the long knife at the gap between gorget and shoulderplate. The assassin set the heel of his palm over his knife's bone hilt, positioned so a sharp blow would puncture both leather and chainmail, and find the jugular beneath. He paused, perhaps sharing my thought that the knight might create quite a clatter if he fell. We held, close enough that I could draw Sir Graeham's ripe stink in with each breath. The wind howled and I drove the knife home. Its hilt stung the hand that wasn't mine, the business end stung Sir Graeham worse, and he fell, twitching. His weight pulled him from the knife.

Again the assassin cleaned his blade. This time on the knight's red cloak, smearing it with a brighter shade. Fastidious, this one.

He found the key on Graeham's belt and unlocked the oak door, iron-bound and polished by the touch of hands. Old as the door was, the archway held more years. My uncle's scrolls spoke of a time when the Haunt was nothing but the east tower, a single watchtower set on the mountain's shoulder with a military camp about its base. And even those men, who fought the tribes of Or and forged a stronghold in the Highlands, did not build the tower. There is writing on that arch, but time has forgotten even the name of the script. Its meaning has passed beyond knowing.

The assassin stepped beneath the archway and beneath the runes deep-set upon the keystone. Pain shot through me, thorns found my flesh, hooking through skin and blood in a manner that promised no easy release, like the barbed arrow that must be dug free, or the lock-hound that needs killing before the muscles and tendons along its jaw can be sliced and its teeth pried from the bone. It hurt, but I found my freedom, torn from the body that had held me. He walked on without pause and I staggered in his wake, following as he mounted the stair. Across the back of his black cloak, a cross had been sewn in white silk. A holy cross.

I ran at him, but passed through as if I were the ghost, though in truth it was me that shivered at the contact. Lamplight offered me his face as I turned, just for a moment before he walked through me and left me standing on the steps. The man held no colour, his face the same pale, drowned hue as his hands, hair oiled to the scalp, the iris of his eyes matching the ivory of the whites. He bore a cross embroidered in white silk across the front of his tunic to echo the one on his back. A papal assassin then. Only the Vatican sends assassins out into the world bearing a return address. The rest of us would rather not be caught using such agents. The papal assassin however is merely an extension of the Pope's infallibility—how can there be shame in executing the word of God? Why would such men cloak themselves in anonymity?

Sprawled in an alcove off the stairwell, Brother Emmer lay dead to the world. The assassin knelt and applied his knife to make sure it was a permanent state of affairs. Emmer had shown little interest in women on the road and had seemed a good choice to watch over my queen. I watched the Pope's man climb the stairs until the turn of the tower took him from view. Emmer's blood washed down, step by step, in crimson falls.

I never fought Katherine, never tried to escape her illusions, but that didn't mean I had to cooperate. Somehow I had broken free of the assassin and I had no reason to watch what else he might do. Murder my queen, no doubt. Miana would be sleeping in the chamber at the top of the stairs if Katherine kept to the castle plan she had mined from my memories. Should I follow like a fool and watch Miana's throat slit? See her thrash in her blood with my child dying inside her?

I stood in the darkness with just the echoes of lamplight from beyond the winding of the stair above and below.

"Truly? You think you can show me anything that would hurt me?" I spoke to the air. "You've walked my rememberings." I let her wander where she pleased when she came with her nightmares. I thought perhaps that daring the long corridors of my memory was more torment to her than her punishments were to me. Even with the key to each of my doors in her hand I knew there were places in me she didn't go. Who in their right mind would?

"Let's play this game, Princess, all the way through. Let's discover if you find the end too bitter."

I ran up the stairs, the contacts between foot and stone were light and without effort, as if only in the assassin's flesh could I properly touch this dream. I caught him within moments, passed him, and won the race to the top.

Marten waited there, crouched before the queen's door, his sword and shield on the floor, his eyes bloodshot and wild. Sweat held dark hair to his brow and ran down the straining tendons of his neck. In one fist a dagger, making constant jabs into his open palm. His breath came in short gasps and blood brimmed crimson from the cup of his hand.

"Fight it," I told him. Despite my resolve I found myself drawn in by his struggle to stay awake and guard Miana.

The assassin came into view, my view, not Marten's. He stopped, sniffed the air without sound, and cocked his head to catch the faint gasp of Marten's pain. Whilst he paused I dived into him, determined to settle around his bones, clinging to anything tangible. A moment of blind agony and I stared once more out of his eyes. I tasted blood. He had shared the hurt of reunion with me and although he hadn't cried out, a sharp intake of breath had passed his lips. Perhaps it would be enough to warn Marten.

The Pope's man reached into his robe, replacing the long bone-handled blade and drawing forth two short and heavy daggers, cruciform and weighted for throwing. He moved very fast, diving into Marten's line of sight whilst at the same time releasing the first of his knives, just a flick of the wrist but imparting lethal force.

Marten launched himself almost in the instant we faced him, slowed for a heartbeat perhaps by the weight of sleep he denied. The assassin's dagger hit somewhere between neck and belly—I heard chain links snap. He passed us with a roar and the assassin's foot lashed out, catching Marten's chin, propelling him into the curved wall. Momentum carried him feet over head over feet, clattering down the stairs. We hesitated, as if unsure whether to pursue and check if any bones remained unbroken. The hot wetness below our knee convinced the assassin otherwise. Somehow Marten had sliced the assassin as he passed. The Pope's man hobbled on toward the door, hissing at the pain now spreading from the cut Marten had left on us. He paused to tie a bandage, a silk sash from an inner pocket, pulled it tight, then advanced up the steps.

Any key had clattered down the stairs with Marten and the Pope's man took out his picks once more to work the lock. It took longer than before, the queen's door boasted a tricky mechanism perhaps as old as the tower. Before it yielded to our patient work the flagstones were pooled with the assassin's blood, red as any man's despite the pallor of his skin.

We stood, and I felt his weakness—blood loss and something else—he strained some muscle I didn't share, but I knew the effort wearied him. Perhaps the all-encompassing sleep had cost him dear.

The door opened without sound. He took the lamp from its hook where Marten had crouched and stepped in. The strength of his imaginings began to reach me as at last his excitement mounted. I saw the pictures rising in his mind. All of a sudden, dream or no dream, I wanted him to fail. I didn't want him to slice Miana open. I had no wish to see the red ruin of my unborn child drawn from her. The fear surprised me, raw and basic, and I knew it to be my own, not some sharing with Katherine. I wondered if it might be an echo of what Coddin warned I would feel for my son or daughter when I first saw them, held them. If that were true then I had my first inkling of how dangerous the bond might be.

On the dresser by the bed a glimmer from the silver chain I gave Miana on her name day. Under the covers a mounded form caught in shadows, wife and child, soft in sleep.

"Wake up." As if saying it would make it happen. "Wake up." All my will and not even a tremble of it on his lips.

Cold certainty gripped me by the throat. This was real. This was now. I slept in my bed in a tent, Miana slept in hers miles from me, and a pale death approached her.

"Katherine!" I shouted her name inside his head. "Don't do this!"

He stepped toward the bed, the second of his throwing knives raised and ready. Perhaps only the size of the lump beneath the covers prevented him from flinging the blade at it immediately. Miana could not be said to be a large woman, even with a baby straining to get out of her. It looked as though she had company in there. I might even have thought it, but for Marten at the door.

Another step, his injured leg numb and cold now, his lips muttering some spell in silence, as if his magics mirrored his unsteady gait and needed support. I had no warning, my arm—his arm—drew back to throw. In that moment the covers fluttered, I heard a muted "choom" and a fist hit my side, hard enough to throw me back, spinning twice before slamming into the wall. I slid to the floor, legs stretched before me, and looked down. Both pale hands covered my side, blood spurting between my fingers, pieces of flesh hanging.

The covers lifted and Miana faced me, crouched around the black mass of the Nuban's crossbow, eyes wide and fierce above it.

My right hand found the bone handle of the longer knife. Spitting blood I crawled to my feet, the world rotating around me. I could see that no bolts remained in the crossbow. Inside the assassin I strained with every piece of my being to still his legs, to lay down the weapon. I think he felt it this time. He moved slowly, but keeping between Miana and her door. His eyes fell to her belly, taut beneath her nightgown.

"Stop!" I held to his arm with all my will, but still it crept forward.

Miana looked angry rather than scared. Ready to do bloody murder.

My hand started forward, lunging with the knife, aimed low,

below the swing of Miana's bow. I couldn't stop it. The gleaming blade would pierce her womb, and slice, and in a welter of gore she would die. Our child with her.

The assassin thrust, and a hand span from finding flesh our arm shuddered off course, all its power cut clean away by a blow that sheared through my shoulder. I twisted as I collapsed, the ironwork of the crossbow smashing into my face. Marten stood behind me, a devil clothed in blood, his snarl veiled in scarlet. My head hit the carpet, vision turning black. Their voices sounded far away.

"My queen!"

"I'm not hurt, Marten."

"I'm so sorry—I failed you—he passed me."

"I'm not hurt, Marten . . . A woman woke me in my dreams."

3

"You're quiet this morning, Jorg."

I crunched my bread: from the Haunt, a day old and slightly stale.

"Still brooding over the chess?" The smell of clove-spice as he came close. "I told you I've played since I was six."

The bread snapped and scattered crust as I broke it open. "Get Riccard in here will you?"

Makin stood, downing his java, a cold and stinking brew the guards favour. He left without question: Makin could read people.

Riccard followed him back in moments later, tramping mud over the floor hides, crumbs of his own breakfast in his yellow moustache.

"Sire?" He offered a bow, probably warned by Makin.

"I want you to ride to the Haunt. Take an hour there. Speak to Chancellor Coddin and the queen. Catch us up as soon as you can with any report. If that report makes mention of a white-skinned man, bring the black coffer from my treasury, the one whose lid is inlaid with a silver eagle, and ten men to guard it. Coddin will arrange it."

Makin raised an eyebrow but came no closer to a question.

I pulled the chessboard near and took an apple from the table. The apple sprayed when bitten and droplets of juice shone on the black and white squares. The pieces stood ready in their lines. I set a finger to the white queen, making a slow circle so she rolled around her base. Either it had been a false dream, Katherine designing better torments than of old, and Miana was fine, or it had been a true dream and Miana was fine.

"Another game, Jorg?" Makin asked. All around, from outside, the sounds of camp being struck.

"No." The queen fell, toppling two pawns. "I'm past games."

4

Five years earlier

I took the Haunt and the Highland's crown in my fourteenth year and bore its weight three months before I went once more to the road. I ranged north to the Heimrift and south to the Horse Coast, and approached fifteen in the Castle Morrow under the protection of Earl Hansa, my grandfather. And though it was his heavy horse that had drawn me there, and the promise of a strong ally in the Southlands, it was the secrets which lay beneath the castle that kept me. In a forgotten cellar one small corner of a lost world broke through into ours.

"Come out come out wherever you are." I knocked the hilt of my dagger against the machine. In the cramped cellar it rang loud enough to hurt my ears.

Still nothing. Just the flicker and buzz of the three still-working glow-bulbs overhead.

"Come on, Grouch. You pop out to badger every visitor. You're famed for it. And yet you hide from me?"

I tapped metal to metal. A thoughtful tempo. Why would Fexler Brews hide from me?

"I thought I was your favourite?" I turned the Builders' view-ring over in my hand. He hadn't made me work very hard for it and I counted it a gift above any my father had ever given me.

"It's some kind of test?" I asked. "You want something from me?"

What would a Builder ghost want from me? What couldn't he take, or make? Or ask for? If he wanted something, wouldn't he ask?

"You want something."

One of the glow-bulbs flickered, flared, and died.

He needs something from me but can't ask.

I held the view-ring to my eye, and once again I saw the world—the whole world as viewed from outside, a jewel of blue and white hung in the blackness that holds the stars.

He wanted me to see something.

"Where are you, Fexler? Where are you hiding?"

I moved to pull the view-ring away in disgust when a tiny point of light caught my eye. A single red dot in all that swirling blue. I pushed the ring tight against the bones of brow and cheek. "Where are you?" And dialled the side of the ring so the world grew beneath me as though I fell into it. I steered and dialled, homing in on my prey, a constant red dot, drawing me to it now, faster and faster until the ring could show no more and the dot held steady above a barren hill in a range that stretched across badlands to the west of the Horse Coast.

"You want me to go here?" I asked.

Silence. Another glow-bulb flared and died.

I stood a moment in the trembling light of the last glow-bulb, shrugged, and made my way up the narrow spiral of stairs toward the castle above.

My grandfather's map room is in a tall tower that overlooks the sea. The map scrolls are held in oiled leather tubes, a wax seal on each set with his sigil. Seven narrow windows admit the light, at least in the months when the storm shutters are not closed against the elements. A scribe is employed to tend the place, and spends his days there from dawn to dusk, ready to open the tubes for anyone authorized to view the contents, and to seal them away again when the work is done.

"You've never thought to suggest a different room?" I asked the scribe as the wind tried to steal the map for the twentieth time. I had been there an hour, chasing documents across the chamber, and was ready to commit murder. How Redmon hadn't taken a crossbow and opened up on the folk below through his seven windows I didn't know. I caught the map before it left the table and replaced the four paperweights it had shrugged off.

"Good ventilation is essential for preserving the vellum," Redmon said. He kept his gaze on his feet, his quill turning over and over in his hand. I think he worried I might damage his charges in my temper. Had he known me he would have worried about his own health. He looked narrow enough to fit through one of the windows.

I located the hills I had seen through the view-ring, and found the general area of the particular hill where the red dot had sat so patiently. I had wondered if there might truly be a red light blazing on that hillside, so bright it could be seen from the dark vaults of heaven, but I reasoned that it had grown no brighter as my view closed in upon it and so it must have been some clever artifice, like a wax mark on a looking glass that seems to override your reflection.

"And what does this signify?" I asked, my finger on a symbol that covered the region. I felt pretty sure I knew. There were three similar symbols marked on the maps of Ancrath in my father's library, covering the regions of Ill Shadow, Eastern Dark, and Kane's Scar. But perhaps they served a different purpose in the southlands.

Redmon stepped to the desk and leaned in. "Promised regions."

"Promised?" I asked.

"The half-life lands. Not a place to travel."

The symbols served the same purpose as they did in Ancrath.

They warned of taints lingering from the Builders' war, stains from their poisons, or shadows from the Day of a Thousand Suns.

"And the promise?" I asked.

"Noble Chen's promise, of course." He looked surprised. "That when the half-life has spent itself these lands will be returned to man, to till and plough." Redmon pushed the wire-framed reading lenses further up his nose and returned to his ledgers at the big desk before the towering shelves of pigeonholes, each crammed with documents.

I rolled the scroll up and took it in my hand like a baton. "I'm taking this to show Lord Robert."

Redmon watched with anguish as I left, as if I'd stolen his only son to use as target practice. "I'll look after it," I said.

I found my uncle in the stables. He spent more time there than anywhere else, and since I'd met his shrew of a wife I had come to understand. Horses made her sneeze I heard it told, worse and worse minute by minute, until it seemed she would sneeze the eyes from her head. Robert found his peace amongst the stalls, talking blood-lines with his stable-master and looking over his stock. He had thirty horses in the castle stables, all prime examples of their lines, and his best knights to ride them, cavalrymen billeted away from the house guard and wall guard in far more luxury, as befits men of title.

"What do you know of the Iberico?" I called out as I walked toward him between the stalls.

"And good afternoon to you, young Jorg." He shook his head and patted the neck of the black stallion leaning out at him.

"I need to go there," I said.

He shook his head with emphasis this time. "The Iberico are dead land. Promised but not given. You don't want to go there."

"That's true. I don't want to. But I *need* to go there. So what can you tell me?" I asked.

The stallion snorted and rolled an eye as if venting Robert's frustration for him.

"I can tell you that men who spend time in such places sicken and die. Some take years before the poison eats them from within, others last weeks or days, losing their hair and teeth, vomiting blood."

"I will be quick then." Behind the set of my jaw second thoughts tried to wrest control of my tongue.

"There are places in the Iberico Hills, unmarked save for the barren look of them, where a man's skin will fall from him as he walks." My uncle pushed the horse away and stepped closer to me. "What grows in those hills is twisted, what lives there unnatural. I doubt your need exceeds the risks."

"You're right," I said. And he was. But when was the world ever so simple as right and wrong? I blinked twice and the red dot watched me from the darkness behind my eyelids. "I know you're right, but often it's not in me to take the sensible path, Uncle. I'm an explorer. Maybe that itch is in you too?"

He rubbed his beard, a quick grin showing through the worry. "Explore somewhere else?"

"I should take my foolish risks while I'm young, no? Better now than when that little girl you've found for me is grown and looking to me to keep her in silks and splendour. If my mistakes prove fatal, find her another husband."

"This is nothing to do with Miana. You just shouldn't do this, Jorg. If I thought it would stop you I would tell you 'no' and set a guard to watch you."

I bowed, turned, and walked away. "I'll take a mule. No sense risking good horseflesh."

"On that we're agreed," he called after me. "Don't let it drink from any standing water there."

I stepped back into the brightness of the day. The wind still raked across the courtyard, cold from the sea, but the sun would burn you even so.

"Visit Carrod Springs first!" Robert's shout reached me as I started for my quarters.

* * *

"Qalasadi and Ibn Fayed." The names tasted exotic.

"A man of power and a powerful man." My grandfather rested in the chair where the Earls of Morrow had sat for generations, facing the sea.

A circle of Builder glass, stronger than the walls around it and a full three yards in diameter, showed us the Middle Sea, the curvature of the Earth making it an azure infinity, white-flecked with waves. Out beyond sight across those depths, across the Corsair Isle, no further from us than Crath City, lay Roma and all her dominions.

Caliph Ibn Fayed might keep his court in the heart of a desert but his ships reached out across that sea, Moorish hands seeking to reclaim these lands that had been passed back and forth between Christendom and the Moslems since forever. Ibn Fayed's mathmagician, Qalasadi, had likely returned to the shadow of the caliph's throne to calculate the optimal timing for the next strike, and the odds of its success.

Far below us a wave slapped the cliffs, no tremor of it reaching the room but a high spray beading the glass. Twice a day they lowered a stable-boy with bucket and cloth to ensure that nothing but age dimmed Grandfather's view.

"Four sails," he said.

I had only seen three. The merchant cog, red-hulled, hauling cargo along the coast, and two fishing boats, bobbing further out.

Grandfather saw my frown. "Out there, on the horizon." A soft-voiced man despite the creaks of age.

A white flash. The sails of some wide-ranging vessel. A warship? A pirate cutter from the Isle? Or some flat-bellied scow out of Ægypt, treasure-laden?

I went closer to the glass, pressed a hand to its coldness. How many centuries ago had it been looted and from what ruin? Redmon surely had a scroll in his windy tower that held the secret.

"I can't allow them to live," I said. The caliph was just a name to me, Qalasadi filled my thoughts. The numbered man.

Grandfather laughed in his chair, the whale-ivory back of it spreading above him like the spray of a breaking wave. "Would you hunt down every man who wronged you, Jorg? However far-flung? However long they run? Seems to me a man like that is a slave to chance, always hunting, no time for living."

"They would have seen you die screaming while the poison ate you," I said. "Your wife too. Your son."

"And would have had you take the blame." He yawned wide enough to crack his jaw and ran the heels of both palms across the grey stubble of his beard.

"Poison is a dirty weapon," I said. Not that I had been above its use in Gelleth. I maintain a balanced view of the world, but that balance is always in my favour.

"We play a dirty game." Grandfather nodded and watched me from his wrinkles with those dark eyes so like Mother's.

Perhaps it wasn't the poison that irked me. Or setting me up for the fall—a chance inspiration surely and none of Ibn Fayed's doing. I recalled Qalasadi in that courtyard the only time we met, his assessment, his calculation as he considered the probabilities. Maybe that lack of malice had made it so personal; he reduced me to numbers and played the odds. Fexler's ghost had been constructed by reducing the true man to numbers. I found I didn't like the process.

"They struck at my family," I said, and shrugged. "I've built a kingdom on not allowing such acts to go unpunished."

He watched me then, with the sunlight streaming around me from the sea window, making me a shadow cut from light. What went on beneath that thin circlet of gold, I wondered, what calculations? We all make them. Not so cold-blooded as Qalasadi's but an arithmetic of sorts nonetheless. What did he make of me, this watering-down of his seed, beloved daughter mixed with detestable Ancrath? Nothing but a name to him a month ago. No child to remember, no soft toddling innocence from years past to blunt the sharp angles of the young killer before him—blood of his blood.

"How would you do it? The Caliph of Liba lives in lands that are not like ours. You would be a white man where almost no white men are. A stranger in a strange land. Marked at every turn. Reported from the moment you set foot on the Afrique shores. You'll find no friends there, only sand, disease, and death. I would gladly have Ibn Fayed and Qalasadi die. Fayed for striking at me in my halls, the mathmagician for his treachery. But if a lone assassin, especially a lone white assassin, could have accomplished it I would have dispatched one. Not in answer to Fayed's raids—as a man of honour I meet war with war—but in response to his assassin."

All men of ambition must pray to be pitted against men of honour. Although I pitied my grandfather at that moment, also it made me happy to know that at least somewhere in the mix from which I sprang there lurked a dash of such a man.

"You're right to say it would not be easy, Earl Hansa." I bowed. "Maybe I'll wait until it becomes easy . . . certainly I need to learn more, consider more."

Grandfather came to a decision. I saw the change as his face hardened into it. He would make a terrible player of poker.

"Leave Ibn Fayed and his creatures to me, Jorg. They struck at Morrow, at me and mine in the Castle Morrow. The vengeance is mine to take and I will take it."

The old man had weighed his odds. In one hand the life of an unknown relative, tainted by bad blood, in the other the chance of destroying an enemy. Whether "unknown relative" had grown into "Rowan's son, my daughter's child" and outweighed the gain, or whether he judged my chances of success so feather-light as to be outweighed by any claim on kinship, I didn't know.

"I will leave them, then." I bowed again. The lie came easily. I chose to believe he saw me as his daughter's son.

* * *

I provisioned well, loading my mule with water-skins and dried meat. I would find fruit on the way: on the Horse Coast in high summer you had only to stretch out an arm to find an apple, apricot, plum, peach, pear, or even an orange. I packed a tent, for shade is a rarity in the dry hills behind the coastlands, and without the sea breezes the land bakes. I'm told the Moors have held the southern kingdoms time and again, Kadiz, Kordoba, Morrow, Wennith, Andaluth, even Aramis. They find it not so different from the dusts of Afrique.

"So the Iberico, is it?"

I finished cinching the load-strap beneath my mule and looked up.

"Sunny!" I grinned at his scowl. Months back I chose the name for the guardsman after he did his best to keep me out of the castle that first day when I arrived incognito.

"Minding my own business I was and up comes Earl Hansa. 'Greyson,' he says. He likes to know all the men's names. 'Greyson,' he says, and puts his hand on my shoulder. 'Young King Jorg is making a trip and I'd like you to go along with him.' 'Volunteering,' he called it."

"Sunny, I can't think of a man I'd rather have with me." I stood and patted the mule's haunches. It seemed a sturdy beast, shabby but strong. The ostler said he was forty years and more, and wise with it. I thought it good to have at least one greybeard in the party.

"This is revenge for making you drink from the horse trough, ain't it?" Sunny said. He had a sour look to him that made me think of Brother Row.

I waggled my hand. "Little bit." In truth I hadn't known I was getting an escort, let alone picked the man. "In any case, you'll enjoy getting out and about," I said. "Surely even the Iberico Hills beat a day standing guard at the Lowery Gate?"

He spat at that, strengthening his resemblance to Row still further. "I'm a wall guard, not a house flower." A stretch of his arm showed off the sun's nut-brown stain. House guards are never so tanned.

With the mule's tether in hand I set off for the gate. Sunny followed. His packhorse stood outside the castle wall in the shade of an olive tree, high laden as if we were bound for a crossing of the Aups.

However reluctant the show Sunny put on, my mule had him beaten. I had to haul the beast past the horse trough. I named him Balky and encouraged him with a stick. In the end I had my way, but the fact that Balky did not want to go where I led was never in doubt. I guess he really was the wise one after all.

5

Castle Morrow, like the Haunt, is set apart from the region's main town. Both castles are placed for defence of their occupants. In the Hundred War the conquering of kingdoms is the business of avarice. The Hundred want their new lands to be rich and plentiful, full of taxpayers and recruits. Most attacks will aim to kill the land's ruler so the aggressor may claim his throne and take the kingdom unharmed. Wars of attrition where the peasantry are slaughtered, cities burned, crops destroyed, are less common and happen most often when the two sides are evenly matched, both struggling to gain the advantage required to assault the foe's castles.

The city of Albaseat rests on fertile plains maybe fifty miles inland from Castle Morrow. It took Sunny and me three days to walk the distance, having started late on the first day, and pausing for frequent stick-based negotiations with Balky. The River Jucca feeds the surrounding farmlands. We approached the city along the Coast Road, which for the last few miles leads along the riverbank, past orchards of every sort, through vineyards, along the foot of slopes thick with olive groves. Turning for Albaseat's gates we walked between tilled fields heavy with tomatoes, peppers, beans, onions, cabbage, potatoes, enough food to feed the world.

The walls and towers of Albaseat shone in the southern sun.

"Makes Hodd Town look like a pile of offal," I said.

"Where?" Sunny asked.

"Capital city of the Renar Highlands," I said. "The only city really. More of a big town. Well, a town anyhow."

"The Renar Highlands?"

"Now you're just trying to irk me." I didn't think he was, though. He blinked and looked away from Albaseat's towers.

"Oh *that* Hood Town, my apologies." It wasn't often that Sunny remembered I was the king of anywhere and it always left him looking surprised.

"Hodd Town!"

The guards at the city gates let us pass without question. It wasn't often that *I* remembered Sunny was Greyson Landless, royal guard from Earl Hansa's court.

Albaseat not only left Hodd Town looking like a tumbledown village, it made Crath City look shabby in comparison. The Moors had ruled Albaseat for generations and left their mark everywhere, from the great stone halls that stabled Grandfather's cavalry to the high towers from whose minarets you could look out over the source of his wealth, laid out in many shades of green. I did just that, paying a copper to climb the winding stair of the Fayed Tower, a public building at the heart of the great plaza before the new cathedral. Sunny stayed at ground level, watching his horse and Balky from the tower's shade.

Even a hundred yards above the plaza's baking flagstones it felt oven hot. The breeze through the minaret was worth a copper on its own. Without the slow green waters of the Jucca the fields would be desert. The green gave over to parched browns as the land rose and I could see the first rolling steps of the Iberico Hills away to the north. Whatever taint they carried seemed to stain the air itself, turning it a dirty yellow where the horizon started to reclaim the hills.

I leaned out, hands on the windowsill, to spot Sunny below. The city marched off in all directions, broad and ordered streets lined with tall, whitewashed houses. To the west grander mansions, to the east the low homes and tight alleys of the poor. My grandfather's people living in the peace of his reign, his nobles plotting, merchants trading, blacksmith, tanner, and slaughterman hard at work, whores aback, maids aknee, washerwomen hauling loads to the river-side meadows where horsemen trained their steeds, the pulse of life, an old and complex dance of many partners. Quick, quick, slow.

To leave all this behind and dare old poisons, to risk an end like those I had given the people of Gelleth, made no sense. And still I would do it. Not for the hollowness inside me, nor the weight of the copper box that held what had been taken, not for the promise of old magics and the power they offered, but just to know, just to do more than skitter about on the surface of this world. I wanted more than I could see from a tower, however high, or even from the eyes the Builders set among the stars.

Perhaps I just wanted to know what it was that I wanted. Maybe that is all that growing up means.

Slow steps brought me from the tower, lost in thought. I waved Sunny to me and bid him lead me to the Lord House.

"They won't want the likes of—" He glanced back at me, taking in the fine cloak, the silver-chased breastplate. "Oh." And remembering that I was a king, albeit of a realm he hardly knew of, he led on.

We passed the cathedral, the finest I'd seen, a stone confection reaching for blue skies. The saints watched me from their niches and galleries. I felt their disapproval, as if they turned to stare once we passed. The crowds thronged there, before the cathedral steps, perhaps drawn by the cool promise of the great hall within. Sunny and I elbowed our way through, pushing aside the occasional priest and monk as we went.

I came sweating to the doors of the Lord House. I would have stripped to the waist and let Balky carry my gear but perhaps that might have created a poor impression. The guards admitted us, a boy taking our animals, and we sat on velvet-cushioned chairs whilst a flunky in foolish amounts of lace and silk went to announce our arrival to the provost.

The man returned several minutes later with a polite cough to indicate that I might put down the large ornamental vase I had been studying and follow him. When my hands are idle they find mischief of one sort or other. I let the vase slip, caught it an inch from the floor, and set it down. Polite coughs leave me wanting to choke out a cough of a different sort. I left Sunny to return the ornament to its niche and bade the servant lead on.

A short corridor took us to the doors of the reception chamber. Like the foyer, every inch of it stood tiled in geometric patterns, blue and white and black, fiendishly complex. Qalasadi would have enjoyed it: even a mathmagician would be hard-pressed to tease out all the secrets it held. High windows caught what breeze was to be had and gave a relief from the heat of the day.

The flunky knocked three times with a little rod he seemed to carry for that sole purpose. A pause and we entered.

The room beyond took my breath, complex in detail but a sparse and simple beauty on the grand scale, an architecture of numbers, very different from the gothic halls of my lands or the dull boxes the Builders left us. The provost sat at the far end in a high-backed ebony chair. Apart from two guards at the door and a scribe at a small desk beside the provost's seat, the long chamber lay empty and my footsteps echoed as I approached.

She looked up from her scroll while I closed the last few yards, a hunched old woman with black and glittering eyes, reminding me of a crow gone to grey and tatters.

"Honorous Jorg Ancrath, King of the Renar Highlands. Grandson to Earl Hansa." She introduced me to herself.

I gave her the small fraction of a bow her rank commanded and answered in the local custom. "You have the right of it, madam."

"We're honoured to welcome you to Albaseat, King Jorg," she said through thin, dry lips and the scribe scratched the words across his parchment.

"It's a fine city. If I could carry it I'd take it with me."

Again the scratching of the quill—my words falling so quickly into posterity.

"What are your plans, King Jorg? I hope we can tempt you to stay? Two days would be sufficient to prepare an official banquet in your honour. Many of the region's merchants would fight for the opportunity to bend your ear, and our nobility would compete to host you at their mansions, even though I hear you are already promised to Miana of Wennith. And of course Cardinal Hencom will require you at mass."

I took pleasure in not waiting for the scribe to catch up, but resisted the temptation to pepper my reply with rare and difficult words or random noises for him to puzzle over.

"Perhaps on my return, Provost. I plan first to visit the Iberico Hills. I have an interest in the promised lands: my father's kingdom has several regions where the fire from the thousand suns still burns."

I heard the quill falter at that. The old woman, though, did not flinch.

"The fire that burns the promised lands is unseen and gives no heat, King Jorg, but it sears flesh just the same. Better to learn of such places in the library."

She made no talk of postponing my trip until after her nobles and merchants had taken their bites of me. If I were bound for the Iberico Hills such efforts would be wasted—money thrown into the grave, as the local saying had it.

"Libraries are a good place to start journeys, Provost. In fact I have come to you hoping that Albaseat might have in one of its libraries a better map of the Iberico than the one copied from my grandfather's scrolls. I would count it a great favour if such a map were provided to me . . ."

I wondered how I looked to her, how young in my armour and confidence. From a distance the gaps between things are reduced. From the far end of her tunnel of years I wondered how different I looked from a child, from a toddler daring a high fall with not the slightest understanding of consequence.

"I would advise beginning and ending this journey among the scrolls, King Jorg." She shifted in her chair, plagued no doubt by the aching of joints. "But when age speaks to youth it goes unheard. When do you plan to leave?"

"With the dawn, Provost."

"I will set my scribe to searching for a map and have whatever he finds waiting for you at the North Gate by first light."

"My thanks." I inclined my head. "I hope to have some new tales to tell at your banquet when I return."

She dismissed me with an impatient wave. She didn't expect to see me again.

6

Five years earlier

Sunny and I made our way to the North Gate of Albaseat in the grey light that steals over the world before dawn. The streets thronged. In summer the Horse Coast bakes and only the earliest hours of the day offer respite. By noon the locals would retreat behind white walls, beneath the terracotta tiles, and sleep until the sun slipped from its zenith.

In the lanes leading to the gate and the wide plaza that lay before it, business had already started. Tavern doors stood open while men bore kegs in upon their shoulders, or lowered barrels into the cellars by the street-traps. Grey-faced women emptied slops from buckets into the gutters. We passed a smithy open to the road so that passersby could see the hammering and quenching and be tempted to purchase what took such sweat and force to craft. A lad hunched at the forge, poking life back into fires banked overnight.

"Oh, to be still abed." Sunny yanked his packhorse away from some tempting refuse.

A cry turned us back toward the blacksmith's. We had gone only a dozen steps beyond it. The smith's boy lay in the street now. He pushed himself up from the flagstones, face grazed, shaking his head, unsteady. The smith paced out from his workshop and kicked the boy hard enough to lift him off the ground. The air left his lungs with a whuff. Under the dirt the boy's hair looked fair, almost golden, rare this far south.

"My money's on the big fellow," I said. My brother, Will, had such hair.

"He's a big one, all right." Sunny nodded. The smith wore just a leather apron from shoulder to knee and leggings held up with rope. The muscle in his arms gleamed. Swinging a four-pound hammer from dawn till dusk will put a lot of meat on a man.

The child lay on his back, one arm half-raised, too winded to groan, a trickle of blood at the corner of his mouth. I thought he might be eight, maybe nine.

"Do I have to kick every lesson into you?" The smith didn't yell but he had the voice of a man who speaks over the anvil. He drove his foot into the boy's head, the force rolling him once. Blood on the smith's boot now, and staining the boy's hair.

"Ah, hell." Sunny shook his head.

We watched as the smith stepped in closer.

"I should stop this," Sunny said, reluctance in every line of him. Something in the smith's face put me in mind of Rike. Not a man to get in the way of.

"Boys get kicked every day," I said. "Children die every day." Some have their heads broken against milestones.

The smith loomed above the boy, who lay curled now as if hunched against the pain. The man drew back for another kick, then paused, reaching a decision. He lifted his boot to stamp the life out of the lad. I guessed he thought him past use, best to finish him off.

"They don't die every day with one of Earl Hansa's guards watching. The Earl wouldn't want this." But still Sunny didn't move. Instead he shouted, "You, smith, stop!"

The man paused, his heel a few inches above the side of the boy's head.

"I've picked up strays before and they both died," I said past a bitter taste. I saw blood in golden curls and felt the thorns' tight hold.

I learned this lesson young, a sharp lesson taught in blood and rain. The path to the empire gates lay at my back. A man diverted from that path by strays, burdened by others' needs, would never sit upon the all-throne. Orrin of Arrow would save the children, but they would not save him.

"He's a street cur," the smith said. "Too stupid to learn. I've fed him for a month. Kept him under my roof. He's mine to end." He brought his heel down hard, his weight upon it.

A loud retort of leather on stone. The boy rolled clear but lacked the strength to get up. The smith roared a curse—it drowned my own—the burn that stretched across my face from chin to brow as if a red-hot hand had branded me, now burned again with the same pain that it first gave. I've been told that conscience speaks in a small voice at the back of the mind, clear to some, to others muffled and easy to ignore. I never heard that it burned across a man's face in red agony. Still, pain or no pain, I don't like to be led or to be pushed. Perhaps I selected Balky as a kindred spirit for I took direction as poorly, even from my own conscience on the rare occasions it made a bid for control.

Sunny passed me, aimed for the smith. He hadn't even drawn his sword.

"I'll buy him from you!" I shouted. Sunny could come in handy and I guessed the smith would break his arms off before the idiot thought to reach for his blade.

That made the smith stop in his tracks, Sunny too, with a sigh of relief, and it quieted the pain. The smith eyed the silver on my breastplate, the cut of my cloak, and thought perhaps that his satisfaction might be worth less than the contents of my coin pouch.

"What's your offer?"

"A contest of your choosing. You win and I pay you this for the boy." I held a gold ducet before my face between index and middle finger. "Lose and you get nothing for him." I magicked the coin away.

He had a good frown at that. The boy managed another roll and fetched up against the wall of the harness shop opposite.

"Perhaps you think you can hold a hot iron longer than I can?" I suggested.

The frown deepened into crevasses topped by the black band of his brows. "Strength," he said. "Who can hold the anvil overhead the longest."

I glanced at the anvil a few yards back into the smithy. Perhaps two men of regular height might weigh as much. "Rules?" I asked.

"Rules? No rules!" He laughed. He flexed an arm and muscle mounded on muscle. The Great Ronaldo would be impressed if Taproot's circus ever made it to Albaseat. "Strength! That's the rule."

"Show me how it's done, then." I walked into the smithy. The glow of the forge fire and of two smoking lamps gave enough light to avoid the workbenches and various buckets. The place had a pleasing smell of char and iron and sweat. It reminded me of Norwood, of Mabberton, of a dozen other battles.

The smith followed. I set a hand to his chest as he passed me. "Your name?"

"Jonas."

He walked around the anvil. I glanced at the ceiling where tools hung from the beams. He would have just enough room. I would have plenty as he stood a hand taller than me.

Sunny stepped up behind me.

"The boy's still alive, I take it? I'm not doing this for a corpse."

"He's alive. Might be hurt bad."

Jonas crouched beside the anvil. He closed one big hand around the horn and set the heel of his other hand beneath the lip of the anvil's face.

"You've done this before." I gave him my grin.

"Yes." He showed his teeth. "I can taste your gold already, boy."

He tensed, building for the explosion that would drive the ironwork upward. That's when I hit him, with a hammer from the nearest bench. I struck the side of his head just by the eye. The noise wasn't dissimilar from his boot hitting the child. The hammer came away bloody and Jonas pitched forward over his anvil.

"What?" Sunny asked, as if somehow he hadn't seen it in the half-light.

I shrugged. "No rules. You heard him."

We left them both lying in their blood. Whatever fire ate at my face I didn't need another stray, and even if the boy could walk, taking him to the Iberico would be more cruel than another month in Jonas's care. At least the boy was sitting up and looking about, which was more than could be said for his master.

A corner and another street brought us to the plaza. We pushed a path through bakers' boys with trays of loaves overhead, between laden farm carts ready to be offloaded onto the stalls already set to either side of the gate towers. The place heaved, late arriving traders made haste to erect their tables and awnings, and the townsfolk came mob-handed to buy, coins clicking in their hip pouches, eyes darting, hunting bargains in the predawn grey.

"We'll be lucky to find the provost's man in all this." Sunny snatched at a passing bread roll and missed.

"Have some faith, man," I said. "How hard is it to spot a king?" I looped Balky's reins over his pack-saddle and ran both hands through my hair, throwing the length of it wide across my shoulders and back.

We reached the gates, the smoothness of the wall stretching above us to the paling sky. Hooves clattered across the flagstones as we led our animals beneath and traversed a dark tunnel through ten yards of wall.

"I'm to ride with you." A voice from the black shadows to the side of the exit.

"There you go, Sunny, we are known." I turned and gave him my grin. The glow from the east caught the lines of his face.

The stranger broke from the shadows, a black clot moving to join us. A woman.

She drew close, her horse a tall black stallion, a dark cloak wrapping her as if she expected to be cold.

"Did you bring a map for us?" I held out my hand.

"I *am* the map," she said. I could make out only the curve of her smile.

"And how did you know us?" I asked, returning my hand to the reins.

She said nothing, only touched her fingers to her cheek. My scars burned for a moment, another echo of Gog's fire no doubt for I had surely forgotten how to blush long before.

Sunny held his tongue, but I could feel the smugness radiating off him behind me.

"I'm Honorous Jorg Ancrath, king of somewhere you've never heard of. The grinning idiot behind me is Greyson Landless, bastard son of some venerable line that holds a few dusty acres along the Horse Coast best used for growing rocks. You can call me Jorg and him Sunny. And we're walking."

"Lesha. One sixteenth of the Provost's horde of grandchildren."

"Her granddaughter? I'm surprised. I had the impression that the Provost wasn't expecting to see us return."

It seemed that Lesha wasn't going to answer for she rode a hundred yards in silence at our side as we led our animals away from the city.

"I'm sure my grandmother's assessment of the expedition is accurate and remains unchanged."

I still could see nothing of her within the folds of her cloak but something in the way she held herself made me sure she was kind to the eye, maybe beautiful.

"So why would she send you, Lady Lesha?" Sunny asked. He broke the silence I'd left for her to fill. Often the lack of a question will prompt an answer, sometimes an answer to a question you might not have thought to ask.

"She didn't send me—I decided to come. In any case, she won't miss me too much. She has plenty of grandchildren and I'm far from being her favourite."

That left a long silence that none of chose to break. Lesha dismounted and led her horse beside us.

The dawn broke, a gentle fading of greys until the eastern sky grew bright with promise. At last the first brilliant corner of the sun poked above the horizon, throwing long shadows our way. I glanced at Lesha then, and lost any sting from when she had touched her cheek to mark my scarring. Each part of her face had been burned as badly as the wound I bore. Her skin held a melted quality, as if it had run like molten rock then frozen once more. The burns surprised me, but less than the fact that she had survived them. She met my gaze. Her eyes were very blue.

"You're still sure you want to go to the Iberico?" She pushed back her hood. The fire had left no hair, her scalp piebald in whites, unhealthy pinks, and beige, holes where her ears lay.

"Damned if *I* am," Sunny gasped.

I reached out and took her reins so we both stopped in the road. Balky stood shoulder to shoulder with her horse, Sunny a few yards ahead, looking back.

"And why are you so keen to return, lady?" I asked. "Why not twice shy, for you've surely been bitten?"

"Perhaps I've nothing to lose now," she said, her lips lumpy lines of gristle. She didn't look away from me.

I closed my eyes for a second and a point of red light blinked against the back of my eyelids. Fexler's tiny red dot, drawing me across all these miles.

"And what desire drew you there in the first place? Did you think to find wealth in the ruins, or to come back to Albaseat a great and famed explorer?" I shook my head. "I don't think so. Those are bad bets—not for a daughter of the provost's family. I think the secrets called you there. You wanted answers. To know what the Builders hid there, yes?"

She glanced away then, and spat, like a man. "I found no answers."

"But that doesn't mean the place holds none." I leaned in toward her. She flinched away, not expecting intimacy. My hand caught her around the back of that bald head, the skin rippled and unpleasant beneath my fingers. "It doesn't mean that asking our questions is not the truest thing that creatures such as you and I can do." I drew her very close though she strained against it. She stood tall for a woman. "We can't be trapped by fear. Lives lived within such walls are just slower deaths." I spoke in a whisper now, bowing my head until a bare inch stood between our faces. I half expected her to smell of char, but she had no scent, not perfume, not sweat. "Let's go there and spit in the eye of any who says the old knowledge is forbidden to us, neh?" I kissed her cheek then, because I feared to do it and though common-sense may occasionally bind me, I'll be fucked if fear will.

Lesha snatched herself away. "You're just a child. You don't know what you're talking about." But she didn't sound displeased.

We rode until noon and took shelter from the sun in the shade of a stand of olive trees. The farmer's wife proved enterprising enough to delay her own siesta and toil up the slopes to offer us wine, cheeses, and hard brown herb-bread. The old woman crossed herself briefly when she saw Lesha but had the grace not to stare. We set to the meal, and sent her back with an empty basket and a handful of coppers, enough for twice the amount of food were it served in a fine tavern.

"Tell me about the Moors," I said to nobody in particular. The piece of cheese I licked from my finger was soft and crumbly both at once. It smelled like something that shouldn't ever be eaten, but had a pleasingly complex and pungent taste.

"Which ones?" Lesha said. She looked asleep, stretched on the dusty soil, head pillowed on her bundled cloak at the base of the tree shading her.

She had a point. I'd seen at least a dozen Moors in Albaseat, wrapped in white robes, most of them all but hidden inside the hood of a burnoose, some trading, some just bound upon their business.

"Tell me about the Caliph of Liba." It seemed a good place to start.

"Ibn Fayed," Sunny muttered. "The thorn in your grandfather's arse."

"Has he many like Qalasadi working for him?" I asked.

"Mathmagicians?" Sunny asked. "No."

"There aren't many like that," Lesha said. "And they don't work for masters in any case. They follow a pure path. There isn't much that men like that want."

"Not gold?" I asked.

Lesha raised her ruined head to watch me then sat up against the tree. "Only rarities hold interest for their kind. Wonders such as we might find in the Iberico, but just as likely old scrolls from the Builder times, ways of calculating, old lore, the sort of cleverness that never seemed to get written down on anything that lasts, or at least that we can read."

"And Ibn Fayed sails against the Horse Coast to raid, or to settle, or is it punishment for not following the Moors' prophet?" I had my grandfather and uncle's views on this but it's good to look at such things from other angles.

"His people want to return," Lesha said.

This was new. The provost's granddaughter took her wisdom from the whole book, not just the current page.

"Return?" I had seen a Moorish hand behind much that stood in Albaseat though no one seemed eager to admit it.

"Caliphs have ruled here as many years as kings have ruled. Before the Builders and after. The scribes today call them raiders, burners, heathens, but there's Moorish cleverness mixed into everything we take pride in."

"Not just a pretty face, then," I said. She read, this one, for her opinions weren't ones that could be formed on what others might think it safe to teach. The church held the Horse Coast Kingdoms and the West Ports close—any closer and they'd choke them. Priests kept a low opinion of heathens, and this far south disagreeing with a man of the cloth often proved to be a dangerous pastime. In every town a church scribe busied himself rewriting history—but they couldn't rewrite what lay written in stone all about them.

Lesha took no offence at my jibe, or at least I think not for her scar tissue couldn't mirror the emotions below.

We lay quiet for a time then. Almost no sound but for the distant clang of a goat bell. Why the old nanny wasn't lying in the shade I couldn't say. The heat wrapped us like a blanket, taking away any inclination to move.

"You were slow to save that boy, Jorg," Sunny said. I thought him asleep for the past quarter hour, but clearly he'd been replaying the morning behind his eyes.

"I didn't save him. I saved you. You're of some use."

"You would have let him die?" Sunny sounded troubled by it.

"I would," I said. "He was nothing to me." Golden curls and blood, the image played over the back of my eyelids. I opened my eyes and sat up. They broke William's head on a milestone, swung him by the feet and beat him on the stone. It happened. The world rolled on regardless. And I learned that nothing mattered.

"I couldn't stand and let it happen while I watched," Sunny said. "You can't kick a child to death in front of Earl Hansa's guard."

"You stepped in for yourself, or for my grandfather?" I asked.

"It was my duty."

I took an olive left at the bottom of the food basket. Firm flesh broke beneath my teeth. The warm and complicated flavour spread as I chewed.

"Would you have stepped in if it hadn't been your duty?" I asked.

Sunny paused. "If he hadn't been so damn big, yes."

"Because you couldn't watch it happen?"

"Yes," he said.

"Don't live by half measures, Greyson." I pushed the dusty linen of my sleeve back until the scars from the hook briar showed—pale sigils against tanned skin. "I heard a priest once speak of the business of salvation. He urged us not to let the fact that we couldn't save everyone from their sins stop us trying to save the people in front of us. That's priests for you. Ready to give up in a moment. Falling over themselves to admit their frailty as if it were a virtue." I spat out the olive stone. "Either children are worth saving just because they're children, or they're not worth saving. Don't let your actions be dictated by the accident that puts one in front of your eyes and hides the next. If they're worth saving, save them all, find them, protect them, make it your life's work. If not, take a different street so you won't even see the one you might have seen, turn your head aside, put a hand to your eyes. Problem solved."

"You'd save them all, would you?" Lesha spoke on the other side of me, voice soft.

"I know a man who is trying to," I said. "And if I hadn't learned better, then yes, I'd save them all. No half measures. Some things can't be cut in half. You can't half-love someone. You can't half-betray, or half-lie."

Silence after that. Even the goat slept.

The shade kept us until the shadows started to lengthen and the white blaze of the sun softened into something that could be endured.

We moved on in the afternoon. Night found our party camped in a dry valley ten miles further north, with a roof of stars and the chirp and whirr of insects to serenade us. The olive groves and cork trees lay far behind. Nothing grew in these valleys except unforgiving thorns, mesquite bushes and creosote, making a rich perfume of the night air but offering nothing to burn. We ate hard bread, apples, some oranges from Albaseat market, and washed it down with a jug of wine, so dark a red as to be near black.

I lay in the night watching the stars wheel, listening to the nicker of the horses, Balky's occasional snort and stamp, Sunny snoring. From time to time Lesha whimpered in her sleep, a soft thing but full of hurt. And rising around it all, the relentless orchestra of night-crawlers, the sound swelling in waves as if an ocean rose about us as the sun fell. I held the copper box in one hand, the other touched the ground, grit beneath my fingertips. Tomorrow we would walk again. It seemed right to walk, and not just to save taking a good horse into poisoned lands. Some places a man needs to have his own two legs take him. Some journeys need a different perspective. The miles mean more if you have travelled them one step at a time and felt the ground change beneath your feet.

At last I closed my eyes and let the multitude of stars be replaced by a single red one. A single star brought the wise men to a cradle in Bethlehem. I wondered if a wise man would follow Fexler's star.

7

Chella's story

Six Years Ago
Defeated in the Cantanlona Swamps

The smell of soil, of earth that crumbles red in the hand, just so, and lets you know you're home. The sun that lit a life from baby to head-strong young man arcs between crimson sunrise and crimson sunset. In the dark, lions roar.

"This is not your place, woman."

She wants it to be her place. The strength of his longing drew her here, with him, riding the wake of his departure.

"Go home." His voice is deep with command. Everything he says sounds like wisdom.

"I can tell why he liked you," she says. She has no home.

"You like him too, but you're too broken to know what to do with that."

"Don't dare to pity me, Kashta." Anger she'd thought burned out flares once more. The red soil, white sun, low huts, all seem further away.

"My name is not yours to conjure with, Chella. Go back."

"Don't order me, Nuban. I could make you my slave again. My toy." His world is a bright patch now at the corner of her vision, detail lost in jewelled beauty.

"I'm not there any more, woman. I'm here. In the drumming circle, in the hut shadow, in the footprint of the lion." Each word fainter and deeper.

Chella lifted her face from the stinking mud and spat foul water. Her arms vanished into the mire at the elbows, thick slime dripped from her. She spat again, teeth scraping the mud from her tongue. "Jorg Ancrath!"

The web of necromancy that she had spun through the marsh month after month until it pervaded every sucking pool and mire, reaching fathoms deep to even the oldest of the bog-dead, now lay tattered, its strength bleeding away, corrupted once more by the lives of frogs and worms and wading birds. Chella found herself sinking and summoned enough of what strength remained to flounder onto more solid ground, a low mound rising from the mud.

The sky held the memory of blue, faded, as if left too long in the sun. She lay on her back, aware of a thousand prickles beneath her, of being too cold on her sides, too hot on her face. A groan escaped. Pain. When a necromancer has spent too much power, when death has burned out of them, only pain remains to fill the hole. After all, that's what life is. Pain.

"Damn him." Chella lay panting, more alive than she had been in decades, barely treading the margins of the deadlands. Her teeth ground over each other, muscles iron, the hurt washing across her in waves. "Damn him."

A crow watched her, glossy black, perched on the stone that marked the mound's highpoint.

The crow spoke, a harsh cawing that took on meaning from one second to the next. "It's not the pain of returning that keeps the necromancer away from life. It's not that which keeps them so far away—as far as they can go without losing their grip on it. It's the memories."

The words came from the crow's beak but they had been her brother's, years ago, when he first taught her, first tempted her with what it meant to be death-sworn. In moments of regret she blamed him, as if he had talked her into corruption, as if mere words had parted her from all that was right. Jorg Ancrath had put an end to all her brother's talking, though. Beheading him beneath Mount Honas, eating his heart, stealing away some part of his strength.

"Fly away, crow." She hissed it past clenched teeth. But memories had started to leak behind her eyes, like pus from a wound, welling up where fingers press.

The crow watched her. Beneath its thin and clutching claws the stone lay lichen spattered, patched in dull orange, faded green, as if diseased. The bird held Chella's slitted gaze, its eyes bright, black, and glittering. "No necromancer truly knows what waits for them as they walk the grey path into the deadlands." It cawed then, harsh and brief as the speech of crows should be, before returning to her brother's voice and to his lessons. "Each of them has their reasons, often horrific reasons that would turn the stomachs of their fellow men, but whatever their motivation, however strange and cold their minds, they don't know what it is that they have begun. If it could be explained to them in advance, shown on one foul canvas, none of them, not even the worst of them, would take the first step."

He hadn't lied. He had spoken the whole truth. But words are only words and they seldom turn a person from their path unless they want to be turned.

"I followed you, Cellan. I took your path." She remembered his face, her brother's face, from a year when they had been young together, children. A happy year. "No!" The pain had been better than this. She tried not to think, to make a stone of her mind, to allow nothing in.

"It's just life, Chella." The bird sounded amused. "Let it in."

Behind screwed-shut eyes images fought for their moment, to hold her regard if just for an instant before the tide of remembering swept them aside. She saw the crow there, dipping its scarlet head into an open corpse.

"Life is sweet." Again the caw. "Taste it."

She snatched for the crow, lunging, one pain-clawed hand reaching. Only to find it gone. No flap of wings, no scolding voice from high above, just one broken and bedraggled feather, as if that was all that there had ever been.

The sun passed overhead, witness to Chella's long agony, and at last, in the dark beneath a host of stars, she sat. Her head throbbed with memory. Not a complete mapping of the life she had stepped away from, but enough meat on the skeleton to match with where she stood upon the threshold of death and life. She hugged herself, feeling at once how her ribs stood out, how sunken her belly, how withered her chest. The coldest fact, though—the harshest judgment, came from the sum of all her remembering. No tragedy had driven her along the path she chose. She hadn't run from any particular horror, no offence too vile to live with, no terror nipping at her heels. Nothing but common greed: greed for power, greed for things, and curiosity, of the everyday cat-killing kind. Such were the needs that had set her walking among the dead, mining depravity, rejecting all humanity. Nothing poetic, dark, or worthy, just the mean little wants of an ordinary little life.

Chella drew a deep breath. She resented having to. Jorg Ancrath had done this to her. She felt her heart thump in her chest. Barely more than a child and he had beaten her twice. Left her lying here more alive than dead. Made her feel!

She picked a leech from her leg, then another, fat with her blood. Her skin itched where mosquitoes had taken their fill. It had been years since she held any interest for such creatures, years since they could even touch her without snuffing out the tiny flickers of life in their soft and fragile bodies.

The marsh stank. It hit her for the first time, though she had spent months in its embrace. It stank, and tasted worse than it smelled. Chella pulled herself up, weak in her legs, trembling. The cool of night on her mud-caked nakedness accounted for some of her shivering, hunger and fatigue for a little more, but most of it was fear. Not of the darkness or the swamp or of the long journey through harsh lands. The Dead King scared her. The thought of his cold regard, of his questions, of standing before him in whatever dead thing he chose to wear, her wrapped in the tatters of her power and speaking of failure.

How had it even come to this? Necromancers had been the masters of death, not its servants. But when the Dead King first rose unbidden amongst the darkest of their workings the necromancers knew fear once more, though they thought it abandoned and forgotten in their path. And not just Chella's small cabal beneath Mount Honas. She knew that now, though for a year and more she had thought the Dead King a demon woken by her delving into places not meant for men, a creature focused on her alone, then on her brother and the few around them. But the Dead King spoke to all who looked past life. Any who reached through and drew back what could be found beyond the veil to refill the remains of those who had passed. All who reached for such power would find themselves, sooner or later, holding the Dead King's hand. And he would not ever let them go.

And why had he sent her against this boy? And how had she failed?

"Damn you, Jorg Ancrath." And Chella fell back to her knees and vomited up a dark and sour mess.

8

In the six kingdoms I took from the prince of Arrow there are many cities larger, cleaner, finer, and in every way superior to Hodd Town. There were cities in my domain that I had yet to see, cities where the people called me king and my statue stood in markets and plazas, that I had not been within ten miles of, and even these were finer than Hodd Town. And yet Hodd Town felt more mine. I had held it longer, taken it in person, painted the streets red when Jarco Renar raised it in rebellion. It was not a place where they remembered Orrin of Arrow. None in Hodd Town spoke of his goodness and vision or voiced the common belief that he would be named a saint before his memory grew cold.

All of Hodd Town turned out to greet our arrival. No one lingers at home when the Gilden Guard ride through their city gates. Highlanders lined the streets cheering, and waving whatever flags they had. Of the Hoddites who would whisper in hoarse voices the next day, heads pounding with the echoes of celebration, not one in ten would be able to give a good account of why they cheered, but in a place like the Highlands it's hard not to get excited over any touch of the exotic or foreign. At least as long as it's just passing through and doesn't look at your sister.

I rode at the head of the column and led it to the gates of Lord

Holland's mansion, the grandest building in the city, or at least the grandest complete building. One day the cathedral would outshine it.

Lord Holland came to throw his gates open in person, a beefy man sweating in his finery, his wife wobbling along behind, a fan of silver and pearls to hide her jowls.

"King Jorg! You honour my house." Lord Holland bowed. His face said his hair should be grey with age so I half expected the glossy black wig to fall as he bent to me, but it stayed in place. Perhaps he kept his own hair and used lampblack on it.

"I do honour you," I agreed. "I've decided to stay the night while I wait on word from the Haunt."

I swung out of my saddle, armour clanking, and waved him to lead on. "Captain Harran." I turned, holding a hand up to stop his mouth. "We're staying here until dawn tomorrow. There's no discussion to be had. We will have to make the time up on the road."

He looked grim at that but we knew each other well enough that after a few moments holding his eyes to mine he turned away and called for the guard to set a perimeter around Holland's mansion.

The Hollands' house guard moved to block Gorgoth's path as he followed Makin and myself to the front doors. I had to commend their bravery. I've seen Gorgoth reach out both hands and crush two men's skulls without effort. Lord Holland paused on the steps ahead of me, sensing trouble. He turned with a questioning look.

"I'm taking Gorgoth through the Gilden Gate in Vyene, so I think he ranks high enough for your front door, Holland." I nodded him on.

The guards stepped back with evident relief and we went inside.

Lord Holland's guest chambers proved to be more than well appointed—even "luxurious" might be too small a word. Thick rugs covered the floor, woven silk shipped from the Indus and worked with all manner of pagan gods. No wall remained without art, either tapestry or oil and brush, and elaborate plasterwork, gilded to a high shine, decorated the ceilings. Holland had offered me his own rooms but I didn't want to live amid his old man's stink. Besides, if they were richer than his guest rooms I'd be hard-pressed to resist stealing stuff.

"Decadence begins when the budget to beautify a man's home exceeds the coin spent to ensure its defence." I turned back to Makin. Gorgoth closed the doors behind him and stood at Makin's side.

Makin smoothed back his hair and grinned. "It's pretty. No doubting that."

Gorgoth let his gaze wander. "There's a whole world reaching into this room."

He had it right. Holland had assembled pieces from all corners of empire and beyond. The works of brilliant men. Years of effort concentrated within four walls to ease the eye of a rich lord's guests.

Gorgoth lifted an elegant chair in one blunt hand, his fingers curled around intricate scrollwork. "The beauty to be found beneath mountains is more . . . robust." He set the chair down again. I imagined the legs splintering if he tried to sit upon it. "Why are we here?"

Makin nodded. "You said bad beds, grinning officials, and fleas. But here we are even so. The beds look fine. Perhaps a little soft and"—he glanced at Gorgoth—"weak, and there may be fleas, though a better class of flea no doubt, and yes, the officials grinned."

I pursed my lips and threw myself back onto the grand bed. I sunk into eiderdown, the coverings almost closing above me as if I had fallen into deep water.

"There's something I need to sleep on," I said.

It took an effort to lift my head to sight Gorgoth. "You two amuse yourselves. I'll send if I need you. Makin, be charming. Gorgoth, don't eat any servants."

Gorgoth rumbled at that. They turned to leave.

"Gorgoth!" He paused before the door, a door so tall that even he would not have to duck beneath it. "Don't let them give you any shit. You can eat them if they try. You're coming to Congression as

King Under the Mountain. The Hundred may not know it yet but they will."

He tilted his head at that, and they both left.

I had my own reasons for bringing the leucrota to Congression, but good as those reasons were it had been the chance to represent his new people, his trolls, that had persuaded Gorgoth, and lord knows he needed persuading, for I couldn't order him. And that in itself made another good reason. I had few men around me that would speak honestly and tell me if they thought me wrong. I had only one man who I couldn't order, who at the very last would twist my head off rather than obey against his instinct. Everyone needs somebody like that around sometimes.

I sat in Lord Holland's delicate chair, at a desk of burr walnut so polished it seemed to glow, and played with the chess set I had filched from the guards' pavilion. I killed a few hours staring at the squares, moving the pieces in their allotted fashion. Enjoying the weight of them in my hand, the glide of them across marble. I have read that the Builders made toys that could play chess. Toys, as small as the silver bishop in my hand, that could defeat any player, taking no time to select moves that undid even the best minds amongst their makers. The bishop made a satisfying click when tapped to the board. I beat out a little rhythm, wondering if any point remained in playing a game that toys could own. If we couldn't find a better game then perhaps the mechanical minds the Builders left behind would always win.

Holland took me at my word and allowed no visitors, no requests, no invitations. I sat alone in the luxury of his guest rooms and remembered. There was a time when a bad memory was taken from me. I carried it in a copper box until at the last I had to know. Any closed box, any secret, will gnaw at you, day on day, year on year, until it reaches the bone. It will whisper the old rhyme—open the box, and face the danger, or wonder—till it drives you mad, what would have happened if you had. There are other memories I would rather set away from me, beyond use and recollection, but the box taught me a lesson. Nothing can be cut away without loss. Even the worst of our memories is part of the foundation that keeps us in the world.

At last I stood, tipped over the kings, both the black side and the white side, and fell once more into the bed. This time I let it swallow me and sank into the white musk of her dreaming.

I stood in the Tall Castle before the doors to my father's throne room. I knew this scene. I knew all the scenes that Katherine played for me behind those doors. Galen dying, but with my indifference overwritten by all her yesterdays so that he fell like an axe through both our lives. Or Father's knife, driven into my chest at the height of my victory, as I reached to him, son to father, a sharp reminder of all his poison, aimed for the heart.

"I'm past games," I said.

I set my fingers to the handles of the great doors.

"I had a brother who taught me a lesson that stuck. Brother Hendrick. A wild one, a stranger to fear."

And no sooner was he mentioned than he stood at my side—like the worst of devils summoned by their name. He stood beside me before my father's doors, with a laugh and a stamp of his boot. Brother Hendrick, dark as a Moor, his long hair in black knots, reaching past his shoulders, lean muscled, rangy like a troll, the pink and ragged slash of a scar from his left eye to the corner of his mouth, stark against dirty skin.

"Brother Jorg." He inclined his head.

"Show her how you died, Brother," I said.

He gave a wild grin at that, did Brother Hendrick, and the Conaught spearman charged again from a sudden rolling smoke. The Conaught spear is an ugly weapon, barbed and barbed again as if it's never intended to come out, cutting blades along the length.

Hendrick caught the spear in his gut, just as I remembered it, right down to the bright sound of mail links snapping. His eyes went wide, that grin of his wider, twisted now and scarlet. The Conaught man had him, stuck on that spear, out of reach of Hendrick's sword even if he had the strength to swing.

"Now I'm doubting that Brother Hendrick could get himself off that spear," I said, over the ghosts of screams and the memory of swords on swords. "But he could have fought it, and maybe just maybe he'd have thrown himself clear. He would have left more yards of his guts on those barbs than remained in his body though. He could have tried to fight it, but sometimes the only option is to raise the stakes, to throw yourself the other way, to force your opponent further down the path they've chosen, further than they might want to go."

Brother Hendrick dropped his sword and shook the shield from his arm. With both hands he seized the spear high along its haft, past the blades, and hauled himself along it. The point sprang black and dripping from his back, a yard of wood and cutting edges passed into his stomach, tearing a terrible wound, and in two driving steps he reached his foe.

"Watch," I said.

And Brother Hendrick slammed his forehead into the spearman's face. Two red hands gripped behind a Conaught neck and pulled him closer still. Hendrick fell, locked to his man, his teeth deep in exposed throat. The smoke rolled over them both.

"That spearman should have let go that day," I said. "*You* should let go now, Katherine."

I gripped the handles to the throne room doors and pulled, not on the metal but on the dark tide of my dreaming, on the fever dreams of long ago when I sweated in the corruption of my thorn wounds. Frost spread from my fingers, across the bronze, over the wood, and from every joint and seam in the doors pus began to ooze. The sweet stench of it drew me to the night I woke in sweat and pain to find Friar Glen's man, Inch, with his hands upon me. As a child of nine I didn't understand much, but the way he snatched back from me, the look on that mild face, the beading sweat as if a fever held him also, all helped me to know his mind. He turned without words and started for the door, hurried but not running. He should have run.

My hands, white upon the icy bronze of the handles, felt not the cold metal but the weight and heat of the poker that I had snatched from before the fire. I should have been too weak to stand but I had slipped from the table where they bled and purged me, let the sheet fall from me, and ran naked to the roaring fire. I caught Inch at the door and when he turned I thrust the poker up between his ribs. He squealed like pigs do when the butcher is killing them. I had only one word for him. A name. "Justice."

I spread the fire not to be warm, though the fever set my teeth chattering and my hands shaking too much to be of use. I set the fire to be clean again. To burn up every trace and touch of Inch and his wrong. To devour all memory of my weakness and failure.

"I meant to stay there," I said, my voice a whisper. She would hear me even so. "I don't remember leaving. I don't remember how close the flames came."

They found me in the forest. I had wanted to reach the girl-who-waits-for-spring, to lie on the ground where I buried my dog and to wait with her, but they caught me before I got there.

I raised my head. "But that's not where I'm bound tonight, Katherine."

There are truths you know but will not speak. Even to yourself in the darkness where we are all of us alone. There are memories you see and yet don't see. Things set apart, made abstract and robbed of meaning. Some doors when they are opened may not be shut again. I knew that, even at nine I knew it. And here, a door that I had closed long ago, like the lid on a coffin, the contents no longer fit for inspection. Fear trembled in my hands and I tightened my grip against it. No part of me wanted this, but I would chase Katherine from my dreams and own my nights once more—and honesty remained my sharpest weapon.

I pulled on the handles to those doors of frost and corruption, I hauled on them and it felt as if I dragged a spear into my guts, inch by bloody inch. And with a squeal of protest the doors opened, not onto a throne room, not to my father's court, but to a dull autumn day on a rutted path that wound away up the valley to where the monastery sat.

"Damned if I will!"

Brother Liar was damned long ago but we none of us mentioned that. Instead we stood in the mud of the road and in the chill of a damp westerly breeze and watched the monastery.

"You'll go up there and ask them to see to your wound," Fat Burlow said again.

Burlow could swing a sword better than most and lay a cold eye on a man. He wasn't jolly with all that lard, but he didn't have the authority that Brother Price used to wield.

"Damned if—"

Brother Rike slapped Liar around the back of the head and he pitched forward into the mud. Grumlow, Roddat, Sim, and the others crowded at Rike's elbows.

"He wouldn't see much," I said.

They turned to look at me, leaving Liar to get to all fours, the road dripping from him. I may have killed Price with three stones but that didn't stop me being a skinny ten-year-old child and the brothers weren't about to take direction from me. That I lived at all came down in equal measures to a quick hand with the knife and to the Nuban's protection. It would be another two years, after Sir Makin had found me, with both him and the Nuban to watch my back, before I would openly make the brothers' decisions for them.

"What's that, runt?" Rike hadn't forgiven me for Price's death. I think he felt I'd stolen it from him.

"He wouldn't see much," I said. "They'd take him to the infirmary.

It's a separate building usually. And they'd watch him because he looks as though he'd be stealing the bandages while they wrapped him."

"What do you know?" Gemt aimed a kick to miss me. He didn't have the balls to risk connecting.

"I know they don't keep their gold in the infirmary," I said.

"We should send the Nuban in," Brother Row said. He spat toward the monastery, lofting the thick wad of his phlegm a remarkable distance. "Let him work his heathen ways on those pious—"

"Send me," I said.

The Nuban had shown no enthusiasm for the venture from the moment Fat Burlow first dreamed it up. I think Burlow only suggested hitting St. Sebastian's to shut Rike's moaning. That and to give the brothers something better to unite behind than his own wavering command.

"What're you a-goin'ta do? Ask them to take pity on you?" Gemt snorted a laugh through his nose. Maical echoed him back down the line, with no idea what the joke was.

"Yes," I said.

"Well . . . it does have an orphanage." Burlow rubbed his stubble, folding himself a few more chins.

We made camp a couple of miles back along the road in a copse of twisted elm and alder, thick with the stink of fox. Burlow had decided in his wisdom that I would approach the monastery a little after dawn when they should be finished with matins prayers.

The brothers lit campfires among the trees and Gains took his cauldron from the head-cart to set over the biggest blaze. The night turned mild with cloud unrolling as the gloom thickened. The aroma of rabbit stew started to spread. We were twenty strong or thereabouts. Burlow moved about convincing men to their duties, Sim and Gemt to watch the road, old Elban to sit where the horses were corralled and listen out for wolves.

Brother Grillo began to pick at that five-string harp of his—well, *his* since he took it from a man who could really play it—and somewhere in the dark a high voice ran through the Queen's Sorrow. Brother Jobe it was who sang that evening. He'd only sing when it got too dark to see much, as if in the blind night he could be another lad in another place and call out the songs they'd taught that boy.

"You don't think we should rob St. Sebastian's?" I asked the darkness.

It spoke back with the depth of the Nuban's voice. "They're your holy men. Why do you want to steal from them?"

I opened my mouth, then shut it. I had thought I just wanted to build my reputation with my road-brothers and to share out a little of the anger gnawing inside me. More than that though . . . they *were* my holy men, these monks in the fortress of their monastery, echoing psalms in its stone halls, carrying golden crosses from chapel to church. They spoke to God and maybe he spoke back, but the wrongs done to me hadn't even rippled the deep pool of their serenity. I wanted to knock on their door. My mouth might ask for sanctuary, I might play the orphaned child, but truly I would be asking "why?" Whatever lay broken inside me had started to wind too tight to be ignored. I would shake the world until its teeth rattled if that was required to have it spit out an answer. *Why?*

Brother Jobe ended his song.

"It's something to do, a place to go," I said.

"I have a place to go," the Nuban said.

"Where?" If I hadn't asked he wouldn't have told. You couldn't leave a gap long enough that it would force the Nuban to fill it.

"Home," he said. "Where it's warm. When I have enough coin I will go to the Horse Coast, to Kordoba, and take a ship across the narrows. From the port of Kutta I can walk home. It's a long way, months, but across lands I know, peoples I know. Here though, in this empire of yours, a man like me can't travel far, not alone, so I wait until fate leads us all south together."

"Why did you come here if you hate it so much?" His rejection stung though it hadn't been aimed my way.

"I was brought here. In chains." He lay back unseen. I could almost hear the chains as he moved. He didn't speak again.

Morning stole through the woods pushing a mist ahead of it. I had to leave my knives and short sword with the Nuban. And no breaking my fast. A rumbling stomach would speak on my behalf at the monks' gate.

"Get the lie of the land, Jorg," Burlow told me as if it had been his idea from the start.

Brother Rike and Brother Hendrick watched me with no comment other than the scrape of their whetstones along iron blades.

"Find out where the men-at-arms bed," Red Kent said. We knew the monks had mercenary guards, Conaught men, maybe soldiers from Reams sent by Lord Ajah, but maintained and kept in coin by the abbot.

"Watch yourself up there, Jorth," Elban lisped. The old man worried too much. You'd have thought as a man's years ran out he'd worry less—but no.

And so I started along the road and let the fog swallow the brothers behind me.

An hour brought me mist-damp and muddy-footed to the bend in the road where we first studied the monastery. I walked another few hundred yards before the fog admitted a dark hint of the building, and in ten strides more it slipped from suggestion to fact, a sprawl of buildings to either side of the River Brent. The waters' complaints reached me as they tumbled through the millwheel before escaping to the farmlands further down the valley to the east. Wood smoke tickled my nostrils, the faintest scent of frying, and my stomach rumbled obligingly.

I passed the bakehouse, brewhouse, and buttery, grim stone blockhouses identified by the aromas of bread, malt, and ale. All seemed deserted, the matins prayers requiring even the lay brothers from their labours in the fields, at the fishponds, or at the piggery. The path to the church threaded the cemetery, headstones all askew as if at sea. Two great trees stood amidst the graves, shouldering the most weathered stones aside. Two corpse-fed yews, echoes of an older faith, standing proud where men played out their lives in service to the white Christ. I stopped to pick a pale red berry from the closer tree. Firm and dusty-skinned. I rolled it between finger and thumb, an echo perhaps of the lost flesh those roots drank, sunk in the ichors of the rotting faithful.

Strains of plainsong reached across the cemetery, the monks coming to the close of matins. I decided to wait.

Burlow had plans to head north with St. Sebastian's treasures. To make the coast, where on a clear day a man could look out across the Quiet Sea and spot the sails of a half dozen nations. The port of Nemla might pay tax to Reams but it paid no attention to Lord Ajah's laws. Pirate lords held power there and a man might sell anything in such a place, from holy relics to human flesh. More often than not the buyer would be a man of the Isles, a Brettan from the drowned lands, sailors all. They said that if all the men of Brettan left ship at once the Isles would not have space for them to stand.

The Nuban once rumbled me a song from the Brettan Isles. Hearts of oak it said they had, but the Nuban told it that if their hearts were of the oak then it was from the yew that their blood had been brewed, a darker and more ancient tree. And from the yew come their longbows, with which the men of Brettan have slain more men in the long years than were felled with bullet or bomb in the short years of the Builders.

I waited by the church doors when the songs ran out, but despite the scraping of pews and the mutter of voices, no one emerged. All fell silent and at last I set hand to the doors and pushed inside into the quiet hall beyond.

One monk remained at prayer, kneeling before the pews, facing the altar. The others must have left through another exit leading into the monastery complex. The light from windows of stained glass fell around the man in many colours, a patch of green across his head making something strange of his baldness. It occurred to me as I waited for him to finish bothering the almighty that I didn't know *how* to ask for sanctuary. Acting had never featured in my skill set, and even as the words I would need sprang to mind I could hear how false they would ring, falling bitter from a cynical tongue. Some tell it that "sorry" is the hardest word, but for me it has always been "help."

In the end I decided to go with my strengths. I didn't wait for the monk to quit his silent moaning and I didn't ask for help.

"I've come to be a monk," I said, with the silent proviso that hell would freeze and heaven burn before I let them give me the haircut.

The man stood without haste and turned to face me, the window colours sliding across the grey of his habit. His tonsure left a garland of black curls around a polished scalp.

"Do you love God, boy?"

"I couldn't love him any more."

"And do you repent of your sins?"

"What man doesn't?"

He had warm eyes and a soft face this one. "And are you humble, boy?"

"I could be no more humble," I said.

"You've a clever way with words, boy." He smiled. The lines spreading from the corners of his eyes declared him given to smiles. "Perhaps too clever. Too much cleverness can be a torment to a man, setting his wits against his faith." He steepled his fingers. "In any event, you are too young to become a novice. Go home, boy, before your parents notice you're gone."

"I have no mother," I said. "And no father."

His smile eased. "Well now, that's a different matter. We have orphans here, saved from the corruptions of the road and educated in the ways of our Lord. But most come to us as infants, and it isn't an easy life, our boys work hard, both in the field and at their studies, and there are rules. Lots of rules."

"I came to be a monk, not an orphan; a brother, not a son." I didn't want to be a monk but just being told "no" lit the corner of a fire in me. I knew myself broken, to burn over every refusal, to feel my blood rise at the slightest provocation, but knowing and fixing are different things.

"A good number of our novices are drawn from boys maintained here." If he sensed my anger he showed no sign of it. "I myself was left on the church steps as a baby, many years ago."

"I could start that way." I shrugged as if letting myself be talked into it.

He nodded and watched me with those kind eyes. I wondered if his prayers were still echoing behind them. Did God speak back to him or did the Old Gods whisper from the yew, or perhaps the gods of the Nuban called out to him across the straits from the crowed heavens above Afrique?

"I'm Abbot Castel," he said.

"Jorg."

"If you follow me we shall at least see that you get a meal." He smiled again, the sort of smile that said he liked me. "And if perhaps you choose to stay we might see whether you really could love God a little more and be somewhat more humble."

I spent that first day digging up potatoes with the twelve orphans currently under St. Sebastian's care. The boys ranged from five years to fourteen, as mixed a bunch as you could want, some serious, some wild, but all excited to have a new boy amongst them to break the monotony of mud and potatoes, potatoes and more mud.

"Did your family leave you here?" Orscar asked the questions and the rest of them listened. A short boy, lean, ragged black hair as if cut in haste, and mud on both cheeks. I guessed him to be eight.

"I walked," I said.

"My grandpa brought me here," Orscar said, resting on his digging fork. "Mam died and my father never came back from the war. I don't remember them much."

Another taller boy snorted at the tale of Orscar's father, but said nothing.

"I came to be a monk," I said. I drove the fork deep and turned up half a dozen potatoes, the biggest of them skewered on the tines.

"Idiot." The largest of the boys shouldered me aside and lifted the end my fork. "Scratch them and they won't keep past a week. You gotta feel the way into the ground, dig around them." He pulled the wounded vegetable free.

I imagined how it would be to lunge forward and impale him, the fork's middle tine nailing his Adam's apple and the other two bracketing his neck. I wondered that the danger didn't even occur to him as he scowled at me over the weapon, pointed right at him. He wouldn't keep past a week.

"Who'd be a monk?" A boy my age came across, dragging a full sack. He looked pale beneath the grime, his grin fixed, as if he knew exactly what I'd been thinking.

"It has to be better than this?" I lowered the fork.

"I'd go mad," he said. "Praying, praying, more praying. And reading the bible every single day. And all the copying. All that quill work, copying other people's words, never writing their own. You want to spend fifty years doing that?" He hushed as one of the lay brothers stomped over from the hedgerow.

"More work, less talk!"

And we set to digging.

It turns out there's a certain satisfaction in digging. Levering your dinner from the ground, lifting the soil and pulling fine hard potatoes from it, thinking of them roasted, mashed, fried in oil, it's all good. Especially if it wasn't you who had to tend and weed the field for the previous six months. Labour like that empties the mind and lets new thoughts wander in from unsuspected corners. And in the moments of rest, when we orphans faced each other, mud-cheeked, leaning on our forks, there's a camaraderie that builds without you knowing it. By the end of the day I think the big lad, David, could have called me an idiot a second time and survived.

We trudged back to the monastery as evening shadows tracked across the rutted fields. They fed us in the fraterhouse with the ordained brothers at one long trestle, the lay brothers at another, and the orphans crowded around a low square table. We ate faggots of potato mash fried in pork fat with autumn greens. I hadn't tasted anything better in forever. And the boys talked. Arthur told how his grandpa used to make shoes before his sight got dim. Orscar showed us the iron cross his da gave him when he went away. A heavy thing with a circle of red enamel at the crossing point. For the blood of Christ, Orscar said. And David told how he might sign up to be a soldier for Lord Ajah, like Bilk and Peter who we saw patrolling along the Brent. They all spoke, often at once, laughing, cramming in food past their words, speaking of foolishness, games they played, dreams they had, "might-have-been's and might-be's." The easy talk that children share, that Will and I had shared. Strange to think of these boys bound about by so many rules and seeming so free, and my road-brothers, unbound by law or conscience, yet so guarded and bitter in their conversation, each word edged and weighted, as if they were every one of them trapped and seeking escape each moment of their lives.

The orphans slept in their own dormitory, a solid stone-built building, slate-roofed, clean within though bare as a monk's cell. I lay among them, comfortable on my straw mattress. Sleep found us all quick enough. Honest labour will do that for you. But I woke in the darkest hour and listened to the night, to the skittering of mice amongst our straw, to the snores and the mumbling of sleep-tied tongues, to the hunting owls and the chuckle of water through the mill. I thought of my road-brothers, caught in dark dreams as their bodies lay scattered between the trees. They would wake soon, blood-hungry, and turn this way.

A monk came for us before dawn so we would be washed and ready for matins prayer.

"No work!" Orscar whispered beside me as he dressed.

"No?"

"It's Sunday, idiot." David used a long pole to heave the shutters open. It made little difference.

"Sunday's for praying." This from Alfred, the peacemaker in the potato field.

"And studies," said Arthur, a tall and serious boy of around my age.

It turned out Sunday held time for studies additional to those the monks arranged for us. First though, I sat through lessons on lettering, instruction on the lives of saints, and a session of choir practice—I croaked like a crow. An elderly monk arrived for the day's last lesson, hunched around a black cane, eyes bright but pale beneath the grey fringe of his hair. He had a sour look to him but the boys seemed to like him.

"Ah. New boy. What's your name, young man?" He spoke quick and high with just a creak of age.

"Jorg," I said.

"Jorg, eh?"

"Yes," I said. "Sir."

"I'm Brother Winter. No sir about it. And I'm here to teach theology." He paused and frowned. "Jorg, eh?"

"Yes, Brother."

"I never did hear of a St. Jorg. Now ain't that a curious thing? St. Alfred, St. Orscar, St. David, St. Arthur, St. Winter . . . ain't you got a saint's day, boy?"

"My mother had it that St. George's day would serve. Jorg being a flavour of George."

"The Brettan saint?" He made to spit and caught himself. "He fell out of heaven when the sea swallowed those lands."

Brother Winter let my name and its ill omens lie after that and taught us theology as promised. He proved entertaining and praised my quick wits, so we parted friends.

In the two hours between vespers and compline we ran free of prayers and lessons. The slightest hint had Orscar begging to show me the monastery—grounds and buildings all. He raced me around as fast as the evening dark allowed, eager to please, as if I were his big brother and my approval weighed more than all the gold in chapel. We crept up the woodpile by the old almonry where peasants came for alms in hard years, and from our vantage spied on Ajah's soldiers who barracked there when not on duty.

"The abbot says we don't need soldiers everywhere." Orscar clambered back down, wiping his nose on his sleeve. "But David says he heard St. Goodwin's—down by Farfield—was raided six months back and burned flat. He heard it from novice Jonas at the smithy."

"If a raid comes, don't trust in soldiers," I told him. "Run for the river and follow it upstream. Don't stop for anything."

I slipped away from Orscar in the dark and made my way to the road, where the monastery lane joined the wider way. Even ditching the boy with a turn of speed in the shadows felt like a betrayal. He'd started to dote on me like Maical with that idiot grin of his following Gemt. Like Justice used to pace after William and me, hour after hour, just happy to be pack with us, overjoyed if we petted him, ecstatic if Will wrapped him in his little arms and buried his face in that fur. The hound would stand there as if he were tolerating the hug, as if it wasn't what he'd followed us half a day for, but his tail couldn't lie.

Elban stood waiting a little way down the road, a ghost in the moonlight. "What's the word, Jorth?"

They'd sent Elban because he didn't look like trouble, but I'd back him against two of Ajah's troopers any day. Well, not in a fair fight, but you don't see many of those.

"The word is precious little gold and more guardsmen than Brother Burlow is going to want to take on, well armed, with strong points to defend. The place is built to hold."

"They ain't gonna like that news, Jorth." "Newth," he said, struggling on the "s." He sounded worried, though he scowled to hide it.

"Tell Burlow you're just the messenger," I suggested. "And keep out of Rike's reach."

"Ain't you coming with me then?" Elban frowned. His tongue slid across the pale flesh of his gums.

"There's a piece or two worth stealing. If I can swipe them, I'll come running. Otherwise I'll join you here tomorrow, same time, and we'll all go."

I left him muttering "they won't like it, they won't like it."

I'd counted twelve guards, none of them much younger than Elban, and the crucifix the abbot wore to vespers on its own was worth the effort to take them down. In truth, despite the cruel lessons taught me by my own father and by the thorns, I had found the whisper of a different way in the fields and halls and sanctums of St. Sebastian, and whilst I listened with a sceptical ear, still I wanted to hear that whisper a little longer.

My father taught me not to love or to compromise, the thorns taught me that even family bonds are fatal weaknesses, a man must walk alone, bide his time and strike when the strength is in his hands. Sometimes, though, it seemed all that bound me to those lessons were the scars they had left on me.

As I trudged back I reasoned that what I wanted from the road, from my road-brothers, wasn't gold and the slaughter of monks. I had come from wealth—I knew how the innocent died. What I sought was the power that lies in hands untied by social strings, not restrained by moral code, chivalric charter, the rules of war. I wanted to earn the edge that the Nuban showed in my father's dungeons, to be forged in battle. And I would find those things in the hard times. I would steer my brothers into the crucible where the Hundred wet their swords, and see what would unfold.

I told myself all that, but unsaid, beneath those words, I knew that perhaps I just wanted a door back to gentler days when my mother had loved me. I was after all a child of ten, weak, stupid, and unformed. I had been taught the right lessons but all teachers know a pupil will backslide if hard lessons are not reinforced by repetition.

The scent of white musk reached me, reached into wherever it is the dreamer stands to watch their nightmare unfold. She stood with me, unseen and untouchable, but close, almost skin to skin as I pulled these old memories through her. And I knew she felt the threat, counted its approach in heartbeats, whilst knowing neither its nature nor the direction of its attack.

I had returned to find the monastery guards setting torches in iron brackets before the chapterhouse. More monks than I had suspected to be housed at St. Sebastian's were already gathered in the shadows by the wall. Evidently not all showed up for meals.

"Where'd you go?" Orscar rushed me from the dark. If I'd had a knife he'd have got himself stuck on it.

"The bishop's coming!" His news proved too important to wait on my answer.

"What bishop? Where?" It didn't seem a very likely story.

"Bishop Murillo! His servant just arrived ahead of the procession to warn us. He's on the north road. We'll see their lights coming up over Jedmire Hill soon enough." Orscar kept hopping from one foot to the other, as if he needed to piss. Probably did.

"Brother Miles said the Vatican sent the Pope's own carriage to collect him." Arthur stood behind us now. "Murillo's on his way to Roma."

"They'll make him a cardinal! For sure!" Orscar sounded far more excited about church politics than any eight-year-old should be.

"Where are all the others?" I asked. Apart from Orscar and Arthur none of the orphans had come for the show.

Orscar blinked. "They must've seen him before. He ministers at St. Chelle. He's visited before. Brother Winter said so."

I didn't let it bother me. I'd seen bishops before. Well, two. Bishop Simon who ministered at Our Lady in Crath City, and Bishop Ferr who replaced Simon when the angels dragged him off one cold night. Even so, I'd wait and have a look-see at this third one. He might have treasures in his carriage that would keep my road-brothers happy. If the other boys had found something better to occupy them, good luck.

"He's the grandson of the Duke of Belpan, you know?" Arthur said.

"The bishop?"

He nodded. I shrugged. Abbots in an order bound to simple living and hard labour might work their way up from an orphan's box abandoned on the doorstep. Bishops in their velvets and palatial residences tended to have been placed there for safe-keeping by powerful relatives, having been plucked from the outer branches of some illustrious family.

It took a while. The torches had started to gutter and the compline bell threatened when at last we saw the procession, armed riders at the front, priests walking, the papal carriage creaking along behind two plough-horses, more clerics trudging behind and finally two more mailed riders with the holy cross in red atop white tabards.

The carriage jolted along the road, halting with its door between the double line of torches that formed a corridor to the chapter-house's grand entrance. The driver of the carriage, a goblin of a man with grey and bushy brows, sat motionless, his pair with their heads down, snorting occasionally like oxen. The grandest of the three priests preceding the carriage came to open the door and to lend Bishop Murillo his arm, although the man seemed unlikely to need it. He squeezed from the gloomy confines, his bulk strained against the purple of his cassock. Once out he reached back in and took the mitre offered from the shadows. I hadn't thought there room for a second passenger. Murillo jammed the hat onto his head, the sweat on his tight black curls immediately soaking into the red band around its base. He stood straight, hands in the small of his back, thrusting that belly. I half expected an enormous belch from his fleshy mouth, but instead he growled and stamped toward the monastery. The head priest and two men-at-arms followed close behind. Although fat, the bishop had a restless energy about him. He reminded me of a boar hunting a scent. A little of Burlow too. His eyes found Orscar, then me, as he reached the door. He smiled at us, a convulsion of the lips, and muttered something to the closer guard before vanishing within.

The bishop's mass kept us from our beds, a droning affair of Latin prayers in the crowded church hall. We orphans stood scattered amongst the monks and saw little but the backs of tonsured heads. Holy or not, monks are an unwashed lot. The old brother ahead of me made frequent releases of evil smells that the rope around his habit could not restrain. He had two fat ticks behind his ear—the image stays with me, two bloated purple pearls.

At last, communion, and the long queue to be dismissed. At the head of the line I saw Abbot Castel take offered cup and drink from its gilt bowl.

"The blood of Christ," the serving priest intoned under the bishop's watchful eye.

Wine. At least it wasn't to be a dry wafer.

We shuffled forward slower than a candle burns its length. In the queue I noted again that most of the orphans were missing, only Orscar stood before me, and somewhere back along the line, Arthur.

I saw the abbot, waiting in the shadows of the wall, as we approached the altar. He had the look of an unwilling conscript gathering himself to draw steel and to fling himself into battle. The bishop in his finery shot Castel a vicious glance. Soft and fat he might be, but another life could have put the bishop amongst my road-brothers, red in tooth and claw. Another life would just have made Castel a different kind of victim to men such as Rike and Row and Liar.

Three more monks until our turn. Two more. One. Orscar stepped up, thirsty for communion wine. The orphans normally got the body, not the blood. And, quicker than I had thought he could, the abbot strode forward, swept the boy up, and bore him from the church. Orscar, made mute by surprise and by the speed of his abduction, didn't manage even a yelp before the door to the chapterhouse swung shut behind them. Every other person in the great hall of the church held still, watching the door until the echoes of its closing died away. Murillo, already red in the face, shaded to purple. Another heartbeat of silence and then the bishop looked my way, furious for reasons I couldn't fathom. He stamped the heel of his crook to the floor. The priest, silver thread tracing the scarf that draped the black velvet of his gown, fixed cold eyes upon me and held out the communion cup, almost empty now. I drank, and the wine was bitter.

More monks, more filing past, more drinking, as we stood and waited. The wine still burned my tongue, as if they had fermented gall rather than grapes. A lethargy rose through me, from the cold stone of the floor, through leg and belly until my thoughts swam in it and the drone of liturgy lost its meaning. And finally, with the witching hour behind us, the bishop spoke those words all children long for in any mass.

"*Ite, missa est.*" You are dismissed.

I staggered on the way to the door, catching at a monk's arm for support. He shook me off, a stony look on his face, as if I were diseased. The church stretched and squashed, the walls and pillars dancing like reflections on a pond.

"What?" I tasted the bitterness again and my tongue ran out of words. My hands sought the knife that should have been on my belt. My hands knew the danger.

"Jorg?" I heard Arthur's voice, saw him bundled away by the monk with the ticks and foul stinks.

Somehow I came to the doors that led outside, and leaned on them. Cold night air would help. They gave, opening by degrees, and I slipped through. Strong arms wrapped me. One of Murillo's men-at-arms. A black hood, taking away the world, throttling hands. I threw my head back and heard a nose break. And fell into a confusion without up or down, without sight, straining against bonds, and drowning, choking, retching in the dark.

Memory gives me only pieces of the time spent in the bishop's chambers, but those pieces are clear and razor-edged. I had never fought Katherine when she pulled me into nightmare. Now I fought her as she tried to leave. I fought her as I drew each part of those broken memories through the channel she had opened—like Brother Hendrick and his Conaught spear, I didn't care if they tore me, so long as she felt some fraction of it too.

The smell of Murillo, perfume and sweat. The corrupt softness of his bulk. The strength that twisted my limbs until they creaked, until the pain reached me through the fog of whatever drug the wine had hidden, and tore thin screams past the gag. I made Katherine watch and share, made her share the pollution, the crude stink of his lust, the delight he took in his power, the horror of being helpless. I let her hear his grunting. I made her understand how dirt can get inside you, too deep to be scrubbed out, too deep to be bled out, perhaps too deep even to be burned out. I showed her how that stain can spread, back across the years turning all a child's memories to rot and filth, out across a future, taking all colour and direction.

I kept her with me, lying soaked in blood and filth and pain, bound, blindfold, sick with the drug and yet clinging to it for fear of the clarity a clear head would bring.

I won't say rage kept me alive. Those poisoned hours offered no escape, nothing so tempting as dying, but perhaps if I could have slid away into death, if it had been an option, then my anger might have been the thing to keep me back. As the drug faded from me and focus returned, a need for revenge started to build, quickly eclipsing all minor desires such as escape, the easing of pain, or the need to breathe.

Chains can hold a man. A well-fastened manacle will require the breaking of bones before the prisoner can win free. Ropes in general cannot be broken, but with determination they can often be slipped. Lubrication is the key. Sweat will normally start the process, but before long the skin will give and blood will help those rough fibres slide over raw flesh.

The bishop didn't wake. I made no noise while I freed my hands, tied behind my back. I eased from the bed, slithering across stained silk sheets. On the floor I took the fruit knife from the bedside table and by the glow of the dying fire sawed at the bonds around my ankles. I walked naked from the room. As if there could be more shame. I took the knife and the poker from the fire with me.

In the small hours of night the monastery corridors lay empty. I walked them blind, trailing the point of the knife along the walls from time to time to count my way. I heard plainsong as I walked, though there were none awake to sing it. Even so, I heard plainsong, pure in its promise, as if all things holy and good were pressed into notes, and spilled from the mouths of angels. I hear it even now when I remember those orphan boys, the digging in that field, mud and potatoes, lessons and games. I hear it as if it were reaching faint through a closed door. And the song drew a tear from me, oh my brothers, not the hurt, or shame, not betrayal, or that last lost chance of redemption—just the beauty of that song. One tear on a hot slow roll down my cheek.

I left by the door to the stables, unlatching it and turning the heavy iron ring. Both the soldiers on the other side turned, blinking away boredom. I felled them with two blows of the poker, first to the left temple of the right guard, then the right temple of the left. Whack, whack. They didn't deserve to be called soldiers, defeated by a naked child. One lay silent, the other, Bilk I think, writhed and groaned. Him I skewered through the throat. That shut his noise. I left the poker in him.

The stables smelled of every other stable. In the darkness, amongst the horses, I could have been anywhere. I moved without sound, listening to the clop of hooves, the restless snort and shudder of disturbed mounts, the scurry of rats. I took as much rope as I could carry and a sharper knife used for working leather. The coils itched my shoulder and back as I returned through the blind corridors.

I left the rope outside the bishop's door and went back for a bale of straw and the soldiers' lamp. The big horses that pulled the Pope's carriage were housed in the stall closest to the stable doors. The larger of the two stepped out when I opened the stall, head down, looking more asleep than awake. I set a tether around his thick neck and left him standing there. He looked as though he would stand forever, or at least until someone gave him reason to move again.

I guessed Murillo's men-at-arms would be billeted with Lord Ajah's soldiers in the almonry for the night. At some point the monks would be on the move for the night prayer. I didn't know when that might happen, nor truly care: I would just kill anyone in my way. The night still had a dream-like quality, perhaps the tail end of whatever poison Murillo had had the priest slip into the wine.

The swinging lamp chased thin shadows across the walls, copies of my limbs. I wedged handfuls of straw beneath the roof eaves where I could reach by climbing on barrel or sill. I wedged more between the split wood, stacked for winter against the chapterhouse wall. There's not much to burn in a stone-built monastery, but the roof is always the best bet. And of course the guest quarters where the bishop slept offered more combustibles, with several tapestries, wooden furniture, shuttered windows. I went into the priests' rooms, two priests in the chamber to the left of the bishop's and three opposite. I cut their throats as they slept, a hand to the mouth while I tugged the sharpness of the leather-knife through skin, flesh, cartilage, and tendon, through vein, artery, and windpipe. Men sliced like that make strange noises, like wet bellows pumping, and thrash before they die, but in the tangle of their bed linens it isn't loud. I set straw and bedding ready to fire in the priests' rooms too.

The high priest, the man who poisoned the cup, ready for Orscar, and drunk by me, I cut. I knew him to be dead but I cut his face and watched the flesh spring open beneath my blade. I sliced away his lips and let the ichor from his eyes, and I prayed, not to God but to whatever devil got to keep his soul, that he would carry the wounds with him into hell.

By the time I returned to Murillo's chambers I was clothed once more, in the scarlet of priests' blood. For a time I watched his bulk within the bed, a black lump in the embers' glow, and listened to the wheeze in and the snored breath out. He posed a puzzle. A strong man who might wake easily. I didn't want to have to kill him. That would be too kind.

In the end I lifted the covers with a gentle hand to expose his feet. I eased the rope beneath his ankles so a yard lay to one side and the rest to the other. A hangman's noose is a simple knot, and I used the loop to draw his ankles together before making the knot tight against them. Then I left with the rope coil, playing it out as I went.

On my route back to the stables I set flame to the various piles of straw and bedding prepared earlier. At the stables I cut the rope and tied the end around the plough-horse's neck. Before I led him away my eye lit upon a fallen hemp bag that lay on the floor with long dark roofing nails spilling from it. I stooped to pick it up.

*   *   *

Brother Gains, who Burlow set to watching the monastery, tells it that I came through the cemetery leading the biggest horse in the world and that all behind me the sky was lit with crimson and orange as fire leapt among the roofs of St. Sebastian. He said I came naked and blood-wrapped and that he thought that it was me screaming, until I drew closer and he saw the grim seal of my mouth. Brother Gains, never a man given to religion, crossed himself and stepped aside without a word when I passed him. He watched the taut rope and shrank back further as the screams grew more loud and more piercing. And out of the darkness, lit by the flames of St. Sebastian, Bishop Murillo came dragging, leaving his own trail of blood and skin on the grit and gravel of the cemetery path, white bone jutting from beneath the rope that bound his broken ankles.

I let Katherine share that night. I let her watch the brothers take to horse and ride whooping up the road toward the distant orange glow. She saw how I bound Murillo and how such terror ran in him that he forgot the agony of his shattered ankles. And I taught her how long it can take to hammer thirteen nails through a man's skull, tap, tap, tap. How night shades into day and brothers gather once again, draped in loot and relics, black with char. The brothers formed my audience, some fascinated, like Rike with his new iron cross around his neck, set with a circle of red enamel at the crossing point—red for the blood of Christ. Some watched in horror, some with reserve, but they all watched, even the Nuban with nothing written on his face but the deep lines of sorrow.

"We're meat and dirt," I told them. "Nobody is clean and nothing can wash away our stain, not the blood of the innocent, not the blood of the lamb."

And the brothers watched as a child learned what revenge can do, and what it can't. Together Katherine and I watched that child learn how a simple iron nail can break a man's mind apart, causing him to laugh, or cry, to lose some basic skill, some memory, or some restraint that made him human or gave a measure of dignity. I let Katherine see how something so simple as hammering home a nail can make such profound changes, to the bishop whose head is pierced, and to the boy who wields the hammer. And then I let her go. And she ran.

My dreams would be my own again. I was past games.

9

I woke to the sound of Makin's voice.

"Get up, Jorg."

In the Haunt I have a page schooled in the art of discreet coughs and a gradual elevation in volume until his royal highness deigns to stir. In Lord Holland's house it seemed "get up" was the best on offer. I struggled to a sitting position, still in the clothes I wore the night before and more tired than when I fell into the bed.

"And a very good morning to you, Lord Makin." My tone made it clear I meant none of it.

"Miana's here," he said.

"Right." I rolled off the bed onto my feet, still woozy with sleep. "Let's go."

"Not shaving?" He offered me my cloak from the chair.

"It's the new style," I said, and went out into the corridor beyond, past the guards stationed outside the door. "Left or right?"

"Left. She's in the blue room."

And yes, Lord Holland had a whole room, the size of a church hall, given over to displaying the colour blue. Miana stood, pale, pretty, her hands across the stretch of her belly, Marten beside her, leaning on a staff for support, his face black with bruising. At the rear of the room, ten men from my guard, cloaks clasped with the Ancrath boar in silver, stood tight around a black coffer, Sir Riccard with them.

I crossed the room and put my arms around Miana. I needed to touch her with my own hands after being locked into the dream with hands I didn't own that tried to kill her. She put her head against my chest and said nothing. She smelled good. Of nothing specific—just good. Makin followed in behind and closed the door.

"I saw the assassin," I said. "A white man, sent from the Vatican, or made to look as though he was. I saw you kill him. You and Marten both." I nodded to him. He knew what it meant to me.

Miana looked up, eyes wide with surprise starting to narrow with confusion, suspicion even. "How?"

"I think he used dream-magics to make the castle sleep, even the trolls below. When you use those methods and spend your power so carelessly, you leave yourself open to others with such skills. Perhaps something of Sageous rubbed off on me when I killed him." I shrugged. "In any case, you know I have bad dreams. It might be easier to fall into such enchantments from a nightmare than from honest sleeping." I didn't mention Katherine. It didn't seem politic to remind her that another woman filled my nights.

"We found these on him." Marten held out a scroll, three gold coins, and a signet ring.

The ring held an intaglio in a silver mount, carnelian worked with an intricate device, the papal seal with one bar. It gave the bearer an authority little short of a cardinal's. I dropped it back into Marten's palm and took the scroll.

"A warrant for your death, Miana."

"Mine!" Outrage rather than fear.

"It's very pretty." The scribe had illuminated it to a high order and not scrimped on the gold leaf. It must have taken a week's work at least. "It's possible they're forgeries, but I doubt it. The trouble the forger would earn for themselves would outweigh any gain. And besides, the Pope does have good reason."

Miana stepped back, her eyes blazing. "Good reason! What offence have I ever given the church?" She clutched herself all the tighter.

"It's to punish me, my dear." I spread my hands to offer up my guilt. "The Vatican must have finally tied me to the sack of St. Sebastian's, and more importantly to them, tied me to the maiming of Bishop Murillo Ap Belpan."

"But you're lord of Belpan now. That line is gone." Anger muddied her logic.

"It's probably the 'bishop' part that has them upset," I said.

"The warrant should be for you, then!" Miana said.

"The church frowns on killing kings. It goes against their views on divine right. They'd rather slap my wrist and show me to be penitent. If that fails then perhaps I might die of an ague over the winter, but nothing so obvious as a warranted assassin."

"What will we do?" Marten asked. He held his voice calm but I think if I'd told him to take ten thousand men and lay siege to Roma, he would have left to do it without further question.

"I think we should open the box," I said. "I hope somebody thought to bring the key."

Miana fished the heavy piece of iron from her skirts and put it in my hand, still warm from her flesh. I waved the guards aside and fitted key to lock.

"Some kind of weapon?" Makin asked. He stood beside Miana now, an arm around her.

"Yes," I said. "Some kind of weapon."

I threw back the lid. Gold coins, stacked and tightly bound in columns, reached nearly to the lid, a sea of them, enough to buy Holland's mansion ten times over.

"That," said Makin, letting his hand fall from Miana's shoulder as he stepped closer, "is a lot of gold."

"Two years of taxes gathered from seven nations," I said.

"You're going to hire your own assassins?" Marten asked.

"You could hire an army with that. A large one." Makin stooped so low the reflected light made his face golden.

"No." I flipped the lid shut and Makin flinched.

"You're going to build the cathedral," Miana said.

"Praise the Lord for clever women. That boy you're cooking for me in there is going to be scary clever."

"Build a cathedral?" Makin blinked. Marten held his peace. Marten trusted my judgement. Too much sometimes.

"An act of contrition," Miana said. "Jorg is going to buy the most expensive pardon in history."

"And of course the Pope is bound by tradition and duty to attend the consecration of any new cathedral." I turned one of the assassin's gold pieces over in my fingers. The word "contrition" nibbled at the edge of my pride.

"Jorg!" Miana narrowed her eyes at me, knowing my mind. She had known it from the start and sought to turn me with talk of diplomacy.

The Pope stared at me from the Vatican gold. Blood gold for my child and wife. Pious CXII. When they showed you fat on money then you must truly be enormous. I held the coin up for inspection. "Don't worry, my dear. I'll play nice. When she comes to see the new cathedral I've built for her I will thank her for coming. Only a madman would threaten the Pope. Even if she is a bitch."

"And what's to stop another assassin coming while you're gone?" Miana asked.

"Nothing."

It's never a good idea to tease a woman near her time, and seldom a good idea to tease Miana in any case, unless you want back worse than you gave. She came at me, fists raised.

"You're coming with me." I spoke quickly, backing around Makin.

"You said wives couldn't come!" Miana mastered the art of the wickedly murderous look at an early age.

"You're my advisor now," I shouted, backing to the door since none of my guard saw fit to defend me.

That mollified her enough to halt her advance and lower her hands. "I can't ride like this," she said.

"You can go in one of the wagons." Each guard troop had a wagon for equipment.

"Well, that'll jolt the baby out of me quick enough!" She sounded cross but seemed to find the idea to her liking. "So I'm to sit all alone in a rickety wagon and be hauled halfway across empire?"

"You'll have Marten for company. He's in no state to ride," I said.

"Marten? So anyone can come along now?"

"Advisor!" I raised my hands again. "Makin, tell Keppen and Grumlow they can go back to the Haunt." I didn't think missing Congression would bother Keppen in the least, and Grumlow had a woman somewhere in Hodd Town that he'd probably rather spend time with.

"So that's settled." I dusted my hands together and cast an eye over the room's lurid blues. "Let's go and make Bishop Gomst a happy man."

We left Holland's mansion in a troop. Gorgoth carried the coffer and it pleased me to see that even his arms strained with the weight of all that gold. Lord Holland, his wife, and retainers flocked about us from the front steps to the gates of their compound. Makin made all the replies and niceties, the dregs of my dreaming still soured the day. At the gates Marten pointed out one of the guard wagons to Miana, an uncomfortably functional vehicle. She made an immediate turn, Sir Riccard jumping to avoid the swing of her belly.

"Lord Holland!" She stopped the man in mid-flow. "I wish to purchase your personal carriage."

I left Miana to secure the deal, guarded by Marten, Riccard, and eight of the ten men who accompanied her from the Haunt. Rike, Grumlow, Keppen, and Kent fell in with us as I led the way to the part-built cathedral of Hodd Town. Gomst had mentioned plans to name it the Sacred Heart after a cathedral of legend that once stood in Crath City. For my part I felt St. George's to be a fine name.

I settled the brothers within the walls of the great hall, dwarfed by the immense pillars that had stood ready to carry the roof for a decade and more. Lesser clerics, choirboys, and the more devoted and well-wrapped of Hodd Town's citizens, watched them with undisguised curiosity. Gorgoth put down his burden, set a bare foot to the lid, and stared back causing several choirboys to make a run for it.

A duty-priest led me to the grand vestibule where Gomst kept his office, due mainly to the fact the chamber had a completed roof. He rose from behind his desk to greet me. From the look of him he slept no better than I did. Gomst never wore his years well and now they hung from him like invisible chains.

"They tell me you do good work here, Father Gomst."

He bowed his head and said nothing. In the six years since we found each other again on the lichway before the ghosts came, the grey had risen from his beard and chased the black from his hair.

"I've brought you enough gold to have the cathedral completed. I want as many men as can fit around the walls to be working here at every hour of every day."

Gomst lifted his head frowning and made to speak.

"On Sundays they can rest," I said.

"You think faith and churches will save us from the Dead King?" Gomst asked.

"Don't you, Bishop?" I thought it would be nice if one of us did.

He drew in a deep breath and set his eyes on me, bright and dark. "It's easier to have faith when you are one of the flock. The closer I get to the top of this long ladder we call the church of Roma . . . the closer to the Holy See where God speaks . . . the less I hear him, the further away I feel."

"It's good that you have some doubt in you, Gomsty. Men who are certain of everything—well, perhaps they're not men at all."

Gomst stepped closer, from shadow into lamplight, and it seemed that I saw him for the first time, set against the memory of another bishop, one more certain of his path and his entitlements. I wondered how long Murillo's shadow had hidden Gomst from my sight. He was at worst guilty of loyalty to bad kings, of a mind narrowed by a life at court, and of pomposity. Not the most capital of crimes, and old crimes at that.

"You remember the ghosts on the lichway, Father Gomst?"

He nodded.

"You told me to run, to leave you there alone. And when they came, you prayed. Faith was your shield. We faced them together, you and I, with all my brothers fled."

Gomst offered a grim smile. "I was in a cage if you recall, or I would have run with them."

"We'll never know, will we?" I gave him the brilliance of my own smile, creasing the stiff burn-scars on my cheek. "And all men are cowards. I may not have run that day but I've always been a coward, never braver than my imagination."

From my belt I pulled out the order he would sign to acknowledge the church's acceptance of my chest of gold. Gomst looked at it.

"I would have run, but for that cage." He shivered.

I clapped a hand to his shoulder. "And here I am building you a new cage, Father Gomst, for just forty thousand ducets."

We sat then, Father Gomst and I, and drank small beer, for the water in Hodd Town is barely safe for washing.

"So here I am, Gomsty, with a box full of shiny metal making a cathedral happen. Making the Pope herself trail out of Roma to my doorstep."

The bishop inclined his head then wiped a touch of foam from his moustache. "Times change, Jorg. Men change."

"And how did I get my box of gold? By setting my will behind a sharp edge and applying an unhealthy amount of determination." I sipped from my flagon. "When you move the big pieces on the board, the world seems more like a game than ever. That illusion, that those at the top know what they're doing—the feeling some folk hold, that the world is safe and solid and well-ordered—well, that illusion wears thin when it's us who stand at the top doing the ordering. I don't doubt that for every step you take toward Roma, God sounds three steps further away."

Gomst's hands trembled on his cup, his big and ugly knuckles paling. "You should watch over those dear to you more closely, Jorg. King Jorg. Triple your guards."

"Yes?" His meaning escaped me. Sweat glistened on his brow.

"I—I hear rumours, among the bishops, from visiting monks, wandering priests . . ."

"Tell me."

"The Pope knows. Not from me. Your confession remains between us. But she knows. They say she will send someone." He set his cup down, rattling it on the desk. "Guard those you love."

I wondered at Gomst, surprised by him after all these years. He'd known me longer than any man I still kept counsel with. After my father burned my dog he called Gomst to instruct me. Perhaps he thought some religion would temper the lesson. Or maybe that hammer, the one I nearly killed him with when he set the fire, had made him think I needed an education in divine right. He may have reasoned that if I thought God stood behind him I would be slower to raise my hand against him the next time. Whatever the reason, he dropped my spiritual welfare into Father Gomst's lap in my seventh year. Or at least he ordered a priest to the Tall Castle for that purpose. It may have been Mother who chose the particular cleric to fill the role.

Strange to say, but Gomst had watched me grow for longer than did my mother, longer than Makin, or the Nuban, or Coddin. He had seen more of my years pass than any of them, Father included.

"The Pope's man has already called, Father Gomst. Two nights ago. He won't be leaving again. Miana will be coming with us to

Congression. In fact, if you play your cards right you can ride with her in Lord Holland's carriage as soon as she's taken it off him."

"I . . ."

"You need to be at the west gate two hours from now. You've got that long to set your priests loose on this project. I will want to see serious progress by the time we get back. Let them know where the gold is coming from. Tell them if I come back from Congression and I'm still not emperor, I'm not going to be in the mood for excuses."

10

Fifty horses churn up a lot of mud. With the season heading into autumn and seven times that number of cavalry we made a river of the stuff. The wagons, set close to the rear of the column, slid through it, their wheels little more than sled-runners often as not. It turned out to be more comfortable than jolting over ruts. In fact if you must travel by carriage I recommend having an army at horse smearing the road out ahead of you.

"Well, this is nice," I said.

Actually for a carriage it was about as nice as it gets. Lord Holland had paid to have almost as much attention lavished on the interior as he did at home. The exterior had been finely worked too, but a thick layer of mud obscured all that.

Gomst sniffed and rummaged for his snot-rag. The bishop had acquired a cold for the journey. As a priest he used to wipe his nose on the black sleeve of his vestment. Bishops have different standards it seems. "I'm surprised you didn't decide to sail, King Jorg," he said.

"I considered it." The voyage of nearly three thousand miles by sea cut the overland distance from five hundred easy miles to a hundred over mountains. As much as I liked my new flagship I couldn't talk myself into such a plan.

Osser Gant sat beside the bishop, sharing his cold. Two old men sniffing and spitting together. Miana, Marten, and I sat opposite, facing the direction of travel. I'd squashed in for a look-see and set my muddy feet on the carpet.

"You need a nursemaid and a midwife," I said. "A bishop, a chamberlain, and a general aren't going to be much help when your time comes."

"I have three nursemaids and two good midwives." Miana fixed me with that stare of hers. "Jenny and Sarah are back at the Haunt. I wasn't expecting to be bundled off to Hodd Town then hauled off to Congression!"

"We'll just have to collect some replacements on the way," I told her.

"Some waifs and strays? Farmgirls skilled in the delivery of cows and sheep?"

Women aren't expected to be reasonable when getting ready to squeeze out a child. I still had my own doubts about the whole process. It seemed as though it would be a tight fit and I was glad I didn't have to do it. "Peasants have babies too, Miana. Lots of them. But no, not a farmgirl. We're going to be travelling through Teutonia. They're at least half-civilized, so I'm told. We'll stop by one of the local lords and prevail on him to volunteer some women of suitable quality and experience."

I peered through the window grille, eager to be back out there. I'd spent a whole minute in the carriage and had had enough of it. Swapping the carriage bench and all its fine cushions for Brath's saddle seemed a fair exchange given that I also got to swap Gomst and Osser for a view, and their sniffing and snotting for a fresh breeze. Outside, the Gelleth lowlands slid past, green and pleasant, fields in the main with occasional strips of woodland splashed in autumn colours. No sign here of the havoc I'd wrecked in the north at Castle Red.

Our route took us across Gelleth under empire pax and would lead on through Attar to bridge the Rhyme at the city of Honth.

From there Captain Harran planned to guide us along the River Danoob through half a dozen Teuton kingdoms until we reached Vyene. A trip estimated at a touch over three weeks. We could make better time and easier travelling on a barge once we reached the Danoob, but with over three hundred horses and their riders aboard most barges have a tendency to sink, and without them aboard, any barge carrying me through Teutonia would be guaranteed to sink. My father held a lot of alliances with the Teuton kingdoms, Scorron in particular, and Teutonia had never liked the idea of the coast kingdoms uniting to the west of them.

"Jorg?" Miana at my side.

"Sorry?"

She sighed and folded tiny hands across her belly.

"Yes." I guessed an answer. It seemed to satisfy her. She nodded and turned to speak to Marten.

It wouldn't be long before he wanted out of there too. A few days for his bruises to fade, maybe a while longer, for he wasn't young, and he would want to be riding. Something niggled at me, guilt perhaps, for being so ready to abandon Miana. It seemed probable that I should want to spend time with her, but I just didn't. I liked her well enough, but not well enough to spend three weeks in a carriage with. I wondered if any man would want to spend three weeks sat next to his wife. Would I feel any different if I'd chosen her? If she had chosen me? If it were Katherine beside me?

"And what are you thinking about, Jorg?" she asked. She fixed me with dark eyes. Not black but hinting green, leaves in moonlight. I'd never taken note of their colour before. Strange what strikes you and when.

"I'm thinking I should take my muddy boots out of this fine carriage and check to see that Harran isn't leading us astray."

She didn't say so but I could see her disappointment at the corners of her mouth. I stepped out feeling less than a king. Life can be complicated enough even when nobody is trying to kill you.

*　*　*

I rode alongside the carriage for a while in a black mood. A fine rain fell, unseasonably warm and light enough for the wind to blow into my face whatever angle I held my head. Makin rode up with his usual grin, spitting out the rain and wiping it from his cheeks.

"Lovely weather."

"People who talk about the weather would be better served by admitting they've nothing to say but like the sound of their own voice."

Makin's grin broadened. "And don't the trees look beautiful this time of year?" I suspected he'd taken a pinch of clove-spice, the stink of it seemed to be on him a lot these days.

"Do you know why the leaves change colour, Makin?" They did look spectacular. The forest had grown around us as we travelled and the canopy burned with colour, from deepest red to flame orange, an autumn fire spreading in defiance of the rain.

"I don't know," he said. "Why do they change?"

"Before a tree sheds a leaf it pumps it full of all the poisons it can't rid itself of otherwise. That red there—that's a man's skin blotching with burst veins after an assassin spikes his last meal with roto-weed. The poison spreading through him before he dies."

"I never knew death could be so pretty," he said, indefatigable.

We rode in silence for a while and I wondered if men were the world's leaves. If as we aged the world filled us with its poisons so as old men, filled to the brim with the bitterest gall, we could fall into hell and take it all with us. Perhaps without death the world would choke on its own evils. The northmen, Sindri's people, have it that a tree, Yggdrasil, stands at the centre, with everything—even worlds—hanging from it. And with Sindri came images of his milk-haired sister, Elin, tall and pale-eyed. Come to me in winter, she had said. I remarked to myself on her eyes in the moment I met her. Miana's after three years. A tree might stand at the centre of an old man's world. Whenever I turned my own face to the centre though, I saw a woman. Most young men do.

Three days later Lord Redmal's soldiers opened the road-gates to let us cross the border into Attar. Redmal's grandfather had built a fort across the road fifty years ago to let the folk of Gelleth know they weren't welcome. Merl Gellethar had flattened it in a dispute a decade before I reduced him to poisoned dust. Attar soldiers now infested the fort's ruins and watched the Gilden Guard with undisguised awe as they streamed past.

On the map Attar is a sizeable land, but the Engine of Wrong still turns and turns at Nathal as it has for ten centuries, and the north of Attar is a wasteland. I'm told it's not a poison or disease that keeps men away from Nathal and the lands around it, just a feeling, just the certainty that nothing there is right.

It took a day to cross the Attar hill country, where they keep the vineyards on the southern slopes and grow the grapes from which the Blood of Attar is fermented, a wine found at many royal tables. On the margins of the wine lands, as the hills smoothed themselves out for tobacco fields and small farmsteads, Red Kent came riding back from the column's vanguard with news.

"Another guard column ahead, sire," he said, as humble and loyal as you please. I think Kent loved being a knight more than anything and, burned as he was, with that scary rasping voice, he made a good king's fist to send into trouble and to end it.

"Not the last we'll see, I suspect. Who is it?"

He paused and then I knew. Who else would it be. I owned every other land east of us until the sea.

"It's from Ancrath, a hundred guard."

The votes of Ancrath and Gelleth, both resting in my father's hand.

I thought again of falling leaves and wondered if it wasn't time for another old man, full to the brim with poison, to make that final drop.

11

Chella's story

Five years of marching back and forth. Five years scurrying to do the Dead King's bidding. Always on the edge of things, as far from his court as one could be and still remain in the empire. Chella spent five years wading through mud and shit simply to rise enough in the Dead King's esteem for him to call her to court and seek an accounting for her failure. And she had come eagerly, racing across the broken empire just to face his judgment, just to stand before the inhumanity of the lichkin and have the Dead King watch her from the flesh into which he had settled deepest. Five wasted years— each one Jorg Ancrath's fault.

"There's a reason I'm having to hurt you."

Chella walked around the stone pillar, a slow circle, hiding her irritation. The young man followed her with his eyes until the pillar took her from sight. She heard the clank of chains as he craned his head to look for her return. He had blue eyes, like many of these Brettan men, and he watched *her* as much as he watched the iron needle between her finger and thumb.

"Where's Sula?" He asked his question again. In the few patches without mud his hair showed blond, a golden hue. He met her gaze through locks matted with dirt and blood. Mire-ghouls had taken him and a woman near the Reed Sea during the Dead King's advance. Sigils on his uniform had marked him as wind-sworn and led him to this inspection.

"Kai." Chella kept her voice tender, moving in quick and close, driving the needle two inches into the muscle of his inner thigh. "Kai Summerson." Her lips close enough to his ear for the blond hair to tickle. "You have to let go of these attachments."

He ground his teeth together, tension bunching around his jaw. After a moment he looked up again. "Where—"

Chella pulled the needle free. "Pain helps remind you of what is important. The first important fact is that I don't have much time to waste on you and if you don't cooperate quickly I will just give you back to the ghouls and let them eat you piece by piece. The second important fact is that you're alive and that pain is not the only thing you can feel. I'm offering you a rare chance. Power, pleasure, a future."

"Where is S—"

Chella slapped him across the face, hard enough to hurt her hand. "Here." She didn't need to speak. She just pulled the thread that bound her to each of her returned. Sula stepped from the shadow into Kai's line of sight. The ghouls hadn't left her pretty. Flesh and skin hung in a wet flap revealing her cheekbone, jaw, broken teeth, and the dark stump of her tongue. The dead girl watched Kai without curiosity. He sucked in a breath, gasping a deeper hurt than the needle had yet put in him. Perhaps she'd been his sweetheart. Surely more than a passing fancy.

"Sula?" Tears misted his eyes.

"Oh, grow up." Boredom and anxiety nipped at Chella's heels and neither would help her turn him. "She's dead. You're not. You can accept her death and find yourself a new direction, or you can join her. The world is changing. Are you going to change with it, Kai?"

Chella flicked her fingers at Sula and the corpse collapsed, ungainly, air belching as her stomach folded.

"Is she still 'your girl,' Kai? Does true love survive where flesh corrupts? What was she to you? A pretty face, a quick panting release? There's no romance in death, Kai, and death's the flip side of our coin." She ran her fingers up into that blond hair of his. "We're just meat on bones, waiting to rot. Find your pleasure where you will, by all means, but don't dress it up in sweetness and promises. There's nothing left to pin your loyalty on any more, Kai. Give it up."

She took his wrist below the manacle and drove the needle through his palm, past clenched fingers. He cried out then, half a curse, half a scream, starting to break. Soon it would be all scream.

"W-what do you want?" He gasped his words past clenched teeth.

"Me? I want what you should want," Chella said. "I want what the Dead King wants me to want. The Dead King doesn't need your loyalty, he just requires that you do what he tells you to do. And when he has nothing for us to do, our time is our own."

Chella pulled the needle free and licked the blood off it. She slid her other hand down across Kai's ribs and the hard muscle of his stomach, sweat slick.

"What do you want me for?" he asked.

Not stupid this one. And a survivor—at his core a survivor ready to do whatever is needed. Lead him slowly though, step by step.

Chella ran her hand lower. Even survivors balk if shown too much of the path at once. There's a road to hell that is paved with good intentions but it's a long route. The quicker path is paved with the kind of ignorance that clever men who just don't want to know are best at.

"You have talents that are rare, Kai."

"The Dead King wants to recruit sky-sworn now?"

"Sky-sworn, rock-sworn, flame-sworn, sea-sworn." Chella pricked his ribs with each word. "They are all sworn, and men who can swear once can swear again. We're the same, you and I, we reach through into other places. What do you think the necromancers are, Kai? Monsters? Dead things?"

"You're dead. Everyone knows necromancers rise from the grave."

Chella leaned in close, close enough that he could bite her neck if he chose, her lips at his ear once more. "Death-sworn."

In five years the Dead King had risen from being simply a new complication in the art of necromancy to a force that would change the world. He no longer bartered with necromancers, no longer manipulated, steered, or simply terrified them into carrying out his will. He owned them. He no longer watched from the Dry Lands, peering into life through dead eyes where they fell, speaking with corpse lips, he inhabited the living world in stolen bodies, walking where he pleased. An army had grown about him. The lichkin had sprung from some untapped well of horror, lieutenants for the hordes of his dead.

While Chella had languished, the Dead King had risen beyond measure. His summons to court could mark a grisly end to the dark little tale of her existence, or a new beginning. She would present herself with Kai as her offering. Fresh meat. Even in the Dead King's forces necromancers were not common. Bearing gifts she would answer his call and answer for her failings with the Ancrath boy—who had also risen beyond measure and expectation.

12

Five years earlier

Carrod Springs stinks. Not a human stink of waste and rot but a chemical offence against the senses, the bad-egg stench of sulphur, combined with sharper aromas fit for turning eyes red and stripping the lining from your nose.

"You see now why the trail detours so far to approach from the west with the prevailing wind," Lesha said.

"Why would anyone live here?" Sunny asked.

A fair question. True enough, water had become a rarity as we trekked north into the wasteland, but the stuff that bubbled up in Carrod Springs could surely not be potable. It had risen hot and steaming from the earth's bowels. And smelled like it.

The settlement, seven shacks and two storage barns, clustered on a rise to the west, a spot where the breeze would offer a clean lungful. If there ever was any breeze. The buildings looked frost-rimed but drawing closer you could see it for what it was: salt, caked to the wood, bearding the eaves. We passed the first barn, doors wide, mounds of salt on display, like grain heaped from the harvest, some piles white, some grey, at the back rusty orange, and to the left side smaller heaps of a deep but faint blue.

Balky had to be encouraged with a stick. None of the animals wanted to be here. They licked their muzzles, spat, and licked again.

I could taste it on my lips too, like the salt spray off the ocean but sharper and more penetrating. My hands felt dry as if the skin on them had died and gone to parchment.

We tied the horses and Lesha led us to one of the smallest shacks—I had taken it to be a privy. A handful of residents watched us from their doorways, all of them veiled, salt crusted on the cloth where they drew breath. One had a huge goitre that wrapped his neck in throttling folds of mottled flesh. At the shack, Lesha knocked and entered. Sunny and I stood by the doorway peering into the gloom. It seemed unlikely we would all fit inside.

"Lesha." A figure, seated in the far corner, nodding to her.

"Toltech." She crouched before him.

Toltech watched her with bright eyes over the top of his veil. He worked the mortar and pestle in his hands all the while, grinding away.

"You're going back in?" He didn't sound surprised.

"Three of us, with three beasts. We'll need pills for a week."

"A week is a long time in the Iberico." Toltech glanced to me then to Sunny. "An hour can be a long time there."

"If it takes us an hour, we'll be there an hour," Lesha said.

Toltech put down his pestle and reached across to a low shelf. He picked up a bowl filled with small wraps of greased paper, tightly bound. Scars ran along his hand. The same molten scars that covered Lesha.

"Take one at sunrise, one at sunset. Swallow them in the paper if you can. The salt steals any moisture in the air and dissolves in it, so these will not last long anywhere damp. Take a hundred. Five silver."

The right salts helped keep out the sickness caused by the echoes of the Builders' fire. Nobody knew why. The required salts could be separated from the waters of Carrod Springs with sufficient expertise. Five pieces of silver seemed a small price to pay. I counted out the coins, one stamped with my grandfather's head, and passed them in to Lesha.

Toltech started to count salt pills into a cotton bag. "If you find anything in the hills, even if it's just broken pieces, bring it to me. I might give you your silver back."

"What have you had from the Iberico before, Master Toltech?" I asked. "I'm something of a collector myself." I leaned a little way in through the entrance. Beneath the salts' astringency the smell of sickness caught at me.

"Small things." He pointed at two short bottles of green glass on the shelf where the bowl had rested. Beside them a tray covered with pieces of fractured plasteek in many colours and shapes. From behind him he took a great cog of silvery metal, stained with age. It looked like an enormous cousin to one of the minute pieces from inside the watch in my baggage. "Nothing of great consequence. The best I sell on."

"And do you know about the Builders, Master Toltech? Do you learn their secrets as you sift through their leavings?" I asked.

"I know only what all of us here know about the Builders. What our fathers knew."

"And that is?" Some men like to be prompted.

"That they are not gone, and that you cannot trust them."

We camped that night on the very edge of the Iberico range where a poisoned stream named the Cuyahoga ran out across the badlands. I swallowed my salt pill, the bitterness escaping despite its wrap of paper. Toltech had had no more to say about the Builders so as we settled down after sunset I quizzed Lesha.

"What does your friend mean when he says the Builders are not gone?"

I felt rather than saw her shrug. We lay close, despite the weight of heat upon us. "Some say the Builders are spirits now, all around us, written into the elements."

"Not just echoes in machines?" I thought of Fexler flickering into life as I came down the cellar steps.

Lesha lifted to face me, frowning, deep enough that her scars buckled into furrows. "Machines? Things of wheels and pulleys? I don't understand."

"Spirits you say?" I decided to keep the engines beneath my grandfather's castle to myself. "Good spirits or evil ones?"

Again the shrug. "Just spirits. In the air, in rocks, running through rivers and streams, even staring at you out of the fire."

"I heard that the Builders took hold of what is real, and before they scorched the world, they changed it," I said.

"Changed what?" I'd forgotten Sunny was even there.

"Everything. Me, you, the world, what *real* is. They made the world listen a little more to what's in men's heads. They made thoughts and fears matter, made them able to change what's around us."

"They didn't make it listen to me."

I smiled at Sunny's grumbling.

"Earl Hansa had a rock-sworn mage work for him," Sunny added. "A young fellow. Must have been ten, fifteen years ago. Arron. That was it. He could work stone with his hands as if it was butter. One time he set a finger to my sword and it got so heavy I couldn't hold it. I couldn't pry it off the floor until the next day."

"What happened to him?" He sounded like a useful man to know, this Arron.

"Sunk."

"Ah."

"Not at sea though. Ortens says he saw it, and Ortens isn't one for lying. He just sunk into the floor one morning. Right out in the centre courtyard. And nobody saw him again. There's just a grey stain where he went into the rock."

"Well, there's a thing," I said.

And we all fell silent.

I lay for a time, on my blanket on the dust, listening to the silence. Something was wrong. I groped for it, reaching like you do in the night when your knife isn't where it should be. For the longest time I couldn't discover what it was that irked me.

"There's no noise." I sat up.

"What?" Lesha, sleep edging her voice.

"Those things, those damned cicadas that screech all night. Where are they?"

"Not here," she said. "We're too close. Nothing lives in the Iberico. Not rats, not bugs, not lichen on rocks. If you want to go back—now is the time."

13

The silence made it hard to sleep. The quiet seemed to have infected us all, even the horses held their peace, barely a snort or scrape of hoof hour after hour. In place of the night's muttering my ears invented their own script for the darkness. I heard whispers from the copper box, a taunting voice just beyond hearing, and behind even that, the sound of my own screaming. Perhaps the death of all those cicadas saved me, burned away by the ghost of the Builders' fire, or maybe built as I am of suspicion and mistrust I would have heard the attackers coming wherever we slept. Somewhere a stone grated beneath the sole of a shoe.

My kick found Lesha first. A stretched hand found some part of Sunny and I pinched it. Had they been road-brothers they would have, depending on their nature, sprung up blade in hand, or frozen where they lay, alert but waiting, until they understood the need. Brother Grumlow would have knifed the hand that shook him, Brother Kent would have feigned sleep, listening. Lesha and Sunny had slept too long in safe beds and started to rise in confusion, grumbling questions.

The predawn hint gave me the enemy as clumps of blackness, low to the dark ground, moving.

"Run!"

I threw my knife into the nearest threat, praying it wasn't a rock, then rolled past Lesha and took off at a sprint. The shriek that went up from the new owner of my dagger did more to convince the others of the danger than did my sudden exit.

Running in the dark is foolish but I'd seen the surroundings before the sun set. No bushes to tangle the feet and most of the rocks not big enough to be a problem. I heard the others behind me, Sunny's boots pounding, Lesha barefoot. Never let an enemy choose the ground. The only consolation in running blind into the night was that whoever meant us harm was now having to do the same.

Memory told me a shallow valley lay ahead, dividing the first swelling foothills of the Iberico. I glanced behind, knowing that if the enemy were too close I would have heard the others go down already. The pursuers had unhooded several lanterns and their lights swung as they ran. Sunny had kept up a good pace and I had a scant twenty yards on him. Already Lesha was lost in the gloom, too stiff in the armour of her scars to run very fast.

I stopped and collared Sunny as he ran past. He nearly gutted me. "Get down." I hauled him to the ground. The Cuyahoga was out there, chuckling along its stony bed and Lesha had advised against wetting your feet in those waters—if you wanted to carry on walking.

"What? Why?" At least he had the sense to hiss his questions.

"The guide!" I kept low, crouched and hoping I looked like a rock. Lesha's feet made an odd noise hitting the dusty ground as she ran. She sounded close, the whoops of pursuit almost as near. She loomed into view and shot past us. I left Sunny to end the first man chasing her as I drove forward into the next two. Behind them the lights of at least four lanterns swung wildly in the hands of running men.

We took them by surprise. I swung left and right, crippled two men, and took off running again. I saw enough to know we had more than a dozen still chasing us, rough irregulars by the look of them. Road-brothers if you like, just not *my* brothers and not *my* roads.

I caught up with Lesha soon enough. They would too. Her only chance had been to get to her horse but there wasn't time.

"Where to?" I shouted.

"Don't know." She panted it out. A useless but reasonable answer.

We let the valley guide us between the hills. Even as we ran the light grew, or rather the greys paled revealing hints at the world. Sunny waited for us where the valley divided, sword in hand, breathing hard. The cries of pursuit rang out behind. Hollers and wolf-howls, as if it were a game to them. It sounded like a lot more than a dozen on our trail.

It occurred to me that we were being herded. I had a couple of seconds to consider the realization before the ground gave way under Sunny. He vanished into a dark hole and I avoided following him by the narrowest of margins. Lesha hit me from behind as I teetered, arms wheeling, on the crumbling edge of the pit, and we went in together.

"Shit."

We landed next to Sunny, our fall broken by a pile of sticks and dry grass. Looking up earned me an eyeful of loose earth sifting down and a glimpse of the paling sky, lighter still now viewed from the depths of a pit. To escape would require a climb of twelve maybe fifteen feet. We'd fallen into some kind of natural sinkhole covered to make a trap.

"Who are they?" I asked.

"Bandits." Lesha's voice came soft with terror. "Perros Viciosos, 'Bad Dogs' in the old tongue. I didn't think they came this close to the Iberico."

"Let them know who you are, Jorg. They'll ransom us." Sunny tried to climb but slipped back in a shower of dry earth.

"*You* don't believe it half the time, Sunny. You think I'll convince this lot they've caught a king?"

The whooping drew closer, louder. Laughter now. "We've got them!"

"Viciosos? That means 'bad'?" It didn't sound quite right.

"Vicious," Lesha said, stuttering out her words. "For what they do to captives."

The pit smelled of char.

"Give me a knife," I said.

"Left mine in a Bad Dog." Sunny patted his side.

"It's all on Garros," Lesha said. She'd left her weapons on her horse. Who sleeps like that?

I drew my sword and made a slow arc to check the space. We had room to swing a cat if its tail wasn't too long. The laughter and mutter of voices increased above. The Bad Dogs were gathering.

I caught Lesha's shoulder and felt the unheard sobs shudder through her. No swift death waited for any of us. "Stand there." I pushed her into clear space, stumbling over the broken branches. She turned to me, just the glimmer of her eyes to mark her in the dark.

Light from above. A torch and a man to hold it. He could have passed for Rike's smaller uglier brother. "See what running got you?"

I swung and severed Lesha's neck in a single clean cut, letting the sword bury its blade in the wall. Before she could fall I had her head in both hands, scarred and heavy, no realization in those eyes yet, and threw it as hard as I could. It struck the bandit square in the face, not on the forehead as I would have liked, but on the nose, mouth, and chin. He staggered one step backward, two steps forward, and fell with a wordless curse. He landed on Lesha's body. I caught the torch.

"What the hell?" Sunny stared in horror and amazement. Mostly amazement.

"Look at the walls," I said. They were black. I stabbed the torch in where the sandy soil would hold it.

The bandit proved as heavy as he looked. I hauled him off Lesha and wrenched my sword clear to hold at his throat. "Get up, Bad Dog." The sharp edge helped him find his feet. "Sunny, get her blood spread around."

"What?"

I kicked the brush around my ankles and set my left hand to the pit wall. "This wasn't put here to break our fall." My fingers came away sooty. "They burn people here."

More noise from above, an angry debate.

"You better lower a rope if you want this idiot alive," I shouted.

A shrill laugh, more heated words exchanged.

"Ah, who am I kidding?" I sliced his throat on the blade of my sword and wrestled him around so the spray of his blood wouldn't be wasted. "Who looks over the edge? It's not as if he knew we didn't have a knife to throw."

Five torches arced in together before the idiot's neck had stopped pulsing. With the brush damped down and our wits about us we managed to get the torches secured and stamp out any burning patches. The smoke covered the stench of blood and soiled corpses. When we were done Sunny met my gaze.

"You killed her so you had something to throw?"

"That would have been enough of a reason—you saw how she moved, she wouldn't help in a fight. But no."

"For the blood?"

"So I didn't have to watch them take as long as they could to kill her. If you knew how these sorts of men work, you'd be asking for me to take your head too."

"But I get a choice?"

"You might be useful yet," I said.

Our prison looked to be a fissure running for fifteen yards or so, three yards across at its widest where we fell into it.

I searched the idiot and found not one but two daggers, one for brawling, one balanced for throwing. I let Sunny have the bigger of the two.

"What now?" he asked. I could feel his fear but he kept it controlled. Holding a sword always leaves you with a little slice of hope.

"Now we wait for them to figure out how to kill us." Anger kept my fear at bay. I wanted to take as many of them with me as could be

managed. Dying in a dusty hole in the middle of nowhere hadn't figured in my plans and knowing that I was going to do just that left a
sour taste in my mouth. How the hell did we manage to run into a
hole with all this space around us in any case?

"You in the pit!" A shout from outside. No heads peeping over
this time.

I kept silent. Two more torches arced in, trailing sparks and
smoke across the pale sky. It seemed pointless given that five hadn't
done the job. The sharp jab in my shoulder came as I was bending
down for the closest brand.

"What?" I heard Sunny's exclamation. If the word "what" had
been taken away from him he wouldn't have had much to say that day.

I could have told him it felt like some kind of venom, but he'd
probably worked that out by then. A numbness had spread over my
shoulder before I managed to stand, turn, and throw my knife at the
dark face behind the blowpipe on the far edge of the pit. I missed.
Another dart hit me in the chest, a little black thing half a finger in
length.

"Fuck."

The third dart set me slumped over my sword, without the
strength to look up. It might be said it's never too hot for armour, but
I'd have run slower than Lesha if I'd kept it on.

Men dropped into the pit and they hauled us out of there like
meat, ropes round our chests, limbs trailing without sensation. It's
not so hard to keep fear at arms' length with a sword. When you're
helpless and in the grip of men for whom your pain is the only decent
entertainment for miles around, you'd be mad not to be terrified.

Two men had hold of my arms, and the creature that darted me
followed along where my heels dragged trails in the dust. My legs
were red to well above the knee, dust caking onto the wet blood. The
creature looked like a girl, eleven maybe, almost skeletal, burned dark
by the sun. She grinned and waved her blowpipe at me.

"Ghoul darts. From the Cantanlona." She had a high clear voice.

"Hard come by," said one of the men on my arms. "You'd better be worth it."

They dragged us three hundred yards or so to a campground. Our horses and Balky were already there, tied to a rail. The horses tugged at their ropes, nervous, thirsty maybe. Balky just looked bored. The encampment seemed semi-permanent, with a few lean-to shacks in even worse condition than those in Carrod Springs, a cart, some water barrels, a chicken or two and in the middle, four thick posts set into the ground. It said a lot about the Perros Viciosos that they had put more construction material and effort into their infrastructure for torture than into their own living arrangements.

I counted about thirty men, as various in their origins and appearance as my own road-brothers, but with a predominance of dark-haired men, Spanards from the interior, an older and more pure bloodline than found in the coast regions, most of them lean and with a dangerous look to them. By my reckoning we'd left five of them dead. None of those in sight bore fresh wounds.

Two men strung Sunny up to one pole then came back for me. The rest watched, or ate, or squabbled over our possessions, or all three. Several men had reached for the box at my hip, but always their hands had fallen away, their interest gone. None of them offered so much as a kick or a punch, as if wanting to keep us in as good health as possible until the fun started.

"That's Jorg Ancrath," Sunny told them. "King of the Renner Highlands, grandson of Earl Hansa."

The Bad Dogs didn't bother to reply, just tightened our ropes and set about their business. Waiting is part of the exercise. Letting the tension rise, like bakers' dough in the tin. Sunny kept talking, kept telling them who I was, who he was, what would happen if we weren't let go. The girl came over to watch us. She held out a hand filled with a large beetle scrabbling to get away.

"Mutant," she said. "Count the legs."

It had eight. "Ugly thing," I told her.

She pulled off two of its legs. The bug was big enough for me to hear the crack as the limbs came free. "All better." She put it down and it took off across the dust.

"You killed Sancha," she said.

"The big ugly idiot?"

"Yes," she said. "I didn't like him."

The men set a fire in the blackened space before the poles. A small one, for wood is rare in the Iberico.

"He's the King of the Renner Highlands," Sunny shouted at them. "He has armies!"

"Renar," I said. The numbness started to fade from my limbs, my strength making a slower return.

A woman came out of one of the shacks, a crone with sparse grey hair and a long nose. She unrolled a hide across the ground, displaying an assortment of knives, hooks, drills, and clamps. Sunny set to struggling. "You can't do this, you bastards."

Only they could.

I knew it wouldn't be long before he was begging me to get him out of this, then cursing me for getting him into it. At least I didn't have Lesha doing the same on the other side of me. I knew what would happen because I'd seen it before. I also knew that the quiet ones, the ones biding their time like me, would scream just as loud and beg just as uselessly in the end. I watched the men as they gathered, catching what names I could, Rael, tall and thin with a scar across his throat, Billan, pot-bellied, a salt-and-pepper beard, pig eyes. I muttered the names to myself. I would hunt them down in hell.

14

Five years earlier

While the old woman worked to expose Sunny's ribs, the girl brought me her latest find. She held the scorpion's claws together in one tight fist and kept the stinger stretched out with the other hand. Eight legs writhed in a fury of motion. The thing had to be a good twelve inches from claw tip to sting. I could see the strain of holding it in the small knots of muscle along her arm bones.

"What?"

"It's not right!" She had to shout to be heard amid Sunny's screaming.

"Mutant?" It looked fine to me, just much bigger than I like my scorpions.

The old woman tossed down another strip of skin and two scrawny chickens chased after it. The men, crowded before the posts, cheered. Most of them sat cross-legged with some kind of liquor to hand in waxed leather tubes from which they sipped. All of them seemed content to let the crone ply her trade. Some chatted between themselves, but most showed an interest and would applaud the deft knife-work at the completion of each stage. I noted that one man had found Lesha's head and held it in his lap, angled toward the posts. There were few among the Bad Dogs who matched the intensity with which she watched us.

"Not mutant. Wrong." She strained to crack the creature's back but couldn't. The legs kept up the frenzy of writhing. "Can't you hear it?"

I could barely hear *her* over Sunny's screaming, let alone her new pet. In truth I think he screamed to take his mind off what was being done, the real hurting had yet to start. Torture is more than pain and the Perros Viciosos knew it. Certainly the old woman knew it. She hadn't really begun on him yet, but the mutilation hurt worse than agony that leaves no mark. When the torturer does damage that obviously won't heal they underscore the irreversibility of it all. This won't get better. This won't go away. It lets the man know he is just meat and veins and sinew. Flesh for the butcher.

The girl, Gretcha, held the scorpion to my face. I craned away, rewarded by a full view of Sunny's chest, the white of rib bones showing through the narrow slots cut to reveal them. Veins stood out in sharp relief across his neck, eyes screwed shut.

I heard it then, the strange whir, click, and tick behind the dry thrashing of legs. It set me in mind of the noise when I put the Builders' watch to my ear, the sound of cogs, of metal teeth meshing with impossible precision. I turned and stared at the thing and for one fragment of a second its black eyes blinked crimson.

Gretcha threw the scorpion down and started to chase it, beating at it with a heavy stick. One blow broke most of the legs along the left side. She vanished from the corner of my eye still chasing the crippled arachnid. I could turn my head no further. The red flash echoed behind my eyelids and for some reason I saw Fexler's red star once more, blinking over the Iberico.

It took the better part of an hour for the old woman to finish her work and in that time she used most of the tools from the wrap she had rolled out at the start. She made an artwork of Sunny's chest and arms, cutting, searing, tearing pieces away, unpeeling layers, pinning them back. He howled at her of course, and at me, demanding release, that I do something, begging me, and before long he swore terrible revenge, not on his tormentors but on Jorg Ancrath who had brought him to this fate.

Fear ran in me—how would it not? Terror ran through me in a hot rush, then as ice along veins, making my fingers and face prickle with pins and needles. But I tried to fool myself that I sat in the audience, watching with the casual cruelty of road-brothers at rest. And to some degree I succeeded for I have sat and watched, on too many occasions, from the times before I really understood such suffering to the times where I understood it and didn't care. The strong will hurt the weak, it's the natural order. But strapped there in the hot sun, waiting my turn to scream and break, I knew the horror of it and despaired.

At last the crone stepped back, red to the elbows, but with scarcely a drop on her clothes or face. She turned to her audience, mocked a curtsey, and went back to her shack with her tools in their roll beneath one arm.

Cheers from the crowd, some quite drunk now. Harsh rasping breaths from Sunny, his head hanging low, one eye wide and staring, the other tight shut. The tall man, Rael, stood and advanced to secure Sunny's head to the post with leather straps. Off by the shacks someone took a piss, another man scattered grain for the hens.

"Gretcha!" The round-bellied man, Billan, called out for the girl.

She came from behind the posts with the slash of a grin on her skull face, dropping a handful of broken insect parts, legs and glossy black plates. Billan set a stool for the girl to stand on, close to Sunny's post.

Gretcha went to the fire without further prompting and took the iron that had been set there. I hadn't seen it placed. She grasped it by the cloth-wrapped end and held the dull orange end toward us. "No!" Sunny understood the leather straps around his forehead. I couldn't blame his struggles. I would be struggling and telling them no when my turn came.

In the fire strange shapes danced. The sun made ghosts of the flame and I had to squint, but I saw them, shapes and colours that had no place there. Delirium setting in from the heat and terror. Perhaps madness would claim my mind before they even started on me.

"You're too loud." Gretcha pushed the hot iron into Sunny's mouth. His clenched lips shrivelled away before the iron's glare. Teeth cracked at the iron's touch. I heard them. They became brittle and shattered as she pushed. Steam poured from his mouth, steam and awful screaming and the smell of roasting.

I looked away, blinded with tears as the little girl put his eyes out. I could say I wept for Sunny, or for the horror of a world where such things happen, but in truth I wept for myself, in fear. At the sharp end of things there is only room for ourselves.

The Bad Dogs whooped and cheered at the sport. Some called out names, presumably of the men who we had killed, but it meant nothing. We would have suffered the same tortures if they had captured us in our sleep without loss.

"Gretcha." Billan again. "Enough with that one. Mary will find something more in him later. Put the other's eye out. Just one. I don't like the way he's been looking at me."

The girl pushed the end of the iron into the hot embers and stood watching it, her back to me. I pulled at my bonds. They knew how to tie a man, not just at the wrists but at the elbows and higher too. I pulled anyhow. Anger rose in me. It wouldn't stand before the iron, but for a moment at least it chased away some measure of the fear. Anger at my tormentors and anger at the foolishness of it, dying in some meaningless camp filled with empty people, people going nowhere, people for whom my agony would be a passing distraction.

When Gretcha turned back I met her gaze and ignored the hot draw of the iron.

"Keep a steady hand, girl." I gave her a savage grin, hating her with a sudden intensity so fierce it hurt.

Are you dangerous? I had asked the Nuban when they held the irons over him. I'd given him his chance, loosed one hand, and he had seized it. *Are you dangerous?* Yes, he had said, and I told him to show me. I wanted that chance now. Let her say the words. *Are you dangerous?*

Instead her smile fell away and her hand wavered, just a touch.

"Stop!" Rael called. "His head isn't bound. You could kill him."

He came across and secured me with more straps. I watched him, trying to commit each detail of his face to memory. He would be one of the last people I saw.

"Give me the iron." He snapped the words out, taking it from Gretcha's hands. "I'll do this one myself." Returning my glare he said, "You might be a lord of some sort. You had enough gold on you. And this." He held up his wrist to show the watch from my uncle's treasury. "But we both know that if you were ransomed you would do nothing but hunt us from the moment you were free and safe. I can see it in you."

I couldn't lie to him. There would be no point. If I were free I would hunt them over any distance at any cost.

"Looks like you've done this before." Rael nodded at my cheek. "Maybe we should start where they left off, just to remind you how it felt."

The red-hot tip of the iron approached the thick scar tissue reaching across the left side of my face. No waver in Rael's hand however fierce my stare. Gretcha stood beside him, her head reaching only a little past his waist.

The heat scorched my lips and dried the wetness from my eyes, but in the scar-tissue no pain, just a warmth, pleasant almost. The burn had killed all sensation in that flesh, I could scratch it with my nails and only feel the tugging in the untouched skin just below my eye. The iron rested a little below my cheekbone with the pressure of a poking finger. Puzzlement reshaped Rael's brow.

"He won't b—"

A sudden pulse of pleasure flushed through the scar tissue, almost orgasmic, and a flash of heat closed my eyes. The stink of my hair crisping filled my nostrils. Rael screamed and when I looked again the dance had him. That dance men do when unexpected agony seizes them, a stubbed toe or blow to that tricksy bone in the elbow will start it off often as not. He held the wrist of his right hand in the grip of his left. And there, seared across the exposed palm, deep enough to reach the little bones that fill the hand, the line the iron had left on him. The iron itself lay in the dust, bright and shining, as white with heat as if it were at the bellows' mouth in a forge, the cloth burning around it.

I had to laugh. What were they going to do if I laughed at them? Hurt me? In the shock of it I had bitten my tongue and I laughed now with the taste of blood filling my mouth and the warmth of it running crimson over my lips.

"Idiot." Billan got up and pushed Rael out of his way. He caught my chin and jaw in a painful grip. "What did you do, boy?"

"Boy?" It hurt to get the word out with his fingers digging into my jaw muscles. I didn't know what I'd done but I was glad of it. I suspected something in the fragments of Gog bedded in that scar had reacted to the touch of so much heat.

"Answer me."

Even now Billan thought he had something to threaten me with. I spat blood into his face. He staggered away with a girlish shriek and that set me laughing all the more. Hysteria had me in its claws. Others among the Perros Viciosos got to their feet. One slab of muscle named Manwa, brother to Sancha who I killed in the pit, took Billan's arm and tried to settle him. A dirty rag set to the blood didn't seem able to wipe it off. Seconds later a better view showed that the skin itself had turned scarlet where the blood touched, and in his eyes the blood had scalded his cornea a milky white. It seemed the necromancy that lurked within me and would kill small things through just a touch of my fingers, really did run in my veins.

"Get Old Mary back!" Billan shouted it in his blindness. The effort to hold himself back, to deny the lust to choke the life out of me, made him tremble. "I want him to scream for a month."

"You won't live a month, Billan. When your brothers understand that your sight isn't coming back . . . how long before they tie you to this post do you think?" I couldn't stop smiling. Hysteria and bravado would be cut from me quick enough when the crone brought her knives, I knew that, but hell, laugh while you can, no?

Manwa pulled out his sword, which turned out to be my sword. "He has a sword of the old-steel and he works magic." He turned the blade in his huge fist. He was a big man but his hands belonged to a giant. "Maybe we should ransom him? The other one said Earl Hansa would pay for them."

Rael spat, his face tight with suffering. A burned hand leaves a man no peace. "He dies. He dies hard."

Manwa shrugged and sat down, my sword across his knees.

Two men led Old Mary back to the posts. I saw them first from the corner of my eye and watched so close that I almost didn't notice the rope go slack around my ankles. Behind the complaints and curses of the Bad Dogs, behind the wet unnatural sobbing from Sunny, I heard a click and whir and a scrabbling like fingers clawing wood. Something fought a path up the post at my back, on the far side. Schnick. The rope around my knees fell away. Nobody noticed.

Mary unrolled her tool-wrap out across the dust again. She gave me a mean look as if I was really going to get it now for disturbing her rest. Again the absurdity of it twitched at the corners of my mouth. She drew the sharpest of her blades, a small cutting edge on a cylindrical metal shaft, the sort of thing Grecko doctors might use for slicing out a canker. Three steps brought Mary to me, unsteady on her feet, sure of hand. She cut away the stained remnants of my shirt. The blade didn't pull as the cloth parted before it.

"That's a very ugly wart you have there, Old Mary," I said.

She paused and looked at me. She had mean old-woman eyes, very dark.

"Oh sorry. I mean the one down on your chin. Ugly thing. Couldn't you just slice it off? With that nice sharp knife of yours? Trim some of those wattles too? We don't want them calling you Ugly Old Mary now, do we?"

Something dry and unpleasant scrambled over my bound hands. I shivered as hard little legs moved over my wrists. It took all my remaining composure not to twitch the thing off me.

"Are you stupid?" Mary asked after the longest pause. She hadn't said a word to Sunny the whole time she worked on him.

"Did I hurt your feelings, Old Mary?" I smiled at her, my teeth crimson no doubt. "You know that however much I shout and beg, those words can't go back in the box, don't you? You are ugly and old. There's nothing we can do about it, Mary. I expect little Gretcha will be doing your work soon enough and you'll be her journeyman piece. I wonder what shapes she'll cut you into?"

The Bad Dogs watched me now, their arguments forgotten. Even Rael and Billan gave up on their hurts for a moment to give me their attention. Victims threaten or plead. Old Mary didn't know what to make of mockery.

Schnick. My wrists were free. Blood started to flow into them. It hurt worse than anything I'd suffered on the torture pole thus far.

Old Mary shook her head and brushed aside a lock of grey hair. She looked annoyed, less sure of herself. Here she was, ready to open me up piece by piece, and I'd made her self-conscious with throw-away commentary on her wartiness. I grinned wide enough to crack my face. I felt pretty sure they'd have to kill me once I got free. The prospect of attacking them rather than expiring on that pole just flooded me with joy. I couldn't stop smiling.

"Cracked, this one." Mary set the point of her knife at the extreme right of my lowest rib.

I strained for the faint noise of my saviour crawling up the pole. If it cut the rope across my chest and upper arms everyone would notice it fall and I would still be secured by the head. They hadn't set a rope around our necks, presumably to stop us choking when straining to get away from the pain.

Mary made her cut. They say sharp knife, no tears. The cutting didn't hurt, but an acid wash of pain followed in the knife's wake. It took all my restraint to keep from kicking her away and betraying myself.

"Ouch," I said. "That hurts."

Mary drew back to make a lower cut parallel to the first. Behind me the creature slipped and fell.

"Oh crap!" I shouted it. Amazingly Old Mary startled back and several of the Bad Dogs flinched. Somehow the creature caught on my hands, a bite or a grip, I didn't know, but I did know it really hurt. "OUCH! Fuck it!"

Mary blinked. I had one thin slice in me—she didn't understand.

"You're going to do the same thing again?" I demanded. The creature released its grip and climbed back over my hands to the pole. It felt like a giant crab, or spider. Jesu, I hate spiders. "You're going to do the ribs all over again like you did on Sunny?" I flicked my eyes his way. "You're supposed to be good at this, to make it interesting to watch! No wonder they've got Gretcha ready to replace you."

"The ribs are boring," somebody called out behind her.

"It's good when she breaks them out." That was Rael.

"We've got one ready for that."

"Something new!"

Slight vibrations as the creature reached the chest rope. Shit. I tensed, ready to struggle like hell when it came free. More vibration and the thing moved on, up, the rope intact.

"Come on, Ugly Mary, show us something new." A dark-skinned youth near the back.

Mary didn't like that at all. She scowled at me, showing yellow stumps of teeth. Muttering, she turned and bent for a thin hook.

The creature moved behind my head. My hair pulled where strands were bound up in the leather. A claw slid under the strap that bound my forehead.

Mary faced me, straightening as much as her back allowed. She kept the hook low as she advanced, at groin level, smiling for once.

Schnick.

I pressed forward and the rope around my chest gave. The creature must have sawed through, leaving just a strand to hold it.

Conjurers will hold your attention where they want it and in doing so can leave you blind to what else is happening before your eyes. Mary's hook held the Bad Dogs' attention. The last rope on me dropped away and, like magic, nobody saw it fall.

The madness in me, some virulent mix of terror and relief, put me in mind to scratch my nose then return my hand behind me. Sanity prevailed. I overcame the temptation to waste the moment by sinking Mary's hook into one of her eyes. Instead I moved forward, very swift, and snatched my sword from Manwa's lap.

I strode into the midst of them.

To avoid grappling and capture it's best to keep to the edge, but they had bows and somewhere, more of those darts. By striking to the middle I kept them disorganized, close. And as I moved through them I laid about me. Before the first of the Dogs gained their feet I had opened wounds on four men that would never close.

There's a freedom in being surrounded on all sides by enemies. In such circumstances, with a heavy blade that's sharp enough to make the wind bleed, you can swing in grand and vicious circles and your only care need be to ensure the weapon isn't locked into the corpse of your last victim. In many ways I had lived most of my life in exactly such a condition, swinging in all directions with no worry about who might die. Experience served me well on the edge of the Iberico Hills.

The Bad Dogs died, parted from heads, from limbs, without time for one man to fall before the point of my sword ploughed a red furrow through the next. Not before or since have I taken such unadulterated joy in slaughter. Some cleared their weapons, swords, knives, sharp little hatchets, cleaver-axes, but none lasted more than two exchanges with me: a swift parry and they went down on the riposte. I got cut, in three places. I didn't know about that until much later, until I found that some of the blood wouldn't clean away.

Once, with men advancing from many directions, I spun and found Manwa in front of me. Instinct wrapped my spare hand around his knife hand and twisted me to the side. Hatred drove my forehead into his nose. He was a tall man, powerful, but I had grown tall, and whether rage multiplied my strength or my muscle matched his I don't know, but his knife didn't find me. In fact I kept it for a dozen more bloody moments, cutting and thrusting, until I left it in Rael's neck.

It helped that many of them were drunk, some too intoxicated on blind-shine even to find their weapons, let alone swing them to good effect. It also helped that I hated them all with such purity, and that I had trained at swordplay for months, day in, day out, until my hands bled and the sword-song rang in my ears.

A fat man fell away from me, guts vomiting in blue coils from his opened belly. Another man, already running, I cut down from behind. Turning, I saw two more Dogs running toward the valley. One I brought down at fifty paces with a hatchet scooped from the ground. The other escaped. The silence was sudden and complete.

By the posts Mary stood with Gretcha at her side. The girl had one small hand knotted in the old woman's skirts, the other holding her blowpipe, levelled at me. I walked toward them. Pfft. Gretcha's dart hit my collarbone. I snatched the pipe from her and threw it behind me.

"We're very much alike, Gretcha, you and I."

I squatted to be level with the girl. The dart came out with a pull and I let it fall into the dust. She watched me with dark eyes. I saw a lot of Mary in her. A granddaughter perhaps.

"I can help." I smiled, sad for her, sad for everything. "If someone had done this for me when I was a child it would have saved everyone a lot of trouble."

Her mouth made an "oh" of surprise as the sword passed through her, grating on thin bones. She slid off the blade as I stood.

"Ugly. Old. Mary," I said.

She still held the hook. I caught her around her scrawny neck but she didn't try to stick me with it. Necromancy tingled in my fingertips, reacting to her age maybe. My fingers found the knobbles of her spine and I let death leak into her, enough to make her crumple to the floor.

Sunny still lived. His gasping made the only sound in that silence that settles over carnage. Some of the Bad Dogs would be wounded but alive. If they were though, they managed to stay quiet about it and sensibly keep themselves from my attention.

Close up Sunny's injuries screamed at me. I sensed the hurt coursing through him in red rivers. Necromancy knows about such things. With a hand against his chest it seemed I knew him blood to bone, that I knew the branching of his veins, the shape of his spine, the beat and flutter of his heart. I had no healing though, only death. Thick mucus, flecked with char, oozed from his eye sockets. His tongue lay scorched and swollen in a broken mouth.

"I can't help you, Greyson Landless."

The effort that raised his eyeless head to me tore through the necromantic threads between us and ripped a gasp from me. I cut his ropes and lowered him to the ground. I wouldn't see him die bound.

"Peace, brother." The point of my sword rested above his heart. "Peace." And I made an end of him.

Greyson's suffering still trembled in my hands. I knelt beside Old Mary, crumpled in the dirt, watching me with bright eyes, dust on the trail of drool across her cheek. With one hand on her scrawny neck and one atop her head I let Sunny's pain free. It seems that a necromancer's fingers can do in moments with strokes and pinches what all her sharp instruments took hours to achieve. Her heart couldn't take it for long and death reached up for her. She died too easy.

Lesha's head lay in among the bodies. I retrieved it, killing one malingerer on the way. Most corpses echoed with some remnant of the person when I touched them. Row's flesh had reeked of him. But

Lesha's head felt empty, not literally, not scooped out, but free of any trace of her, a shell. Somehow it pleased me, that she had gone beyond reach. Somewhere better I hoped.

I set her head beside Sunny, ready to bury. First though, I walked around the posts. The scorpion, missing three legs on one side, some armour broken away from its back, clung motionless to the rear of the post I had been bound to. The leather strap that held my head still hung from its claw. The scorpion's head lifted a fraction as I approached it, and once more the dark beads of its eyes glowed crimson.

"Fexler?" I asked.

It twitched twice and fell from the post, landing on its back. One more convulsion and it wrapped tight with a loud crackling noise, its armoured plates seizing in permanent embrace.

"Damn."

15

Chella's story

"Tell me again."

He's chained and bleeding in a dungeon surrounded by walking dead, and up above there's all manner of worse things, mire-ghouls and rag-a-mauls the least of them . . . and he keeps asking questions!

"You're an unusual man, Kai Summerson." Chella paced around the pillar once more. She couldn't seem to keep her feet still. Too much life in them perhaps.

"This from a necromancer with my woman's corpse on the floor."

Chella leaned in close, the iron needle in her hand, but she knew the balance had slipped away from her. Somewhere along the line this unusual young man had deduced that she needed his cooperation. Maybe it had just been too obvious that she would have killed him if her need hadn't been so great.

"What is it that you didn't understand?" She whispered it into his ear. He couldn't know how much she needed a success, anything to move her from the cold shadow of the Dead King's disdain.

"Sula's in heaven . . . and also here?"

A sigh escaped her, sharpened by frustration. Even clever men could be fools. "What will not pass into heaven may be returned to the body. How much is returned depends upon the person, and upon the call. It doesn't take much to get a fresh corpse on its feet. A little hunger, greed, some anger maybe. Sula had plenty of greed."

"So not everyone can be returned. Some people pass on clean and whole?"

"A saint maybe. I've never met one." Also children. But she didn't say it. Whatever the road to hell is paved with, the key is to take one step at a time.

"And having reminded me of heaven you expect me to damn myself to eternity in flames just to avoid a painful death?" Kai spat blood onto the floor. He must have bitten his tongue. He didn't seem nearly as scared as he should be. Probably it felt like a dream to him, a nightmare, too much strangeness too quickly. If she had time Chella would leave him a day or two. Fear seeps into a man. In a cold dark place, alone with nothing but imagination for company, terror would gather him in. But she didn't have two days, or even one.

"Death is broken, Kai. Hell is rising. How long do you think heaven will keep you safe? The Dead King is putting an end to all of that. Eternity will be here, in this world, in this flesh. All you need to decide is whether to feed the fire or be the fuel."

16

Perhaps the Engine of Wrong had found a new gear for nothing felt right after Kent brought news that my father's carriage preceded us. I rode to the front of our column, Makin and Rike falling in around me. At Captain Harran's side a few minutes later, cresting a low rise, I saw the dull gleam of the Ancrath column ahead. It takes more than a river of mud to keep the Gilden Guard from shining.

I pulled up to stare at the carriage bumping along amidst the horsemen. I last rode in it when I was nine. The old bastard had salvaged it.

"He scares me too," Makin said.

"I'm not scared of my father." I showed him my scowl but he only grinned.

"I don't know how he puts the fright in a man," Makin said. "I mean, I swing the better sword, and yes he's got a cold temper on him and harsh ways, but so have a lot of kings, and dukes, and earls, barons, lords—hell, any man you give command to is likely to put an edge on it just to keep hold. He's not even given to torture: his brother, his nephews, all well known for it, but Olidan he'll just have you hung and be done."

Rike snorted at that. He'd seen my father's dungeons from the wrong side. Still, Makin had it right, there were plenty around who made Olidan Ancrath seem a reasonable man.

"I said I wasn't scared of him." My heartbeat told the lie but only I could hear it.

Makin shrugged. "Everyone is. He puts the fright in you. He's got the look. That's what does it. Cold eyes. Makes you shiver."

I've been known for bold moves at times, for daring the challenge even when I've known I shouldn't. Under that grey sky though, with a cold wind blowing wet from the north, I felt no inclination to catch up to the carriage labouring ahead of us and demand an accounting for the past. My chest ached along the thin seam of that old scar and for once I found myself wanting to let something lie.

We rode without talking, the column moving around us, so many guardsmen in their fine armour, so sure in their purpose. The chill breeze nagged at me and all my yesterdays crowded at my shoulder, wanting their turn to rattle in my skull.

"Cerys," I said.

Makin pushed back his helm and looked at me.

"Killed when she had three years to her. Tell me." I had thought that if we ever spoke of Makin's daughter it would be in maudlin drunkenness in the small hours before dawn, or perhaps as with Coddin it would take a mortal wound to turn our conversation to matters of consequence. That it might happen riding in the mud in the cold light of day surrounded by strangers had not occurred.

Still Makin watched me, jolting in the saddle, unaccustomed stiffness in that flexible face of his. For the longest moment I thought he wouldn't speak.

"My father had lands in Normardy, a small estate outside the town of Trent. I wasn't the first son. I got married off to a rich man's daughter. Her father and mine settled some acres on us and a house. The house came a couple of years after our official marriage. Something less than a mansion, more than a farmhouse. The sort of place you might have raided when you led the brothers on the road."

"It was outlaws?" I asked.

"No." His eyes glittered, bright with memory. "Some official dispute, but too petty to be called a war. Trent and Merca quarrelling over their boundaries. A hundred soldiers and men-at-arms on each side, no more. And they met in my wheatfield. We were both seventeen, Nessa and me, Cerys three. I had a few farmhands, two house servants, a maid, a wet-nurse."

Even Rike had the sense to say nothing. Nothing but the clomp of hooves in mud, Gorgoth's heavy footfalls, the creak of harness, dull chinks of metal on metal, the high sharp arguments of birds invisible against the sky.

"I didn't see them die. I might have been lying in the dirt by the main door clutching my chest. Nessa likely got cut down while I lay there looking at the clouds. I blacked out later. Cerys hid herself in the house and the fire probably reached her after I'd been dragged unconscious into a ditch. Children do that, they hide from the fire rather than run, and the smoke finds them.

"Took me six months to recover. Stabbed through a lung. Later, I raided into Merca, with a band who survived that day. I found out that the lord's boy who led that raid had been sent to a cousin's in Attar to keep him safe. We met a year later. I tracked him to a little fort-town about twenty miles north of here.

"My route back took me through Ancrath, and I stayed there. In time I found service with your father. And that's all there is to it."

Makin didn't have a grin on him, though I've seen him smile at death time and again. He kept his eyes on the horizon but I knew he saw further than that. Across years. "That" is never all there is to it. Hurt spreads and grows and reaches out to break what's good. Time heals all wounds, but often it's only by the application of the grave, and while we live some hurts live with us, burning, making us twist and turn to escape them. And as we twist, we turn into other men.

"And how long does it take for a child that you cross nations to avenge, because you couldn't save her when saving her was an option, to become a child that you knife because you couldn't accept him when accepting him was an option?"

Makin gave half a grin then, though he didn't look away from whatever past held him. "Ah, Jorg, but you were never as sweet as Cerys, and I was never as cold as Olidan."

Another day passed and we trailed the Ancrath column through Attar's heartlands. Everywhere peasants came on rag-bound feet to watch us pass, wreathed in the smoke from fields where red lines of fire ate the stubble. They abandoned the harvest's funeral rites, the laying and the stacking of crops, the pickling and the drying for winter, to watch the Gilden Guard and see the pennants of jet and gold flutter on high. Empire meant something to them. Something old and deep, a half-forgotten dream of better things.

In the late afternoon, sunshine broke through a fissure in the clouds and Miana emerged from Lord Holland's carriage to ride a sedate mile side-saddle as we plodded through a ford town with the unlikely name of Piddle. Marten took to saddle as well and when Miana retired he kept at my side.

"She's finding it difficult, sire," he said, unprompted.

"More difficult than being at the Haunt waiting for guests from the Vatican?"

"It's hard work carrying a child in the last month." Marten shrugged but I felt he cared more than that.

Sometimes it cuts to see other men more passionate than I about the things that I should care for. I knew that if the Pope's assassin had killed Miana and our unborn child I would have grieved. But also I knew that some terrible part of me, down at the core, would have raised its face to the world with a red grin, welcoming the chance, the excuse, for the coming moments of purity in which my revenge would sail upon a tide of blood. And I knew that rage would have swept away everything else, including sorrow.

"It's a hard world, Marten." He glanced across, confused for a moment as we'd ridden a quarter mile since he last spoke. "It shouldn't be easy to bring someone into a hard world. It's too easy to make a new life, too easy to take an old one. It's only right that some part of the process present a little difficulty."

He kept his gaze upon me, a right earned over and again in my service, and the weight of his judgment built upon me.

"Dammit." I snorted my exasperation. "I feel outnumbered in that carriage."

Martin smiled. "A married man is always outnumbered."

I spat in the mud and pulled on Brath's reins with a curse. Five minutes later I sat in the carriage once more beside Miana.

"My father's carriage is just ahead of us," I said.

"I know."

It felt odd to be talking about him, especially with Gomst and Osser sat watching us. Gomst at least had the sense to pull out his bible, a book near big enough to hide the both of them, and engage the older man in discussion of some or other psalm.

"Coddin wants me to vote with my father at Congression. To make peace with him." The words made my mouth dirty.

"And you would rather . . . not?" A smile quirked at the corners of her lips but I didn't feel mocked.

A snatch of Gomst's conversation reached me. "'Father, where is the lamb that is to be sacrificed?' And Abraham replied, 'My son, God will provide the lamb.'"

"I have many reasons to want him dead. And almost as many reasons to want to be the one to do it."

"But *do* you want to do it? The Jorg I know tends to do what he wants to do, and if reasons oppose him he changes them."

"I—" I wanted to understand how it all worked, this business of living and of raising children. I wanted to do the job better than he had. "Men will tell our son how it was between me and my father."

Miana leaned closer, raven-dark hair falling around her pale face.

"So what will they tell our child?" She refused to call him "our son" until he came out to prove himself.

"Even the king can't control men's gossip," I said.

Miana watched me. She wore a circlet of woven gold but her hair did as it pleased, taking at least two maids and a handful of clips to constrain. At last my incomprehension drove her to explain. "How can a clever man be so stupid? How it was between you and Olidan isn't finished. The story that will be told is not yet written."

"Oh."

I let her shoo me out of the carriage.

Not until chance took a hand though did I finally find the stones to ride to my father's carriage. A guard captain came with news and found me skulking mid-column, Gorgoth at my side. Gorgoth always proved good company if you didn't want to talk.

"The Ancrath carriage has broken an axle." He didn't bother with my title. "Can room be found in yours? There's some objection to using one of the baggage wagons."

"I'll come and discuss the matter." I suppressed a sigh. Sometimes you can sense the current of the universe flowing and nothing can deny its will for too long.

All my men rode in my wake. Word had spread fast. Even Gorgoth came, perhaps curious to see where a son such as I had sprung from. We passed the Gilden Guard in their hundreds, all halted on the trail. Every head turned our way. And in a narrow stretch of road, unremarkable save for the stream on whose rocky bed my father's carriage had broken its axle, I came once more to speak with the King of Ancrath.

I felt Coddin at least would be pleased. I may not have taken his advice but fate seemed to disagree with my decision, pushing the Ancraths one step further along the path of the old prophecy. Two Ancraths working together were required to break the power of the hidden hands and here were the last two Ancraths. Well, you can lead a horse to water, but I choose what I damn well drink and I hold a low opinion of prophecy. It would take more than hell freezing over to see me allied to my father's cause.

They had dragged the carriage some twenty yards up the slope from the stream. I dismounted close by, my boots sinking six inches into churned mud. A breeze tugged the bare twigs in the hedgerows, a taller tree overreached us, black-fingered against a pale sky. The hand on Brath's reins shook as if the wind pulled on it too. I bit off a curse at my weakness and faced the carriage door. A thousand years ago Big Jan had pulled me through that door, from one world into another.

I stood there, cold, my bladder too full, a tremble in my limbs, turned in heartbeats from the king of seven nations bound for Congression to a scared child once again.

The guard captain of the Ancrath column applied his mailed knuckles to the wood. "Honorous Jorg Ancrath requests audience."

I wanted to be anywhere else, but stepped closer. None of the guard but the captain had dismounted to prevent violence. Either they didn't know the stories men told of me, or they didn't care. Perhaps they saw their job as retribution for breaking pax rather than prevention of such breaches.

The door opened and from the dark interior emerged a slim and pale hand. A woman's hand. I stepped forward and took it. Sareth? Father had brought his wife?

"Nephew."

And she stepped out onto the riding board, all whispering silks and stiff lace collars, her hand cool yet burning in my grip. The carriage behind her lay empty.

"Aunt Katherine," I said, my words once again in short supply.

17

Six years had only made her the more beautiful. What Katherine Ap Scorron hid in dreams stood before me on a cold day at the edge of winter.

"Katherine." I still held her hand, raised between us. She took it back. "My father sent you to Congression? In his stead?"

"Ancrath is at war. Olidan stays with his armies to ensure that the war is not lost."

She wore black, a flowing gown of it, satin folds reaching to a broad hem of black suede from which the mud might be brushed when dry. Lace around her neck like ink tattoos, earrings of silver and jet. Still mourning her prince.

"He sent you? With two voting seals and no advisors."

"Nossar of Elm was to come but he fell sick. I have the king's trust." She watched me, hard eyes, her lips a tight line in a pale face. "Olidan has come to appreciate my talents." Half a challenge—more than half. As if she might favour father over son and replace her sister at his side.

"I've come to appreciate your talents myself, lady." I sketched her a bow if only to gather my thoughts. "May I offer you a place in the Renar carriage? Father's repairs to this one seem to have been poorly judged." I drew on Brath's reins, bringing him close enough that she could mount from the riding board.

Katherine left the carriage without further encouragement, stepping up to ride side-saddle to accommodate the length of her dress. For one moment satin lay taut across the jut of her hipbone. I wanted her for more than the shape of her body—but I wanted that too.

Kent dismounted quick enough so that I could take his horse and ride with Katherine back along the column. I rode close, wanting to speak but knowing how weak my words would sound.

"I didn't mean to kill Degran. I would have fought to save him. He was my—"

"And yet you did kill him." She didn't look my way.

I could have spoken of Sageous but the heathen had only put the rope in my hands, the fact he knew someone would get hanged hardly excused me. In the end I could only agree. I did kill my brother.

"Orrin also deserved better from his brother," I said. "He would have made a good emperor."

"The world eats good men for breakfast." She shook her reins to coax Brath a little faster.

The words sounded familiar. I kicked Kent's horse and caught her. She pulled up beside Lord Holland's carriage. "I didn't know your tastes were so grand, Jorg."

"My wife's choice," I said.

I nodded to the guardsman by the carriage door and he knocked to announce Katherine. His knuckles barely made contact with the lacquered wood before the door sprang open and Miana leaned out, dark eyes on Katherine, lips pursed. She looked unaccountably pretty.

"I've brought you a midwife, dear—my aunt Katherine."

It's my sincere hope that Katherine's look of shock was more spectacular than the one I wore when taking her hand five minutes earlier.

I entered the carriage first and sat between the young queen and the older princess. I didn't trust in Gomst to be able to stop the bloodshed should things go badly.

"Queen Miana of Renar," I said, "this is Princess Katherine Ap Scorron, my father's representative at Congression and widow to the Prince of Arrow. We met Arrow's army two years back, you may recall." I waved a hand at the old men. "Osser Gant of Kennick, Lord Makin's advisor, and of course you know Bishop Gomst."

Miana settled her hands on her belly. "I'm sorry for your loss, Katherine. Jorg tells me he killed the man who murdered your husband."

"Egan, yes. Orrin's younger brother. Though the best deed that day was in putting an end to the heathen, Sageous. He poisoned Egan's mind. He wouldn't have betrayed Orrin otherwise."

I pressed back into the cushions. Two women, each given to speaking her mind and to trampling any social niceties that stood in their way, are wont to have short conversations that end interestingly. The fact that Katherine allowed for Sageous's hand in Orrin's fratricide seemed harsh when she gave me no room to hide in such excuses. In truth, though, I couldn't hang my guilt on him.

"The firstborn are often the best that the tree will offer," Miana said. "The ancients offered the first fruit to the gods. It might be that the first child carries whatever goodness their parents have to give." She laced her fingers over the greatness of her womb.

A slight smile touched Katherine's lips. "My sister is the firstborn. Anything gentle or kind went her way rather than mine."

"And my brother who will one day rule in Wennith is a good man. Any wickedness or cunning that my parents had came to me." Miana paused as the carriage lurched into motion, all the columns starting to move now. "And you have Orrin and Egan to support my theory."

"Of course that would make Jorg the Ancraths' paragon." Katherine glanced at Gomst who had the grace to look away. "Tell us, Jorg, what was William like?"

That surprised me. I had been happy letting them spar across me. "He was seven. It was hard to tell," I said.

"Tutor Lundist said William was the more clever of the two. The sun to Jorg's moon." Gomst spoke up but kept his eyes down. "He told me the child had an iron will such that no nurse could sway him from his chosen path. Even Lundist with his eastern cunning couldn't divert the lad. They brought him before me once, a boy of six determined that he was setting off on foot to find Atlantis. I talked about his duty, about God's plan for each of us. He laughed at me and said he had a plan for God." Gomst looked up but he didn't see us, his eyes fixed on the past. "Blond as if he came from the emperor's own blood." He blinked. "And iron in him. I believe he could have done anything, that boy—had he been allowed to grow. Anything. Good or ill."

My own memories painted a softer picture but I couldn't dispute Gomst. When William set his mind, when he decided how a thing should be, there was no arguing with him. Even when Father was called upon he would hold his nerve. And despite what I knew of my father's ruthlessness, when it came to William, it never occurred to me that the matter was yet settled even when we heard Father's footsteps in the corridor. Perhaps the reason my father hated me lay as simple as that. I had always been the weaker of the two. The wrong son died that night, the wrong son hung in the thorns.

Miana spoke into the uncomfortable silence. "So tell me, Katherine, how is my father-in-law? I have yet to meet him. I'd like to get to know him. I had hoped he might be at Congression so Jorg could introduce us."

That painted a picture. What would Father make of my tiny child-wife who incinerated her own soldiers to tear a vast hole in the enemy?

"King Olidan never changes," Katherine said. "I've spent years at his court and don't know him so I doubt you'd learn much if he had come to Congression. I'm far from sure my sister knows him after six years in his bed. None of us know what his dreams for Ancrath are."

I read that code clear enough. She hadn't managed to work her night-magics on Father, and perhaps Sageous hadn't either. Maybe Father's was the only hand on the knife that stabbed me. All presuming Katherine wasn't lying of course, but her words rang true, it didn't seem she would consider me worth sullying her lips with falsehoods for.

"How goes his war, Princess?" Osser Gant leant forward. He had quick ways about him for a greybeard, his eyes dark and cunning. I could see why Makin valued him.

"The dead continue to press from the marshes, seldom great numbers in any one place, but enough to drain the land. Peasants are killed in their villages, their bodies dragged to the bogs, farmers die in their homesteads. The dead hide in the mud when Ancrath's troops pursue, or they shelter in Ill-Shadow, in any place where the land is too poisoned for men. Gelleth has such places." She looked my way once more. "The attacks sap morale, leave food in short supply. Before I left there was talk of a lichkin walking the marsh."

Gomst crossed himself at that.

"And what do they say in Olidan's court about the direction of these attacks?" Osser asked. A question of considerable interest to all Kennick men for although they had lost the marshes to the dead many years before, very little of the predation was on the Kennick dry lands. Makin's troops had little cause for worry as long as they kept their feet on firm ground.

"They say the Dead King hates King Olidan," Katherine said.

"And what do you say, Katherine?" Miana leaned across me, lily-scented, our child kicking my legs through her belly.

"I say the black ships will sail up the Sane estuary and disgorge their troops into the marshes when the Dead King is ready to strike. And that from there they will move through Ancrath, sheltering in the scars the Builders left us, Ill Shadow, Eastern Dark, Kane's Wound, what your people call 'promised lands,' Queen. He will move into Gelleth along the paths Jorg opened with his destruction of Mount Honas, and continue by such means, gathering strength from many sources, until they reach Vyene where Congression's endless voting will cease to matter."

"And is this what King Olidan has sent you to tell the Hundred?" Gomst asked. He held his crucifix so tight that the gold bent in his grip, a zealot's fire in his eye. Such passion made a stranger of the man after so many years of empty piety. "It is what the holy say. God tells them this."

A brittle laugh escaped Katherine. "Olidan knows the black ships will sail his way. He says Ancrath will hold, that this new contagion will be stamped out, that Ancrath will save the empire. He asks only that his right to the throne be acknowledged and whilst he leads his armies to save the Hundred they set the crown upon his lap and restore the stewardship. Of course he asks in more tactful language, in many messages suited to many ears, calling in old debts and promises." Her green eyes found me, our faces close, my leg pressed to hers and generating heat. "Filial duties remembered," she said.

"Why—"

Katherine cut me off. "Your father says he knows the Dead King. Knows his secrets. Knows how to undo him."

18

Chella's story

"What you've seen so far will not prepare you for this. Make a stone of your mind. Swear any oath that is asked of you." Chella straightened the collar of Kai's robe and stood back to look at him again.

"I will."

Ten years had settled on the young man overnight, tight lines around his mouth, lips narrowed. He wore the weariness around his eyes and in them. She hadn't broken him. You can't make necromancers from broken men. It's a contract that must be entered into of one's own will, and Kai had just enough of an instinct for self-preservation to will it. Beneath his charm and easy ways Chella imagined a hardness had always waited. She walked on and he followed her along the corridor.

"Don't look at any of them. Especially not the lichkin," she said.

"Christ! Lichkin!" He stopped and when she turned he backed away, the colour running from his face. For a moment it seemed that his knees would buckle. "I thought the king's court were necromancers . . ."

"The lichkin should be the least of your concerns." Chella couldn't blame him. You had to meet the Dead King to understand.

"But . . ." Kai frowned. She saw his hand move beneath his robe.

He would be holding the knife she gave him, taking comfort in a sharp edge. Men! "But if they're dead, shouldn't we be the ones to give the orders?"

Fear and ambition, a good combination. Chella felt her lips twist, a sour smile. He had barely started to sense the deadlands, this one, made his first corpse twitch only hours before, and already he thought himself a necromancer and reached for the reins. "If they were fallen then yes, a necromancer would have raised them and a necromancer would rule them."

"They're not dead?" Again the frown.

"Oh they're dead. But they will never be ours to command. The lichkin are dead—but they never died. It's given to us to call back what cannot enter heaven and restore it under our command to the flesh and bones it once owned. But in the deadlands, where we call the fallen from, there are things that are dead and that have never lived. The lichkin are such creatures and they are the Dead King's soldiers. And in the darkest reaches of the deadlands, amongst such creatures, the Dead King came from nowhere and crowned himself in fewer than ten years."

She walked on and after a moment's hesitation Kai followed. Where else had he to go?

They passed several doors on the left, and shuttered windows on the right. A storm-wind rattled the heavy boards but the rain had yet to fall. Two guards waited at the corner, dead men in rusted armour, a faint aroma of decay about them overwritten by the eye-watering chemicals used to cure their flesh.

"These are strong ones. I can feel it." Kai paused, lifting his hand toward the pair as if pressing against something in the air.

"Not much of these passed on," Chella said. "Bad men. Bad lives. It left a lot to be called back into the body. Cunning, some measure of intelligence, some useful memories. Most of the guards here are like this. And when you find a corpse you can refill almost to the brim, well, you don't want it to rot away on you now, do you?" The dead men watched her with shrivelled eyes, their dark thoughts unknowable.

More corridors, more guards, more doors. The Dead King took the castle only months before from the last Brettan lord of any consequence, Artur Elgin, whose ships had sailed from the port below for twenty years and more, terrorizing the continental coasts north and south. Artur Elgin's days of terror weren't over. Indeed they had very much begun, though now he served the Dead King, or rather what had been called back from the deadlands did, and Chella suspected that was pretty much all of the man.

Chella sensed the Dead King always, from a thousand miles she felt him as something crawling beneath her skin. In the castle where he laid his plans no place was free of the taste of him, bitter on the tongue.

At last they came to the doors to Artur's court, slabs of old oak with black iron hinges scrolling out across them. The bog-stink wrinkled her nose. Mire-ghouls watched them from the shadows to either side, some with black darts clutched in stained hands. Before the doors two giants, each more than eight foot tall, freaks from the promised lands, their dena scorched by the Builders' fire so that they grew wrong. Big but wrong. And now dead. Meat-puppets held by the necromancers' will.

The giants stepped aside and Chella moved toward the doors. The presence of the Dead King overwhelmed that of his court, reaching through stone and wood to swamp her senses. In the fullness of Chella's necromantic power, when she stepped as far from life as a person can and still return, she knew the Death King's presence as a dark-light, a black sun whose radiance froze and corrupted but somehow still drew her on. Now though, dressed only in the tatters of her former strength, with her blood pumping once again, Chella felt her master as a threat, as something sculpted from every memory of hurt or harm or pain, screaming hatred in a register just beyond hearing.

She set her hands to the doors and found them trembling.

*   *   *

The stink of lichkin hits flesh like ink hits blotting paper: it sinks bone-deep, overriding irrelevances such as the nose. Men are busy dying from the moment they're born but it's a crawl from the cradle to the grave. Being near a lichkin makes it a race.

The Dead King's court lay in darkness but as Chella pushed the doors open a cold glow began to spread within the chamber. Ghosts, tight-wrapped around their masters, began to unfurl, like an outer skin, flayed from the lichkin by the presence of life. The spirits burned with the light of their own misery, pale apparitions, delicate tissues of memory, membranes of misused lives. The lichkin them-selves were blind spots on her living eyes, as if patches of her retina had died, folding the room's image over itself in those places. In times when the necromancy ran deep in her and her blood lay still, Chella had seen the lichkin, bone-white, bone-thin, the wedge of their eye-less heads filled with small sharp teeth, each hand dividing into three root-like fingers.

"Kai!" She felt his retreat. The sound of his name made him stop. He knew better than to run.

The Dead King sat on Lord Artur Elgin's driftwood throne. He wore Artur Elgin's robes. They fitted him well. Blue-leather shoul-ders, a laced front fixed with silver clasps each set with sea-stone, the leather giving over to thick velvet of a deeper midnight blue. He wore Artur Elgin's body too, and it fitted him less well, hunched and awk-ward, and when he lifted his head to Chella the smile that he made with the dead man's mouth was an awful thing.

19

Five years earlier

Two knives broke in the effort to uncoil the scorpion. When I locked its tail in place with Old Mary's clamps and levered it apart using a sword, the corpse opened in a series of jerking releases, accompanied by crunches like glass breaking under a heel.

"You're something made," I told it. "A clever piece of clockwork."

I could see no cogs or wheels though, no matter how close I squinted. Just black crystal, traces of clear sparkling jelly and multitudes of wires, most of them so thin as to be on the edge of invisible.

"Something broken." I put it into Lesha's saddle-pack to take with me.

It took hours to dig two graves. My wounds stung and smarted. Later they ached and throbbed. I used an axe to break up the ground and a shield to scoop the soil away. The earth tasted sour, worse than the salts from Carrod Springs.

I buried Greyson first. I found a visored helm, scoured it out with sand, and put it on him to cover his face. "You be sure to grumble, wherever you find yourself, Sunny." Two shield-loads of dust and grit stole the detail from him. Just another corpse. Four more and he made little more than an undulation in the earth. Ten more and I smoothed the ground over.

I set Lesha's head against her neck. I felt it the right thing to do since I had separated them in the first place. The pieces didn't seem to fit.

"All the king's horses and all the king's men couldn't put Lesha together again."

I sat beside the grave without looking at her, watching the sun drop toward the west. "These men, they weren't any different to me and mine." My cuts stung and throbbed. I thought of how much hurt I'd escaped and the complaints went away. "Being at the sharp end of the stick changes your view on the business of poking, sure enough— you'd have to be pretty stupid not to see that one coming though." I stopped talking. It wasn't so much that there wasn't anyone to hear. When you've got death in you and you're surrounded by corpses, well, you're always going to have some kind of an audience. It was more that what gripped me was too fluid, too uncertain to be captured and spoken. Words are blunt instruments, better suited to murder than to making sense of the world. I filled the grave. It was time.

The sun clung to the horizon with crimson fingers. I straightened and paused mid-step. Red eyes watched me, the sky reflected in the gaze of the fallen. Too many heads lay turned my way for chance to have set their course. Coldness pulsed from the old wound in my chest, necromancy, a numbness like the ghouls' darts brought, or a detachment maybe, as if some unseen hand were closing around me, walling away the world's vitality. Close by, Rael lay, a knife in his throat, skewering the old scar where some past attempt had failed. I took my step and his eyes followed the motion.

"Dead King." The words bubbled up, the blood so dark it ran purple over his teeth.

"Hmmm." I picked up the sturdiest of the discarded axes. The Perros Viciosos had favoured axes. The heft of it held a certain comfort. A quick shake rid me of wearies and I set to my task. It's hard work taking the limbs off a man. The legs especially take a lot of hacking, and flesh is much tougher stuff than you might imagine. As soon as you lose the edge on an axe it tends to bounce off a leather-clad thigh if your stroke is anything but perfect. With luck you'll break the bone in any case, but to hew the whole limb off? Think cutting down trees: always far harder than you think it should be. By the end my breath came in gasps and sweat dripped from my nose. I settled for taking off hands and feet from the last ten men before collapsing in a cross-legged slump before Rael once more.

"Life was much easier when death held on to what it was given," I said.

I couldn't tell if Rael still watched me but the Dead King's presence lingered in the stink of old blood.

"I'm thinking if you could stand these lads up again you would have done it by now, but better safe than sorry, neh?"

Still nothing. The Dead King seemed to have Chella under his thumb, so that made his interest in me . . . unsettling.

I leaned in over Rael's corpse and rapped on his forehead. "Hello?" Gathering my own traces of necromancy and reaching in didn't seem like the best idea, rather like using your fingers to take a bone from a hungry dog.

Nothing. Perhaps the king had a lot of dead eyes to peer out of—too many people to scare for more than a quick name check with each. I shrugged. At the bottom of it the Perros Viciosos weren't any more frightening dead than alive. It didn't mean I wanted to spend my night sleeping among them though. They surely smelled worse dead.

I led Lesha's horse away from the camp and settled a hundred yards off over a low ridge. Despite myself I slept poorly, haunted by Sunny's screams and prodded awake by each small noise in the darkness.

*   *   *

Dawn found me back at the Bad Dogs' camp. I blessed the Iberico's poisons for the lack of flies and rats. What beauty there is to war is in the moment. After a day any battlefield is little more than carrion and scavengers. In the Iberico at least the carrion doesn't swarm with flies. In fact, apart from my own indulgence with the axe, the dead looked untouched with only the occasional large and hardy cockroach digging in for breakfast.

I collected my bits and pieces. Balky favoured me with a reproachful stare as I loaded him. I tethered the mule to Lesha's stallion, and led them both off into the promised land.

Without Lesha's guidance I had nothing to stop me walking into the invisible fires that had scoured her so badly. We walk a knife-edge each day though, and most don't know it—at least in the promised lands, in the Iberico, in Kane's Scar and Ill-Shadow back in Ancrath, in such places there's no pretence, no lie of safety, no deception that like the ancients' song, "love is all you need." At a single false step you can and will burn. As always.

At times I let Lesha's horse precede me, but horses like to be led and prodding him along made for slow going.

The first time I saw it I wasn't sure what my eyes were telling me. On a slope to our right a shoulder of weathered Builder-stone broke through the shale. Above and around it the air shimmered in a heat haze. The burned side of my face throbbed with it, and in the moment I closed that eye with wincing—the haze vanished. Looking once more, and only with the eye so nearly blinded when Gog burned me, I saw the shimmer again, like the ghosts of flame that had danced on Jane beneath Mount Honas.

"Get along." I pulled Balky up on his tether. He let out a hee-haw loud enough to crack rocks. The notion to push him through that shimmer came and went. Other considerations aside, I'd have to carry my own kit. If one of those mouse-sized roaches had been handy I would have tossed that through. A stray thought occurred. I dug out the view-ring from my pack and held it up to watch the phenomenon through. In an instant, shades of red wrapped the world, painted in thick crimson around the shoulder of old stone, fading to less violent hues further down the slope. Along our path at the bottom of the dry valley the ring showed occasional regions of dull orange hanging mist-like.

"Damn but that's handy. What else can you show me?"

And like the genie from Aladdin's lamp, Fexler Brews stood before me on the road, no larger than life and no smaller. I took a step back, the kind of step that seeks no permission and springs from the days when men's fear was written into the marrow of our race. The kind I always regret. I held the ring aside and Fexler vanished along with the shades of red and orange. Brought back and he returned with the ring.

"What am I doing here, Brews?" I felt silly talking to something seen only through a small loop of steel, even out in the wilds with none but horse and mule to watch me.

Fexler spread his hands. He wore the same whites he had back at Castle Morrow, not a speck of dust on them.

"Why the mystery? Just tell me plain and—"

He turned and walked away down the valley.

"Hell." And I followed, hauling Balky after.

20

Five years earlier

Fexler Brews' ghost led me through the Iberico Hills. We walked from well before noon until well after, long enough for me to grow weary and for the cuts on my back, just above my hip, to start with that nagging ache and heat that speaks of infection.

The hills held every colour from bone-white through the greys to ochre. Baked mud, crumbling earth, exposed rock. And from time to time some rusting hulk, eroding in that stubborn way that Builder works have about them, refusing the elements century after century. Most of them blocks of metal with no hint of function, looking like steel, pocked and pitted, some large as houses, some askew as if pushed aside by giants, all stained with corrosion in trickled green and powder-white. We passed one that buzzed, a high whine that hurt my teeth, and Fexler vanished until it lay well behind me. In another place a leaning metal column, half-buried, or maybe nine-tenths buried, sang in a voice of staggering beauty and a language unknown to me. I stood with the sun's heat beating against me and the hairs on end across my neck, just bathing in it.

I saw Fexler only through the viewing ring and perhaps the ring just drew him for me, overriding the scenery like a painting on glass. Either way he guided me through the dry washes and dusty gullies of the promised land, without speaking, pausing only when I paused.

We passed one machine where the metal sheeting had torn away to reveal spinning cylinders, wheels turning in wheels, all moving in silence, gleaming. It reminded me of the interior of the watch in my pack. Fexler wouldn't speak of it.

The shadows had grown long when our path following a gully came to a dead end hemmed in by crumbling walls of earth and sand. Fexler came to a halt, watching me.

"Why have we stopped?" I asked. Not that I wasn't happy to have stopped—there just seemed no reason for it.

Fexler vanished.

Banging the view ring against the hilt of my sword didn't restore him. I made a slow turn, completing the circle with my arms spread. Lesha's stallion watched with mild interest. Balky just looked vacant.

I stepped toward Fexler's last position and stubbed my toe. A day early an expert had tortured me, albeit very briefly. Stubbing my toe proved more intense and more shocking. I reached shoulder-deep into my well of obscenities and released a string of quite spectacular examples. It deserved a better audience. In time, after all the hopping and cursing, I hobbled over to discover what had lamed me.

With some kneeling, scraping, and brushing, I uncovered a lid of Builder-stone, circular and about a yard across. Rusty stains indicated that the thing had once been secured in place by more than its weight. The spare sword I'd strapped to Lesha's horse proved useful for levering the lid up the few inches necessarily to shunt it by degrees to one side. It took half a skin of water to replace what the effort had sweated out of me. The sun in those hills is without mercy.

Beneath the lid a shaft led down, unlit, smooth as far as I could tell, and without any odour rising from it. I took a small rock and dropped it into the darkness. It's not something I could resist doing even if I had no reason for it. The pause before the distant clatter told me that I didn't want to follow the rock.

"You could have told me to bring some damn rope!" I had some despite Fexler's lack of warning, but I doubted it would be enough.

In a shaft as narrow as the one before me you can brace your back against the wall and your feet on the opposite side, and edge down. However, if the shaft widens, or enters a room, or is smoother than you'd hoped . . . getting back up might prove difficult. I had come into the Iberico prepared to dare invisible fires. Somehow though, getting stuck in a hole and dying of thirst seemed too pathetic an end to be risked.

I dug the tinderbox from my kit and took off the bandage I'd wrapped around the wound on my upper arm. I had to peel it away, and where the linen stuck it stank, sickly sweet. The dry ends took the flame well enough and burned as it fluttered after the rock I'd dropped in. The sides looked to be parallel all the way down. I guessed it to be some forty-foot deep. I thought a tunnel led off from the bottom but it was hard to tell from my position.

I squeezed the uncovered wound, trying to force the pus out of it. "Christ-on-a-bike!" One of Makin's oaths, that. I don't know what a bike is but it sounds painful. The edges of my flesh looked an unhealthy pink, rimmed in black crusts. I couldn't imagine the two halves ever knitting together again.

The Bad Dogs had plenty of rope at their camp and I'd taken a fair bit of it with me. Never go questing without a bit of rope, at least that's how the stories have it. My three pieces knotted together reached about two thirds of the way down the hole. I tied a larger knot in one end and secured it under the stone lid rather than trust to my equine companions for anchorage. On my belt I tied the lantern I'd taken from the camp and a spare flask of oil. I squeezed flint, steel, and tinder into a pocket. Better not to carry a light for the descent or a fall might find me with broken legs *and* on fire.

A tired achiness made each action clumsy. I swallowed another bitter pill of Carrod Springs' salts and took the rope in both hands. One more glance at the dusty hills, at the worn blue of the sky, and I started down.

Out of the sun I felt cold enough to shiver, though that may have owed more to fever than to the drop in temperature. I climbed down hand over hand, clutching at the rope with my knees. When my knees discovered they had nothing left to clutch, the top of the shaft, part occluded by the lid, offered a bright crescent of sky. A shudder took me, along with the sudden conviction that someone would slide the lid back and seal away the light.

Groaning with the effort, I lifted both feet to brace against the side of the shaft and pushed until my shoulders and upper back wedged against the opposite side. I had no great conviction that the pressure would keep me from falling if I let go the rope, but even less conviction that I could manage the climb back.

I let go.

Inch by strained inch I slid down the shaft. My legs shook with the effort and I felt sure I must be leaving a trail of skin and blood on the Builder stone: my shirt couldn't have lasted long against the friction.

Sufficient daylight reached down to let me know when the shaft ran out of wall, and soon enough I found that whilst the soles of my boots still gripped the stonework, my heels had nothing to rest on. When a decision is inevitable you may as well take it as quick as possible so that you still have something left to deal with whatever consequences may arise. I dropped, doing my best to swing my feet below me. The effort proved a partial success and ended with bruised heels, banged-up knees, elbows slammed to the ground, and finally the side of my head fetching up against the floor. An inch or so of dust covering the stone floor served to lessen the impact, saving me from a cracked skull and leaving me conscious, choking, and with a river of blood flowing from my nose. I levered myself up so I could sit cradling my knees, and set my back to the nearest wall.

"Ow." The complaint came out nasally.

Pain led my fingers to a piece of the lantern glass embedded in my thigh. I pulled it out and held the wound closed until the blood stopped pulsing around my fingertips. In time I found the lantern wick, set it into the oil flask, and with steel and flint and more fumbling than necessary I set a flame to it. The tunnel led off to front and back, circular in cross-section and looking suspiciously like a sewer. The end of my rope dangled three yards above my outstretched hand and getting back into the shaft would require gymnastics I thought beyond me even without wounds or fever.

On the assumption that water had once flowed along the tunnel I made my best guess at which direction it might have taken and started to walk "upstream." When you're in a dark place, and your light is going to run out before too long, you get on with things. It's a wonder to me how few people apply that same logic to their lives.

Three times new tunnels joined mine and on each occasion I studied my choices through the Builders' view-ring, which shed some light on the matter, a red blinking light that demanded I turn right twice and then follow straight on. At two of the turns traces of rust hinted that metal grilles once blocked the way. A great sage once said there are few problems that won't go away if you ignore them long enough. Fortunately these obstacles had been pre-ignored for a thousand years.

Toward its end the pipe rose at a steep angle and brought me into a circular room, empty in the main but littered with fragments of plasteek. Brittle with age, they made a satisfying crunch underfoot. Some of the pieces could have been the arms of chairs, small wheels, others lay bonded to the remains of metal cabinets. A corridor led off and I followed it, shadows dancing all around. The place had no odour to it, as if even that staleness which haunts abandoned rooms had given up and left.

A long corridor led me past many doorways all open and dark, decorated with the fragments of the doors that had guarded them. In the ceiling flat strips of whitish glass punctuated the walk and at one point, as I passed below, two of them tried to flicker to life like the glow-bulbs in the Tall Castle.

I've wandered the ruins of forts where generations lived, seen the march of empty centuries across the old stone, wearing away the sharpness that defined lives. In those places, at every turn, those lost inhabitants are remembered. The scuffmark where a door closed decade after decade, steps sagging with wear, the deep-scored name where a child set his stamp upon a windowsill. You can read such ruins, however tumbled, almost see the soldiers at the walls, stable-boys leading horses out to exercise. But in the dry corridors of this Builders' den, untouched by rain or wind, undisturbed, I saw nothing but puzzles and sorrow. I might be the first man to walk here in a thousand years. A thousand more might pass before the next. In such a place silence and dust wait whilst men's lives slip past. Without the flicker of my flame to count the moments hours could race by, years escape, and I might crawl away ancient and unwise.

The corridor ended in a large hall with many doors, these seemingly of wood but untouched by age.

Silence.

In the times that I have reached after the dead to pull back what is needed to make them rise, it seemed I reached into such a place as this. When I drew Row back into his corpse it was into dry lands that I followed him despite his dying in the mud of the Cantanlona bogs. I thought for a moment of William, of my little brother falling into such a place after they broke him. When I lay as dead after Father's knife touched my heart I imagined an angel came for me and I refused her. I hoped that years before that day she had descended to the dry lands to make those same offers to William. And that he had not refused.

My head snapped up, jerking me from my half-doze.

"Enough of this!" Delirium had started to reel me in. I shook it off and focused. I moved on, snorting at the thought of William and the angel. Even at seven he could probably have given her a harder time of it than I did at fourteen.

At the far end of the hall an archway led into a smaller lower hall. It caught my eye since the Builders weren't given to arches. A dozen or more cubicles opened to either side of the lesser hall, like monks' cells, each of them layered in dust, scattered with plasteek fragments and pieces of corroded metal. I picked up a sliver of metal. Lighter than expected, not iron, and not rusted but powdery with some white residue. Oxidation. The word floated up from Lundist's instructions on alchemy.

The seventh cell on the left held a wonder. A man waited there, without motion, his back to me. And from the side of his head a spray of scarlet blood, fragments of bone tumbling through the air . . . all frozen in the moment. A picture, but not a picture. Something real and solid but standing outside time. Where each of the other cells had a ring of corrosion in the centre of the ceiling, this one had a collar of silver metal, bound in places with copper, and surrounding a white light. The man sat in his grey tunic directly below the light. Somehow, no illumination escaped into the hall—and yet I saw the light. He sat on a chair that looked too thin to support him, odd in its slim and flowing form, without decoration or device. Beside him, part of a bed. Not a broken piece or a component but a section as if cut out like biscuits from dough, ending at some unseen perimeter that surrounded it and the man both. Beyond this small circle at the cell's centre, holding the man, the chair, and part of the bed, the remainder of the room lay in dusty ruin like all the rest.

I walked in to touch the man—or the image—perhaps it was an image, like Fexler's data ghost, just more convincingly drawn. Something the Builders considered art? Invisible glass stopped my fingers. I couldn't get close to the man. My hand slid across an unseen surface, cool and slick to the fingertips.

The cell proved large enough for me to edge around the forbidden area, stepping through the dust at the margins of the room. The man's hand came into view, holding a complex piece of metalwork to his head, an iron tube projecting from it to touch his temple.

"I know this." The oldest of my father's books held pictures of objects similar to this one. "It's a gun."

Another step and I saw the face, captured in the instant, imagining the pain but not yet feeling it despite the plume of blood and brain and bone behind him.

"Fexler!" I'd found the man himself. Not the memory.

The view-ring showed only the room, with Fexler lit red by the light, as if all the time that red dot pulsing amid the Iberico Hills had been this time-locked circle.

I made another circuit around the tableaux. "You stopped time!" I thought about it, then shrugged. They say the Builders could fly. Who knows which is the more difficult, the stopping of time or taking to the skies? I thought of the watch buried in my baggage on Balky's back. A device of the ancients—perhaps if I stopped its hands turning I would stop time just as they had.

"You brought me here, Fexler." I spoke to the man. "What do you want? I can't fix you."

Obviously I couldn't fix him. What had Fexler's ghost been thinking? The answer came easy enough. Jorg breaks things. Fexler didn't send me to fix this—he sent me to end it.

Of course breaking things that are sealed away behind unbreakable glass can prove difficult. As the point of my knife slid over the invisible barrier I started to doubt the glass existed at all. It seemed clear that something had to stand between a space where time flowed and a space where it did not. Zeno's paradoxes sprang to mind. The Greeks loved paradoxes. Maybe they used them as currency. In any case I made no headway.

I walked away, a slight tremble in me from the fever. In every other cell nothing whole survived. I guess that the device in the ceiling had stopped time and in doing so had stopped the process of its own decay.

Memory stole me back beneath Mount Honas. In the Builders' halls I had seen the remains of many narrow pipes, most just faint traces of verdigris, some bedded in the stone, some running against walls, some so thin that they could only have been strands of wire.

The histories have it that the secret fire of the Builders ran along such paths to wake their devices. My watch needed no such fire but perhaps a coiled spring would not suffice for such mechanisms as that which held Fexler. Certainly it had not unwound over all the centuries. Did the machine need to be fed to keep time stationary?

A slow and minute inspection of the walls revealed no sign of hidden paths bringing fire to the ceiling ring. It took an age of hunting the corridors to find something to support me so I could check the ceiling. In the end I found a collection of bottles, like wine bottles but clear and cylindrical and slender as my arm. Binding all nine of them side to side with my shirt I made a very precarious platform on which to stand. Of all the Builders' artefacts only glass had seen off the years without loss.

From my shifting, clinking platform I discovered that the barrier which enclosed Fexler narrowed as it rose so that at the ceiling I could get to within an inch or so of the metal ring. I used my knife to jab at the stonework around it. Poor treatment for a good weapon, but I had spare blades stashed on Lesha's horse if I ever got back to him, and nothing else to work with.

Once before, in Gelleth, I had driven a blade into some magic of the Builders, a spirit trapped behind glass in the room before the weapon hall. A shock had run through the sword and thrown me twitching to the floor. The memory made me have to steel myself for each scratch and jab as I scored a circle around the ceiling ring. My muscles remembered the shock and kept trying to refuse to dig out a chance at renewing the experience.

The Builder stone started to flake and powder under my attacks. It took an hour maybe, possibly a day. It felt like a day. Sweat ran down me in hot streams and my arm ached, growing weaker by the moment as arms do when used overhead for more than a few minutes. I jabbed and scored, scored and jabbed. Without warning a deafening bang exploded around me, the light went out, and I fell with glass shattering below.

And for the second time since climbing down the shaft I lay bruised and aching in the dark with broken glass embedded in my leg. My makeshift lantern must have been knocked over and doused when I fell. Instead of searching for it I held the view-ring to my eye. The ring showed me the cell in greenish tones, revealing almost as much detail as I might see in daylight. Fexler lay on the floor, sprawled at my feet, the gun still clutched in his outstretched hand, a wisp of smoke escaping the barrel. Around his head a black and spreading pool of blood.

"Thank you." Fexler—my Fexler from Castle Morrow, a projection of white light—stood beside the corpse, watching the splayed limbs, face unreadable.

"Fexler, good to see you," I said. And it was. Any company in such a place is welcome. I drew a deep breath, taking in the stink of chemicals and fire from the gun, the tang of blood. The Builder halls felt real at last.

"Why all the silence and mystery?" I edged through the glass and dust to set my back to a wall, in part for support, in part because it's good practice.

"The men of my time lived amongst wonders but they were made no differently from their forefathers who wore skins and ate raw meat in caves, or from their descendants who carry iron swords and live in ruins they can't comprehend. In short, they had the same instincts as any man. Would you trust a copy of yourself?"

"So they set spells on you such that no data ghost could kill the person from whom they were copied?" I asked.

"So that no data echo could harm any human, or ask for them to be harmed, or take actions that might lead them to hurt. It has taken a thousand years of subtle manipulation, of twists and sleights of logic, for me even to reach the stage where I could point someone like you in this direction, Jorg."

"And why would you?" My hand settled on the fallen oil flask. I gave it a swirl. Maybe a fifth of it remained.

"Data echoes are not just forbidden from harming their original template. In fact whilst the person whose data created any particular echo still lives there are an enormous number of restrictions placed on that echo, for the convenience, privacy, and peace of mind of the person in question. In the world that I inhabit I have been very much a second class citizen for considerably longer than your empire has existed."

"In Castle Morrow?" *The world that he lives in?*

A tight smile, quick and gone. "Imagine an ocean wider and deeper than all others, full of wonder and variety, and on the surface a thickness of ice broken only here and there. The echoes that the Builders left behind, 'data ghosts' if that's how you want to call us, we echoes swim in such an ocean and the places where we may be seen in this thin world of yours are like the holes in the ice where we can surface. We exist in the joined complexity of the Builders' machinery, and in places such as the terminal at Morrow we may be seen."

"So why aren't you?"

"Why aren't we what?"

"Seen? Why was it just you haunting that cellar?"

Another smile, more of bitterness in it than of friendship. "Second class citizen. The menial duties fell to me. Keeping an eye on the savages."

I had to remind myself that the Fexler who shared anything with me lay on the floor, his blood cooling around him. The Fexler talking to me was not a man, just the idea of a man, an idea held in a machine. I reached out a foot to nudge the dead man. Fexler's echo shuddered as if the action disturbed him.

"So why did he kill himself?" I asked. "And what stopped him?"

"He started a war," Fexler said. "And finished it."

"Hell, I lit up one of your suns, it didn't make me take a knife to my throat straight after."

"The weapons Fexler Brews launched could not be detonated with a fire."

"You saw that?" Fexler's ghost had been watching me six years back, under Mount Honas?

"Our weapons burned like suns—exactly the same way. Each needs a trigger to ignite it, a smaller, more primitive implosion. Your fire at Silo Eleven using weapons relocated from Vaucluse melted the implosion components into a critical mass. What you saw was a partial ignition of the trigger that would then light the sun. The fuel for the 'suns' is short-lived, it's a matter of half-life, the fuel for the rockets that bore them lasts little longer. All that remains now are the triggers."

I wondered if the original Fexler had liked the sound of his own voice so much. In any event it was a sobering thought to know I laid waste to Gelleth with a fraction of the spark that would light a true Builder Sun. And despite my words, the dead of Gelleth *had* haunted me, literally and in dreams. To have burned the whole world in such fashion would have been . . . uncomfortable.

"And even with his gun he didn't manage to kill himself?" With such toys at their disposal it seemed unforgivable for any Builder to fail in the act of taking a life.

"These cubicles were designed to hold key personnel in stasis until conditions improved to the point where life might be sustained outside again. Fexler was perhaps not thinking clearly as he sat here wrestling with his conscience. Maybe he didn't appreciate that the automatic systems would kick in to preserve him or perhaps he just didn't realize how quickly they could act."

"Either way, he left you in the shit along with all the real people in the world."

"He did." Fexler's image flickered, a frown above his eyes.

I grinned. It must have been odd to spend a thousand years cursing the man you were copied from. "So now I've freed you and you get to swim in your sea with the big fish, and not waste time watching the savages. What do I get out of it?" Still holding the view-ring to my eye I pulled the gun from Fexler's warm, dead hand, careful not to point the business end my way. He seemed reluctant to let it go.

"Unfortunately we need to watch the savages even more these days," Fexler said. "The machines that still keep running won't run forever, and unless you people get past swords and arrows there's never going to be anyone to maintain them. Maintenance requires civilization, and we're not going to get civilization again until all the wars stop."

"You couldn't stop your own wars, Fexler."

"He couldn't." Fexler looked down at his corpse. "I'm another matter."

I pursed my lips. "Either way—it sounds as though you'd like there to be an emperor on the Gilden Throne."

21

Five years earlier

In the dry and deathless halls of the Builders, beneath the poisoned dusts of Iberico, I sat half-delirious with fever and spoke to a ghost who had helped me kill the man from whom he sprang.

"And *who* do the ghosts in your machines want to rule this empire of servants for them?" I asked.

"Orrin of Arrow is favoured by our projections," Fexler said. "A peacemaker. A man of progress."

"Hah!" I spat from a dry mouth, aching in every limb. "So you've no real interest in my leaving here to stop him then?"

"Projections favour Orrin," Fexler agreed.

I kicked the warm corpse at my feet again. "Are you . . . is he likely to stand back up? I seem to have made a new friend, the Dead King. Takes an unhealthy interest in me. I find him watching out of any pair of dead eyes that are handy. Would it upset you if I dismember him . . . you . . . a little? Just to be sure?" Part of me hoped Fexler would object and save me the effort of all that hacking. He shook his head as if the matter were unimportant.

"Projections favour Orrin, but some of us prefer to bet on longer odds for greater rewards," Fexler said.

"Why so? What rewards? I'd bet on Orrin too if I had a stake." The words tumbled from numb lips, the poison pulsed in me,

I could smell my wounds. That's what happens when you stop. Take a rest and the world catches up with you. Lesson in life—keep moving.

"You may recall"—Fexler stepped closer, edging between me and his earthly remains—"that we spoke about a wheel. About how my generation's greatest works were nothing to do with new ways to scorch the earth but how to change the rules of everything, how to alter the way in which the world worked?"

"Vaguely." I waved a trembling hand. "Something to do with making what we want matter." It didn't seem to have worked. I wanted him to shut up now and leave me alone, and *that* wasn't happening.

"Almost." Fexler smiled. "The physicists called it an adjustment of quantum emphasis. But the effect was to change the role of the observer. Of you and me. For the will of the observer to matter. So man could control his environment directly through the force of his desire, rather than through machinery."

I had the feeling that if I died he would carry on saying his piece to my corpse.

"Unfortunately that wheel wasn't just turned—it was set turning. It hasn't stopped. In fact, like so many things in nature, the process has a tipping point and we're reaching it. The fractures in the world, in the walls between mind and matter, between energy and will, between life and death, they're all growing. And *everything* is in danger of falling through the cracks. Each time these powers, the ability to influence energy or mass or existence, are used, the divergence grows. These are the magics you know as being fire-sworn, or rock-sworn, or as necromancy and the like. The more they are used, the easier they become, and the wider the world is broken open. And this Dead King of yours is just another symptom. Another example of a singular force of will being used to change the world and, in doing so, accelerating the turn of that wheel we released."

A sigh, and a panel I hadn't seen before opened on the wall to my left. Enough light came from the cavity behind to illuminate the room. I lowered the view-ring but Fexler vanished, so I set it back to my eye.

"Take the pills." Fexler pointed to the cavity. "Swallow two a day until they're gone. They will cure your sepsis."

I got to my knees and scraped the handful of yellow tablets from the alcove. They were the only thing there, and I saw no means of delivery. My throat hurt as I swallowed two of them. They could be poison but Fexler likely had a thousand ways to kill me if he wanted that.

"So what do you want from me, Fexler?"

"As I've said, there are many ghosts in the Builders' machines." I saw his frown as he tried to shape his words to my understanding. "These ghosts, these echoes, pay your kind scant attention. But their eyes are turning back to the now, to the dust and dirt where we all started. Many of them favour supporting new civilization so that the deep networks can be maintained and repaired. A growing number, however, now care more about the imminent threat as the veils thin. The problems of decay seem less pressing. They feel that the only way to stop the wheel turning, to maintain the barriers that keep earth different from fire, life different from death, is to destroy all mankind. And they've had a thousand years to circumvent the rules that once kept them from such acts. With none to wield these powers, with none left to have a will to exercise, the damage will be undone, or at least halted."

"So poor Fexler's only fault was that he didn't light up quite enough suns? If he had killed off the last few people there would be no problem?" I snorted. "It doesn't pay to start a job and not finish it."

Fexler flickered as if he were a reflection disturbed by the arrival of a stone in a pond. He frowned.

"And which camp are you in, Fexler? Make us your servants to fix your carriage, or kill us all off quick before we break the world?"

"I have a third way," he said.

He rippled again, mouth twisting as if in pain. The light wavered in the space behind the panel, and died.

"An alternative the others don't yet acknowledge—ah!" He faded, almost vanished, returned too bright, making me squint.

"Take the control ring to Vyene. Beneath the throne there—"

And he was gone.

22

Chella's story

"Jorg of Ancrath sends you back to me again, Chella."

Something in the grinding of Artur Elgin's jaw set Chella's teeth on edge. Something in the way the Dead King ground that jawbone when he moved it to shape his words.

"I've brought Kai Summerson to court, sire, a necromancer seeking service—"

"Were you not to Jorg's tastes, Chella? Did he spurn your proposal?"

Just the grinding of that bone, hinge and socket, made her skin crawl. That and the glitter of his eyes. She thought of times when she had swum in foulness, of corpse-work in the darkest places, of hunting men's remains in the deadland borders, enough horror to take almost anyone's sanity . . . and yet here she cowered from nothing but the sick click and crunch of a dead man's jaw.

"Chella?" A gentle enough reminder but lesser reprimands than that had sent the Dead King's servants to the lichkin.

"He refused me, sire." More than five years on and still the Dead King wanted her old failure replayed.

"And you still think him a foolish youth with more luck than judgment?"

"No, sire." Though she did. Whatever strange emotions the boy might stir in her Chella could see little of genius in his actions. When men bet on long odds in sufficient numbers some of them will walk away with the prize. It doesn't mean those winners will win tomorrow.

"I want him here, Chella, to stand before my court and to answer to me."

"Yes, sire." Though what Jorg Ancrath might have to answer the Dead King for she had no idea. A "why" trembled on her lips but she knew it would never take flight.

"Bring Kai Summerson before me."

Chella turned to motion Kai forward, drawing a breath of relief to be released from the Dead King's stare if only for a moment. In the coldness of wraith-light Kai aged another decade as the Dead King's regard fell upon him.

"Kai." The name dropped like a dead thing from Artur Elgin's lips. "Sky-sworn. Have you flown, Kai? Have you touched heaven?"

"No, lord." Kai kept his gaze to the floor. "I saw what the eagle sees, but only with my mind. And now I am death-sworn."

"Death can ride the winds, Kai. Remember that. Why did you not fly? Was it beyond you? Did you not truly hold the sky within you?"

"Fear kept me on the ground, lord." Passion in his words now, the Dead King's talent for touching each raw nerve. "Fear of losing myself." Chella knew few sky-sworn who took flight ever returned. The winds claimed them. They lost substance and danced in storms, spread too thin to be contained in flesh again. She watched Kai, his knuckles white, nails biting. Did he wish now that he had lost himself in the pitiless blue?

"It's your will, the power of your desire, that counts in this world—in all worlds." For a moment the Dead King seemed almost tender, something more awful than anger coming from Artur Elgin's dead lips. "The force of your conviction can anchor mind to flesh if your sense of who you are, your command of what you are, is stronger than the wind. It's that same power of will that reels in the silver cord and draws a necromancer back from their travels in the dry lands. That same sense of self returns what won't pass into heaven back to the shell of a man's body, to what carried him through life, to the groove he scored in the world, be it corrupt flesh, or even bare bone, and when at last bone is lost, it returns him to a place maybe, a home, a room, to haunt the living, because misery loves company and so do all its friends."

Kai lifted his gaze against the weight of the Dead King's stare. "Fear held me."

"Fear holds many men, fear keeps them from their duty, fathers abandon sons, one brother leaves the next to die."

"Yes, lord."

"When the storms come, Kai Summerson, show me death on wings." Artur Elgin's fingers flicked to motion Kai away.

Until the doors closed behind Kai no further words were spoken. Chella remained, the only living thing in the vaulted throne room. Perhaps hers was the only curiosity. The Dead King had need of her. Why else after all this time was she here once more, within the inner circle, humiliating reminders of her failure the only price of admission.

"Chella Undenhert." The Dead King formed the name with care.

"Sire." The last to know that name died six years back on Jorg Ancrath's blade. None had spoken it in decades.

"Some might think necromancy a threat to those of us who step out of the dry lands, out of the dust beyond, competition at the very least."

"Never that, sire." Kai's words returned to her. *Shouldn't we be the ones to give orders?*

"Do you know what I want, Chella?"

She truly didn't. "Jorg Ancrath?"

"I want what he wants, what all of our kind need. To rule, to own, to hold the highest ground, to have our will prevail."

"To be emperor?" Chella knew the hunger of the dead, but ambition came as a surprise, though all the signs lay before her. A dead king in a dead king's throne.

"The empire will be a start. Remade, it can be a step from which to take everything. I am not called king of here or king of there, they call me Dead King, lord of all that does not live. Do you think in this world I would sit content with 'Lord of Brettan'? Or 'emperor' of an empire beyond whose borders lie lands unclaimed?"

"No, sire." For all the horror of him a child's greed and child's pride lay about the Dead King. Perhaps his interest in the Ancrath kings lay in the mirror they held up to him.

"Do you know why the Hundred have not united against me, Chella?"

"They hate each other too much, sire. Gather them on a ship and let it sink—no hand would be spare for bailing or for swimming, they'd all be locked on throats, choking away the air before the waters could."

"They have not united because they don't fear me." Artur Elgin rose from the Dead King's throne. "The returned cannot breed, they rot, they know more of hunger than of caution, they can stand against armies only where the ground favours them. It is a wonder that I have taken what I now hold with nothing but corpses to play with." Artur's hand settled on Chella's shoulder and it took all her control not to flinch it off.

"Empires are won in many ways. Do you know of tactics, Chella?"

"A little, sire." If he would just take that hand away . . .

"And what are the only two tactical advantages of my legions, Chella?"

"I— I— They know no fear?"

"No." An exquisite agony bled into her shoulder and the Dead King returned Artur's hand to his side. "A man without fear is missing a friend. An old ghost once told me that.

"My troops have two tactical advantages. They don't breathe and they don't eat. That means that any swamp, lake, or sea, is a stronghold and that I need not maintain supply lines. Past that they are poor servants at best. And it is these advantages that have given me the Isles and allow us to assault Ancrath from the Ken Marshes.

"Beyond this, my ambitions require new strategies if they are to be met on a timescale to my liking."

The Dead King settled once more in Artur Elgin's driftwood throne. He ran white fingers along the chair's polished arms, and Chella heard the screams of sailors drowning.

"Thantos, Keres."

Two lichkin detached from their brethren and moved to flank the Dead King. Still Chella's eyes would not see them, returning only glimpses of ghost-wrapped bone.

"Chella." He leaned Artur's body toward her in the chair. "Choosing a strategy is like deciding upon a weapon. And a weapon needs a point if it is to pierce the foe, neh? You, Chella, are going to pierce the belly of the empire for me. I'm sending you on a journey. Brother Thantos and Sister Keres will keep you safe. The remainder of your escort is on a ship approaching the harbour as we speak."

23

We made progress, not good progress but enough. Sometimes the guard didn't get their charges to Vyene on time, but it hadn't happened in my lifetime. Even when a member of the Hundred died en route, their corpse would make a punctual arrival.

When towns and villages lay at convenient points we spent the night in commandeered accommodation, otherwise tents were pitched in fields or clearings. I liked those nights best, Katherine and Miana lit by firelight in woods where cold mists threaded the trees, each woman framed by the fur trim of winter robes, all of us huddling close to the heat. Gomst and Osser in their chairs with wine goblets in hand debated as old men do, Makin and Marten kept by the queen ready to make up for my failings, Kent sat quiet, watching the night. Rike and Gorgoth bookended our little band, soaking up the warmth, both looking meaner than hell.

On one such night, with the crackle of the fire and the glow of many others dotted about us through the wood, Miana said, "Jorg, you sleep so much better out of the Haunt, why is that?" Her breath steamed before her in the night and though she faced me it was Katherine that she watched.

"I've always loved the road, dear," I told her. "You leave your troubles behind you."

"Not if you bring your wife." Rike snorted and kept his gaze on the fire, immune to the sharp look Marten sent his way.

"In the Haunt you always talked in your sleep." Miana turned to face Katherine now. "He practically raved. I had to set my bed in the east tower just to get some rest."

Katherine made no reply, her face still.

"But now he sleeps like a sinless child, without murmur," Miana said.

I shrugged. "Bishop Gomst is the one with night terrors. Should we worry when our holiest rest uneasy?"

Miana ignored me. "No more 'Sareth,' no more 'Degran,' and no more endless 'Katherine! Katherine!' "

Katherine arched one eyebrow, delicate, expressive, and delicious. Miana had been irritable all day in the carriage, but then if I'd swallowed a whole baby and it insisted on kicking the hell out of my insides I might be less than my normal tolerant self.

A stick popped with a loud retort, sending embers from the fire.

Defence is always a weakness and I didn't feel like attacking, so I waited. Katherine had so many options open to her—I wanted to know which she would take.

"I trust King Jorg only called my name out in torment, Queen?"

I wondered what her hands were doing under that fur wrap. Twisting? Sliding toward a knife? Still and collected?

"It's true." Miana smiled, quick and unexpected, her frown erased. "He never did seem pleased to see you."

Katherine nodded. "My nephew has many crimes to answer for, but the darkest are against my sister, Queen Sareth and her child. Perhaps as he says his sins are left behind on the road. Maybe when we stop at Vyene they will catch up with him once more."

None around the fire made any move to defend me from the charges.

I spoke up for myself. "If there were any justice, lady, God himself would reach down and strike me dead, for I am guilty as you say.

But until he does, I will just have to keep moving on and doing what I can in the world."

Gorgoth surprised me then, his voice so deep at first you might think it a trembling in the ground itself. It took me a moment to understand he had started to sing, something wordless, elemental like the crackle of the fire, and captivating. For the longest time we only sat and listened, the stars wheeling overhead, frosty in the night.

For three nights and days rain thundered from leaden skies, drowning out conversation in the carriage and attempting to drown pretty much everything else outside. The roads before us became rivers of mud. The rivers themselves grew to dark and swirling monsters wielding trees and carts as they surged past. Captain Harran led his force along the alternative routes planned out against such eventualities, taking us through larger towns, through cities where the stone bridges had ridden out many a flood.

I took to Brath's saddle again. After days pressed against the warmth of Katherine's cool indifference I could do with a cold shower.

"Making your escape, Jorg?" Makin rode up beside me as I pulled away from Holland's carriage.

The road led like a causeway through a sea of flooded pasture, the waters broken only by half-drowned hedgerows. Hours later the rain failed and the sky cracked open along a bright fault-line. The still waters all around became mirrors, every lone tree reflected, bare fingers reaching below as well as above. So much of the world is about surfaces, the eye deceived, with the truth in the unknown and unknowable depths beneath.

"Damn." I shook my head. I'd come out of the carriage to think about something other than Katherine!

"My lord?" A guardsman close at hand.

"It's nothing," I said.

"My lord, Captain Harran asks for you at the head of the column."

"Oh." An exchanged glance with Makin and we picked up the pace to pass those ahead, already slowing.

In the west the sun started to edge beneath the cloud bank to tinge the floodwater crimson. We reached Harran after five minutes of mud and splatter. A small town lay ahead on a rise, an island for now.

"Gottering." Harran nodded to the distant houses.

Marten and Kent joined us.

"Is the road impassable?" I asked, the route dipped beneath the flood before rising again just as it entered Gottering.

"It shouldn't be too deep," Harran said. He leaned forward and touched his horse's leg to indicate the level.

"What then?" I asked.

Marten drew his sword, a slow action, and pointed to the fencing on our left. I had thought it the normal detritus that a flood will wad into any fence or decorate the bushes with, but a closer look told a different story.

"Rags?"

"Clothes," Harran said.

Kent slipped from his horse and squelched a few steps forward along the road. Bending he retrieved a handful of mud. He held a grimy palm up to me.

I'd noted the white specks but not really paid attention. Inches from my face I could see them for what they were. Teeth. People's teeth, long-rooted and bloody.

The waters burned red now with the sun drowning in the west. The air held a chill already.

"And does this mean anything to you, Harran?"

"The guard travel many places. I've heard stories." An old scar beneath his eye burned very white. I'd not noticed it before. Harran wore his years this evening. "Best get that bishop of yours here. He may have more to tell."

And so, minutes later, Makin returned with Gomst behind him in the saddle. And Kent who had gone to escort the bishop, not for safety but because of the piety that got burned into him at the Haunt, returned with Katherine.

"You could have let the princess have your horse, Sir Kent. I'm sure she didn't want to cuddle up to a crispy bloodhound like yourself."

"I wouldn't let him wade after us in the mud." Katherine leaned around Kent's shoulder and shot me a venomous look.

"You showed Bishop Gomst your evidence then, Kent?" I ignored Katherine. I could feel her daring me to say she should have stayed where she was.

Makin let Gomst down on the verge where the ground rose to the ridge along which the fence ran.

"This is a bad thing." Gomst staggered and almost slipped over on the wet grass before he reached the dark shrouding of rags. His hand kept questing for the support of his crook, left back atop Holland's carriage. "Like St. Anstals . . . I had a report." He patted his robes in search, then abandoned the effort. "And the ruin of Tropez." Wild eyes found me. "The Dead King's work has been done here. Ghouls and rag-a-mauls if we're lucky."

"And if we're not so blessed, old man?"

"Lichkin. There might be a lichkin." He couldn't keep the terror from his voice.

Harran nodded. "The monsters from the Isles."

"Mother Ursula saw in visions that the lichkin would cross the waters. A dark tide would bear them." Gomst hugged himself against the cold. "They say that the lichkin have only one mercy."

"What mercy is that, your grace?" Kent rasped.

"In the end they let you die."

I looked over at the black shapes of Gottering, roofs, a church tower, chimneys, a tavern's weather vane. It pays to choose your ground and I would rather choose the town than a thin strip of mud amid a vast lake. But had the enemy already chosen Gottering, already laid their traps? Or was too much being read into some rags and a scattering of teeth.

"Count them," I said.

"My lord?" Harran frowned at me.

"How many teeth, how much clothing? Did three peasants brawl here and bring the Gilden Guard to a halt, or is this the scene of a massacre?"

Harran waved at two of his men and they climbed down to inspect more closely.

I nudged Brath closer to the captain. "If it's corpses we're to fight, best to do it with our feet dry and space to see them coming. How deep is the water around us? I'd say two feet? Three? Not drowning deep? Even if the dead crawled through it a man might mark the ripples in their wake?"

"Deeper in places," Harran said. Another captain disagreed. Harran and two more guard captains, Rosson and Devers, started to argue the lie of the land.

Marten rode through a gap in the fence, down into the flood. He stood in his stirrups to face us in the gloom, the water lapping his toes. "It's about this deep, sire."

"Dozens," said the man checking the fence, peeling the garments from it. "Scores maybe."

"We'll stay here," I said. "And ride into Gottering with first light."

I accompanied Katherine and Gomst back to the carriage. "I'll sleep in here tonight," I told Miana as she opened the door. "I want a sword close to you."

"I'll marshal the guard around the carriage," Makin said from the saddle.

"Put Kent on the roof. Rike and Gorgoth by the doors. Let Marten organize patrols through the fields. Better a drowned guardsman or two than being taken by surprise."

Cold woke me in the night. Even with Miana pressed against me beneath a bearskin throw, and with Katherine's weight through the thickness of her own furs, the cold opened my eyes. The faint slosh of horses moving through the standing waters became a fractured sound, a brittle tinkling and a creaking. Ice.

I leaned toward the nearer window, across Katherine, and found her watching me. In the dark her eyes made a gleam without colour. She drew aside the window cover and together we squinted through the perforations of the grille, the steam of our breath mixing.

The screams started faint and grew no louder, but with each passing minute the horror mounted. Screams reaching across the skin of ice, all the way from the dark shapes of Gottering. I knew it for pain. Terror has a different quality and pain will scare away fear quick enough.

"I should go out."

"Stay," she said.

So I did.

Katherine sat up, straight-backed against the cushioned rest. "Something's coming." I reached for my sword—she shook her head. "Coming a different way."

For a moment, before she closed her eyes, I swear I saw them: green, grass-green, lit from within. She sat still, ice-still, painted in black and pale by moonlight through the window grille. I thought her perfect and need trembled in me. Screams I had heard before.

She sat without motion as the long night marched past, her lips twitching with an occasional word, muttered and indistinct. Miana and the old men slept, uneasy in their dreams but not tormented, and I watched Katherine, listening to the distant howling, to the crackle of ice, and to the drawing of her breath.

24

We came into Gottering at first light. The water sloshed around the carriage floor at the deepest point and brought the smell of the river to us, but we didn't have to get out.

I climbed from the carriage in the town square, with the flood trickling down the step behind me. The place showed no signs of damage, a pleasant enough town in the most prosperous region of Attar. Bunting from the harvest festival still hung across the main street from rooftop to rooftop. A child's hoop beside the carriage wheels. Birdsong.

"Did it seem to the patrols that the screams came from town?" I asked.

Harran nodded. "Couldn't be more than an hour since they stopped."

A sniff of the air spoke of rot and shit, cold against the sinuses, what you expect from any town. And something else.

"Blood," I said. "There's slaughter been done here. I can smell it."

"Search the houses." Harran waved his men on. Dozens of them set off, ducking through doorways, the dawn light gleaming on their mail.

The first of the guard re-emerged within minutes. He held some kind of garment out before him, a pale and wrinkled thing, his face, almost as pale, kept stiff in a mask of revulsion.

"Here!" I called the man to me and put my hands out to inspect his prize.

He placed it in my arms without waiting for further invitation.

Even with it draped across my forearms, with the weight of it, the raw scent, and the faintly obscene warmth still clinging there, it took several moments before I understood what I held. It took an effort not to flinch and drop the thing in that instant of realization. I lifted it up, let the arms hang, the scalp flop.

"It takes some skill to flay a man so completely," I said. I scanned the company, meeting the gaze of each soldier. "Terror is a weapon, gentlemen, and our enemy understands its use. Let's be sure that we also understand this game."

I let the skin drop to the cobbles. A wet sound. "Find them all. Pile them here."

I rode the empty streets with Red Kent and Makin, circling the town at the water's edge, finding nothing. By the time the sun cleared the rooftops Harran's men had made a heap of one hundred and ninety skins, taken from cellars, bedrooms, stables, chairs before hearths, all across town. Each of a piece with just the three slices that a practised huntsman would use to take the hide from a deer. Men, women, young and old, children's skins lay there, all faces wrinkled now. I picked up the hoop toy from by the carriage and fretted it through my fingers as the guard built the pile.

Marten escorted Miana and Katherine from the carriage into the Red Fox Inn, Gottering's only such establishment. Miana waddled, her belly impossibly large, discomfort written across her face. Marten saw them installed in cushioned chairs and kept their company while they waited, with a fire lit and guardsmen about them, Gorgoth at the door. Outside, Gomst read a benediction over the remains in the square. I trusted Katherine to maintain whatever wall she had erected to keep the lichkin out of our heads, but she would have to sleep eventually.

"We should move on," Harran said, pulling his white mare to Brath's side. "This is not our concern."

"It's true. The Duke of Attar would not thank us for policing his lands on his behalf."

Harran pushed the gratitude from his face so fast many would have missed it.

"Prepare to move out!" he shouted.

I would have been happy to ride on as well—but it felt like being pushed.

Through the small leaded panes of the inn window, stained a faint green by the Attar glass, I saw Marten start to his feet and take Miana's hand with concern.

"However," I said. "Are you not expecting other guard troops to come this way? The flooding narrows the options for travelling from the west. How many of the Hundred are to follow in our wake?"

"There may be some." Honour wouldn't let him lie. A problem that never troubled me.

"And aren't the guard bound to the whole task, to getting the Hundred to Vyene, not just to those in their immediate charge?"

Harran stood in his stirrups. "Strike that! I want the victims found. I want each house secured." With a growl he rode off to oversee.

"Whoever has still to travel this way is unlikely to be voting in your favour at Congression." Osser Gant levered himself from the shadows of stable block, his gaunt frame supported on a silver-topped cane, a nice piece of work in the shape of a fox's head.

"So why am I reminding Harran of a duty he would rather have forgotten?" I asked.

Osser nodded. "And risking yourself."

"You've spent a lifetime on the edge of those stinking marshes, Gant. How many lichkin have you seen?"

"An old man like me doesn't stray far from his master's hall, King Jorg. But you won't meet many men who've seen a lichkin. You might find the corpse of a man who has seen one, and that corpse might try to kill you, but the man will be long gone." Osser nodded, as if agreeing with himself.

"Not a one in all these years?" I asked.

"The lichkin may be old," Osser said. "I don't know. But they're new to the Ken Marshes. They've roamed there for ten years at most. Maybe not much more than five years. Even in the Isles they are a new plague."

Marten came to the inn's door and beckoned to me. Something important. Sometimes you just know. I swung out of my saddle and stepped down. Walking after an age in the saddle puts an unfamiliar edge on something you do every day of your life—just for a moment as your leg muscles remember how they were made. I opted for a slow crossing of the square. Something told me it might be a short walk but it was taking me a long way.

Marten leaned in close. "I think it's her time. Sarah was like this."

"She can't wait?" I said. "Hold it in?"

"It doesn't work like that, Jorg." The flickered hint of a smile.

"Hell." I raised my voice. "I want more guards around this inn. Secure all the exits."

I peered through a glass pane. Miana had stretched back in her chair, Katherine in close, blocking my view. I didn't want to go in. There was a time when I was pleased to find that something still scared me. As the years stacked up I kept finding new things to worry over. Pleasure turning to dismay. It seems men have far more to fear than boys.

I went back to Osser. Makin finished tending his horse and came across with Kent to join us.

"And how many lichkin are there, Chancellor Gant?" I asked.

"I heard tell there were seven in all the world," Kent said, his gaze flicking to the bishop praying before the mounded skins. "Seven is too many."

"There may be seven," Osser said. "The bishop has a list of seven names written by the sisters of the Helskian Order."

"I thought the Pope called for all the seers to be killed. She said the nunneries weren't built to shelter witches." The decree had stuck with me—an example of the lengths to which the Vatican would go in order to avoid unwelcome facts.

"Her Holiness called for the sisters of Helsk to be blinded," said Father Gomst, having finished or abandoned his prayers. "And they were blinded. But their visions continue."

A glance toward the inn's window revealed little but Marten staring out. Katherine moved across the room with a steaming bowl and a cloth over one arm, becoming lost behind Marten's broad shoulders.

Rike returned to the main square, a black oak coffer under one arm overflowing with silverware and fine silk. A few of the guards stationed at the entry points gave him disapproving stares but none went as far as to challenge him. Gold armour or not, I would be surprised if any professional soldier would turn down a choice piece of loot when searching Gottering. Even so, something was wrong with the picture. I pursed my lips and frowned.

"Brother Rike." He walked over, sullen despite his takings.

I reached out and plucked at the silk, a lustrous orange I'd not encountered before. "What is it with you and fabric, Rike? I'm not sure I've ever seen you leave a burning building without a bolt of stolen cloth. Something you're not telling us?" The idea of Rike in a dress painted as nasty a picture as the heaped skins. But that wasn't the problem. The answer struck me. "You can carry more than that." When did I last see Rike stop looting before the weight of his takings made it impossible to gather any more?

Rike shrugged and spat, colour coming to his face. "I'd had enough."

"You never have enough, Brother Rike."

"It's the eyes." He spat again and started to tie the coffer to his horse. "I don't mind the fingers—but the eyes don't look dead."

"What eyes?"

"Every house." He shook his head and fastened another strap. "In the drawer with the knives and forks, on a shelf in the cupboard, behind the jars in the larder, everywhere you go to hunt out something worth taking. I don't like them." He tightened the last strap.

"Eyeballs?" Makin asked.

Rike nodded and I shivered despite myself. No doubt they were removed as neatly as the skins. I think the precision of it unnerved me. I've seen a raven pluck a ripe eyeball from a head black with decay and kept right on eating my own meal. But something in the lichkin's neat slicing felt unnatural. I shook it off.

Marten came from the inn, banished by Katherine. A moment's hesitation took me. Could Katherine be trusted alone with my child when she held me responsible for her nephew's death? Might she have saved Miana from the assassin's knife just for the chance to twist the life from my infant son? I threw the thought away. Revenge is my art, not hers.

Martin stopped beside Rike and me, ignoring us both, staring at the heap of skins, some lost question leaving his mouth open.

I shrugged. "Men are made of meat. Lichkin like to play with the pieces. I've seen worse in a fleshmonger's shop. Hell, I've seen worse when men take against their captives." That last bit was a lie, but the truth was that it wasn't conscience that stopped men short of the lichkins' excesses—men just weren't such accomplished butchers.

I watched Rike rather than Marten. Nothing natural put the fear into Rike. Some things might set him running, but he'd be angry as hell while he ran and planning his revenge all the way. The last time I'd seen him run in terror had been from the ghosts on the lichway. Fingers and eyeballs stashed away in peasant houses wouldn't do it. I'd seen him take both, and he hadn't much cared if the former owners had finished using them.

My gaze returned to the skin heap. Something in my imagination kept making it seem to crawl. "Burn that," I said. "It's not as if it's needed any more."

I went to the inn. Time to step through that door.

"Damnation! Jorg where the fuck have you been?" Miana snarled that "Jorg" past small white teeth. I always said she had a pretty face and a foul mouth. And they say even the most proper of maids can swear like a sailor when labouring over a child. What words would she find when it came to push and shove? Strange to say that we're born to our mothers' cursing but ever after they think the young have tender ears and can hear only what might be said in church. I closed the door behind me, leaving it just an inch or two ajar.

Inside the inn smelled of wood smoke, hot and close, and older less pleasant taints, perhaps of murders done here before the sun rose.

"Sweet Jesus!" Miana gasped and spat, clutching herself. She lay back in a great armchair heaped with cushions. Sweat-beaded skin, tendons straining in her neck. "I don't want my baby here. Not here." Katherine glanced at me across the swell of Miana's breasts. On the walls brown smears where skinless bodies had touched rough timbers.

I hadn't wanted my child born on the road. It's a hard enough place to live, and not a fit place to enter the world, not even with a gilded carriage and an honour guard decorated just as richly. And this village of the dead bore even worse omens. I thought of Degran small, frail, broken in my hands. The lichkin held Gottering in its hands— waiting—and Miana was ready to deliver.

Gorgoth turned from the doorway of the inn, taking more wood for the pyre in the square. A thick log in each hand, lifted from those racked against the wall. Guardsmen had joined in, tearing shutters from windows, breaking up an abandoned cart. Others came from the inn's cellar with flasks of brandy and urns of lamp oil to quicken the flames. I pulled the door open and followed Gorgoth.

"Get back in here, you whore-born bastard!"

I closed the door on Miana, watched by the Gilden Guard to either side. Eyebrows raised.

"The queen is not herself," I said.

Six golden-helmed heads snapped back front and centre as I passed between them.

The lichkin held the town, held us all, though many of our number didn't yet know it. Perhaps a little fire might loosen its grip and cleanse the air. Gottering was a spell now, an enchantment, a single great rune set out in pieces of men. Blood-magic.

When the timbers lay doused and heaped around the pile of flayed skins I drew Gog from his scabbard. The blade gleamed in the winter sun so's you could imagine flames dancing on its edge. I set it to the wood. "Burn," I said. And flames really did dance on that keen line.

The blaze took fast, leaping amongst the broken wood, devouring the oil and spirits, sinking hot teeth into timber. Almost at once the meaty tang of burned flesh reached out, stronger than the smoke. Memory took me to the Haunt, walking out between scorched corpses to meet Egan of Arrow. And just a moment later, another memory, the shrieks of those the fire had left alive. Only—not memory.

"What?" I tilted my head to locate the sound. A high keening.

Captain Harran broke into the square on horseback. "It's from that copse, on the ridge to the west. Hollow Wood."

As we came into Gottering there had been another island in the flooded fields, three hundred yards to the west, a few acres of tangled woodland.

The lichkins' mercy, Gomst had said, *is that in the end they let you die.*

But not yet.

The people of Gottering still lived. They still felt it. Somewhere in that wood close on two hundred townsfolk, flayed, without fingers or eyes or teeth, howled as I burned their skins.

"Jorg!" A shout edged with scream. Katherine at the doorway, pale, framed by auburn curls.

I ran, sword in hand. I pushed past her.

"It— It got stronger. I couldn't stop it," Katherine said behind me.

Miana lay before the fireplace and the crackling logs on bedding from the inn rooms, skirts hitched around her hips in many layers.

Pain had twisted her limbs. The firelight shone on skin stretched too tight across her womb. White against that red flesh, set over my hidden child, the print of a three-fingered hand.

"Miana?" I stepped close, slamming Gog back into his scabbard. "Miana?" A cold touch flickered across my chest. Perhaps that same three-fingered hand, reaching in. I have no truck with poets and their flowered words but in that moment my heart truly froze, turning to a heavy and clenched wound to see her there—a physical pain that staggered me. A weakness the lichkin infected me with, no doubt.

"Miana?" The eyes she turned my way did not know me.

I swung around for the door, almost knocking Katherine down. "You're leaving?"

"Yes."

"She needs you." Anger. Disappointment. "Here."

"The lichkin is reaching for both her and my son," I said. "And wherever this lichkin is it is not here."

I left her, left Miana, left the inn. I hastened past the pyre where skins bubbled and melted, fats running and steaming over the flagstones.

With the brothers at my heels I ran to the corner by the bakers' kilns, to a step that offered a view west across bright waters toward the bare trees where my enemy waited. I paused, willing my limbs to stillness, letting heartbeats count out time—time for judgment and clarity to catch me up. Moments passed with nothing but the distant howling and the black reflection of branches reaching out toward Gottering.

"Surfaces and reflections, Makin," I said. "Worlds divided by such thin barriers, unseen, unknowably deep."

"Your pardon, sire?" Makin took sanctuary in formality rather than try to follow me.

Every fibre of me screamed for action. My wife lay marked and tormented, a stranger to me, a prison for my son. My son!

My father would tell me, "find a new wife." Nail the pair, mother and babe, to the floor with one sword thrust and ride on. Let the lichkin choke on that. And I would do it too, if no better choice remained. I would do it. I told myself I would do it.

I held still, just a tremble in my fingers. "Consider the problem in hand, Lord Makin. The good bishop tells me there are at least seven lichkin, maybe more. And we know they're striking across Attar for the first time. Maybe they're attacking along other routes into Vyene? Spread thin? It seems that if there were many and they were confident of victory over soldiers rather than peasants, they would have come to us last night. That or they're toying with us, cat to mouse.

"Well, I would rather find out about a new enemy by first encountering one on their own, so this is a chance not to miss, rather than a horror to run from," I said.

It wanted us to run. All this—all this was about fear. It wanted Miana bundled into a carriage and half a thousand guardsmen to gallop off along the road to Honth.

"And if it's the cat toying with the mouse?" Makin asked.

I smiled. "What better chance will the mouse ever have to kill the cat?"

I drew Gog and the fire that burst out along the sword made pale all flame that had ever burned there before. I set off toward the black trees and the weakening screams of Gottering, wading through dark waters with the brothers treading in my wake. And I walked rather than ran, though a fire burned in me near as fierce as that on my blade, because surfaces divide known from unknown, and though I might walk where angels fear to tread, I try not to rush in like a fool.

25

Floodwater always has the same stink to it, of earth after rain but gone too far, tainted with rot. The coldness of it made me clutch at my breath, rising by inches as I waded on. My face blazed with the heat of the fire on Gog's blade, reflecting in dark and hungry water. Some foolishness made me think of the River Sane's gentle meander through Crath City, at the bend past the Bridge of Arts where stone pillars jut from the slow current to mark an area for swimming. Mother would take us there in the high summer heat when the Sane still remembered winter. As tiny boys we would edge in, inch by inch, squealing. That shriek and gasp as the river took our privates in icy hands—I felt it again and bit down the exclamation.

"Brisk!" Sir Makin said behind me. "Don't think my balls will be coming back down for a month."

"Why are we even going?" Rike from the back.

I glanced over my shoulder, at Gorgoth almost naked despite the cold, pushing a bow wave before him, Red Kent, his short sword and hatchet held out above the water, Makin with a grin, Rike with a sour sulk on him, Marten frowning, determined, the device on his shield the black spars of a burned house on a green field.

"Why?" Rike repeated.

"Because it doesn't want us to," I said, pressing on.

I made a mental note to change my ways. If, every time an enemy demands you sit down, instead you jump up, well, that predictability becomes a ring through your nose by which you can be pulled when pushing fails.

"Enjoy yourselves." Rike sounded further behind me.

I stopped and turned. Rike had never really taken to the business of me being king. I might have seven nations where men bent their knee to me in their thousands, through love or fear, mainly fear, but with Rike the only knee-bending took place when not to do so would get that knee broken.

"Do we have to do this now, Brother Rike?" I asked.

He sneered. "What are you gonna do? Cut my skin off and scoop out my eyes?"

Apparently the lichkin scared him more than I did.

"Of course not." I shook my head, showing him the old smile. "I'm a king!" I took a stride toward him. Lowering Gog's point to the water so it sizzled, jumped, and spat, the steam rising between us. "I'll have a professional do it. Somebody who really enjoys it. Kings don't dirty their hands."

Gorgoth let out a deep laugh at that. Makin joined him. In the end even Rike gave that "hur" of his and we carried on. Jokes come hard when you're past ball-deep in icy water and heading toward hell, but fortunately my audience wasn't too discerning. Also I wasn't joking.

Closer to the copse now, water around my waist, each step sinking into hidden softness. Three times I caught myself from falling, tripped by some submerged briar or fencepost. Makin went down once and came up cursing and spluttering.

The water seemed colder closer to the trees, plates of wafer-thin ice gliding in our wake, and a mist rising, tendrils reaching to mix with the frosting of our breath. The mists rose with us as the gradient led us from the flood among the outermost of the black and dripping trees.

I saw the first ghost only as a glimpse between trunks, a figure moving fast but not stirring the calf-deep water. Just a glimpse, ragged black hair, muddy, a child. The name Orscar floated through me, though I couldn't place it. I turned to warn the brothers, sword still levelled at where the boy had been. And of course found only mist to meet me. Mist and an iron cross, a pendant hanging from a low branch, a blob of red enamel at the crossing point. For the blood of Christ.

"I know this game of shades, dead-thing!" I swung Gog in a slow circle, mists shrivelling back before the flames. "Bring my dead mother, William, the baby if you must. Bring the dead of Gelleth, bring Greyson's ghost with his eyes gone, bring Lesha carrying her head. You're playing the wrong hand against me. I've known worse."

"Have you now?"

A sharp pain took me in the chest. I turned again and the fire on Gog died, blade dropping as the strength left my arm.

Father stood, wolf-robed, iron crowned, iron in his hair, winter in his eyes.

"You're not dead." The words left me, soft and without emotion. "Not a ghost."

"Am I not?"

"You're not!" Beneath my breastplate blood spilled, pumped from an old wound, soaking my shirt and the woollens over it, running in hot rivulets down across my belly. "The Tall Castle wouldn't fall to marsh corpses." I shook my head. "And your men are too scared to slit your throat." I blinked. He stood there, the water rippling around his high boots, solid and meaner than nails, not some grey spectre.

"You'll be a father within the hour, Jorg." He looked at his hands, spread them before his belt, turning them palm to back, back to palm.

"Don't—" Loose fingers found a tighter grip on Gog's hilt. "How do you know that?"

"Ghosts know what they know." He turned to stare into the fog.

"You're not dead." It wasn't possible. He couldn't die. Not that old man. And not without me being the one to do it. "How——"

"The wrong son died, Jorg." I never knew anyone to match Father's talent for cutting across a man's words without raising his voice. "It should have been William taken from the thorns. He had my strength. You were ever your mother's whelp. Better Degran even than you. Better even him."

"Who killed you?" I made it a demand.

"Who?" Those eyes found me again. I had thought it cold before. "My heart gave out, pounding that pretty Teuton of mine. What was it you called her? The Scorron whore."

The waters rose about us, swirling, eddying around the trees. Knee-deep, thigh-deep.

My strength left me with each heartbeat, limbs icy, the only warmth that of the blood spilling from the old wound, the one Father gave me, the one that should never have healed. "You'll be a father soon, Jorg. That little southern wife of yours will push out a son. In slime and blood, shouting at the world. Just like mine did. The Pope's man failed. I told her, 'send three, two at the least,' but the silly bitch sent just the one. Said he was her best. I had high hopes, but he failed."

"You knew?" The flood reached my chest. Without its support I doubted I could stand. When it touched the wound I felt the coldness pour into me, as if black water were filling me like a hollow gourd.

"It's good that you won't see your boy," my father told me. "You're too weak to raise a son." His wolfskin lifted on the flood but it meant nothing to him. He watched me with just the hint of a smile, a thing as cold as his regard.

The water spilled around my neck, putting a chatter in my teeth, my hair floating around me, drawn by the current. The weight of my armour, of the sword held in a numb hand, the pull of the mud, all held me down.

I thought of my child, of Miana with the white hand seared on her belly, and a spark of anger lit in me despite the cold. "You were mine to kill, old man." I snarled it before the water closed my mouth and swallowed me.

I looked up at a distant surface through dark weeds—the tangled drift of my hair. Far above me, impossibly far, a rippled surface fracturing the daylight to send weak glimmers down into the icy depths. A hand hung over me, limp, reaching for the sky. My hand. The dim and greenish light moved ripple patterns across my fingers.

I stared. Stared at that distant sun. It could be a million miles away. Lundist had said a million. More than a million. The waters held me. I hung limp and stared until that twinkling patch of green-tinted light became all I could see, became my world.

Shapes resolved. Green-tinted. And it seemed, though the water held me, though my chest ached for air and my heart pounded behind my ribs, that I looked not at the sky through water, but through the faint green stain of Attar glass into an inn room. A room where a fire burned in the hearth, where Miana lay, and Katherine crouched at her side.

I saw the lichkin come for them, the door flying apart in splinters. It walked in, slow and measured, a bone-thing, shrouded in dead space where the eye can't see. The creature had left us a trap in the Hollow Wood and waited for us to leave. While we lay drowning the lichkin slipped into Gottering.

Guardsmen came hard on its heels. On her heels. Somehow I knew the lichkin for a she. They fell choking, perhaps drowning with their own ghosts, strangled by lost loves, choked by disapproving parents, or whatever tawdry fragments of their past haunted them. We all carry the seeds of our own destruction with us, we all drag our history behind us like rusted chain.

Katherine rose to meet her.

"You shouldn't have come." Somehow Katherine's voice reached me, cut through to my dying brain, past the thunder of my heart.

The lichkin advanced on Katherine, only its hands clear to me, white, bone-like, root-like. My vision pulsed and prickled. In a moment I would take the breath my body screamed for.

"You don't know much, dead-thing." Katherine stood before it, the muted reds of her travel-gown swaying around her. Even dying I saw her beauty. Without desire—just as a statement, like the glory of a stained-glass window, or the play of light and shadow across mountains. I saw her fear too, and the strength that held it down.

Those hands reached for her, fast but slowing, as if finding some invisible resistance.

"You can't be very old, dead-thing," she said. "It's written in the oldest books. Sleep and death are brother and sister. The Bard knew it. For in death's sleep what dreams will come? And believe me dead-thing, I know dreams."

The lichkin howled and raised a grey swirl around Katherine. Her skirts whipped about her. At Katherine's feet Miana twisted and moaned. Shapes moved in that swirl. Shapes and suggestions.

"Enough," Katherine said, sharp voiced. "Ghosts, is it? But dreams are populated by ghosts and little else. Ghosts are made of dreams, dead dreams, lost dreams, bad dreams, dreams that get stuck in tight little circles, that carve their own rut in the fabric of the world and won't let go."

Katherine's hand snaked out and caught something from the swirl, held it by the throat. To me it was Orscar from the monastery, Sunny lashed to the Bad Dogs' pole, Lesha wanting me to save her, the boy in Albaseat beaten by the smith. You can't save them all so why save any? She choked it, fingers turning white with strain. At the last Father's face hung there, black with blood. And then, poof, it was gone, a wisp of smoke, nothing more.

Katherine stepped forward, a quick step. And the lichkin flinched. It turned to run. But she caught it. Caught its bone-white hand in hers.

Katherine held the lichkin, rigid with effort, hand growing white, veins growing dark and darker still, but she refused to release it.

"You shouldn't have come."

And I broke the surface. Retching and gasping, I sat up, the water about me a foot deep, eighteen inches maybe. No more. I drew in the sweetest breath and parted the black veil of my hair. All about me, at the edge of the Hollow Wood, the brothers sat, choking and gasping, spitting water, purple in the face.

26

Chella's story

The carriage jolted across frost-stiffened mud and Chella cursed again. On the bench opposite, Kai looked far more comfortable, on the edge of sleep almost, as if bounced in his nurse's arms. She clutched the armrest, fingers white on the leather. Five years starved of necromancy, five years since the Ancrath boy had drained her, shrivelled up her power in the firestorm of his ghosts. She had thought the Dead King merely cruel to punish her so, to leave her stranded once more on the shores of life, plagued by the everyday aches and pains of flesh, mocked by trivialities like temperature. Now she appreciated his cunning too.

"Damnation." Chella hugged her furs close about her. "Who made the autumn so chill?"

"Who decided to hold Congression on the edge of winter?" Kai asked. "That's the more reasonable question."

Chella felt cold, not reasonable. Kai's easy manner irked her. She returned often now to the day the mire-ghouls had dragged him and the girl to her through the reeds. Mud and slime in their hair, horror frozen into their fresh young faces. Each display of his returning confidence, each hint of the mild contempt that hid behind his smile, made her regret deciding to use him the more. Better he had died with his pert little strumpet.

Necromancy at its heart is a guilty pleasure, a surrender to the darkest instinct. The fact that Golden Boy had picked up his old self-assurance again, his charm and his winning smile, as if he just dabbled in a secret vice, a necessary evil, dug at her moment to moment. That he proved so good at it made her want to claw the face off him. He seemed to think it something he could set aside when no longer required, like he had that girl. What was her name? Sula? She wondered if Kai could still remember it.

Necromancy has to cost you. It had certainly cost Chella. Jorg might have taken a bite for free, but all he got was a taste. Golden Boy on the other hand had picked it up as though it were nothing but juggling, and had yet to drop a ball.

"I hate being alive," Chella spoke to the passing world through the carriage grille, hedgerows edged with hoarfrost so thick that every twig bristled with thorns of ice.

"And yet we hang to it so dear," Kai said. "Sometimes by fingertips."

He had walked the dry lands now. Thought he knew it all. Thought he knew both sides of the coin from his stumbling in the borders where newly dead sometimes lost their way. Chella wondered how the deep voyaging would change him. What it would be that took the ease from his smile. Somewhere past Absolution, in the places where angels fear to tread, maybe even across the black sands to the caves where lichkin dwell. It waited for him out there—and on the day of his dark epiphany she would forgive him his slights and his superiority for they would be broken things that no longer held use for him. Until that day, though . . . one more cheerful encouragement and she would take his face.

The roll and rock of the carriage made her stomach jump. Her bones ached so it hurt to sit. And the cold, the damp, insidious cold! She wiped her nose, leaving a glistening trail across the back of her hand, then sniffed, noting and pretending to ignore Kai's look of faint disgust.

We play with corpses and my mucus offends him!

Being so alive made her petty and weak.

The carriage rolled to a halt, the coachman banging three times on the roof.

Kai looked up. "Trouble?"

Chella sensed nothing but in her diminished state that meant little. She shrugged, leaned forward, and opened the carriage door.

Axtis stood in the mud, his golden armour bright in the winter sun, hurting her eyes. More of the Gilden Guard pressed around him on horseback. "Smoke rising over the town ahead."

"Which town?" Chella squinted. Leaving the carriage didn't appeal, the sun promised warmth, but it lied.

"Gottering."

"Never heard of it. Send riders ahead and drive on." She leaned back into the carriage and closed the door. "Two hundred and fifty men! Worried over smoke. If the place was one big bonfire we could ride through."

"Perhaps our friends have been here before us." Kai caught the mist of his breath and shaped it into a question mark, fading between them. Old tricks.

"Lichkin are no one's friends, Wind-sworn. You'd do well to remember that."

The carriage juddered into motion again and before long rolled on into smooth mud and tinkling ice crusts.

"The road is flooded—we're fording." Kai, head back against the rests, eyes closed. "There's a pyre of sorts in the town square. No bones."

Kai had told her his wind-sight grew hand in hand with his dead-sight. She hated him the more for it. His eyeballs twitched beneath his eyelids, looking ahead of them, seeing what she could not. Still, she allowed herself a smile. There were things ahead that Kai would not see coming, however far his vision rode the wind. The Dead King's cunning had set them on this path. Two necromancers sent to Congression. The necromancy necessary to his purpose, and just as necessary the fact that they stood close enough to life to pass as untainted, Kai too new to his calling to raise alarm, and she too distant from her old power to seem a threat.

Dark waters seeped around the door join as they went, the carriage half-floating now. Then, as it seemed they would sink, the wheels found the road once more and they jolted back onto dry land. Chella caught the stink of roast meat.

"It's a funeral pyre."

"There are no bones," Kai said. "And the festival flags are out. A celebration maybe?"

Chella knew death. She shook her head.

Stepping from the carriage she jumped to the ground before it came to a halt.

"What is it?" Kai dropped down behind her.

Chella raised a hand to silence him, not that she listened with her ears, but it felt good to shut him up.

"Screaming . . ." she said. Horrible agony. Her skin burned with it. A hand rose before her face and for a moment she didn't recognize it as hers, hanging on invisible thread, one long finger, bony in the knuckle, pointing. The questing hand settled, indicating the open waters between the town and a nearby copse. "There."

"I can barely sense it," Kai said.

"It's hiding." Chella brought her hands together before her, shaping her will. She might have only an echo of her power but she wielded what she held with lifetimes of experience. "Help me bring it out."

Drawing forth dead things from behind the veil always put Chella in mind of the cesspit back in Jonholt. A hot summer and the stink rose between the boards, acrid, strong enough to make her eyes water that day, the day she dropped Nan Robtin's brooch. "Dropped" was the wrong word. She had pinned it carefully to her smock, piercing coarse wool with the steel pin. And even so, it fell, turning in the air, sparkling, making diamond fractures of the light, though it was only glass and mirror. She missed the brooch twice in the air, fingers brushing it, then fumbled it, sending it skittering across the boards and down the dung hole.

For the longest time Chella had stood and stared at the hole. The image of the sparkling brooch falling into darkness played across her vision. She hadn't asked to take it. Nan would have said no. *It's borrowing if you bring it back*, she had told herself.

"Stealing if you don't," she whispered, there by the cesspit behind the scrub lilacs.

She had lain flat upon the boards, nose wrinkled, breath held against the physical force of the stench. Cheek to the wood, arm reaching down, the stained boards scraping her bicep through her smock. Fingers found the filth, the coldness surprising, a crawling sensation of revulsion as she dipped in, stomach heaving, her hand enveloped now, wanting to make a fist and yet stretching out, questing.

The need to draw breath built in her chest, a hammering demand. Eyes screwed tight. Toes curled, legs drumming, hand questing. YOU WILL BREATHE. And in the end the body's wants prove stronger than the mind's and you always take the breath.

Chella had lain gagging, a thin spill of acid spew drooling from her panting mouth, and still her fingers hunted in a cold world, half-solid, half-liquid.

And after all that—the sudden bite of the brooch pin made her scream and whip her hand out, empty, splattering filth.

"The trick," she muttered to Kai, "is to let it bite."

When the bite came Kai fell shrieking, and Chella endured with grim satisfaction, hauling to bring out what was lost and hidden. Weak as she was, Chella used the life that filled her to tempt and anchor her prey. At the last, when her bones threatened to tear through flesh and skin if she did not release her hold, Chella pulled harder still and a mist began to coil about the surface of the flood. Frost patterns spread beneath the mist, racing in wild, angular profusion over dark water.

It rose in a splintering of ice, something both more white than the frost, blacker than the waters, a creature of bone-pale limbs cast with midnight shadow, blade-thin, hands dividing root-like into three fingers. And somehow, despite the lack of defining features, undeniably female. Mouthless, her pain scaled a different register, resonating in an ache deep in the sockets of Chella's teeth. Men of the guard staggered around her, choking, tearing at their eyes.

"Keres!" Chella named the lichkin, sealing it back into the world.

"What happened?" Kai climbed to his feet, hauling in a breath. "I can see it. What's changed?"

"I—" Something *had* changed, the lichkin lay revealed, stripped of its shroud of ghosts.

Kai clenched his jaw against the lichkin's resonating agony.

The ghosts were gone—flayed away.

And in that moment Chella understood.

"She's been skinned."

27

Five years earlier

I lay a long time in the dark, gripped by fever. I lay in the dust beside the fresh corpse of a thousand-year-old man and from time to time, when my mind grew clear enough to understand the slurred demands of my leathery tongue, I drank.

Without light and without sound, dreams cannot be told from delirium. I talked to myself—mutters and accusations—and sometimes to Fexler, face-down, the back of his head a wet mess of soft and sharp. I held his gun—my totem against terrors in the night. In the other hand I clutched the thorn-patterned box, refusing the urge to open it even in the madness of fever.

I spoke to my demons, addressing each with long and dreary monologues as I twisted in the dust. Lesha's head watched me from the alcove where the pills had been, her skin luminous, blood oozing black from the stump of her neck. Sunny came eyeless to stand vigil, the words from his seared tongue as incoherent as mine. William came hand in hand with Mother, her eyes worried, his hard as stones.

"I tried to save you." Same old story—no new excuses from Jorgy.

He shook his head, blood and curls. We both knew thorns would not have held him.

The dead of Gelleth came to stand watch, and my brothers from the mire, collected by Chella just for me.

And in time Fexler's medicines worked their slow magic, my fever broke, and dreams faded into darkness, William's eyes the last to go, hanging like an accusation.

"I'm hungry." The bones of my spine grated as I sat up.

I didn't know how long I'd lain there—long enough for Fexler to smell the wrong kind of sweet. But even that didn't stop the growling of my stomach.

I made a meal of the hardtack in my pack, finding it with blind fingers and chewing in the dark, spitting out the occasional inedibles fished out by mistake. I looted Fexler without squandering my light, a fingertip search discovering and exploring his many pockets. In one hand I held my blunted knife ready, not trusting his cold and stiff corpse to suffer my attentions without protest. He lay quiet, though. Perhaps the Builders had the means to defend their halls from such influences just as the seals the mind-sworn place on royal tombs hold their charges safe. I found a lightweight rectangular box, like a card case, with heavy, rattling contents, elsewhere several flexible cards that felt like plasteek, tubes that might have been writing instruments in his breast pocket. All of them went into my pack.

At last, when I felt ready to move, I relit my flask-and-wick lamp.

Getting into the shaft proved every bit the nightmare I had imagined it. Climbing up to a point at which I could snag the rope proved worse. Missing the rope, falling, and having to repeat the process nearly ended my tale with a dusty skeleton at the bottom of a deep, dry hole.

When I heaved myself out into the noonday sun, bloody-handed, panting, too dry to sweat, Balky and the stallion were waiting where I left them, offering the same looks they had seen me off with. The stallion had flecks of white foam on his muzzle and both carried the signs of dehydration, sunken flesh and an unhealthy glitter to the eyes. I stood before them, bent over with exhaustion, heaving in my breath, eyes screwed tight against the brightness of the day. I wondered if the Builder-ghosts felt this way when they came out into one world from another. Did they have to struggle from the deep places of their strange existence to emerge like Fexler did, painted by machines for human eyes? Those old ghosts watched me as I straightened, as one hand lifted to shield my gaze. I sensed their attention. As blank and unreadable as the mule's and surely more alien.

The last of the water from the skins on the stallion's back did little more than take the edge from our thirst when split three ways. I would have taken it all, of course, had I not thought we could all three make it out and back to the Bad Dogs' barrels.

The Bad Dogs' camp held few signs of its former masters. A split bone here and there, the weapons, tatters of cloth, scraps of armour, all filmed over with dust. I stayed long enough to take one of Toltech's bitter pills and fill my water-skins.

I took a look through the view-ring before I left. Part of me wanted to see Fexler there, to tell him how much his freedom had cost, to see if he cared. The ring showed nothing, just the world through a hoop of silver-steel. As I took it away the view flicked to the one seen from the lower slopes of paradise, nations laid out in browns and greens, without regard for the boundaries on men's maps, the oceans swirled about in deepest blue. And there, on the coast to the south, on the thin arm of sea that divides our lands from Afrique . . . a red dot, burning.

"I'm not your toy, Fexler. You can't set me chasing across empire to join your little dots."

Balky snorted, as if wondering whether I'd gone mad in the heat. I put the ring away. "Dammit." I'd been planning a journey to that exact spot.

*   *   *

"King Honorous Jorg Ancrath." The flunky with little rod for rapping doors afforded me the introduction he omitted on my first visit.

The provost sat in her ebony chair as if she had remained there since I left, seated the whole time with her ledgers and tallies, amid the geometric splendour of her Moorish halls. The writing desk beside her lay empty, the scribe perhaps dismissed while the provost checked his work. She watched me cross the floor with sufficient interest to pause her quill-scratching.

"Sanity prevailed, King Jorg?" she asked. "You turned back before the Hills? When I sent Lesha to guide you I had hope that it would be her scars that showed you the way—back through the city gates."

"Your granddaughter was both a caution and an inspiration, Provost." I came to the step of her dais and offered a deeper bow than she merited. I carried bad news after all. "She was an explorer. Our world needs more like her."

"Was?" The old woman didn't miss much. I felt rather than heard the tensing of the two men at the door.

"Outlaws attacked our camp while we slept. Perros Viciosos."

"Oh." That made her old, those two words. Years that had only toughened now for a moment hung their weight upon her head. "Better to have found the fire a second time."

"Lesha died in the struggle before we were taken, Provost. My man, Greyson, was not so lucky. His was a hard death."

And yet you survived. She didn't say it. The Hundred and their spawn have an instinct for survival and it never pays to ask the cost.

The provost sat back in her chair and set her quill on the armrest. A moment later she let her papers fall. "I have sixteen grandchildren you know, Jorg?"

I nodded. It didn't seem the time to say "fifteen."

"All bright and wonderful children who ran through these halls at one time or other, shrieking, laughing, full of life. A trickle of them at first, then a tide. And their mothers would put them on my lap, always the mothers, and we'd sit and goggle, young to old, a mystery to each other. Then life would sweep them on their way, and now I could more quickly tell you the names of the sixteen district water marshals than of those children. Many I wouldn't recognize in the street unless you told me to watch out for one.

"Lesha was a bold girl. Not pretty, but clever and fierce. She could have done my job maybe, but she was never meant for city life. I'm sorry now that I didn't get to know her better. More sorry for her father, who knew her even less well perhaps but will weep for her where all I have are excuses."

"I liked her. The same force pushed us both. I liked Greyson too," I said.

It struck me that finding someone I might call a friend had been a rare thing in my life. And in the space of three short months I'd discovered and lost two.

"I hope whatever you found proves worth the sacrifice."

The gun hung heavy at my hip, wrapped in leather. Almost as heavy as the copper box on the hip opposite. The provost took up her quill again. No talk now of receptions, feasts with merchants, mass with the cardinal. Perhaps she first wanted to tell her son that his daughter was dead.

"A man who can't make sacrifices has lost before he starts, Provost. There was a time when I could spend the lives of those around me without care. Now, sometimes, I care. Sometimes it hurts." I thought for a moment of the Nuban falling away after I shot him. "But that doesn't mean that I can't and won't sacrifice absolutely anything rather than allow it to be used to rule me, rather than have it be made into a way to lose."

"Well now, there's an attitude that will serve you well at Congression, King Jorg." The provost offered me a grim smile, tight in the creases of her face.

"Your granddaughter though was not something I gave up to advance my cause. I did my best to save her from pain."

The provost took a scroll and dipped her quill. "These Perros will face justice soon enough." She shot me a cold look. "These road-brothers. This order will send enough of the city guard to hang them all."

"They're all dead, I believe. Perhaps one or two escaped." I remembered flinging the hatchet, the man's arms thrown up as he fell, the second runner vanishing over the rise. "One." I wanted to go back and hunt him down myself. With effort I unclenched my jaw and met the provost's gaze.

"We know of the Perros Viciosos in Albaseat, King Jorg. Tales are brought through our gates, many tales."

"Well, let them add that to Lesha's own story. At the last she brought an end to the Bad Dogs and saved many others from their predations. And I was the end she brought them." I thought perhaps Lesha might have approved of that.

The provost shook her head, just a fraction, telling me her disbelief without words. "It can't be that there are less than scores in that band, not with the trouble they have caused, the atrocities . . ."

"Two dozen, a few more perhaps." I shrugged. "It doesn't take many hands or much imagination to build a reputation on blood and horror."

"Two dozen—and yet you killed all but one?" The provost arched a brow and set her quill down again as if unwilling to record a falsehood.

"Dear lady, I killed them from youngest child to oldest woman, and when I was done I blunted three axes dismembering their corpses. I am Jorg of Ancrath—I burned ten thousand in Gelleth and didn't think it too many."

I gave her my bow and turned to leave. The men at the door, wide and gleaming in the black scales of their armour, stepped aside sharply.

28

Five years earlier

I turned fifteen on the voyage to Afrique. I had always imagined such a journey as an endurance at sea, like the storm-tossed odysseys of legend that end clinging to a raft of wreckage, hidden from the sun by a square of tarpaulin, on the point of drinking your own urine as the faint haze of land rises over the horizon.

The truth is that from Albaseat you can travel by good roads through the kingdoms of Kadiz and Kordoba and come to the Kordoban coast where a promontory ends in a vast rock miles wide—Tariq's Mountain. Look south from the watchtowers on the heights of this wave-lapped mountain, across two dozen miles of ocean, and the shores of Afrique may be seen, bare peaks rising in challenge above a morning sea mist. Look west, across Tariq Bay and you'll see Port Albus where many ships wait to carry a man with gold in his pocket to whatever corner of the Earth he desires.

It isn't that Afrique is so far away that gives her mystery. From the realms of the Horse Coast you can almost reach out to touch her, but as I've learned with Katherine, touching is not knowing. The fringes of Maroc may be seen from the watchtowers of the Rock, but the vastness of Afrique sprawls south so far that at its extreme are regions more distant from the Horse Coast than the frozen north of the Jarls, as far as Utter in the east, as far even as the Great Lands of the West across the ocean.

In short then I was at sea for only a day, and on that day, midway between two continents, out of sight of all land—thanks to the persistence of the coastal mists—the hour of my birth came and went and I entered my fifteenth year.

I had arrived at Port Albus burned dark by the Kordoban sun, which in truth is much the same as the sun of Kadiz and of Wennith and of Morrow, though the Kordobans like to claim it as their own. I negotiated passage across the straits on quays thronged with as many Moors, Nubans, and men of Araby as with men of the Horse Coast or Port Kingdoms. Captain Akham of the *Keshaf* agreed to carry me that morning. I waited while thick-muscled Nubans, black as trolls, brought ashore the last of his cargo. They stacked up white salt-blocks thick as a hand span and a foot square, carried from the unknown across great deserts on camel trains. And beside them, baskets of fruit from the groves of Maroc. Lemons larger than any I'd held, and objects picked from no tree I had seen before. I had a stevedore name them for me, pineapple, star fruit, hairy lychee. I bought one of each for two copper stallions, both a little crimped, and went aboard an hour later with sticky hands, sticky face, sticky dagger, and a mouth wanting to taste more of foreign shores.

While I waited and ate my fruit a man joined me at the barrel-stack, just opposite the gangway. A man stranger than any on the quay, though by no means the furthest flung.

"Sir Jorg of Conaught." I sketched him a bow. "And you'll be a Florentine?"

He nodded, a curt motion beneath the tall cylinder of his hat. No part of his flesh showed, save his face, a plump and pasty white beneath the two-inch brim of that hat. How it didn't burn scarlet I don't know.

"I've not met a modern before." I hadn't liked the curtness of that nod so I spat out any politeness with the tough skin of the pineapple chunk I'd been chewing on.

He had nothing to say to that and looked away to where two men struggled with his luggage, a large trunk, covered with the same black fabric his frock coat, trews, waistcoat, and shirt appeared to have been cut from. A symphony in black with only his white cotton gloves and, of course, his pale face, to sour it. Sweat trickled along the side of his nose, his coat looked thick with it, shiny with human grease.

"A Florentine banker bound for Afrique with not a bodyguard in sight?" I asked. "I'll keep the footpads off you for a few days if you have the coin." I thought I might attract less attention as the guard to a man even more out of place than myself.

He glanced my way, failing to keep his distaste hidden. "Thank you, sir, no."

I shrugged, yawned, and rolled my head. I imagined the wideness and wildness of the world must be a shock to any of the banking clans after the swordless peace their clockwork soldiers maintained in Florence. The next piece of pineapple glistened on the point of my dagger—gone in one noisy mouthful.

"Your name, banker," I said.

"Marco Onstantos Evenaline of the House Gold, Mercantile Derivatives South."

"Well, good luck, Master Marco." I turned my back on him and followed his trunk onboard. He would probably need all the luck he could afford, but reason demanded that he must have something to him or he wouldn't have survived to get this far from the counting tables of the Florentines.

On the bleached white decks of the *Keshaf* I spent hours watching the swelling sea from the prow and discovered that though the south had stained me I would never be so dark that the sun couldn't burn me that bit more. The second half of the voyage found me skulking in the sails' shade.

"My lord?" The captain's boy with water in a leather mug.

I took it. Never refuse water in dry places—and there is no place more dry than the seas off Afrique. "My thanks." Thirst made me grateful.

I travelled as a down-at-heels knight rather than a king, with letters from my grandfather to ease passage where needed. Losing the weight of my title made life far more simple. I sipped the water and leaned back against coiled rope, more at ease than I had been in an age. I had had enough of formality in Albaseat, even if I did escape the threatened receptions. Better to learn the ways of empire incognito, from the streets, from the sewers if need be, than amongst the fountains and scented shade of the rich.

At times like these, finding peace in anonymity, I could only wonder, if I gained such pleasure in slipping the bonds of kingship why I kept repeating my claim to a greater throne, a heavier crown? With the creak of timbers about me, the flapping shade of the sails, and a cool sea-breeze to take the sweat away, replying to such questions came hard. My fingers found the answer. A copper box, thorn-patterned. Even here, in the wide blue sea, driven by restless winds, the child would find me, and though the box might hold the worst of my crimes, enough of them still roamed free, such that if I ever lingered too long, however bright a paradise I may have found, the past would catch me up, rise around me in a dark tide, and devour peace.

If you must run, have something to run toward, so it feels less like cowardice. And if you must run to something, why not make it the empire throne? Something suitably distant and unobtainable. After all, getting everything you wish for is nearly as dire a curse as having all your dreams come true.

Yusuf Malendra came to stand beside me at the ship's rail. A tall man, slim, the wind billowing his loose cottons around him. Captain Akham introduced us as I boarded, the only other passenger other than Marco and me, but since then he'd hidden himself away—a difficult feat on a small ship. The modern, Marco of the long title, had thrown up over the side almost before we left harbour, nearly losing that fancy hat of his. He vanished below decks soon after. Perhaps Yusuf had been hidden down there too.

"Impressive is it not?" He nodded toward the Rock—Tariq's Mountain, miles behind us yet still huge.

"Very. This Tariq must have been a great king," I said.

"Nobody knows. It's a very ancient name." He gripped the rail in both hands. "All our names are ancient. The Builders wrote their names in machines and now we can't read them. The suns burned all that was written on paper except the oldest of writings, that were stored in deep vaults, did you know that? The writings we found were the most precious, valued more for their antiquity than the secrets they held. When the lands became habitable and men crept back to them most of the records they recovered were the works of Greeks and Romans."

"So we're behind the Builders in all things, even names?" A short laugh escaped me.

For a while we watched the gulls wheel, listened to their cries.

"You are visiting a relative in Maroc?" he asked. "Getting married?"

"You think your ladies would like me?" I turned my burns toward him.

Yusuf shrugged. "Daughters marry who their fathers tell them to."

"And are you getting married?" I lifted my gaze from the slim and curving sword at his hip to the dark mass of his hair, an expanding confusion of tight curls, imprisoned with bone combs.

He threw his head back and laughed. "Questions for questions. You're a man who's spent time at court." He let the swell lean him back into the rail and shot me a shrewd look. "I'm too old for more wives, Sir Jorg, and you perhaps think yourself too young for the first?" Dark lips framed his smile, darker than the caramel of his skin. I guessed he might be thirty, certainly no older.

I shrugged. "Surely too young for any more. And to satisfy your curiosity, Lord Yusuf, I am merely travelling to see what the world has to offer."

A wave slapped the hull sending up an unexpected spray over both of us.

The Marocan wiped his face. "Salty! Let's hope the world has better to offer than that, no?" Again the grin, teeth long, even, and curiously grey.

I grinned back. An odyssey would have been all right with me, barring the drifting wreckage and the consumption of urine. One day at sea was too few. Besides, entering a new world deserves a journey of consequence, not just a hop across a thirty-mile channel.

"You will come and stay with me, Sir Jorg. I have a beautiful home. Come with me when we disembark. Let it not be said Maroc offers a poor welcome. I insist. And you can tell us what you hope to find in Afrique."

"You honour me," I said.

We stood without speaking for a time, watching the gulls again and the white-flecked waves, until at last the distant mist and haze offered up the mountains once more, the jagged coast of a new world. I wondered what I would tell my hosts when they asked at table what brought me there. I could give away my rank and speak of Congression, of how the provost of Albaseat put into my mind that in Vyene the empire throne might be won in a different kind of game, with less bloodshed and more lying. And that to play in this new game I needed to know more about the key figures in the Hundred, more than they chose to show before the Gilden Gates. I could perhaps speak of the Prince of Arrow. Of how, more than the wind in the *Keshaf*'s sails, his derision drove me to see the borders of empire for myself, to know what I would own, to give me better reasons for wanting it. And at the last, if foolishness took hold, I might speak of Ibn Fayed and of a mathmagician named Qalasadi. I had spent years in pursuit of revenge against an uncle who killed my mother and brother, and here was a man who would have slain all my mother's kin in one night and left me holding the blame. Surely he deserved no better than Uncle Renar got?

The port of Kutta sprawled across a long and dusty arc of coastline, hemmed between the sea and mountains that launched skyward, browns and dark clumps of greenery soon giving way to bare rock. We stepped ashore onto a long and rickety quay crammed with so many people it seemed that at any given moment a dozen of them threatened to fall into the water. I let Yusuf forge a path. The balance between the force that may be exerted in such endeavours and the nature of the response when offence is taken varies with geography. Rather than pitch headlong into a pointless fight mere yards into what I planned to be a long journey through Afrique, I let myself be led, and kept close and watchful.

There seemed no reason for the crowd, all of them but the half-naked Nubans swathed head to foot in robes, either white or black, most turbaned in the Maroc way, the shesh covering head and face, leaving just eyes to contend with. The noise also! A wall of sound, a harsh jabber, half-threat, half-joke. Maybe the peace of the voyage made it seem so, or it's that a throng is more raucous when the language is unknown to you, or perhaps just the heat and press of bodies amplified the clamour. Struggling behind Yusuf in that mass of humanity I knew that for the first time I had stepped into somewhere truly foreign. A place where they spoke a different tongue, where minds ran different paths. Maroc had been part of empire for centuries, its lords attended Congression still, but for the first time I had entered a realm that bordered kingdoms not ever part of empire. A place where "empire" would not suffice but needed to be qualified with "holy" for they knew of other empires. In Utter they call us "Christendom" but in Maroc we are the Holy Empire, more fitting since nineteen in every twenty of Maroc's people answer the adhan call when the muezzin sing from their minarets.

The crowd even had a different stink to it, spices overwriting any odour of unwashed bodies, mint, coriander, sesame, turmeric, ginger, pepper, others unknown, carried on the men themselves as if they sweated it out.

"Keep up, Sir Jorg!" Yusuf grinned over his shoulder. "Show but the slightest interest and you'll be penniless by the time we reach the java house, laden down with rugs, brass lamps, enough dreamweed to kill a camel, and a hooka to smoke it through."

"No." I pushed aside embroidered rugs from two salesmen, passing between them as if through a curtained entrance. "No." They spoke empire tongue well enough when a sale stood in the offing. "No." Once more and we were through, crossing a wide and dusty square pursued by barefoot yammering children wearing dirty linens and clean smiles.

Hemming the far side of the square a dozen or so java houses opened with tables sprawling out into the shade from awnings in faded green and red, behind us the quays and ships—boats mainly, the larger ships tying up at more substantial quays before great warehouses further around the bay.

Apart from the children in their whites, and what could be old women or old men hunched in black wrappings, set on various slow journeys along the shaded margins of the square, nothing moved. The crowds through which we forged a path remained resolutely jammed along the narrow stilted walkways, their cacophony hushed behind us, mixed with the gentle threshing of ocean waves against breakwaters. The sun's heat pushed down, an immense hand, making even the flies struggle, stripped of their frenzy, languid almost.

A man approached us from one of the alleys between the shops, leading three horses, a tall araby stallion and two mares, all pale. Five such stallions had been part of the compensation Father accepted for Mother's and William's deaths.

"My man, Kalal. We can ride to my estate, or sit awhile first and watch the sea." Yusuf gestured at the nearest and grandest of the java houses. "You'll like the java in Maroc, Sir Jorg. Hot and sweet and strong."

I didn't like the java in Ancrath or Renar, cold and sour and weak, and expensive, above all expensive. I doubted increasing its strength would change my opinion. Yusuf must have read my frown, though I had thought myself good at writing on my face only what I chose.

"They serve teas also. And I could introduce you to our national sport," he said.

"Tea sounds promising." Never refuse a drink in a dry place. "And this sport, does it involve camels?"

Both men laughed at that. Kalal, perhaps a kinsman, had the same colouring and, when he laughed, the same faintly grey teeth.

"Dice, my friend." Yusuf set an arm about my shoulders. "No camels. It is the game of twelve lines. Do you know it?"

"No," I said. "Show me."

Yusuf steered me toward the tables where old men sat in white robes and red fez, smoking from their water-pipes, sipping from small cups, bent across their boards of triangles, counters, and dice. He barked two harsh words in the Berber tongue and Kalal led the horses off with one last grey grin.

"A game of chance?" I asked. Dice rattled in their shakers as we approached.

"A game of calculation, my friend. Of probability."

I thought then of Qalasadi's black smile, of how the mathmagicans despite their science of numbers still kept to tradition and mystery to instil a magic beyond mere arithmetic. I wondered how such teeth might look with the stain of the betel leaf scoured away. Grey perhaps?

"Yes," I said. "I would like to play such a game. Tell me the rules. I always like to know the rules."

29

Five years earlier

The board lay between us, the game of twelve lines, counters marshalled, dice ready in the cup. I knew the rules well enough: we had the game in Ancrath, almost the same but named battamon. Yusuf's explanation of the mechanics gave me time to study him, to consider my options. The way he spoke of the game, of the combinations, the scatter of odds, and the basic strategies, all marked him out as a mathmagician. If not for the teeth though I might not have done my own arithmetic and added the two and the two.

"Why don't you go first?" I said.

He took the shaker and rattled the dice.

Clearly they had done their sums, worked a little magic, and anticipated me. Had they predicted me with certainty, or just mapped out the paths that I might take, weighted them with probabilities, and deployed their resources appropriately? Either way it unsettled me to find myself the subject of calculation.

Yusuf threw the dice, a three and a three. His hand moved almost too fast to see, clicking counters along the board.

"Don't expect me to do well, I'm a slow study." I took the shaker and dice from him.

The Moor seemed relaxed. He could afford to be if he had me figured out, if he knew before I did what course I would take. How many slates had they covered with their equations, how many men passing their calculations back and forth to balance and simplify my terms? Did they know already at what point I might draw steel for an attack? Did a man stand ready for it at a dark window, crossbow wound and aimed at the spot I would choose? Did they know the hour when I might elect to slip away, or the direction I would take? If they all had Qalasadi's skill I would not be surprised to find they had already written down the next words to come from my mouth.

"Well, that's not good!" A one and a two. I advanced my counters.

Yusuf shook the dice. All around us men played the game, smoked, sipped their dark and bitter brews. From time to time a face would turn my way, lined and sun-stained, usually the grey hairs outnumbering the black. No smiles for the traveller here, nothing to read from those incurious eyes. I wondered how many of them worked for Qalasadi? All of them. Only Yusuf and his servant?

I could stand and make for the *Keshaf*, still tied at the quay. But they already knew if I would or not. Maddening.

Yusuf threw and took his move. White counters sweeping around the board. My tea arrived, and his java. Would it be poisoned? I lifted it to my lips.

"Oranges?"

"It is scented with the blossom of the orange tree," Yusuf agreed.

If they had wanted me poisoned the deck-boy on the *Keshaf* could have put powders in the water he brought me. I touched the cup to my lips, a thin work of porcelain set round with a delicate pattern of diamonds. They would want me as a hostage for Ibn Fayed's war against my grandfather.

The tea tasted good. I threw the dice and made my moves, taking longer than I needed to puzzle them. Yusuf's next moves seemed wrong to me, not foolish, but overcautious. I reminded myself that even mathmagicians are fallible. They had meant to poison Grandfather, and yet he lived. They had meant to further Ibn Fayed's cause, and yet a dozen and more highborn deaths along the Horse Coast were now piled at his door, dishonourable killings. The stench of them tainted his house.

I rolled the dice. Six and four.

Beneath the table my fingers curled around the hilt of my dagger. "Do you know what I'm going to do next, Lord Yusuf?" I asked.

I could have the blade in his throat quicker than quick.

A slow smile. "No, but I can guess."

I took my move.

Yusuf hesitated a moment before scooping the dice into the cup. A frown creased his forehead. Perhaps he was recalculating.

While the Moor took his go I made a mental list. A list of six options, choices other men might make.

1) Rike: Reach out, catch Yusuf behind the head and slam his face very hard into the table. Go with the flow thereafter.
2) Makin: Make a new friend. Turn on the charm.
3) Gorgoth: Part company without fuss. Take a path to protect those most depending on me.
4) Father: Purchase whichever loyalties can be bought.
Dispense whatever justice can be paid out without loss.
Return home to consolidate my strengths.
5) Gomst: Pray for guidance. Follow Yusuf, obey the rules, run when a chance presents itself.
6) Sim: Show no defiance. Go with Yusuf and his man. Murder them both in a lonely spot. Continue on disguised as the Moor.

The dice came my way again. I picked one out. If I let the die choose, if I let chance decide among unlikely options, that might break the network of prediction that had me snared.

"Maybe one at a time will improve my luck," I said.

Yusuf smiled but said nothing, watching with intent.

I rolled the die. Predict this!

A two. Make a friend? Damn that!

I set the second cube spinning across the table. *Alea iacta est*, as Caesar put it. The die is cast. I would tie my fate to this one.

It spun for an age on one corner, caught an edge, clattered off the table. Yusuf bent to follow it and brought it up in his hand. "Another two!"

Damnation.

I moved my counters, hoping for some kind of inspiration. Yusuf was already pretending to be my friend. How to turn that into something real I hadn't a clue. In fact I wasn't entirely sure I understood the difference.

A disturbance in the white heat outside caught my eye. A hunch-backed giant in black mobbed by a sudden crowd? No, mobbed by children, a man surrounded by ragged children as he dragged something across the square.

"Your pardon, Yusuf." I stood, rewarded by momentary confusion in the Moor's eyes.

Short steps and sharp turns brought me through the clustered tables and into the sunlight. The modern in his blacks, his hat dangerously askew, pulled on his trunk whilst the children, mocked, taunted, threw pebbles, or tried fishing in his pockets.

"A friend in need . . ." I shrugged and strode across, raising my arms and doing a passable impression of Rike scaring chickens to death. The children scattered and the modern managed to slip, losing his hat in the process. I scooped it up and had it ready as he got to his feet.

"Marco Onstantos Evenaline of the House Gold, Mercantile Derivatives South," I said. "How the hell are you?" And I handed over his ridiculous hat.

I hadn't formed an impression of the modern's age on the ship and even now it was hard to pin down. Beneath that hat Marco maintained a wispy comb-over, pale hair failing to hide a fish-belly scalp. The style demonstrated a talent for self-deception—such a man could forgive himself anything.

"My thanks."

I'd never heard thanks offered with less gratitude.

After close and suspicious examination of his headgear Marco settled it back in place and dusted down his jacket.

"The House Gold can't stretch to a porter and a guard?" I asked, watching a couple of the boldest urchins edge from the shadows again.

"Not one at the quay could speak the empire tongue." Marco frowned. "They wouldn't take my coin."

"Well, I already told you I'd take your coin, banker." I gave him what I hoped might be a friendly smile. I'm not used to pretending to like people. "And I speak six languages." I didn't mention that none of those were Moorish, but I find hand gestures and a sharp edge go a long way toward cutting through misunderstanding.

"No," he said, quick enough that I thought he must have seen me for what I was the moment he laid those small black eyes upon me.

"I'll help you without charge, gratis, pro bono." I tried a different smile, imagining Sir Makin stepping ashore with a joke to hand. "You could use a friend, now couldn't you, Marco?"

At the last, still heavy with mistrust, the banker managed a smile, as ugly as mine felt. "You can bring my trunk and find us some transport." He held out a hand in its white cotton glove. "Friend."

I met his grip, a soft one, moist despite the glove, and released him quick enough. "And where are we bound, Marco?"

"Hamada." He pronounced the word carefully.

"And what's in Hamada?" I kept close watch on that pasty face, wondering once more if I were playing a game of chance or if chance were playing a game with me.

"Banking business," he said, pressing thin lips thinner.

I nodded. Ibn Fayed had his palace in Hamada. There would be no banking business in that city that was not also Ibn Fayed's business.

The banker's trunk weighed far more than I had expected. I put my back into it and hauled it toward the java house, with new respect for the modern's strength. I'd worked up a good sweat by the time we reached the shade.

"If you'll attend the trunk for a moment, Marco, I will make my apologies to Lord Yusuf."

I found Yusuf studying the board, his java cup resting at his lips.

"I'm not a lord you know, Sir Jorg. We have our rulers on the north coast, sultans, caliphs, emperors, all sorts. And below that we have a vast array of princes, more than you can count, some as poor as mice. Anyone you meet with silks or a jewel who does not declare themselves a merchant will be a prince. And beneath the princes, beneath the ones with lands and great houses at least, you have the friends of princes, most often soldiers, but sometimes sages. When our patron calls we are at their service—when they do not call we are our own men.

"So, you will journey with this modern? You should come to my home, meet my wives, eat pomegranate, try roast peacock. But you won't. Travel with the modern then, and take a care, my friend. The man is not welcome. No harm will be done to him but the desert is a hard place without the support of fellow men. And strangers, men like yourselves from gentler lands, will die in the Margins before you even reach the sand."

I held out my hand and he took it, his grip firm and dry. "Sometimes men must take their chances," I said, and leaning in I took the nearest die. "If I may. You never know when one of these might save your life."

"Go with God, Jorg of Ancrath," he said and returned to the study of the board.

30

Five years earlier

Marco stood beside his trunk, stiff, uncomfortable in his frock coat.

"Is there a law says you can't take that off?" I grinned and took hold of his half-ton trunk.

"Your breastplate must chafe in this heat, Sir Jorg?"

I had strapped it back on as we came into port. Not something to go overboard in, but worth suffering ashore.

"The blacks will stop a dagger thrust?" I asked.

"Tradition will stop anyone from trying," Marco said.

The banking clan privileges hadn't meant much to me as a road-brother but certainly in the courts of the Hundred and in the corridors of Vyene they were afforded protections above that of kings.

"Let's find us some transport." I nodded down the largest of the alleys leading from the plaza. All the streets in Kutta looked to be narrow, hemmed in by tall buildings to manufacture shade. A tight fit for wagons, but the serious cargos would be unloaded further down the coast at Tanjer, a larger and more commercial port.

Marco followed me, keeping his distance as if spurning my protection and putting me firmly into the role of porter. Perhaps he was safer than I. Men everywhere knew that to strike down a modern was to open an account with the clans, and that gold would spill from Florentine coffers until the debt had been paid, the ledgers balanced.

In a broken empire though, the promise of eventual death on an assassin's blade proved less protection than the bankers might have hoped when set against the certainty of immediate gold. Perhaps in less wild and more honourable lands the moderns' traditions offered more surety. Certainly the Moors held merchants in high esteem and kept better order than we did in the lands closer to Vyene.

Dragging that trunk in search of stables, my decision to leave Brath safe in the care of a Port Albus farrier seemed more foolish by the yard. By the time we reached what I was looking for the curses were spitting from me, sweat dripping, arms burning. It appeared to be a stable of sorts. Camels lounged around a covered water-trough, mangy beasts with clumped collars of moulting fur and cracked skin around their knees. I'd met a camel before, long ago in Dr. Taproot's circus. A surly creature, ungainly and given to spitting. These looked no better.

"Wait there." I stood Marco out of sight.

I knocked at a door of bleached and fractured planks, answered in time by an old man with one milky eye. In the shadows behind him I heard the snort and clomp of horses.

"*As-salamu alaykum.*" I wished peace upon the old thief. All horse-traders are thieves. "Two mounts and a pack-mule." I held up three fingers and in the other hand a gold florin stamped with Grandfather's face, and I finished with, "*Insha'allah.*" Thereby exhausting all the local phrases I'd learned from Yusuf on our crossing.

He watched me with his good eye, running fingers over his chin, white stubble, skin the colour of java and milk. A shadow fell across us, a man on camelback. I glanced at him, a warrior riding high on the saddled hump, all black wrappings, just the flash of eyes in the slit of his shesh. He moved on.

"Two horses," I repeated.

The old trader spouted gibberish at me and waved his hand in negation. He knew what I wanted, nobody with something to sell in Kutta lacks the rudiments of empire tongue required to conduct a sale.

"Two!" I added a second coin and rubbed them between finger and thumb.

It hurt him to do it but he shook his head and stamped off muttering. The door shuddered closed.

"They really don't want you getting to Hamada, Marco."

I crossed over to him. He scowled each time I said his name, flinching at some breach of manners, some over-familiarity. "Marco," I said, leaning close enough to smell the sourness of him, "it's a long walk. Have you no friends in Kutta?"

"No," he said.

I wondered if he had any friends anywhere. Heading off across the desert to Hamada with him, horses or no horses, seemed a fool's errand. Someone with influence, quite possibly Ibn Fayed himself, did not want Marco to get there. Moreover, at least three mathmagicians appeared to have anticipated my arrival, which meant that Ibn Fayed knew my intentions. The only sensible course of action was to turn around and sail for Port Albus. Except that such a move would be encompassed in the calculations carried out long before my arrival by Yusuf, Qalasadi, and others. To behave as predicted would only draw me deeper into their net. Perhaps into an arrest at the docks, or an accident at sea—arranged for my return trip whilst I had been playing the game of twelve lines and sipping tea. Coming here in the first place had been a misjudgment—in truth an arrogance, a child's conceit.

"So what would you have me do, Marco?" Abandoning him to his fate seemed the most sensible choice. But the die had told me to make a new friend, and sensible choices were predictable choices, which this far into the net would like as not get me killed.

"I'll need a room."

"That I can do."

I went alone, collared a street urchin and let a copper coin lead us both to a guesthouse. The heavy and ancient door the boy took me to looked unpromising, sitting alone in a wide blank wall. When I knocked, a woman glared at us through the grille. A crone, older than the bleached wood and rusted nails she hauled open. Too wrinkled and bent to need a veil to keep her modest she cast a disapproving eye over me and led on in. The interior surprised me. A short corridor led to an inner courtyard where lemon trees grew in the shade of balconies rising four storeys on each side. Enamelled tiles decorated all surfaces, blue and white, geometrically patterned. An illusion of coolness, if not actual coolness.

I took two rooms, paid in coppers from half a dozen nations, and went to fetch Marco. He had waited where the crone couldn't see him through the grille and I let her complaints, the sharp and the guttural, run off me as I hauled his trunk through, the modern following in my wake.

"It's too small," Marco said. Sweat ran off him in rivers but it didn't seem to bother him. I'd yet to see him drink. I wondered if soon he'd start to shrivel. Something about him called to the death-magic in me, to the necromancer's heart. It tingled at my fingertips.

"Too small for what?" I collapsed onto the trunk. Dragging it up two flights of stairs had half-killed me.

Marco scowled. I had expected bankers, especially travelling bankers, to be closer to diplomats, masters of their own demeanour, but this one made no effort to hide his distaste for me. Perhaps he hoarded his charm along with his gold, for I'd yet to see so much as a glint of either.

"You owe me for the room, and the guide, banker."

"Guide? A child in rags led you off."

"A child that I paid," I said, still flat out on the trunk.

"I am keeping tally, Sir Jorg. Now, if you will afford me some privacy . . ."

I levered myself up and went to my room where I collapsed again. I lay with closed eyes imagining the sharp winds over the icy shoulders of Halradra. In six months I had crossed half the empire. And like Goldilocks with her bears and porridge, I'd found parts too hot and parts too cold. And for the first time I wanted to be back in the Highlands, back where it felt just right. For the first time I thought of my kingdom as home.

When you stare at the cracked blankness of a ceiling your mind will wander. Mine made a list. A list of reasons that brought me here. A list of the answers I would give to that question. None of them sufficient on their own but together a compelling force that had driven me into this foolishness. Orrin of Arrow had sent me, with his talk of oceans and distant lands. Perhaps I thought that with broad horizons of my own I could capture some of whatever magic he held. Fexler Brews had sent me with his little red light, now blinking over the caliphate of Liba. Curiosity had led me into the Iberico and tied me to the Bad Dogs' torture pole. It would be fair to say curiosity had its hooks in me. Short of opening a certain box curiosity could get me to do most things. Qalasadi had sent me with his treachery. Ibn Fayed with his threat. Grandfather when he judged me worth saving and told me not to go. In the end perhaps, though I called it vengeance, it was not this time the need to strike back that drove me but the need to defend. I had a family.

Long ago my mother had charged me to look after William, to keep my little brother safe. And though I have failed many duties since, that was the first of my failures and the one that bit deepest— deeper than the thorns whose scars record the event. Like Marco I had ledgers to balance, and though this duty was a poor substitute, I would see it through. I had a family once more. That old man in his castle by the sea. The old woman who loved him and who had loved my mother. My uncle, soldier though he was. And no thorns to hold me back. A threat hung over them and this time nothing, man or monster or ghost, would keep me from saving them.

Clarity of vision is a thing much prized. I find when you turn that clear sight upon yourself—and see through to the truth behind your own actions—it might be better to be blind. For the bliss of ignorance I would tell myself that only vengeance drew me, as it did of old, when choice lay black and white like pieces on a board, and life was a simpler game.

The heat, the immediate quiet, and the faint sounds that distance made familiar—smoothed of their alien edges—all conspired to lull me to sleep. A buzzing brought me to my senses, reaching for the knife at my hip. Something on my chest? I slapped a hand to the hot metal of my breastplate. The buzz again, as if a huge fly had crawled beneath the armour and become trapped.

Cramped fingers found the buzzing thing between iron, cloth, and sweating flesh. I fished it out. The Builders' view-ring! I took the thong that held it from around my neck and let the ring make slow revolutions. It buzzed once more, tiny vibrations seen only as a blur-ring of the surface. I held it to my eye and at once the whole of the wall between my room and Marco's became overwritten with pulsing red light.

"Curious."

I moved to the wall and set my ear to it. The sounds of a conver-sation reached me, too indistinct to make out the words or even the language. Outside my window the balcony overlooking the lemon trees served all the rooms. I slipped out and edged to Marco's win-dow. He had the shutters closed.

Any in the courtyard below who chose to look up, or any guest on their balcony, would see me. However, the banking clan seemed less popular than genital warts in Kutta so I thought it unlikely that anyone would complain about my spying. In fact the lack of attention I was getting made me sure that they were all busy spying on me.

I set an eye to the shutter slats. I shouldn't have been able to see much, looking from the brightness of the day into the gloom of a shuttered room. The Builder ghost glowed with its own light though, described in whites from bone to magnolia, and so I had no trouble seeing it, or in seeing Marco, cast into pasty relief by the pale illumi-nation.

Spying is well and good, but in general I don't have the patience for it, and what patience I do have is soon lost when it gets hot. I dug my fingers between the slats and wrenched the shutters open. The catch came free and skittered across the floor, fetching up against the polished leather of Marco's shoe. I stepped in and closed the shutter behind me.

"So sorry." I sketched the faintest of bows. "But I really wanted to see what you were up to."

The modern staggered back, his face twisted halfway between murder and terror.

The trunk lay open at the centre of the room, the bed set on end and leaning against the door to make space. Inside, the sharkskin exterior gave over to metal, plasteek, and muted patterns of light beneath glass that reminded me of the hidden panel at the weapon vaults beneath Mount Honas.

"Ah, the aberration." This Builder ghost spoke with none of Fexler's warmth, dropping each word stillborn. He looked younger, maybe thirty, maybe forty, hard to tell in a picture drawn from shades of pale. His clothes too were different, many layers, close-tailored, buttons along the front, a breast pocket.

"Aberration? I like that. I've been called many things, but you're the first to use 'aberration.' And what should I call you, ghost?"

"Kill him!" Marco hissed, his hat held to his chest like a talisman.

"Well, that's no way to treat a friend." I gave Marco my smile, the one with edges, then looked to the data ghost. "Instead of that why don't you tell me how it is that you need Marco here to drag you halfway across Maroc when you should be able to look out of a thousand hidden eyes, step out of all manner of hidden doors in scores of nations? And what do you want with Ibn Fayed?"

"You may call me Michael." The ghost grinned, a smile selected from one of thousands stolen from the Michael made of flesh, a man now centuries old dust. A real smile but somehow wrong, as if sewn into position on a dead man's face. "And I need to be carried because

Ibn Fayed has a new faith—one that bids him seek out any trace of the Builders and erase it. Which of course answers your question about my business with him, Jorg."

"Well and good then. I too have business with the man. It's just the getting there that is proving problematic. Perhaps you have some wonder of the ancients that will fly us all there like birds?"

Marco snorted, managing contempt. But the Builders had flown. I knew it from my father's library.

"Well?" I asked. If this turn of events lay within the mathmagicians' calculations then I may as well have admitted defeat—but given that I didn't think it did fall within their plotting, I found renewed interest in crossing the desert to the court of Ibn Fayed with my two new friends.

"I can do better than that, Jorg of Ancrath," Michael said. "We can go by ship."

31

Sleep became a rare commodity after the arrival of our newest travel-ling companion. Day by day Gottering fell further behind us. On the fifth day, Captain Harran declared we would push on through the night to reach Honth by dawn. On that long and rumbling journey a moment of quiet visited and exhaustion dragged me down quicker than the mud of Cantanlona. Jolted by rutted miles, the occupants of Holland's carriage exchanged partners periodically. I rolled open a sleep-burred eye at one such bump to see Osser Gant's grey head cradled in the bishop's lap. Another lurch took my head from Miana's shoulder, another still put Katherine's head on mine.

In the darkness of my dreaming Katherine's skin burned against me, but we shared nothing save warmth. When she lifted me from my quiet nightmare of thorns and rain she gave no warning.

"Katherine?" I knew her touch. Perhaps my show and tell of childish woe hadn't scared her from my dreams as well as hoped. Perhaps like me she merely thought how stupid I had been to let old Bishop Murillo capture me in the first place. I have the church to thank for teaching me that last lesson in reading the signs, in seeing the trap rise around you, in never lowering your guard. A lesson that has served me well.

"Katherine?"

A dark hall. I moved through bars of moonlight behind shuttered windows. My head turned for me, my fingers trailed the wall without asking permission. Familiar. All of it familiar, the hall, the smell of the place, the roughness of the wall, and of course, the being trapped in another's head. Steps down, a long and winding stair.

"This is like that night at the Haunt—when the Pope's man came calling," I said, though no lips moved to speak my words.

The end of the stair. I turned a corner. Familiar, but not the Haunt. More steps down. My hand—his hand—took an oil lamp from its niche.

"Katherine!" I made my silent voice louder, more demanding.

"Ssh! You'll wake him, you idiot." Her voice seemed to come from a deep place.

"Wake who?"

"Robart Hool of course! Your spy back at the Tall Castle."

A door. Hool's fingers on the black iron of its handle.

"If he's my spy why are you using him?" Espionage was never my forte but I had been rather proud of having a man so high in the king's guard on my payroll. Until now.

"Sageous opened him up to true-dreams," Katherine said from her well. "He sleepwalks and the castle guard know not to wake him or there can be trouble. He's good with a sword. I use him so I can watch over Sareth when I'm not there."

"And now—"

"Ssh!"

"But—"

"Shut. Up."

Hool moved through the doorway and along a corridor, shadows swinging around him. We came to the Short Bridge, a yard of mahogany crossing over the recess from which a steel door could be summoned to seal the vaults. He crossed over and started down the steps beyond.

It grew colder. We were no longer in the keep of the Tall Castle but below it in a long Builder-made corridor that leads by zigs and zags through the upper vaults to an ancient annex excavated by the dear departed House of Or. Built to house their dead. Less ancient than the castle itself of course, but having the decency to wear its years more openly. In the tomb-vault the walls ran with cracks and in places the stone facings had fallen to reveal rough-hewn rock scarred by pick marks.

Hool's feet slapped bare on cold stone, his nightclothes thin comfort against the subterranean chill, but his scabbard bumped against his legs, a better kind of comfort altogether. Sleepwalking or no, a swordsman always buckles on his blade. Makin taught him well, back in the days of wooden swords in the courtyard. I hope he'd learned the lesson I taught him too, that afternoon in the duelling square when I stepped outside the rules of the game and felled him with a punch to the throat.

Hool's footsteps echoed and his breath steamed before him. When the Ancraths displaced the Ors my ancestors were quick to empty the mausoleum, turning out each sepulchre ready for fresher occupants. And in time we started to fill the place. The old statues were replaced, or sometimes just altered. With creditable economy and lack of sentiment my great-grandfather had the masons chip the moustache from the founder of the Or dynasty, reshape his nose a little, and stand over my great-great-grandfather's corpse in passable representation of the man.

If Katherine used Hool to watch over Sareth, why were we in the tomb vault? Unless of course Sareth had died? What did Katherine want to show me? Another death to stain my hands? Or was she leading me to the place where she had me dragged on the day I returned from Gelleth, where she took me to keep my father from finishing what he started? Reminding me of the life I owed her? He would have cut my heart out if that had been required to stop it from beating, I know that much. Were we returning to Mother's tomb?

The image of a sunlit surface woke in me. A surface high above me. The pressure of cold water. And floating from those depths came a memory that seemed less real now in the Tall Castle, in the house of the Ancrath dead, than it had in the mists of Gottering. My father was dead? I hadn't spoken of it to anyone. Katherine had shown me ghosts were made of dreams. The lichkin could have lied to me—she must have been lying to me. That old man was too mean to die. Especially a soft death in the comfort of a bed. Was that where we were going? Had we come for that? To see him in his tomb?

We turned a corner to see a light vanishing around the next turn thirty yards ahead. I caught a glimpse of two men at the rear of the party before the corner took them. Something wrong about them— something familiar. The air held a sour reek.

People heading to the tombs. To where Mother and William lay beneath marble lids. Behind enchanted seals.

Hool sped up, no urgency in his movement, just a quicker pace, Katherine's touch light enough not to wake him, firm enough for acceleration. At the next turn we had clear view of the last three figures. Each a thing of sunken flesh, stained dark, not by sun but by mire, hair lank and patched, hanging down across black rags. They carried pipes and darts. Mire-ghouls.

How would such creatures have penetrated the castle? Why hadn't Katherine raised the alarm when she had the chance?

Another turn, the end of the Builder corridors, entering the decaying works of Or now.

Why hadn't Katherine raised the alarm? Because that would wake Hool up and she'd lose her eyes in Ancrath, she wouldn't know the reasons. And after all, reasons can be worth their weight in gold. Fexler had sent me to his tomb to put a proper end to his remains, to bring him into his full strength. The dead were not so different. Necromancers returned them to their flesh or bones to find their strength once more. But what drew them here?

Dust hushed Hool's footsteps now. Unlike every other cellar in

Crath City, mouldering and dank, some magic in the Builder foundations kept the vaults dry as bones. A parched and whispering place like the dry-lands where souls fall.

The oldest of my relatives lay furthest back, great-great-grandfather, great-grandfather, grandfather, wives, brothers, sisters, also lesser-born Ancraths who were, despite the cardinal sin of their birth, great champions. A horde of them, all but forgotten. Statued relics staring into dark infinity above old bones. But the glow came from a closer set of steps leading to a chamber better known to me.

Robart Hool's fingers closed around the hilt of his sword.

"Don't! He'll wake up!" Katherine's voice, in my ear or in his, I couldn't tell.

The sword whispered from its sheath, a decent blade from the forge of Samath down by the Bridge of Change, runed for sharpness. Ahead of us the ghouls would be entering Mother's tomb.

"I won't let him." Quite how I would stop Hool waking wasn't something that concerned me. Perhaps just wanting it enough would make it happen in this world the Builders had left us. Though whatever Fexler said it seemed that wanting seldom made it so.

Katherine had set Hool striding—I made him sprint, whipping his sword in a figure eight to get a sense of its weight and balance. I don't know quite how I worked his strings. It's possible Katherine took pity on me and lent her strength, but I've found that when my blood kin are threatened, even when they're dead already, my will takes on an edge.

When you've committed yourself to violence it takes an almost inhuman effort to stop short. It's one of those things that once you've started need to be finished, rather like coitus, interrupting that's a sin, even the priests say so. I stopped though, and Robart Hool didn't wake. Charging in would likely provide a fresh corpse for the ghouls, and whatever friends might be accompanying them, to play with. But to raise the alarm might take us too far away, take too long, and let the invaders escape with whatever prize they came for.

Instead I ran Hool back up the corridor, up the steps, to the Short Bridge. He reached it breathing more heavily but not winded. In wall recesses to either side of the bridge lay silver panels with smooth silver buttons. Some combination of the buttons would raise the door, an implacable slab of Builder steel from which a thousand swords might be forged—one of the Ancrath treasures.

I'd never seen the door raised. No one had ever told me which buttons to push.

"Father never dreamed the combination for you I suppose?" I asked.

Katherine didn't reply but Hool shuddered for her. I wondered if Father's dreams were too dark for her to tread.

"Fuck it."

I drove Hool's blade through the panel. The door slammed up with such speed that one of the balanced planks hadn't time to fall away. It became splinters. Along the corridor behind me glow-bulbs flickered on in several places, creating islands of reddish light. In some distant place a siren started up, sounding for all the world like the voice of the Connath watchtower, though I doubted three strong men had taken to the winding handle of some similar device. This voice came more crisp, more clear, the work of a more ancient machine. Where the running and the stabbing and the crashing of steel doors had failed, this distant wailing started to undo my grip on Hool, peeling my fingers back one at a time, lifting him from sleep as if he were a diver in some dark sea now struggling for the shimmer of the surface. I pressed him down again, the action pushing me toward that surface, at once both close and far away. The sounds of the carriage started to leak into my ears, the creak of the frame, rumble of wheels, Gomst's snores.

"No."

Hool and I ran back, bare feet slapping, following the turns as if remembering a waking dream that is slipping through your grasp even as you seize it.

Close now. One more corner.

Darts came hissing out of the darkness. One struck the oil lamp and glanced away. The other sunk into Hool's chest, the thick pectoral muscle on the left. A small red circle grew around the black shaft of it.

Keep running. Keep dreaming.

Hool proved to be too fast on his feet and the line of sight too short for a second volley. He threw the lamp and raced after it rather than run while splashing oil with each step. The lamp shattered against the wall where the corridor turned, the bloom of fire silhouetting two ghouls, lurking at the corner, quick fingers pushing new darts into their blowpipes. He reached them as they drew breath for their shots. The swing of his sword destroyed both pipes. They moved swift and sure, these creatures, different from the dead men Chella set walking, corrupt but alive, once men perhaps but shaped by the poisons of the promised lands.

Both leapt for us, and Hool's next slash opened one in the air, shoulder to hip, pale grey guts slopping out in a welter of black blood. The other bore him to the ground, talons in his shoulders, grey teeth filed to points snapping before his face. With the sword trapped between us and the ghoul Hool could do little but roll and push. The creature hadn't much weight to it, maybe half of what a grown man might weigh, but its wiry limbs held a fearsome strength. Its breath stank of graves, and those teeth straining so hard to close on flesh put a horror in me even though it wasn't my face it wanted to eat off the bone.

Desperation lent Hool the brute force needed to win free. He lifted himself off the ghoul using the sword between them as a bar. Its talons raked his shoulders, the blood spattering down across its chest. Panting and cursing Hool pinned the ghoul with his knees and turned the blade to skewer it through the neck.

He cast around, wild, lost. It occurred to me that despite the blood spilling down our chest, soaking scarlet into our nightshirt, I felt no pain.

"Jorg! Wake up!" Katherine's voice in my ear, the warmth of her breath on my neck, the rumble of the carriage behind her.

No.

Hool turned to follow on.

No.

I pushed the image of the dart into his eyes, hanging to him by fingertips.

He reached to pull it free. The thing held tight, tenting his flesh around it as he tugged. *Just a thorn! One sharp yank, rip it out barbs and all, let it bleed clean.* And he did.

"God damn it!" He spat blood, looked around again. "Where the hell?" I felt his lips move, felt Katherine shaking me half a thousand miles away.

Images from his dream got him moving again. Things he'd seen with his own sleeping eyes. The door sealing the vaults, a third ghoul, maybe more entering the Ancrath tombs. I fed him my anger too, burning against the numbness that would be tingling in his fingers by now.

Not so far ahead, the sound of a hammer striking iron, again and again.

Somehow I hung on as he ran, leaving the dying glow of the broken lamp behind us. A hard left into darkness and ahead of us, in the stolen burial chambers of the House of Or, another glow. Slower now. Slow, up the steps to Mother's tomb, the intruders' light catching gleams from Hool's blade, still slick with the black blood of ghouls.

And there in the light of a single lantern, a third ghoul and three dead men, their stained flesh marked with the scale tattoos of Brettan sailors, all of them watching the fifth of their party, a pale man, black-cloaked, black-cowled, kneeling by the smaller of the two sarcophagi, chipping with hammer and chisel at the runes set around its lid.

To his credit Hool made no challenge or battle-cry. He moved in behind them without hesitation, lined up his swing, and carved half-way through the ghoul's head. Even as Hool attacked I wondered at the dead men watching. The minds of such things are filled with the worst of what once lived there, and idle curiosity is not a sin, at least not one dark enough to return to a corpse. And yet they watched the tomb, avid, careless. Hool wrenched his blade free and hacked the head from the first of the dead men before the other two turned. Not a perfect swing, but he had some skill, did Master Hool and while his sword kept its fine-honed edge it would forgive him his minor errors.

The dead men came at him, faster than I had hoped. Released from their fascination with my brother's tomb they proved a different proposition from the shambling dead more often encountered. Hool chopped the arm from one, taking it at the elbow. The dead man caught Hool's sword arm in its remaining hand, and the second threw itself at his legs.

As Hool went down, the necromancer rose.

I may not have counted Robart Hool high in my esteem, but he died well. He took the sword from his trapped arm and rammed it left-handed through the neck of the corpse man falling to cover him.

Pinned by the one-armed corpse, grappled at the legs with the other dead man biting flesh from his thigh, Robart roared and fought to rise. The necromancer came in fast and touched cold fingers to the wrist of the hand straining to free the sword. All the fight left Robart. Not the pain, not the horror of the dead man's teeth chewing at the tendon high on his thigh, but the fight. I knew what a necromancer's touch could do.

The dead sailor kneeled then stood, its grin crimson, blood dripping from its chin. The eyes that watched us weren't the eyes it first saw us with. Something looked through them. The necromancer kneeled, paler now, more pale than I thought a man could be.

"My lord," he said, not lifting his gaze from the flagstones. "My king."

"My lord!" Gomst's shrill voice.

"My king!" Osser Gant.

"Wake up you fool boy!" A sharp slap and I found myself looking into Katherine's eyes.

"Damn you all!" Miana said, and the baby started howling.

32

"Hold the baby, Jorg."

Miana thrust our son at me, red-faced in his swaddling cloths, drawing breath for a howl. She clambered onto the carriage bench and knelt up at the window to peer out. The walls of Honth made a dark line to the west.

Little William reached capacity and made the slight shudder that presaged a yell. He couldn't manage much volume yet but the mewl of babies has been designed with great cunning to tear at an adult's peace of mind, parents especially. I shoved the knuckle of my little finger into his mouth and let him forget the scream while he gave it a vicious gumming.

Katherine sat beside me watching my son with unreadable eyes. I hugged him close, my breastplate now strapped to Brath's saddlebags in its wraps of lambskin and oilcloth. I'd found babies don't appreciate armour. William spat my knuckle out and drew breath for another attempt at yelling. He'd come into the world red-faced, bald but for black straggles, skinny in the limbs, fat in the body, more of a little pink frog than a person, drooling, malodorous, demanding. Even so, I wanted to hold him. That weakness that infects all men, that is part of how we are made, had found a way into me. And yet my own father had set it aside, if it ever once found purchase on him. Perhaps it became easier to set me aside as I grew.

The howl burst out of William's little mouth, a sound too big for such a small frame. I jiggled him quiet and wondered just how large a stick I'd given the world to beat me with.

I watched Katherine for a moment. We hadn't spoken of the night's dreaming. I had questions and more questions, but I would ask them without an audience and at a time when I could take a moment to settle around whatever answers she might have. She didn't meet my gaze but studied my son instead. I had worried once that she might mean him harm but it seemed hard to imagine now, with him in my arms.

"There's someone close by who would kill that child given the slightest chance." Katherine looked away as she spoke, her voice low as if it were a small matter, almost lost in the rattle of the carriage.

"What?" Miana turned from the window grille, fast, eyes bright. I didn't think she had been listening, but it seemed she paid close attention to whatever passed between my aunt and me.

"If I explain, I want your word that this person will be safe from you and your men, Jorg," Katherine said.

"Well, that doesn't sound like me, now does it?" I made an effort not to let the tension in my arms crush William. Miana reached for her baby, but I held him closer. "Suppose you tell anyhow."

"Katherine!" Miana reached across me for Katherine's hand. "Please."

For a moment I saw the red explosion of Miana's firebomb in the Haunt's courtyard. It would not go well if Katherine refused her.

"The man rides under the Pax Gilden," Katherine said.

The guard would kill anyone who tried to attack him, hunt down anyone who succeeded in killing him. Just as they would intervene in, or avenge, any violence in our carriage.

"You're not Father's only representative." I should have realized from the start, but finding Katherine in the Ancrath carriage threw off my game. "He found a replacement for Lord Nossar."

She nodded. "Jarco Renar."

"Cousin Jarco." I leaned back in my seat and unclenched the fingers knotted in William's cloths. I'd heard no report of the man since he escaped his failed rebellion in Hodd Town. That had been a year before the Prince of Arrow arrived at my door. We had us a murderous little struggle: civil wars are always brutal, old wounds left too long festering get to spill out their poison over new generations. The battles left the Highlands weakened, short on men, and empty-coffered. I had thought Jarco's funds came from Arrow, but perhaps Father had been spending my inheritance.

Nothing would please Jarco more than getting his hands on my son. After all, I killed his brother at Norwood, took his father at the Haunt, and usurped his inheritance. And of course he had his fair share of the family flair for vengeance. I wondered if he were riding as one of the guard. Perhaps he convinced them it was the only way to keep him safe from me. Or they might have him hidden among the straggle of camp-followers reaching back behind us. Finding him would not be easy.

"How could you not have mentioned this before?" Miana asked, hands whitening around Katherine's. "He could have attacked any of us."

"William is not under the guard's protection," I said. Jarco wouldn't sell his life just for a chance at mine, but he could kill my son and have the guard defend him. That might strike him as an opportunity too good to miss. Quite the joke.

"Well, put him under the guard's protection!" A certain shrillness entered Miana's voice. Katherine winced, though whether from the volume or beneath Miana's grip, I didn't know.

"Children may not be advisors or representatives." She knew the rules as well as I. On the bench opposite the old men nodded their heads.

"But—" Miana hushed as I gave her back our child and went to the door. I hung half-out, over the mud and ruts, and hollered for Makin. He rode up sharp enough.

"I want you all around the carriage—Jarco Renar is armoured in gold and looking for a way to reach Prince William."

Makin glanced around at the nearest riders. "I'll kill him myself."

"Don't. He's under the Pax." As I said it I wondered whose life I might be prepared to spend for Jarco's death. I waved Makin closer and leaned in so only he would hear me. "On second thoughts, I always knew I kept Rike around for a reason. Tell him there's a hundred gold ducets for him if he kills Jarco. He'd best be prepared to run afterward, though."

Makin nodded and hauled on his reins.

I called after him. "A hundred gold and five Araby stallions." It seemed fitting somehow.

"You!" I shouted to the nearest guardsman. "Get Harran here."

The man nodded his golden helm and spurred off toward the head of the column.

"Give me Makin and Marten and we'll ride home to the Highlands," Miana was saying behind me.

"I would give you Rike and Kent and Gorgoth as well and you still wouldn't be safe, Miana. We're too far from home in lands that love us not."

By the time Captain Harran drew level, flanked by two other troop captains, Katherine and Miana were arguing in fierce whispers with William interjecting the odd protest.

Harran lifted his visor. "King Jorg."

"I will speak with Jarco Renar," I said.

"Jarco Renar is under my protection. I have advised him not to show himself to you, in order to avoid any unpleasantness."

"Oh I can assure you, Captain, there will be far more unpleasantness if you don't bring him before me."

Harran smiled. "Jorg, I have nearly five hundred of the emperor's best soldiers here precisely to make sure that you can't hurt Jarco Renar and Jarco Renar can't hurt you. Getting our charges to Vyene is what we do. By my count you have four men with you capable of bearing arms. Best let us get on with our job, no?"

"That's King Jorg to you, Captain Harran," I said.

The four men he mentioned had joined us now. In truth I had three since Gorgoth was his own man and would be as likely to stand with the guard as with me.

A slap to the carriage's side brought us to a halt. "Would you hand me that, Lord Makin?" I pointed to the Nuban's crossbow, tied to Brath's saddle.

I took the bow, stepped down into the mud, and crossed to the bank beside the road. The weight of their attention settled on me as I bent to wind the bow.

"The guard here are assigned to protect myself, Lord Makin, and my advisors?" I didn't look up.

"Yes," Harran said.

"And they would offer me violence under what circumstances?" I knew the rules. I wanted to hear Harran speak them.

"Quarrel," I said, hand outstretched. Makin slapped an iron bolt into my palm.

"If you attempted to harm any of the Hundred, their advisors, or delegates." Harran's stallion gave a nervous whinny and stamped.

"Makin, if you would be good enough to foreswear the need for any protection from me, as my banner-man. Just so there's no confusion." I set the bolt in place.

"I do so swear," he said.

I looked up, held Harran's dark stare, took his measure one last time. "I like you well enough, Harran, but my son is in that carriage and Jarco Renar will like as not try to kill him since he is not under your protection. So, I need to speak with my cousin in order to reach some arrangement."

"I've explained King Jorg, that cannot—"

I shot Harran in the face. He half-lurched, half-leapt from the saddle. Caught by his stirrups he came to rest at an odd angle, almost jutting from the side of his horse. The beast took flight, cantering back along the line, dragging Harran through the leafless hedges. His golden helm caught in the thorns and ripped free, blood dripping from it.

"Quarrel," I said, hand out. Makin supplied one.

I started to wind the bow again.

"Captain Rosson is it? And Captain Devers?" My question caught them with blades half-drawn. "Why are you baring steel at me when your single most holy duty to the empire is my protection?" All around me the guard were reaching for their swords, others urging their horses in closer to discover the cause of unrest.

"You just shot Harran!" Rosson, the man on the left, spat.

"I did." I nodded. "I'm going to shoot you next. I figure I'll be able to kill twenty of you before I need to start digging the bolts out of your corpses in order to continue. Now must I repeat my question? On what grounds are you drawing steel against me? I'm sure Captain Harran would not have approved. He at least knew his duty!"

"I—" Captain Rosson hesitated, his blade not yet clear of the scabbard.

"Your duty, Captain, is to protect me. You can hardly do that by hacking at me with your sword now can you? The only circumstance that would permit you to attack me is if I threatened another of your charges. But I'm not doing that. I'm just going to kill the few hundred guard assigned to me."

"King Jorg—you—you can't be serious," Captain Rosson said.

I failed to see how I could be more serious, but some men take time to adjust to unfamiliar circumstances.

ChooOOOooom.

Rosson hit the mud with a dull splat. At a range of two yards no breastplate, however fancy, is going to stop a crossbow bolt from a mechanism as heavy as the Nuban's bow.

I set to winding again, starting to feel the ache in my bicep. "Captain Devers? Are you going to bring Jarco Renar to speak with me? Remember, if I try to kill him you can cut me to pieces."

Rosson twitched in the mud. He tried to say something but only blood came out.

Miana and Katherine crowded the carriage door, Gomst peering over the pair. Osser Gant appeared to prefer his ledgers.

"Jorg!" Katherine's hair fell around her in dark red curls, a heat in those eyes. "These are honourable men!"

"And I am not." I held my hand out. "Quarrel."

"Men with families, lives to live . . ."

Miana said nothing, her face held tight against emotion, my son clasped to her breast.

I ignored Katherine and addressed the guard instead, lifting my voice to carry on the cold afternoon breeze. "I quite liked Captain Harran. You saw where that got him. The rest of you I hardly know. My newborn son is at risk. I hunted down a lichkin to ensure his safety. Do you think I will flinch at murdering each and every one of you?

"I suggest Jarco Renar be brought before me, or this will not end well."

Viewed along the length of my crossbow Captain Devers looked pale and unhappy. He had flipped up his visor to reveal a thin face decorated with scars and pockmarks, a short, dark beard hugging his chin.

"Bring Renar here!" he shouted.

While we waited I mounted Brath and backed him in a tight circle. He had been well trained and the smell of blood didn't bother him. Captain Harran's helm came free of the hedgerow thorns and I held it in one hand, the crossbow in the other, steering Brath with my knees.

Sir Kent clambered from his horse onto the top of the carriage. Choosing the right position had kept Kent alive more times than any armour or skill with a blade.

"Bring me some more captains." I raised the crossbow toward Captain Devers again.

"No, wait!" He put up his hands, as if that would stop a quarrel. "He'll be here!"

"But you will not." I squeezed the trigger, but before I'd applied sufficient pressure the guard ranks parted and Jarco Renar sat before me on a roan mare in golden armour. I turned the crossbow toward him.

"I would have sent out someone else," I told him. "Just to see if I knew what you look like." It happened that I knew what he looked like, though we had never met.

Jarco hadn't his brother's chubbiness, or that deceiving amiability Marclos had. A taller man, broader in the shoulder, he had more of my uncle's look about him, more of the Renar wolf.

I advanced Brath toward him. Hands tightened on sword hilts all around me.

"Here." I gave Captain Devers the loaded crossbow, leaning in for a conspiratorial whisper. "If he attacks me be ready to shoot him. You're here to protect *me*, remember. Cousin Jarco has his own defenders, the guard who rode with him out of Crath City."

I pulled Brath's head around. "Jarco, so pleased you could join us."

"Cousin Jorg." His horse stepped around Captain Rosson who was taking a damned long time to die for somebody shot through the chest.

A squeeze of the knees brought Brath in closer. Harran's empty helm dripped dark blood on my leg.

"I'm not happy with you, Jarco," I told him.

"Nor I with you, Cousin Jorg."

"That rebellion of yours left me weak in the face of my enemies, Jarco." With the soldiers lost taking Hodd Town back under control, the defence against the Prince of Arrow would not have been quite so desperate. The battle had left Hodd Town rather the worse for wear too, and it had been ugly to start with.

"You sit in my throne, Cousin." He had a touch of Father's coldness in his eyes, and some of Uncle's wildness. I would have paid well to be a spy at court the day Jarco came to beg King Olidan's favour. How had my father greeted his nephew? "You rule over my people," Jarco said.

"They love me well." I smiled to irk him. Jarco knew it for truth. Kings who bring victories are always loved and the price paid soon forgotten. The Highlanders had found new pride at being the centre of a realm of nations. As Uncle's subjects they had been a footnote in the business of empire, forgotten often as not. Happier, safer no doubt, but men will spend such coin to hold themselves in better esteem, for we are shallow creatures, brutish and raised on blood.

"What is it you want of me, Jorg?" He faked a yawn and stifled it.

"I note that you worry over your inheritance, Cousin, but you seem to have forgiven me for your father." A shrug and a tilt of the head to show my puzzlement. "And your sweet brother."

"I do not forget them." Muscles bunching around his jaw.

"Perhaps you would like something to remember them by, to remember your lost heritage? Your lost pride. It can be hard to lose your family." I slid Gog from my scabbard, hilt toward my cousin. The blade had been Uncle Renar's, ancient work, forged from Builder steel and brought into Ancrath hands by my father's grandfather when he took the Highlands for his own as the empire crumbled.

Jarco took the sword, quick as you like. Better to have it in his hands rather than mine. I could see the hate burning in him. To some men there's no poison worse than a gift, none worse than a measure of pity. I would know.

"Of course," I said. "Should some harm befall me, should the Highlands ever cry for a trueborn Renar on the throne, it wouldn't be you who gets to wear the crown."

The blade stood between us, his ancestral steel.

He frowned, black brows crowding. "You make no sense, Ancrath. I hold title before that mewling babe of yours." William let out an obliging cry before Miana stuffed his mouth again.

"But even in your grasping for your father's title, Jarco, you would admit that *his* right to it outweighs your own?"

"My father . . . ?" The point of his sword, of the blade I'd named Gog, aimed at my heart. My breastplate lay neatly wrapped behind me, strapped to the saddlebags.

"I should have let Uncle die. A better man would have. But I do so enjoy our chats. Enough to walk down all those steps to the dungeon several times a week. He speaks of you often, Jarco. It's hard to understand his words these days, but I don't think Uncle Renar is well pleased with you."

It took one more smile to make him crack. He had a quick arm, I'll give him that. Even deflected with Harran's helmet Jarco's thrust ran through my hair as I ducked.

ChooOOoom! And Captain Devers did his duty.

Jarco fell backward off his nag, feet coming up out of his stirrups. I had to laugh.

Katherine jumped down beside him in the mud, careless of her skirts. Miana offered me a wordless stare. The look of someone who's got what they asked for, bitter or not, and knows it.

"You didn't have to kill him." Katherine looked up with murder in her eyes. I like people who have the grace to show their anger.

"Captain Devers killed him," I said, and took my bow back from the man in question and slung it over a shoulder.

"My apologies, Brother Rike." I handed him Brath's reins and slid from the saddle. A few strands of cut hair floated down with me.

I scooped Gog from the dirt and wiped the blade clean on Rosson's cloak. He watched me from a white face.

"Did anyone ever once tell you I was a nice man, Rosson?"

He didn't answer. Dead at last perhaps.

Gorgoth loomed over me, silent, watching.

I looked up. "I might have grown past the killing of men on a whim, Gorgoth, but be damned sure I consider the safety of my son more than a whim."

I sheathed Gog then climbed back into the carriage. Miana waited with William, Osser with his ledgers, Gomst with God's judgment. I spoke to Katherine instead, down in the mud with Jarco.

"You know he had to die. Or at least you will know it in an hour, or a day. What makes us different is that I knew it from the moment you spoke. And in the end, my way is quicker, cleaner, and fewer people get hurt."

33

Five years earlier

"Very funny." I wiped the camel spit from my leg.

My unnamed steed curled its lip, showing narrow and uneven teeth, then turned to face the backside of the camel ahead.

"When we're through with this journey I plan to buy you and eat your liver," I told it.

Riding a camel is nothing like horse riding. You're a yard higher in the air and perched on a creature that regards you as an unforgivable insult. The beast's natural gait is designed to throw a passenger off at each stride, lurching you first forward and to the left, backward to the right, forward to the right, backward to the left, in endless repetition.

Omal, one of the drovers for the camel-train, came alongside. "Sail him, Jorg. You came by sea, no? Sail him. Not horse—camel."

Michael promised me a ship. The drovers' agents who came to our lodging to collect us for the "train" had laughed at that. "Camel! Camel! Ship of the desert, effendi." And grinning like loons, as if to humour us, they had loaded Marco's trunk onto one of the beasts then led us away to join the caravan.

How Michael arranged to have us travel with the caravan I didn't know, but it seemed clear that whilst Hamada might be blocked to the Builder-ghosts, they still had ways into Kutta at times of need. I hadn't asked him. Instead I had seated myself in a wicker chair that looked too frail for the task and said, "I would guess you're one of the ghosts that wants the Prince of Arrow for emperor so he can earn us the peace we need if we're to school ourselves for service to your machines."

Marco's tight little mouth dropped open at that. Despite the common saying, there are few men whose jaws actually do drop in surprise. Marco's did, dry lips parting with an audible pop. I could have held tight to my knowledge, for such snippets can be a valuable commodity and the banking clans do so love to trade. However, Fexler had left me such meagre scraps I thought it better to spend them carelessly in the hope that scattering my crumbs might convince others I had reserves of such lore and should be treated with respect.

I added, "If you stood with those that want to burn all life from the world, well, I'm sure you know of other places like the vaults in Gelleth where you could find enough fire and enough poison for the job?"

Marco's open mouth snapped closed and he turned to Michael, eyes blazing. It didn't seem to occur to him that I could be lying. An observation that I tucked away for future need.

I continued, "In fact I'd like to know what stops them, these scorched-earthers, from wiping the slate clean? Does a war rage in all the Builder relics, humming to themselves in the dusts of the promised lands, scattered and hidden in cellars, secreted in luggage . . . ?"

Michael's eyes were the least convincing part of his illusion, as though something wholly alien watched me through two holes punched into a man's face. I wondered what the real Michael had been like, and how far a thousand years had moved this creature from its starting template.

"It's very easy to kill most of the people," Michael said. "And very hard to kill absolutely all of them. To do so would require a consensus, cooperation between all, or almost all, of my people. Rather like Congress. Perhaps on the day you finally elect a replacement for your dead emperor you should start to worry that my kind might find a similar unity of purpose."

"And what of Fexler Brews?" I would play a closer hand here. Fexler spoke of a third way, and neither of the first two were to my liking.

"Brews?" It heartened me to see the Builder ghost sneer. At least that much humanity persisted in the data echo. "A servant, barely more than a maintenance algorithm. He is free to act now, but after a millennium on the margins of our world he is hardly the spokesman for you to listen to. Would you want me to judge you by the man who winds open your gate to let me in?"

As I swayed through the Margins, only a little more easy in my saddle than Marco lurching on the mount ahead of me, I knew Fexler Brews for what he was. A glorified gatekeeper with delusions of grandeur.

The Margins of the Sahar Desert are a vast and barren wilderness of cracked mud. A fissured geometry stretches across these lands, repeating at ever-larger scales, dust-blown, unbroken by mountain, lake, tree, or bush. In places the cracks are paper-thin, elsewhere you might stick your arm down them, and there are others still that would swallow a camel. Twisted creatures skulk in the fissures, hiding from the sun at surprising depths where the mud still remembers ancient rains. In the darkness they emerge.

Our train comprised six score camels and fifty men to ride them, the desert Moors or Taureg as they called themselves. Most of the Taureg were traders, or drovers like Omal in their employ. They sold goods from the Port Kingdoms in Hamada, and returned with salt blocks. The salt they purchased from factors who in turn bought it from the Salash, almost-men, capable of enduring the oven heat of the deep Sahar where even the hardiest of Moorish tribes could not travel.

Along with the merchants and their workers, a dozen Ha'tari

accompanied us, warriors from a mercenary clan of great repute. They slouched on their mounts by day, dead to the world, and earned their keep at night, driving off predators that emerged from the cracked landscape.

On the first night of our journey around the camel-dung fires of Taureg we sat with our backs to the night and sipped hot java from cups no bigger than thimbles. I still hated the stuff but the expense made it an insult to refuse. The stars gave more light than the fire, a white-hot blaze of them across the sky. The Moors chattered in their harsh tongue, and in whispers I quizzed Marco. The discovery that not only was I known to the Builder-ghosts, but knew of them, had moderated his opinions somewhat and if he still held me in contempt at least he made some effort to disguise the fact.

"Ibn Fayed must know we're coming," I said. "He made efforts to thwart us, and yet he allows our progress now. Surely a dozen Ha'tari aren't going to stop his men?"

"Clearly his objections to my audit are not sufficiently large to incur the bad feeling that slaughtering a Taureg salt caravan would engender. Those objections were, however, large enough to motivate efforts to deny me transport." Marco sipped his java, sucking it through his teeth.

"And he has no objections to my visit?"

A large dung beetle scurried over my boot. Eight legs, a mutant. For a moment little Gretcha watched me from the fire-glow. I scowled and the fire flared then dimmed, causing the drovers to shift back, muttering.

"Your visit? Why should he even know of it?" Marco's permanent frown deepened.

"Yusuf knew of it."

"And what is Lord Yusuf to you or me?"

For someone who dragged the means to speak to a Builder ghost around with him, Marco seemed to know very little.

"Yusuf is a mathmagician."

Marco raised an eyebrow at that. "Abominations, all of them. But Ibn Fayed doesn't own such creatures. They have their own agendas. Don't think the only reason the numbered men may seek you is in the caliph's service."

Beneath my travel cloak I toyed with the view-ring, rotating it through my fingers. A thought struck, a bolt from the diamond-scattered night, piercing me skull to toes. The fingers around the ring closed in a grip that might have crushed it if it were only a little less robust.

"Why do you have to drag that trunk with you, Marco? Why is it so damn heavy?"

The banker blinked at me.

"It weighs more than the two of us!" I said.

He blinked again. "How heavy should it be?"

I clutched the view-ring and thought back to a time when it had taken both Gorgoth and Rike to carry a work of the Builders from a vault deep beneath the Castle Red.

The trip through the Margins took three days, our journey punctuated by the crossing of the widest fissures on a bridge of three planks, carried for the purpose, laid down and picked up, time and again. We travelled without landmarks, beset with dust storms, always too dry, always too hot. At one point we passed the carcass of a vast beetle, its hollowed carapace large enough to stable camels. In three days those remains were the only thing to break the monotony of flat, cracked mud.

The desert announced itself as ripples on the horizon. With remarkable speed the hardpan and dust gave over to sand, rising in white dunes to heights I would not have imagined possible.

In the desert the Tauregs' skills became obvious. The way they navigated counting the dunes as if they were landmarks rather than identical shifting masses. The way they trekked up the lee of each white mountain, threading the path of least resistance, finding the firm-packed sand for good-footing, finding the best respite from the wind, and in the evening, blessed intervals of shade.

An unease rose in me. Each mile took us further into a prison. Neither Marco or I could leave again without the goodwill of men such as these: the desert trapped us better than high walls.

The white sands multiplied the sun's heat and made a furnace in which we cooked. Marco made no concession to the temperature, wearing all his blacks, the frockcoat, waistcoat, his white gloves. I began to think him changed, like the Salash of the deep Sahar. No human could endure as he did. And beneath his tall hat his skin stayed paste-white and unburned.

By night, shivering beneath the cold blaze of the heavens, we sat among the merchants with the dunes rising all about, ghost pale, huger than the waves on the roughest sea. On such nights the merchants would tell their tales in murmured phrases, so little animation in them that it was hard to tell who spoke behind their shesh, until at some punch-line the storyteller would start to wave his hands and the whole circle joined in with harsh jabber and raucous laughter. Behind us in the drover circle the men played the game of twelve lines on ancient boards, silent save for the chatter of dice. And around the fire circles, phantoms in the night, walked the Ha'tari, passing a low and haunting song between them, and guarding us from dangers unknown.

34

Five years earlier

Somewhere in the loneliness of the Sahar, amongst the twenty days of our crossing, we passed unnoticed from Maroc into Liba. The Taureg spoke of a land that had lain between the realms long ago, devoured by nibbles until Maroc met Liba in the sands. A land of people who would have done well to heed the saying about inches given and miles taken, or as the locals have it, "beware the camel's nose" after the story of the camel who begs his way by inches into the tent, then refuses to leave.

Hamada rises from desert sands in low mud buildings, rounded as if by the wind, and whitewashed to dazzle the eye. They look at first like pebbles half-bedded in the ground. There is water here: you can taste it on the air, see it in the stands of karran grass that stabilize the dunes and hold back their tides. As you begin to move among the white buildings you see grander structures beyond, nestling in the slight hollow that holds the city. In some ancient time a god fell to earth here and fractured the deepest bedrock, bringing to the surface the waters of an aquifer untapped in any other place.

"I don't think I've ever been as far from anywhere, Brother Marco." I shaded my eyes and watched the city through the heat-shimmer.

"I'm not your brother," he said.

Omal, riding between us, snorted. "Far from anywhere? Hamada means 'centre.' This is the heart of Liba. Hamada."

We rode in with the morning sun throwing our shadows behind us, hauling on our reins to keep the camels from bolting for the water. Even so, they picked the pace up, snorting and blowing, licking at their muzzles with coarse tongues. Faces appeared at shadowed windows and the drovers called out halloos to old friends. In the shade of tiny alleys scrawny children chased scrawnier chickens.

Deeper in, the streets of Hamada boast tall houses of white-washed plaster over brick with high turrets to catch the wind. Further still and our column came in sight of great halls in white stone, public buildings to dwarf the works in Albaseat, constructed to the sparse and grand arithmetic of the Moorish scholars. Libraries, galleries for sculpture, pillared baths where desert men might settle in the luxury of deep waters.

"Not too shabby." I felt like the dirty peasant come to court.

"Gold has been made and spent here." Marco nodded. "Gold and more gold." For once the sneer had left him. It's an unsettling business having to re-evaluate your world view. Neither of us were enjoying it.

Our caravan turned from the centre road and entered a vast market square with pens partitioned for camels, goats, sheep, and even a few horses. Here black-clad crowds thronged, merchants anticipating the camel train and ready to haggle. Omal and his comrades helped Marco down and set his trunk on the sandy flagstones before him. He approached it with the bandy gait of a man too long in the saddle.

"I'm not dragging that thing again," I said, glad to be off my own camel. "It's been carried twenty days and more, it can be carried for the last mile."

Rattling a few coins soon found a toothless old rogue with a donkey willing to help us along to the caliph's palace. The beast looked as ancient as its master and I fully expected its legs to fold beneath it as the three of us lowered the trunk to its back. It proved as contrary as Balky, though, and just hee-hawed its complaints whilst the old man secured the load.

Standing in the heat, sweating while I watched the old man work, the worries that eluded me in the emptiness of the desert returned in force. Since that moment in the Kutta java house when I understood the nature of the trap, it seemed that like Brother Hendrick, impaled on that Conaught spear, I had been driving the blade deeper. Sensible hope of revenge, not that it ever had been sensible, had gone out the window as soon as I realized they knew me, realized I was anticipated. Now in the midst of a desert that could hold me prisoner on its own, I aimed my path at the enemy's court, set no doubt just a few score yards above the dungeons I would soon rot in.

"Here's to you, Brother Hendrick."

"Your pardon?" Marco poked at the brim of his hat to peer at me.

"Let's get this done," I said, and started walking. Beneath desert robes the copper box, the gun, and the view-ring all rubbed at me, uncomfortable in the heat. It seemed unlikely that any of them would offer salvation.

Broad streets, where the wind scoured only a whisper of sand, brought us past bathhouse and library, law court and gallery, to a steeper dip where beneath the steel sky of the desert a wide and flawless lake reflected the caliph's palace. Between us and the waters the pillared ruins of an amphitheatre rose from a scattering of rubble. Some work of the Romans, unimaginably old.

"And what's that?" I pointed to a tall tower, the tallest in Hamada, set apart from the palace yet casting its dark shadow down across high walls into the heart of the compound.

"Mathema," the old rogue said over his gums.

"Qalasadi?" I jabbed my finger at it.

"Qalasadi." He nodded.

"We'll go there first," I said. Revenge had brought me here. The need to strike back when struck. Ibn Fayed owed me a debt of blood, but Qalasadi, his debt had a face on it and I would settle that first.

"Go where you like, Sir Jorg," Marco said. "My business is at the palace."

"And what business is that, Marco? Come now, friend, you can tell Brother Jorg. We've travelled many a mile together." I showed him my teeth.

"We're not brothers—"

I fished into my robes. For an instant Marco flinched, as if he thought I would pull a knife on him. Instead I drew out Yusuf's die.

"On the road we are family, Brother Marco."

I knelt and set the die spinning on the flagstones, whirling like a top on one corner.

"I've come to collect a debt," he said. "From Ibn Fayed."

The die rattled across the ground. A two.

"Go with God, Brother Marco," I said.

I came alone to the door of the mathmagicans' tower. No guard stood there, no windows overlooked it. The tower reached a hundred yards above me, an elegant spire, maybe twenty yards in diameter at the base. The first windows opened about halfway up its length, stepping in a spiral toward the heights of the spire, the stone too smooth for scorpion or spider.

The door had been fashioned of black crystal, flaws glimmering in its upper layers where the sun reached in. I knocked and where my knuckles struck, a circle of numbers appeared, written in gleams, the ten digits the Arabs first gave us.

"A puzzle?"

I touched one digit, the "two," another grew brighter, the "four." I touched that. The circle vanished. I waited. Nothing.

A harder knock, but my knuckles made no sound against the crystal, just summoned the circle of numbers again. I pressed, chasing the glowing numbers in ever-quicker circles, trying to read the patterns, keeping track for a few seconds then losing the thread.

"Damn it, I didn't come to play games."

The place lay deserted. A few figures moved among the distant ruins, Marco and other visitors toiled up the broad steps before Fayed's palace, and a thin crowd loitered around the sandy margins of the lake, but not a soul lay within earshot.

I tried again. Then again. Clearly whatever it took to be a math-magician I wasn't made of the stuff. The glowing numbers danced their perimeter, fading as I watched. I scowled at the door, and that didn't work either. More out of frustration than judgment I knocked again and as soon as the number circle appeared I tore the view-ring from its thong and slapped it dead centre. Immediately the procession of numerals sped up, sped again, and blurred into a circle of light. The door began to emit a hum, high pitched and rapidly scaling the octaves. Small lightnings started to fork through the crystal, spreading from the points where the view-ring touched it. My fingertips buzzed with the vibration. Hum became whine became shriek. Vertical became horizontal. And I found myself trying to rise amongst jagged black chunks of what had been a most impressive door.

With ringing ears and numb fingers I located the view-ring amid the sparkling rubble and hastened through the doorway. A corridor led straight ahead, appearing to divide the ground floor. At the far end I glimpsed steps—presumably the stair that wound around just inside the tower walls. Half a dozen young Liban men in white tunics headed toward me from arches to either side of the corridor, their looks those of scholars, astonishment rather than anger on their faces. I drew my knife and let the sleeve of my robes fall around it. Looks can be deceiving.

"Something's wrong with your door." Without pause I strode between them.

On reaching the stairs, which led off down and up, I chose up. I retied the view-ring on its thong, fumbling the knots, fingers still buzzing.

I had it from Omal that the mathema was more by way of a university, a place of study for the mathmagicians. Qalasadi was some sort of teacher. A tutor to the caliph's children, a guide for students come to study at Hamada, an arbiter in the affairs of lesser lights amongst the numbered men, as they liked to call themselves. The tower was not his home, not his domain or fiefdom, but even so, somehow I thought I might find him at the top.

Equations kept pace with me as I walked the worn steps, climbing the mathema tower knife in hand. Some ran the full length of the spiral stair, others started and ended within a few yards to be replaced by fresh calculations, all carved into the stonework then inlaid with black wax to make them legible. I passed door after door, each set with a letter from the Greek, starting with "alpha," next "beta." By "mu" I had reached the first of the windows and a cooling breeze spiralled up with me. I passed two mathmagicians coming down, both old men, wrinkled like prunes and so deep in conversation I could have been on fire and gone unremarked.

And finally, where the last window offered Hamada in a broad, bright panorama, the steps ended at a door set with "omega," inlaid in brass into the mahogany. I gave myself a moment. I'd rather climb mountains than steps.

I let my sleeve hide the blade once more and pushed the door. It swung open with a soft complaint of hinges and there, leaning over a wide and glossy desk at the centre of a single circular room, Qalasadi, Yusuf, and Kalal. They looked up in unison and the moment of surprise written on those three faces proved all the reward I could want for my long climb. Yusuf and Kalal immediately bent their head back to the papers as if hunting for an error amidst their scratchings. Both men clutched quills, their fingers stained as black as their teeth.

"Jorg." Qalasadi recovered his composure in the space between two breaths. "Our projections indicated the front door would take you considerably longer to pass."

Yusuf and Kalal exchanged glances, as if asking what other errors may have crept into their calculations.

"Your projections? For men who want to put out the Builders' eyes you surely sound a lot like them."

Qalasadi spread his hands, empty, ink-stained. "It's our actions that define us, not the manner in which we reach the decision to act."

I threw the dagger, moving my arm across my body so the action would not be telegraphed. The blade bedded in the gleaming table, hilt quivering, a hand's breadth from Qalasadi's groin. I'd been aiming for roughly that spot but it was a tricky throw, a flat angle and an awkward motion. I'd thought it a reasonable chance the knife would glance off and end up in his scrotum.

"Is that on your papers? Had you figured that one out?" I strode toward the table. "Did you have the knife's trajectory plotted?"

Qalasadi put a hand on Yusuf's shoulder. The younger men ceased their scribbling and looked up, still hung with frowns as if more concerned by their calculus than my sharp edges.

"Can I get you a drink, King Jorg?" Qalasadi said. "It's a long climb up all those steps." The ivory wand he'd used to write in the dust of my grandfather's courtyard lay in his hand now.

I came to the table, just its width between us, my knife skewering a sheath of papers, all covered with tight-packed symbology, and spoke in a calm voice, as reasonable men do. "Part of being in the business of prediction, a large part perhaps, must be the art of giving the impression that things are unfolding according to your expectations. A victim who believes himself anticipated at every turn is not only crippled by uncertainty but also easier to predict."

All three men watched me without reply. No sign of nerves, save perhaps Qalasadi's fingers rubbing at the short curls of his beard, and a faint sheen of sweat across Kalal's brow. Yusuf had taken the combs from his hair and bound it all back, tight to the skull. He looked older now, more clever.

"You must have known I would decide to hit the table with that throw or you would have tried to stop me . . . unless you didn't know I would throw the knife at all?" I found myself digging into the crippling uncertainty I'd just spoken of.

"And the drink?" Qalasadi said.

I did have a thirst on me, but that was too predictable. Besides, you don't cross nations to hunt down a poisoner and then drink what he gives you. "Why did you try to kill my mother's kin, Qalasadi? A friend told me the mathmagicians have their own purposes. Was it just to please Ibn Fayed? To keep his good will and stop him turfing you out of this rather fine oasis?"

Qalasadi rubbed his chin across the top of his palm, closing his fingers about his jaw in consideration. He had the same even pace to him that he showed in Castle Morrow. I had liked him from the start. Perhaps that's why I showed off for him, maybe gave him the information he needed to deduce my story. Even now, with vengeance a sword thrust away, I had no hatred for him.

"It's an irony of our times that men seeking peace must make war," he said. "You know it yourself, Jorg. The Hundred War must be won if it is to stop. Won on the battlefield, won on the floor of Congression. These things are of a piece."

"And Ibn Fayed is the man to win it?" I asked.

"In five years Ibn Fayed will vote for Orrin of Arrow at Congression. The Earl Hansa would not. The vote will be close. The Prince of Arrow will bring peace. Millions will prosper. Hundreds of thousands will live instead of dying in war. Our order chose the many over the few."

"That was a mistake. They were my few." A heat rose in me.

"Mistakes can be made." He nodded, thoughtful. "Even with enchantment to tame the variables the sum of the world is a complex one."

"So you still intend to gift the realm of Morrow to Ibn Fayed? To let the Moorish tide back yet again into the Horse Coast?" I watched Qalasadi, his eyes, his mouth, the motion of his hands, everything, just to try and read something of the man. It maddened me to have them stand there so calm, as if they knew at each moment what was on my tongue to speak, in my mind to do. And yet did they? Was it part of their show of smokes and mirrors?

"We intend that the Prince of Arrow win the empire throne at Congression in the 104th year of Interregnum." Yusuf spoke for the first time, his voice edged with just a touch of strain. "The Congression of year 100 will be a stalemate: that cannot be changed."

"It may be that the caliph's domains can more easily be expanded in other directions." Kalal spoke, his high voice at odds with a serious mouth. "Maroc may fall more easily than Morrow or Kordoba."

The amount of relief that suggestion brought surprised me. "I came to kill you, Qalasadi. To lay waste to your domain and leave behind ruination."

He had the grace or commonsense not to smirk at my apocalyptic turn of phrase. Most likely they knew of Gelleth even in Afrique. Perhaps they saw the glare of it, rising above the horizon. Lord knows it burned bright enough, and high? It scorched heaven!

"I hope that you will not," said Qalasadi.

"Hope?" I drew my robe aside, setting hand to hilt. "You don't know?"

"All men need hope, Jorg. Even men of numbers." Yusuf pressed a smile onto his lips, his voice soft, the voice of a man ready to die.

"And what do your equations say of me, poisoner?" My sword stood between us now. I had no recollection of drawing it. The rage I needed flared and died, flared again. I saw my grandfather and grandmother laid out pale on the deathbed, Uncle Robert in a warrior's tomb, hands folded across the blade upon his chest. I saw Qalasadi's smile in a sunlit courtyard. Yusuf wiping the sea from his face. "Salty!" he had said. "Let's hope the world has better to offer than that, no?" Words spoken at sea.

I slammed my sword hilt onto the table's polished wood. "What do your calculations say?" A roar that made them flinch.

"Two," Qalasadi said.

"Two?" A laugh tore out of me, sharp-edged, full of hurting.

He bowed his head. "Two."

Yusuf ran a finger across pages of scrawl. "Two."

"It's what the magic gives us," Qalasadi said.

Something cold tingled at my cheekbones. "Why two?"

And the mathmagician frowned, as he had in the courtyard at Castle Morrow, as if trying once again to remember that lost sensation, to recall a forgotten taste.

"Two friends lost in dry-lands? Two friends to be made in the desert? Two years away from your throne? Two women who will own your heart? Two decades you will live?" The magic lies in the first number, the mathematics in the second."

"And what is the second number?" Anger left me, the remaining image two sad mounds in the dirt of the Iberico, fading.

"The second number," Qalasadi said, without checking his papers, "is 333000054500."

"Now that is a number! None of these twos, threes, and fourteens you plague me with. What the hell does it mean?"

"It is, I hope, the coordinates where you abandoned Michael."

35

Five years earlier

It came as something of a relief to discover the order of mathmagicians didn't require my death, as it seemed likely they could have arranged to take it, certainly after I'd delivered myself into their hands with such cunning. Also good to learn that they now considered there were better routes than those that led to Morrow, other ways to place the necessary voting power into Ibn Fayed's hands and to assure the Prince of Arrow's ascendance. It meant that I in turn did not require their death.

It is true that I had a bad record with soothsayers and the like predicting glory for Orrin of Arrow. For once, however, I felt able to step around it and move on. Maybe I was growing up. I comforted myself with Fexler's words about the changing world and the power of desire. Perhaps for those whose burning desire was to know the future rather than live in the present, perhaps for them it was that desire more than the means they employed that gave them some blurry window onto tomorrow. Whether it be Danelore witches casting rune stones, or clever Moors with equations of fiendish complexity, maybe their raw and focused desire delivered their insights. And if my desire were the greater, maybe I would prove them wrong.

The need for vengeance, for retribution against Qalasadi after his attempt on my family, had never burned so bright as the imperative that took me to Uncle Renar's door. In fact it felt good to let it drop. Lundist and the Nuban would have been proud of me, but in truth I liked the man and it was that rather than any new-found strength of character that allowed me to set it aside.

In some chamber above us a mechanism whirred and a great bell began to sound out the hour of the day.

"Yusuf and I will accompany you to the caliph's court," Qalasadi said, voice raised.

"He won't want to execute me? Or lock me in a cell?" I asked.

"He knows you are here, so whether you go to court with us, or are taken there later under armed guard, is unlikely to change events," Qalasadi said.

"Though if his soldiers have to drag you there, projections do slide toward less desirable outcomes," Yusuf added.

"But you have already calculated what will happen?" I frowned at Yusuf.

"Yes." A nod.

"And?"

"And telling you will make the outcome less certain." Qalasadi closed the book he had just opened and picked it up. Yusuf threw an arm over my shoulders and steered me toward the door.

"And Kalal stays here?" I asked above the tenth and loudest intonation of the bell.

Yusuf grinned. "The sums don't do themselves, you know."

To their credit neither Qalasadi or Yusuf raised an eyebrow at the tower's lack of a front door, and I guessed it was not one that would be easy to replace. The younger men in their whites, still with the blackened teeth, alarming in their wrongness, had gathered the fragments together in a small sad heap to one side of the doorway, and others from within the mathema had joined them. Several dozen of the students sat in a circle, murmuring, passing crystal pieces amongst

one another, the occasional cry going up when they found two fragments that matched. They fell silent as we passed.

"I see you found a new solution to the door, Jorg," Yusuf said, his
voice dry.

"It presents a better puzzle now," Qalasadi said, "though one that
is less of an obstacle."

We crossed the plaza under the sun's blaze. You could almost see
the lake boiling away, but it put a hint of coolness in the air, a blessing
worth more than gold in the Sahar. The steps up to the caliph's gates
were broad and many, larger than steps made for men, deceiving the
eye so that as you climbed the true size of the palace became apparent
in a slow dawning.

Supplicants queued on the steps in the shade of a grand portico.
Gates, that looked to be made of gold, towered above us all, and royal
guards in polished steel stood ready to receive the caliph's visitors,
bright and faintly ridiculous plumes bobbing above conical helms.
Qalasadi and Yusuf bypassed the score and more of black-robed peti-
tioners. I spared a smile for Marco, wedged in the midst of the locals
and struggling to heft his trunk up another step.

"As-salamu alaykum." Qalasadi wished peace upon the giant who
stepped to bar our way. A sensible wish given the size of the scimitar
at the man's hip. Hachirahs, Tutor Lundist's book had called them,
their blades sufficient to hack a man in two.

"As-salamu alaykum, murshid mathema." The man bowed, but not so
low that one might stab him unawares.

More words exchanged in the shared tongue of Maroc and Liba.
I had enough of it to judge that Qalasadi was assuring the guard of
my royal status, despite appearances to the contrary. It might have
been politic to spend some time and some gold cleaning off the desert
and dressing the part, but it seemed wiser to meet with Ibn Fayed
before Marco gained an audience.

We entered by a gate within the gate and three plumed guards led
us along marble corridors, marvellously cool. The silence of the

palace enveloped us, a peace rather than the sterile absence of sound in the Builders' corridors, and broken on occasion by the tinkle of hidden fountains and the cry of peacocks.

The caliph's palace had nothing in common with the castles of the north. For one thing, it had been built for pleasure, not defence. The palace sprawled rather than towered, its halls and galleries wide and open, running one into the next, where they should divide into bottlenecks and killing grounds. And we passed not a single statue, painting, nor any but a few tapestries depicting only patterns in many bright colours. The men of the desert lacked our obsession with raising our own images, setting down our ancestry for the ages in stone and paint.

"We're here." Qalasadi's warning felt redundant. Double doors faced us, taller than houses, fashioned from vast slabs of ebony inlaid with gold. Wood is a rarity in the desert: the ebony spoke more loudly of the caliph's wealth than did the gold.

Palace guards with polearms stood in alcoves to each side, the bladed ends elaborate in shape and catching the light from small circular windows in the ceiling far above.

"Well," I said, then ran out of words. I have stepped into the lions' den before, but perhaps not since I walked alone into Marclos of Renar's personal army had I put myself so deeply into the hands of an enemy. At least with Marclos my brothers were just a few hundred yards away in a defensible position. I stood now in a well-guarded palace in an alien city amidst a vast desert in a strange land a continent away from home. I had nothing with which to bargain, and no gifts to offer, except perhaps for the trick I had played in the desert. I couldn't say if Qalasadi's coordinates were correct, but I did know that the Builder ghost, Michael, would not be accompanying Marco to court.

"We will wait here. Your audience is to be a private one." Qalasadi set a hand to my shoulder. "I can't tell you that Ibn Fayed is a good man, but he is at the least a man of honour."

One of our escorts stepped forward to knock three times upon a boss set across the join of the doors. I turned to face the two math-magicians.

"A pity it wasn't three friends your spells predicted I would make in the desert." I could do with a friend like the caliph, even if that friendship only extended to letting me leave.

Behind me the great doors stole into motion. A breeze ran cool across my neck and I turned to face my future.

"Good luck, Prince of Thorns." Yusuf spoke at my ear, voice soft. "We became friends at sea, you and I, so you still have a friend to make in the desert. Choose well."

The walk from doors to throne, along a silk runner the colour of the ocean, took a lifetime. In the vast and airy marble cavern of Ibn Fayed's throne room, walking between sunlit patches as if through the light and shade of forests, ideas, phrases, lines of attack, all bubbled up in fragments, roiling one over the next whilst all the time my gaze rested on the figure in his seat, first distant, drawing closer. Around the perimeter of the chamber great window arches stood to catch the breeze, each screened by elaborate shutters, more perforation than wood.

The whole expanse of the throne room stood empty. Only on the dais was there any sign of life. Fayed in his sic-wood throne amid the glitter of gemstones, on either side Nuban servants wafting him with fans of ostrich feathers on long poles. A circle of imperial guard on the lowest step, ten men. A wild cat of enormous size on the third step, and a heavy-muscled man to hold its chain, crouched beside it, both ready to spring.

Still I had no plan. No idea of what words might flow when my mouth opened. I prepared to surprise myself. Maybe I would tear Fexler's gun from my hip and lay waste. I doubted that had figured in anyone's calculations. Save perhaps those of Fexler himself.

A thin man in close black robes rose from his cushion on the step below the throne. Sun-stained but perhaps not from birth, not young, but with his years hidden. Like the very fat, the very thin play games with their wrinkles and disguise their age.

"Ibn Fayed, Caliph of Liba, Lord of the Three Realms, Water-Giver, welcomes King Jorg of Renar to his humble abode." Spoken in empire tongue with no trace of accent.

"I'm honoured," I said. "Hamada is a jewel." And in truth, standing there in the warmth and light of the caliph's palace I couldn't imagine what he would make of the castles and cities of the north. What would Ibn Fayed see in the great houses of my homeland, cold, cramped, and dirty, places where men spilled blood over narrow and muddy tracts of land, all smoke and filth.

"The caliph has wondered what would bring the King of Renar so far from his kingdom, unattended?" The Caliph's Voice kept any judgment from his tone but his eye twitched across my raggedness in disapproval.

I watched Ibn Fayed, deep in the grasp of his throne, so clearly a warrior despite his silks. He met my gaze, eyes hard and black. Of an age with the Earl Hansa, the years had grizzled him, a beard cropped so close as to be little more than stubble trekked white across the darkness of his skin, reaching for his cheekbones.

"I came to kill him for the disrespect shown to my grandfather."

That reached him. For a moment his eyes widened. No need of a translator to whisper behind his throne—he knew my meaning.

Where my honesty won a moment of surprise from the caliph it almost set his Voice back on the cushions. For the longest moment he stood slack-jawed and staring. Not a twitch from the guards though— they heard only the gabble of a northman.

Ibn Fayed muttered something and the thin man found his tongue.

"And is that still your intention, King Jorg?"

"No."

Another mutter then, "You no longer believe you can achieve your goal?"

"I doubt I could escape afterward. I think the desert would defeat me," I said, drawing a grunt of amusement from the caliph. "Also, I have gained new perspective on the matter and think perhaps that there is a third way."

"Explain." The Caliph's Voice clearly knew his master's ways well enough not to require a prompt at every turn. His terse command convinced me that he truly was to be treated as nothing more than a conduit, speaking exactly as Ibn Fayed would if he cared to raise his voice.

"By coming close to the source of the attacks upon my grandfather's house I have gained distance from the Castle Morrow. Even the Horse Coast has grown small from so far away." I thought of Lord Nossar in his map room at Elm, inking back the faded and forgotten lines on ancient charts, laying claims that would see Martin's son and little girl into the ground. "I see that actions taken at such a remove may still be those of an honourable man though when viewed from the halls of my grandfather's castle they cry for justice and retribution. I see that the Prince of Arrow was right when he told me to travel, to meet the peoples against whom I might make war."

"And if assassination was the first way, what are the second and the third?" asked the Voice.

"The second way is war. For my grandfather to turn the wealth of his lands into more ships, a greater navy to scour the coasts of Liba." I didn't speak of invasion. While the Moors might find a foothold along the Horse Coast it seemed to me that the lands of Afrique would swallow armies whole without the need for the natives to do more than wait for the sun to work its will. "The third way is alliance."

Now Fayed laughed out loud. "My people have ruled here four thousand years." His voice so dry it almost creaked. He waved at the thin man who carried on without pause.

"A chain of civilization stretching back unbroken across millennia. And you come here ragged, empty-handed? Only through the knowing of the mathema do we recognize you as king. It is true that charts render small what may hold many lives, but in our map room Renar may be found only after careful search and can be covered with the thumb." He made the appropriate gesture, as if squashing my kingdom like a bug. "Whereas a man may scarcely cover Liba with his hand." The thin man spread his fingers. And with the hand still raised, open and turned toward me, "There is a saying in the desert. Don't reach for friendship with an empty hand."

"What would the Earl Hansa pay to have you back, boy?" Fayed's croak from the throne.

I made the least of bows. "My hand only looks empty, Ibn Fayed." I didn't know what my grandfather might pay, but I guessed Fayed would ask for more than coin. Even if I survived the negotiations, to return dragging such a failure with me would undo any ties I had made in Morrow.

"What then does it hold?" the Voice asked.

"Tell me, Excellency, did you need your magicians to tell you I was coming?"

The Voice bridled at being questioned, anger written into the sharp lines of his face. Fayed made the briefest wave and the answer came, calm and without offence. "Hamada is a fortress that needs no walls. Only by caravan can the dunes be crossed. And rest assured that all who travel the salt roads are known in this palace before they come in sight of the city. Known by name and feature, their cargo known, down to the last fig in their saddlebags."

"And if you knew of my approach you would know also of my travelling companion," I said.

"Marco Onstantos Evenaline of the House Gold, Mercantile Derivatives South. A Florentine banker."

"He is waiting at your gates, Caliph. Why is he here?"

Again the wave to quell his Voice's objections. When a man doesn't bother to keep secrets from you, you know that you're in trouble.

"He comes to claim against a contract. Our payment for an old debt sunk off the Corsair Isle. Though the Florentines had agents aboard and had taken the monies into their care they say that under the agreed terms no payment is properly transacted until docked in Port Vito."

"Interesting," I said. "And although his visit is not welcomed or encouraged, you afford him the protections and diplomatic privileges agreed for the clans under empire law."

"Yes."

"And those old agreements might allow him a secret fig or two in his saddlebag . . . Perhaps you should bring him in and I could show you what's in my hand . . ."

The Voice had no answer. A long silence, nothing but the wafting of feathers as Ibn Fayed considered. The faintest of nods.

"He will be summoned."

Our audience proved less private than advertised for no further order was issued. And yet I assumed it was being acted upon.

"An interesting cat you have there, Excellency." I don't count small talk amongst my skills but we couldn't just watch each other for the next ten minutes waiting on Marco.

"A leopard," the Voice replied. "From the interior."

A long pause. I'm really not good at idle chat.

"So you're destroying all the Builders' works? I'm interested in hearing the reasons why."

"It is no secret." The Voice looked uncomfortable even so. "The caliph's proclamations have been called out after prayers across Liba for close on a year now. This new wisdom came to him in a dream at the end of the Holy Month. On the Day of a Thousand Suns there came a dawn so bright that many of our ancestors who died that morning could not see the way to paradise. They sought the darkness of their machines to hide from that unholy light. But they became trapped there, djinns, haunting the relics of their past. It is out of mercy that we act. We break open their prisons and set them free to ascend to their reward."

He delivered his lines with conviction. Whether he believed them, or whether he could have made a great actor, I didn't know.

"Let us hope those trapped souls understand the mercies that you heap upon them," I said. "And whose idea was it? Some scheme out of the mathema?"

"Mine." Ibn Fayed laid the claim from his throne, his hands closing into fists.

A distant, hollow sound, repeated, and again. I glanced back along the silk runner to see the doors open. Marco Onstantos Evenaline stepped through, in his blacks as ever, but with his hat in his hand. He must have been plucked from the line shortly after we passed him and have followed in our footsteps.

We all watched his slow advance across the width of the hall. Ibn Fayed really did have a hell of a throne room. It occurred to me that a large portion of the Haunt would fit into it, and certainly the entirety of the villages of Gutting and Little Gutting.

At last Marco drew up alongside me, looking pleased for the first time since we met. The absence of his trunk had changed him, he stood taller, more proud.

"Ibn Fayed, Caliph of Liba, Lord of the Three Realms, Water-Giver, welcomes Marco Onstantos Evenaline of the House Gold, Mercantile Derivatives South to his humble abode."

"As well he should," Marco said. "Though courtesies will prove no shield from the consequences of his actions."

"You dare?" The Voice may have spoken an alien tongue but the volume and tone drew ten curved blades from the scabbards of the imperial guard.

"Harsh language to use over an unpaid debt, Marco?" I did my best to ignore the glittering steel a foot to my left, the guardsmen having included me in the insult. "By the look of things I would say the caliph is good for it?" I didn't wave my arm at the opulence of our surroundings, concerned that someone might lop it off.

"You wallow in ignorance, Jorg of Renar, like a pig in filth. It will please me to see you burn."

"Marco! I thought we were friends?" I tried not to smile but I was never the actor.

He looked away from me toward the throne. "Ibn Fayed, you are sentenced to die. All of Hamada is forfeit."

Two long steel bolts appeared in Marco's chest, jutting out at diverging angles. I took a moment to recognize them as projectiles, fired from some overlarge crossbows that must be concealed in galleries above us.

Marco staggered half a step and raised his hands. "Die." Joints crackled as he formed a fist. It put me in mind of that scorpion in the Hills as I unwound it. For a heartbeat he hypnotized all of us, stood there impaled on those bolts, his hat rolling on its brim at his feet. Fist slammed into palm.

And nothing.

Though perhaps it seemed brighter for a second, as if the sun had peeked out from behind clouds.

Marco pounded fist into palm a second time. "No!" He swept us with a wild gaze, looked down at the shafts in his chest, and collapsed.

"This is what is in your hand?" the Voice asked. "A madman?"

"Look out of your window, Ibn Fayed." I pointed west.

A sharp clap sent one of the guards running to haul open the shutters.

The man pulled on a concealed rope and the screens parted, the brightness of the day dazzling us. For long moments we stood blinking in the desert light, trying to see into the brilliance of the outside world. And there it rose, boiling upward over the dunes, a fierce column of orange and black, fire threaded with night, opening into an inferno, mushrooming above the sands, and above that, impossibly high, a white halo of cloud spreading, outpacing the flames.

The burned half of my face pulsed with warmth, a heat on the edge of pain, the light of it filling my eye and making something new of the flame-cloud, lending it an ethereal beauty and the aspect of a gate, or fissure in the world, opening onto something that could be heaven or could be hell.

"It would take you two days on camel back to stand dead centre beneath that explosion," I said.

"I don't understand." Ibn Fayed stood from his throne.

"Have Marco's trunk brought here," I said.

The caliph nodded. His Voice called out the command.

We had no need of small talk while we waited. The explosion demanded the eye. None of us spoke. Even the servants laid down their feathered poles to watch. And after five minutes we saw the dunes rise, the sand leaping into the air, one after the next, bang, bang, bang, faster than an arrow in flight. The sound hit us, a wall of it, loud enough to take every shutter from its hinges and leave a finger's width of sand across each inch of the marble floor. The rumble that followed drew out for an age, deep and full of terror.

Qalasadi and Yusuf came through the great doors, six guards behind them carrying Marco's trunk. If they knocked we didn't hear them.

They set the trunk beside Marco's corpse.

"You have checked this?" The Voice pointed at it.

"We have." Qalasadi nodded. "In any event, nothing of the Builders' magic can pass the gates and seals set upon this palace."

"That's n—" I bit off the words and patted my chest. Gone! The view-ring wasn't there. "How in hell—"

"I cut the thong just before we left the mathema," Yusuf said. "Kalal stayed to pick it from the floor."

"A light touch, Brother Yusuf. I hadn't taken you for a thief." It unnerved me to think he had held a blade at my neck, but I supposed they had had me in a noose since I set foot on the quay at Kutta port.

"Theft is about timing, Jorg, and timing can be calculated." He seemed unashamed.

I remembered the bell sounding as we left the tower, holding my attention, drowning out other senses, overwriting the clink of viewing-ring striking floor.

"Besides," Yusuf continued. "It would have been detected and taken at the palace gates, casting you in a very bad light. A friend couldn't let that happen to a friend."

I shrugged. There seemed little else to do. In any event, they hadn't detected my gun. Perhaps when they spoke of the Builders' works they meant the ones with more magic and less mechanics. The ones where lightning ran trapped in metal veins.

"Open it." Ibn Fayed, returned to his throne, gaze flicking from window to trunk, trunk to window.

Qalasadi kneeled, undid the catches, worked some magic on the lock—a lock I knew to be very tricky—and threw back the lid.

"Sand?" The caliph leaned forward.

The desert taught me many things. Two of those things were about Marco. The desert is a quiet place. Not silent. There is always the wind, the hiss of sand, the plod of feet, and the complaint of camels. But it is a place where a man can be heard and where a man can listen. When I listened to Marco I noticed that he whirred, he creaked, and he ticked. All these sounds existed on the edge of hearing, but once noted could be found in any quiet moment, especially if he exerted himself, then I would hear it more clearly, that whirring, like the cogs in my watch.

And in discovering this strangeness I found myself watching Marco Onstantos Evenaline, the white man in his black suit, unburned by the sun, sweating but never wilting, a man curiously unsuited to what should be, excluding the harshness of ledgers, a business of warm handshakes and human bonding.

The second thing I learned at night, watching the infinite stars. I noticed that they shimmered. Only to be expected, of course. Stars twinkle. But it seemed to me, in the dead of night, with the sands about us cooled and the air cold enough to set me deep into my blankets, that the stars above Marco's camel twinkled too much. And I remembered that heat haze I had seen in the Iberico Hills, with just the eye ringed by the burn that Gog left me by way of a thank you. The haze I saw with a second sight. The haze that warned of secret fires.

A week later, in the dead of night, two days out from Hamada, I rose from my blankets. The Ha'tari were used to men leaving the caravan to water the sands. In the Margins we had a trench cut to save us wandering out amongst the fissures and the horrors that lurked there, but in the desert we could find a quiet spot among the dunes. It was far less common that a man should lead his camel out into the sand. And I wasn't even leading mine, I was leading Marco's. Perhaps they thought me a city boy, too long without the company of women, and tempted beyond reason by the twitching rear of the camel ahead. Probably they thought I wanted to steal from the banker. Either way, none of them liked him, and they liked my gold.

I didn't go far. In the dip between two moon-pale dunes I hefted the trunk from the camel's back and set to working at its tricky lock with tiny picks I keep from my years with the brothers. There's little call for anything more sophisticated than an axe when faced with a lock on the road, but they always fascinated me and I learned a few techniques from men in our band who had found their way into disgrace through less violent paths than mine. I worked veiled, with the sand gauze across the eye-slit, using only touch.

In time I had the case unlocked. I dug a grave in the sand, more of a dent—you can't scoop a deep hole in the dunes any more than you can dig in water. It took much of my strength to tip the trunk onto its side. The view-ring's capabilities told me plain that only a fraction of the machinery before me was required to manufacture Michael's image. I had to wonder at the weight of the rest and the wisps of hidden fire rising from it.

I guessed that the contents would separate from the container easy enough. No ancient's hand had stretched the sharkskin over its frame, nor wood panelled the interior. Marco would want to be able to change the casing without effort in order to disguise his cargo when required.

I opened the lid from the side and tipped the trunk forward so it fell open-mouthed into the pit . . . into the dent at least. Some fiddling, the application of my knife's point in two places, and enough shaking and grunting to alarm Marco's camel, soon won the trunk free of its contents. I used a stolen plate to heap sand over the rectangular block of silver-steel and plasteek. The machine buzzed once during the process then fell silent.

With sand mounded smoothly over the device I turned my attention to filling the trunk. Half an hour later, sweaty and dry-mouthed, I near killed myself hauling the thing onto the camel's back once more.

"How did you know the Builder-ghosts would not just explode the device while you were burying it?" Qalasadi asked.

"How could they know what was happening? And such things are of immense value—they cannot be made again. They would not destroy it unless all hope of recovering it had gone," I said.

"Why would they allow the banker to detonate it if it were not close enough to the palace to destroy Ibn Fayed?" Yusuf asked.

"I didn't know for sure that they would," I said. "It seems though that the Builder-ghosts see less than we might think, especially in the desert and where their works have been targeted for destruction. They must have placed their trust in Marco to act in their interest. Even if they knew where the device lay, they could not with certainty say that the caliph had not entered the radius of destruction. Or perhaps they expected it to be more devastating."

"More?" The Voice drew a deep breath.

I shrugged. "In any event, Marco didn't need to bring his trunk into the throne room to do its work, or into the palace. He could have destroyed Hamada from a mile off amongst the dunes. Whether his bravado before the throne was on the Builders' instructions or what he felt to be a fitting exit from the world, I don't know."

"The Builders threw their suns from one side of the world to the other on tongues of flame, and where they burned whole countries were reduced to char," Qalasadi said. "Why have one lone banker haul the weapon here on a camel?"

"There's not much that still works after a thousand years." I closed the trunk and sat on the lid. "The rockets and the greatest of their weapons are spent and useless. Only the triggers are left intact . . . the sparks that lit the suns, if you like. They need to be moved by agents to the city that is to be destroyed."

"And this is their vengeance for my . . ." Ibn Fayed looked old, a tremor in his hands. "I was too proud. For my people's sake I will—"

"You may have put yourself at the head of the queue, Caliph, but I think there is more to it than that. Michael, he called himself. It may not be chance that he shares his name with the archangel, warlord of God's armies. The Builders have larger worries than one desert ruler breaking what machinery he can find above the dunes. Some among them plan to kill us all. Hamada was to be a demonstration. A model to be repeated."

"Lucky for us that you arrived on our shores when you did then, King Jorg." Qalasadi bowed his head.

"Was it luck, magician?" I tried to see his eyes but he kept his face down. "You knew the Builder-ghosts were mounting some kind of attack. You thought it involved me . . . and you let me into the caliph's palace, albeit declawed. And perhaps there was another hand pointing my way, working on that timing you all seem so proud of . . ." I wondered, had Fexler played me, pushed me here and there across his board with the most gentle of nudges and the occasional flash of red light glimpsed through a steel ring? Had he delayed Marco, or sped his way, so that we found Port Albus together? Had I been Fexler's agent in some contest with Michael . . . with the whole of his faction?

"Explain to me," Ibn Fayed said, "why this assassin would risk so much just to let me know his mind before we all died? If my archers had not both contrived to miss his heart, he could have died without igniting . . ." His gaze returned to the windows. "That."

"I don't think there was any danger of him failing," I said.

"But he died just moments after completing his mission," Ibn Fayed said, sharp eyes beneath grey and bushy brows.

"Oh, Marco's not dead," I said. "Are you, Marco?"

The modern's head snapped up. The speed of it shocking, like a length of flexed metal flicking straight, murder in his eyes.

"I'm far from sure he was ever alive." I stepped back, not drawing my sword in case over-zealous archers threaded bolts through my chest as well.

Marco got to his feet in a quick series of jerky motions. He pulled the bolts from his body and dropped them to the floor, blood-smeared but not dripping. The imperial guard drew their swords again.

"You just wanted to hear how you were tricked, didn't you, Marco? Before you found a good moment to finish at least part of the job."

He ignored me and leapt at the caliph, careless of the guardsmen blocking his way. Bright blades flickered in motion, feet scrabbled on the sandy floor, blood sprayed, gobbets of flesh flew and Marco surged to within a yard of Ibn Fayed before the weight of men took him to the ground. He fought with the same frightening speed demonstrated when he raised his head, fingers rending muscle and fat, throwing grown men away as if they were less than children. The swords that fell on him sliced his blacks to tatters but beneath the red butchery of his flesh metal gleamed, copper and silver-steel. Whirs and clicks accompanied his movements, audible through the screams, the clash of steel, and the leopard's spitting howl. The noise of teeth-through-ratchets as fingers closed on necks with the inexorable strength of the vice.

Men died. Marco found his feet again. Ibn Fayed and his Voice moved to shelter behind the throne as Marco climbed the third step, blood running down the stone in red trickles. Injured guardsmen clung to both legs, others hewed at him as though he were a tree. Before the throne the leopard and its handler hesitated. The cat had been straining at its chain, ready to attack. Now it sat back, ears flat to its skull. Sensible beast.

More guardsmen were running in from the great doors, and more behind them, but like all things it was a matter of timing. Marco had enough of it for his purpose and they had insufficient for theirs. He would kill the caliph before they stopped him.

I mounted the three steps, careful of my footing in the gore, pulled the gun from beneath my robes. With the barrel set to the back of his pale skull I put four bullets through the metal casing and into whatever clockwork served him for a brain.

He fell twitching amongst the dead and wounded as the echoes of the last shot died away.

I held the gun up. "Old technology." I pointed it at Marco. "New technology. You might want to rework those seals, Qalasadi." I spun the gun around my finger and caught it flat in my palm, displaying it to Ibn Fayed, "And this, Caliph, is what I have in my hand."

36

Five years earlier

Ibn Fayed had them set a throne of silver one step down from the summit of his dais and when I returned to court, clean and refreshed, dressed in silks and a heavy chain of gold, he bade me sit there.

"These are sorry times when the ghosts of our ancestors reach out to take our lives." He spoke to me direct now, slow with his words as if fishing them from the dust of memory.

"They are not agreed, those ghosts. A war, of sorts, rages among them, deep in their machines. But few if any of the Builders have good intentions for us. Even our saviours would make us slaves," I told him.

"Then you will join me? Dig out and destroy what can be found of them? Start a new era free from the ghosts of the past?" Ibn Fayed sounded curious rather than eager.

"A wise man told me that history will not stop us repeating our mistakes, but will at least make us ashamed of doing so." I remembered Lundist's smile when he said it, as much of sadness in it as amusement. "Will you argue your case at Congression, Ibn Fayed?"

"It would seem foolish to attend. What better place for the ghosts to destroy us? Can we trust the Gilden Guard to keep all agents such as the banker from coming within several miles of the Gilden Gates?"

I steepled my fingers before my mouth to hide the laugh rising there. "Caliph, I would bet my life that the last emperor, all his fathers before him, and every Congression since the stewardship has sat above a device more powerful than the one Marco carried toward Hamada. The Builder-ghosts would want to know they could end the empire any time they chose. The fact that they have not done so just tells us that Michael's faction do not yet hold command amongst their brothers nor have unfettered access to whatever controls such weapons.

If the ghosts ever unite to a degree sufficient to destroy Vyene then nowhere will be safe. Marco only failed here by poor luck and by the intervention of other ghosts." I felt sure now that Fexler had aimed me at the modern, or clockwork soldier, or whatever the hell Marco really was.

"And when you go to Congression, Jorg, how will you cast your vote?" Ibn Fayed asked, affording me the courtesy that one lone vote might matter.

"For myself, of course." I grinned, creasing the stiffness of scar tissue. "And you, Caliph?"

"Orrin of Arrow is a good man," he said. "It might be time for such a man."

"Wouldn't an emperor grate on you? Don't you prefer to rule the desert with a free hand?"

Ibn Fayed shook his head, croaking a dry laugh. "I live on the very edge of the Holy Empire. To the south, as far away as Vyene, is another emperor, a Cerani emperor, and his domain reaches to my borders, as vast as our broken empire ever was at its heights. Soon enough, maybe not in my lifetime but surely before my grandson takes this chair, the Cerani and their allied tribes will come out of the desert and swallow Liba whole. That is unless someone is crowned at Vyene to remake our strength."

I passed a month in the desert city. I learned what I could of their ways. For some weeks I studied in the mathema, even pieced together a little of their door. Qalasadi returned the view-ring to my keeping, on the understanding that it must never enter the palace and must leave Liba with me.

I sat one evening in the mathema tower, closeted alone in a windowless chamber on the floor behind the door marked "epsilon." A simple earthenware oil lamp lit the book before me, equations and more equations. I have the head for mathematics but no love for it. I've seen a formula bring tears to Kalal's eyes with its elegance and the sheer beauty of its symmetries. I grasped the formula, or thought I did, but it didn't move me. Whatever poetry such things hold I am deaf to it.

On the table beside the book, the view-ring, a shiny and inert lump since the explosion, or since Qalasadi's intervention, although he said they did nothing to it. I yawned and slammed the book hard enough to make the flame jerk and shudder, and to set the ring dancing like a spun coin at the very last of its rotations. But unlike a coin the ring kept its oscillations going. I watched it, hypnotized.

"Jorg?" And Fexler's image rose above the ring, painted in whites as always, not quite opaque. If the Builders had set themselves the task of recreating ghosts from the stories told to children they could have done the job no better.

"Who's asking?"

He focused on me as I spoke, his image growing sharper. "Can't you see me?"

"I can see you."

"Then you recognize me. Fexler Brews."

I laid my hand flat across the book. "It says here that a prediction will diverge from the truth. The further the prediction is carried, the larger the discrepancy. Wraps it all up in statistics and bounds, of course. But the message is clear enough. You're a prediction. I doubt you're anything like the man I saw die any more."

"Untrue," Fexler said. "I have the original data. I don't need to rely on fading memories. Fexler Brews is alive in me as true and clear as ever."

I shook my head and watched him. The shadows danced everywhere but across him. On me, on the walls, the ceiling, only Fexler constant, lit by his own light.

"You can't grow if you're constantly defined by this collection of frozen moments that you keep returning to. And if you can't grow, you're not alive. So either you're Fexler, and like him you're dead. Or you're alive, but you're someone else. Something else."

"Are you sure it's me we're talking about?" Fexler raised a brow— very human.

"Ah . . ." It closed on me like steel jaws. The worst traps are the ones we lay for ourselves. All these years and it took a nothing, a web of numbers, to show me to myself. I could count on one hand the brief and personal passion plays that nailed me to my past. The carriage and the thorns. The hammer and Justice burning. The bishop. Father's knife jutting from my chest. And at my hip, in a copper box, perhaps one more. "I liked you better before, Fexler. Why are you here?"

"I came to learn your plans," he said.

"You don't watch me enough to know them?"

"I have been . . . busy, elsewhere."

"Vyene is calling me," I said. "I mean to take ship to Mazeno and travel by road to the Gilden Gates. It will probably be a quicker return journey than the one that brought me here. And besides, I have a memory from a fever dream, a memory of you asking me to go there, something about the throne, and my view-ring, only you were calling it a different name. Control ring? Is that a true memory?"

"It is a true memory, but I won't speak of it now. It is probable others are listening. Go to Vyene: it will be a good education."

I sat back, ran my eye across the books ranked along shelves from floor to ceiling, all that knowledge. "These mathmagicians, they're the champions of that effort to recivilize us, aren't they, Fexler? The start of a new understanding, so we can repair what the Builders built."

"One of several such starts." He nodded.

"I've looked at the scraps left from your time. Almost nothing was ever written down . . ."

"It was written into machines, into memory. You just lack the means to read it." Fexler looked around at the books too, as if he needed to use his eyes to see them. One of many deceptions, no doubt.

"I've looked at those scraps and nowhere does it speak of heaven and hell, of a life beyond death, of church or mosque or any place of worship."

Fexler looked down at me, floating as he was a foot above the desk, his head near touching the ceiling. "Few among us concerned ourselves with religion. We had answers that didn't require faith."

"But I've spoken with an angel." I frowned. "At least I think I have. And for damn sure I've reached into the deadlands chasing after pieces of men's souls. How can you—"

"For a clever boy you can be very stupid, Jorg." Something in his voice carried a faint echo of that angel, timeless, tolerant.

"What?" Spoken too loud. My anger is never more than a moment away. It makes a fool of me more times than I can say.

"Our greatest work was to change the role of the observer. We put power into the hands of men, directly into their hands. Too much power as it turned out. If the raw strength of one man's will, the right man's will, can bring fire from nothing, part the waters, pulverize stone, command winds. What then of the unfocused desire and expectation of millions?"

"You—"

"Your afterlife is what you expect it to be, what the thousands, the millions around you expect, what legend builds, told, retold, refined, evolving. In this place, amongst the sands, they fashion themselves a different paradise and different paths to it, some dark, some light. All of it is fabrication, constructed over the reality my people lived in. Whatever waited for a man after his death in those times, it was not mentioned in our calculations. Our priests, when they could

find anyone to listen, described something more subtle, more profound, and more wonderful than the mishmash of medieval supersti-
tion your kind have built upon."

"We made it?" It didn't seem possible. "We built heaven and hell?"

"Oh yes. If your priests ever discover what power lies at their fingertips with the will of their flock behind them . . . well, pray that
they do not, or every word of fire and brimstone, of last judgments
and devils with pitchforks, will become the gospel truth, rising up on
all sides. Why do you think we have worked so hard to reinforce the
church's hatred of 'magic' and its practice?"

The worst of it was that I believed him. It sounded like truth.
Without pause, I took the book of calculus and set it down on the
view-ring, hard. Fexler's image vanished like a spot of light when you
put your hand over the hole that casts it. There's only so much truth
I can listen to in one go.

Qalasadi and Yusuf came to the edge of Hamada to see me off into
the desert. I had made my farewells to Ibn Fayed in the coolness of
his throne room, accepting gifts of gold, diamonds, amber, and of
clove-spice for the journey. "There is always pain," the caliph told me,
closing my hand around the spice.

Omal waited with the camels, ten altogether, three tall, white
ones—gifts to me from the caliph—good breeders and from fine
bloodlines by all accounts. To me they were as ill-tempered, ungainly,
and foul-smelling as the rest of them. Along with Omal we had three
more drovers and a guard of five Ha'tari.

"Safe journey, King Jorg." Qalasadi bowed, one hand folded
across his stomach.

"I've yet to have one of those, but let's hope this will be it." I
grinned and inclined my head a fraction.

"Next time you will come to my house, meet my wife, see what I
have to suffer," Yusuf said, a smile on him, eyes bright.

"Next time I will." I turned to go, but paused. "And the Prince of Arrow? Don't your predictions tell you to erase me so that he might have a clear run?" For a cold moment I wondered if the nine men accompanying me had orders to bury my corpse in a dune.

Yusuf's grin became a little fixed and he shot an embarrassed glance at Qalasadi. The older man laced his fingers and brought both hands to his chin.

"Our projections show no significant probability of you imped-ing the Prince of Arrow, King Jorg. As such we are rescued from hav-ing to wrestle with the problems of the one over the many and the many over the one."

"If he comes to Renar, Jorg, don't get in his way." An edge of pleading in Yusuf's voice. "It would not be wise."

"Well." The revelation left me a little nonplussed despite saving me from conflict with the mathmagicians. "That's good then." And I went to mount my camel.

37

Chella's story

Keres had left a brittle feeling in her wake. The carriage creaked like an old man's joints and every place she had touched lay rough, discoloured, dry enough to suck the moisture from skin.

"She'll find her way back to the Dead King." Chella turned away from the road, Kai kept close at her shoulder.

The lichkin would follow fractures and fault-lines, places where the veils hung threadbare between the world and death's dry dominion. She would travel in coffins, shadow the sick, drift with plague spores, and in time she would enter the Dead King's court, wrapped again in unquiet spirits, snatched up on her journey.

"We should be moving, delegate." Captain Axtis of the Gilden Guard had marshalled his troops a mile down the road whilst the necromancers tended to Keres' needs. Although the guard remained ignorant of the lichkin its presence unsettled them, sapping morale. Axtis seemed keen to move on, to leave Gottering to the dead.

"Let us do that." Chella hauled herself back into the carriage. "Be as quick as you like, driver."

They lurched into motion even before Kai shut the door behind him. He caught the side of the bench to stop the fall carrying him into Chella's lap, and held himself for a moment, twelve inches separating their swaying bodies. Her pulse beat fierce in the veins of her wrists.

Swift hands. For a moment Chella savoured the thought of such entanglement. Kai found his balance and his seat at the same time she pushed him away—a mutual decision. She closed her hands, nails sharp in her palms, and put her head back against the rest. *What would I want with a pretty blond thing like him in any case? Unseasoned meat.*

"We will be in Honth soon?" Kai asked.

"Yes." He knew that. The living just liked to chatter—they would spend long enough silent in the grave. The same need twisted her lips, wanting her to add more. She pressed them tight.

"Then along the Danoob," Kai said. "Have you ever seen it, Chella?"

"No."

"They say if you're in love the waters look blue."

Before Jorg she had never travelled, never strayed from Gelleth, just that short journey from Jonholt to the mountain. A scant few miles in three lifetimes, but oh the things she had seen on that trip.

The span of three lives spent digging into death, unravelling mysteries, stepping away from life in all its mess and clutter and squabbles. And here she sat, rattling her way toward the heart of empire, sick with being alive, stomach roiling at the jolting motion and at the thought of what lay ahead. Not until the Dead King announced her as his representative and pressed five voting seals into her hands had she ever doubted his genius. Now she knew it for insanity.

At the town of Wendmere Captain Axtis halted the column for lunch. The guard set their five times fifty warhorses, their pack animals, and the steeds of the column-followers to grazing in the meadows, careless of who farmed them or what need the grass was set against. The ragged tail of followers still straggled in as Kai and Chella seated themselves beside the hearth in Wendmere's finest inn. Chella noted the armourers' wagons rolling by, the carts of the farriers, the troop's leather workers, the seamstresses' tiny wagon. Kai paid more attention to the whores, an ever-changing population trailing the guard, girls on mules, girls in open buggies and gigs, more in

Onsa's wheel-house. Each band with some cut-faced rogue to guard and guide and chivvy and negotiate. Chella could almost see the chains of hunger and misery that towed them behind the golden men of Vyene.

Guards brought in goblets and platters in their velvet-lined cases from the goods train, each piece set with the imperial eagle. Only the Gilden Guard themselves could be trusted to serve their wards, to serve the Hundred or their representatives. Chella found herself wondering if these gleaming warriors could handle their swords as well as they handled the silver cutlery being set before her.

"What do you think of the empire's elite, Kai? You served in an army, did you not?"

Kai lowered his goblet from wine-darkened lips. He frowned at the man standing to attention ready to refill it. "Who says the guard are 'elite'? Every petty noble's third son who's too dumb to make it in the clergy gets shipped off to Vyene where each grows fat on bribes as an over-valued 'watchman,' and each fourth year they get to go on a little trip to collect the Hundred. Pretty armour doesn't make a warrior."

To their credit, the men around them hid their offence well.

"I guess the truth lies somewhere between," Chella said. "I hear they train hard, these men of Vyene. They are, perhaps, as well-forged as a weapon can be without fire."

She looked out, through the distortion of the small and puddle-paned windows, across the rooftops, to distant smoke. Their true protection stalked out there somewhere, Thantos, more cautious than his sister and more deadly.

Keres had been skinned, though! A chill crept over Chella, despite the fire, despite the wine. If the lichkin could have told them what happened—her mind would be at better ease. A trouble named is a trouble tamed.

Captain Axtis came in, stamping against the cold and brushing rain off the shoulders of his cloak.

"Tell me, Captain," Chella said. "When were the guard last called on to defend the Gilden Gates, when did they last take to the battlefield?"

"Sixtieth year of the Interregnum, Madam Delegate." Without hesitation. "The battle of Crassis Plains, against the Holy Roman army of the false emperor Manzal."

A generation ago. "Were you even born then, Axtis?"

"I was two years of age, Madam Delegate."

And showing grey hairs under that helm today. Chella wondered how they would stand against the dead of her master's army, the quick and the slow, with the ghouls and the lichkin.

"I came to say we should be moving on if you're set upon a full escort the whole way to Vyene."

"Oh we are, Captain." Chella set down her goblet and stood. It would serve Axtis very well to put her and Kai upon one of those golden barges. To let the Danoob carry his problems away, to discharge his responsibilities to the river, and if the barge should sink with all hands, a small price to pay to keep Congression beyond the Dead King's reach for another four years.

The carriage rolled on amidst the guard column, past woods and fields, town and cottage. Chella found herself watching the scenery, enjoying the warmth of rare sunshine between the rains, breathing in the scents of the countryside, the stink of farms. When the cry of "Honth" shook her from her thoughts she bit her tongue to let the pain sharpen her. Life casts more spells than any necromancer and they can be twice as deadly in their softness.

"How far?" she called out to the driver.

"A mile, two maybe."

They creaked on for a few more minutes before rolling to a halt.

"We can't be there yet." Kai opened the door. Hedgerows, cattle lowing beyond. A surge of horse and gold-armoured bodies, and Axtis dismounted before them.

"Lady Chella, another delegate—"

"Get out of the way." A louder voice overriding the captain's. "You can't stop me—I'm on a peace mission."

Axtis slammed the carriage door in Kai's face.

"You have no authority here, sir!" Axtis used the shout he reserved for his men. "I suggest you return to the forward column."

The sound of someone jumping from their horse. "I'm on a diplomatic visit, Captain. Your job is to facilitate such intercourse. If we delegates come to blows you may intervene."

The carriage door rattled, a hand on the handle. Kai blocked the grille, staring down at the scene outside.

"This has to be the representatives from the Drowned Isles, no? Who else would be following from the west?" A loud sniff. "Doesn't smell like the Dead King—who've you got in here, Captain?"

Kai opened the door. And backed away, half-pushed, half of his own accord, as Jorg Ancrath, clad in the blacks and reds of a road tunic, clambered in.

"Chella!" The boy turned one of his dangerous smiles on her, ignoring Kai.

"Jorg."

He sat on the bench opposite them, legs stretched out, boots muddy on the floor, at perfect ease. He flicked the long black tangles of his hair back across his shoulders, watching her with dark eyes, amusement touching the sharp angles of his face, the ugly burn a reminder of his extremes.

"Two of you?" Again that sharp grin. "Is that all the living that can be mustered from the Drowned Isles? And Chella, you're no Brettan. I would have heard it in your voice."

"*The* Jorg?" Kai turned her way.

"A Jorg, certainly." Jorg leaned in, elbows on his knees. Outside, the guard clustered. "And it does seem I'm the object of unhealthy fascination in certain quarters. Isn't that so, Chella?" He let his hand fall to rest on the black skirts over her thigh. "I am of course married now, dear heart, so you must put romance from your mind."

"The Dead King—" Kai began.

"The Dead King loves me too, I think," Jorg said, fingers closing on her flesh. "He has watched me for years. Sent his minions to raid my brother's tomb." He turned to face Kai, very quick. "Do you know why?"

"I—"

Jorg turned back, fixing Chella with his stare. "He doesn't know. Do you?"

"No."

"How frustrating for you." Jorg released her and leaned back on the bench. Her leg burned where his fingers had been. "Shall we carry on? My column is just ahead waiting to cross the Rhyme at the Honth bridge."

Kai stamped for the carriage to proceed. "From what I've heard, I am surprised that you would choose to ride in the Lady Chella's company, King Jorg."

"She's been telling tales, has she?" Jorg leaned forward again, with the air of a conspirator. "Truth be told— Wait, I don't even know your name. I know you're a man of the Isles, I have one of your countrymen in my carriage, a Merssy man, Gomst they call him. I'm pleased to see the Dead King has sent at least as many Brettans to Congression as I have. But your name?"

"He's Kai Summerson," Chella said, anxious to gain some control. "So why are you riding with us, Jorg?"

"Can't I just enjoy your company? Might I not be pining for my lady of the mire?" Jorg cast a lascivious eye along the length of her. Despite herself Chella felt the blood rise in her cheeks. Ancrath noticed immediately and grinned all the wider. "You look . . . different, Chella. Older?"

She kept her lips sealed. They jolted another hundred yards before he spoke.

"In truth? I could think of no easy way to kill you all. And so to keep my son safe from you I need to watch you. Closely. If that should prove impossible I would of course have to resort to killing you the hard way."

"Son?" Chella found it hard to imagine, and imagination was something that had returned in strength when the necromancy faded from her. "You have a son?"

Jorg nodded. "Even so. Another William, to make his grandfather proud. Though I don't know if Olidan of Ancrath lived long enough to be a grandfather?"

"If he's dead I know nothing of it." Time was she felt each death as ripples in a pond, and the King of Ancrath would have made quite a splash—now though, she might have new eyes for the living world, but she lay deaf to the deadlands. Jorg's fault, of course. She said it to herself again, hoping to believe it. Jorg's fault.

Jorg frowned, just for a moment, replacing it with the smile he wore in place of armour. "No matter."

"I've no designs on your son, Jorg," Chella said. It surprised her to find that she didn't.

"And you, Kai Summerson? Are you a child killer?" Jorg asked.

"No." A sharp reply, the offence written on his face. It seemed laughable that a necromancer should rail against such a suggestion, but then she remembered Kai had killed no one since she took him. When you learn the dark arts amid the corpse-hordes of the Isles murder is no longer a pre-requisite.

"Me, I have taken the lives of children, Kai. Baby boy, small girl, it means little. The lives of men even less. Do not cross me." Careless words scattered like broken glass for the Brettan to pick a path through. Chella came to Kai's aid before he cut himself.

"Does your son make you happy, Jorg?" The question felt important. Jorg Ancrath with a baby boy. Chella tried to picture him with the infant in his arms.

Jorg flashed a dark look her way. He bowed his head, shielded by the hair that swept about his face, and for the longest time she thought he would not reply.

"There are no happy endings for such as us, Chella. No redemption. Not with our sins. Any joy is borrowed—laughter shared on the road, and left behind." He turned to Kai. "I have killed children, Kai Summerson. In such company you will too." Something familiar lay in his voice, in the framing of his words. She could almost taste it.

Returning his gaze to Chella Jorg watched her face awhile, sorrow in his own. "We have both walked black paths, lady. Don't think that mine leads back into the light. Of all those that tried to guide me, of my father, of the whispers from the thorn bush, of Corion's evil council, the darkest voice was ever mine."

And in a moment of recognition Chella knew who the Dead King was.

38

When Makin reported the Isles' contingent catching up our own golden host I had known Chella would be amongst their number. Known it blood to bone, without evidence or reason. And I left our carriage, my wife, my child, my tantalizing aunt, with more swiftness than was seemly, and with less trepidation than when I went to my father's carriage, though this one might hold the Dead King himself. I closed the door on them all, on all my weaknesses. Despite my tempering of years some foolish part of me still reached for the happiness of family, the redemption love might bring. Broken hopes that would not serve me. I closed the door on them and rode toward what I knew best—toward the damned. My past lay black, the future burned, and in the thin slice between, the world expected me to be a father, to hold a son, to save him, save them all? Too much to ask of a man so dark with sin. Too much to ask of any man perhaps.

The Dead King's carriage, whilst not so grand as Lord Holland's, had nothing funereal about it. Even the presence of two necromancers hadn't tainted the atmosphere. In fact I didn't know for sure if Kai Summerson practised the arts of reanimation: he seemed too young, too full of life. And Chella herself had changed. Beyond a doubt. In past encounters she had burned with an unholy joy, so fierce that its light became an after-image on the memory, obscuring truth. In the swamps and caverns an ambiguity of the flesh made her all things to all men, or at least to this one, ripe with the darkest juice. Now it seemed that a stranger sat opposite me, more old, more pale, still with a beauty to her, hair very black, high and delicate angles to her face, an elegance not seen before, her eyes dark with secrets and in unguarded moments becoming wounds.

"I still mean to kill you," I said, in part to pass the time as we rumbled through the streets of Honth.

She shrugged, less easy in her indifference than of old. "The Nuban forgave me. You should too."

That made me start. "He did not!" But he probably did. The Nuban never held grudges—said he had enough to carry and a long way to go.

"So, tell me about the Dead King," I asked Kai and he shuddered at the words. Just for a moment, quickly suppressed.

The Brettan looked out of the window before he answered, as if seeking the reassurance of daylight, comfort in the passing of narrow homes in plaster and thatch, each stuffed with lives, mother, father, squalling brats, toothless elders, bristling with argument and laughter, every flea hopping.

"The Dead King is the future, King Jorg. He closed his hand around the Drowned Isles and soon he'll reach out for the world. He rules in the deadlands, and we all will spend longer dead than we do living."

"But who is he, Chella? What is he? Why the interest in Ancrath?" She knew something. Perhaps she would tell me in the hope it would make me suffer.

"Ancrath is the gateway to the continent, Jorg. You're a clever boy, you should know that."

"Why me?" I asked.

"You make a lot of people take notice. Destroying mountains, holding huge armies at your gates. All very grand. And of course the

Dead King knows you have your eye on Ancrath. It's bad enough that your father proves so stubborn in his resistance, to have the son there in his place would be worse still, maybe?"

"Hmmm." It sounded plausible, but I didn't believe her. "And surely this Dead King can't think to win friends at Congression? He expects diplomacy? Negotiations with dead things crawled from slime and dust?"

Chella smiled to herself, a gentle thing that made her pretty. "There are worse monsters at the emperor's court, Jorg. The Queen of Red is on the road to Congression. The Silent Sister with her, to advise, and Luntar out of Thar with them. You've met Luntar I understand?"

"Just once." I had no memory of him, but we had met. He had given me that copper box, and filled it. "They might be monsters, perhaps worse than me, but they are born of women, they live, they will die. Tell me, where has this Dead King come from? Don't the dry-lands slope ever down? Don't they reach hell? Has he escaped Lucifer and climbed from the abyss?"

"He's no demon." Chella made a slow shake of her head, as if it might have been better to have a risen demon among us. "And what happens here, in the mud and dirt of this world, matters very much to him. Heaven, hell, and earth, three that are one—there can be no change above or below that isn't mirrored here. This world, where our lives are spent, is both a lock and a lever. That is what the Dead King says."

"And doesn't the Devil object to this vagrant camping on his very doorstep? Stealing what is his?" It seemed absurd to be debating the politics of hell, but I had reached into the dead-lands with my own hands, tasted the air, and I knew them to be a path to Lucifer's door.

"The Dead King plans to break open the gates of heaven," Kai said. "You think that he cares what else may come?"

"Everything is changing, Jorg." Chella bowed her head. "Everything."

"You still haven't told me where he came from, this messiah of yours. Why don't the ancients speak of him? In what books is he recorded?" I asked, still hoping for grains of truth in her lies and madness. "How old is he?"

"Young, Jorg. Very young. Younger than you."

39

Chella's story

The bridge at Tyrol spanned the Danoob in seventeen arches, a broad carriageway riding across stone pillars. The great bridge back at Honth had leaped the Rhyme in one breath-taking arc, but Chella liked the Tyrol bridge better. She could imagine it being built, see in her mind's eye the men who laboured here.

"How does the river look to you, Chella?" Jorg watched close for her answer.

"Brown and churning." She reported it faithfully. "What do you see, Kai?"

Kai half stood, peering through the window grille, swaying with the motion of the carriage. "Brown."

"Are there no lovers amongst us?" Jorg asked. "The legend that the waters look blue to those in love is older than this bridge."

"The river is brown. Shit brown. It's a matter of silt and drainage and the sewers of Tyrol, not of the sick-making fantasies that people want to wrap their fucking in." Chella saw no reason to keep the sourness to herself.

"Not so," Jorg said. "If the right man loved the right woman he could make that river run blue."

"Water-sworn." Kai sat back into the shadows, nodding.

"Meh." Jorg shook his head. "All this swearing. All these narrow paths. A man can reach into anything and turn it to his cause. It's not want, or desire, just certainty. Only be assured that whatever you reach into will reach into you in turn."

He set his boots across the gap between seats, resting between Kai and Chella. "Did you ever love, Kai? Was there a girl that would turn the waters blue for you?"

Kai opened his mouth then bit back on the answer. He started forward, then slumped. "No."

"Love." Jorg smiled. "Now there's something that will reach back into you."

The carriage rumbled from the bridge down onto the north bank where the roads lay better tended.

"Perhaps you should go back to your own carriage, Jorg, to your queen, and see if you like the view from there any better." Chella found herself not wanting him to leave, but tormenting him was all she knew. For a moment she saw the needle she had used to stick Kai, and felt it sliding into flesh again.

He pulled in his feet and leaned in toward her, close, hand resting once more upon her thigh. "What is it you're hoping to achieve at Congression, Chella? The Dead King can't think to win any converts, surely? I'm not even certain that Master Summerson here is a proper convert. So what is the point?"

"The point is that we have a right to attend and that the Dead King wishes us to. Either should be enough for you, Jorg of Ancrath." Chella winced at the grip on her leg. Life and pain walked hand in hand, neither to her liking.

He narrowed his eyes—how many had seen that look and then nothing else ever again?—and moved closer, his breath tickling across her cheek. "You're here to show us the human face of the dead-tide? To put Congression at its ease? Flatter old kings, a pretty boy to flirt with their queens and princesses?"

"No." Anger bubbled up in her, hot under the coolness of his breath—her hands made claws. "We're here with trickery and treachery and deceit and murder, just like you, Jorg of Ancrath, what else can broken things like us bring to the world?"

"Renar."

"What?" Her thigh burned, again, where he touched her, again.

"Jorg of Renar."

"Doesn't it gall you to take his name, the one who murdered little William? Sweet mother Rowan?"

"Better than to take my father's name."

"Instead you wear his brother's name? A man you keep in dark torment? Don't snarl so, I hear the guard speak of it, of how you murdered Harran, and another good man to get to the son."

He leaned in close. "Maybe I keep the name to remind me of the colour of my soul." His breath out, her breath in. She tasted cinnamon.

"Was that all I needed to seduce you, Jorg? To just be a touch less damned?"

He turned from her, staring at Kai in his shadowed corner. "Get out."

And he did, a quick unwelcome flash of daylight, cold and drear, and Kai was gone.

"I'm still going to kill you," Jorg said, very close.

Chella closed his mouth with hers.

She ran her fingers across his shoulders, plunged her hands down then up under the pleating of his road-tunic, across the heat and hardness of muscle laid over his back, stippled by old scars, the slice of a heavy blade, nicks and cuts, a hundred thorn wounds. He moved over her, tall, heavy, the dark wave of his hair falling about them, the scrape of his burned face as his mouth found the hollow of her neck.

Something hot and wet and vital ran through her, a sudden flood that took her breath and lifted her. The life-force she'd been resisting, rejecting, washed away all resistance, implacable as spring. She tore at him, angry, fierce, wanting. He lifted her, without pause or effort, slamming her back against the padded wall. Some small fragment of her worried that the driver might think it the sign to stop, and the guard would gather round. Jorg surged against her and all other voices quieted. His desire woke an answer in her, the need bled from every line of him, spoke in the ragged breaths he drew.

Their bodies came together in a savage recognition of flesh, her limbs strained under the weight of him, hand splayed one second, clenched the next, cushions shredded. Outside, the uneasy snort of horses, the whickering of mares, the stamp of stallions reacting to stray energies, to the scent of their lust. Jorg slammed her against the wall once more, harder, and the carriage lurched forward, the team breaking into a trot despite the driver's cries. Black skirts gathered around her hips.

Jorg entered her, brutal, quick, wanted—an ungentle coupling, both of them torn by rough need. Chella rose to meet him, all her strength locked against him, riding and ridden, no comfort offered or given. They coupled like wild cats, instinctual aggression kept at bay, a truce imposed by some deeper, older imperative, but unable to stop the violence bubbling over, ready to part squalling at the moment of release.

"Enough!" Jorg threw her off him and lurched backward onto the opposite bench, beyond the reach of her nails, panting, blood at the corner of his mouth.

"I— I'll say when it's enough, King of Renar." She spat the words between her gasps. She wanted more, but it might kill her. Every inch of her tingled, burned with a fire of new-woken life. Jorg had been the key to turn the lock. Perhaps any man might have served, but it seemed right that it had been him.

Jorg pushed back sweat-plastered hair and tied up his trews, the belt too broken to hold. "I'm far from sure you can even stand, madam." The flash of a grin, full of mischief. He looked very young in that moment.

"So that's how diplomacy is conducted at Congression?" she asked, heart still thumping, lying back in warmth and wetness.

"When we get there we'll see." Jorg scooped some stray buttons from the floor and set a hand to the door. "And when I'm crowned we'll have our last kiss."

As if she'd ever bend the knee and kiss his hand. The arrogance of it made her snarl.

"Back to your lady love now, Jorg?" Chella set a smile on her lips but it didn't fit well.

"She's too good for the likes of me, Chella. I'm soiled goods, past repair. I belong with our kind." He flashed that smile again and pushed out the door. "Come near my son and I'll kill you, Chella." And he was gone.

40

I kept Brath to a gentle trot, passing the guard of the Drowned Isles delegation and drawing ever closer to the golden army surrounding the delegations of Ancrath and Renar. Katherine with Father's two votes, me with my seven.

Katherine would know. Somehow she would know, even if she didn't trespass in my dreams she'd smell Chella on me. Miana would just shake her head in that way that makes her look like someone's mother rather than the child she is. "Never tell me, never let me be told." That's all she ever asked of me. And I've held to it as far as I know. Clearly, she deserved better, but it would require a better man to give it.

I found a foolish smile on my lips and wiped it away. My tongue ached and I had lines of fire across my back. Nail wounds always hurt more than the shallow cut of a blade. Taking Chella had been ill advised, but my whole life has been a series of dangerous choices wrestled around to better outcomes. Not that it had been a choice, not truly. There are times when we realize we're just passengers, all our intellect and pontification, carried around in meat and bones that knows what it wants. When flesh meets fire it wants to pull back and does so whatever you might have to say about it. There can be times, when man meets woman, that the same forces work in reverse.

Makin rode with me from the rear of our column to Holland's carriage.

"You're leaving them alone to plot now?" He had a suspicious look on him, as though he knew I'd been up to something.

"A judgment call," I said. "I don't judge they'll be calling on us. And if they do . . ."

"Missing our company, were you?" Makin pulled alongside, shoulder to shoulder, putting the faint scent of clove-spice in the air. It worried me he took so much, blunting the true Makin, but I could hardly counsel sense. Red Kent joined us as we moved further up the column. "Missing us?" he echoed Makin.

"Missing you? You remember Chella from the leucrota halls, from the swamp. How long would you like to ride in her carriage?"

Both men rode in silence for a minute, staring out across the fields. Which part of those encounters they might have been visualizing I couldn't say. Holland's carriage came into view as we rounded a slow bend.

"Just long enough," Makin said, answering my forgotten question. "I'd ride with her long enough."

Kent reached out and tugged up the collar of my road-tunic, not something he'd done since I was ten, and certainly not since I was king. "Mosquito bite," he rasped in that burned voice of his, and touched his neck. "Big one from the looks of it, like what we had us back in the Cantanlona marsh."

I climbed to the carriage footplate from Brath's saddle without having the driver stop.

"Did you miss me, Father Gomst?" I slammed the door behind and threw myself between Katherine and Miana, one scrambling to get her book out of the way, the other hauling my son clear.

"Did Orrin ever tell you about the day we met on the road, Katherine?" I didn't give the good bishop a chance to reply.

She closed her book, some small and battered tome in red leather. "No."

"Hmm. And there was me thinking I'd made an impression."

"But Egan did, several times. And Egan was a man of few words," she said. Behind me, William started to fuss for the breast.

"He said Orrin was a fool for toying with you, for letting you live, said he would have killed you in three heartbeats."

"Well, I was only fourteen," I said. "In the end I bested *him* in less than three heartbeats. In any case, I had a friend with me that day who would have roasted Orrin in his armour by way of a victory prize. So once again, even with hindsight, Orrin was the wisest man there."

As the carriage rumbled on I took the view-ring out and used it with practised ease to zero in on the Tall Castle. Years of such watching had revealed little about my father's plans save to tell me they hadn't been written in letters six foot tall and left upon the roof. Now, I saw palls of smoke trailing down across the city. Even from heaven's heights the black work of the fires could be seen, stamped across the Tall Castle, across the streets of Crath. It seemed the Dead King was burning my past just as the Builders planned to burn our future. If his dark flood turned into a tide the Builders would end us all before such magics tore the world open.

Closer study found black sails on the Sane, columns marching along both shores. I followed their progress. The Dead King's legions had reached through Gelleth already. Forcing their pace night and day there existed a possibility that they might catch us before the gates of Vyene. Estimating the size of the horde proved difficult, strung out and loose along the banks as it was, tens of thousands perhaps. More might join with it along the way. Even so. Dead men against heavy horse and city walls? It seemed a rash move.

"What do you see?" Gomst asked as I made my count.

"Trouble."

The thought of the dead things marching, despoiling the garden

lands of Ancrath—it put a thin blade between my ribs and let it
twist. I wondered if even the graves at Perechaise had yielded their
dead. I might not have stood to keep the Dead King's horde from
the Tall Castle but in a different time, beside the girl-who-waits-for-
spring and the grave in which I buried Justice, I would have made
such a stand.

I leaned back, my eye aching after two hours and more of staring
through the ring. Miana slept, our child on her chest. I thought of my
father, seated in his throne, iron diadem upon his head. The old bastard was dead? I didn't know what to do with that. It didn't fit, no
matter how I turned it. He had been mine to kill, mine to end. Fate
had been drawing me to that moment all these years . . . I rubbed my
sore eye, slumped forward, elbows on knees, chin on knuckles. Father
couldn't be dead. I set the matter aside, to chew upon when it seemed
more palatable.

Across the carriage Bishop Gomst dozed, grey hair straying,
mouth ajar. Osser Gant watched me though, silent and with a
bright eye. Makin's chancellor, brought for his advice, yet holding his
tongue.

I thought then of Coddin, my chancellor rotting back in the
Haunt, of Fexler Brews lost in his machines, both of them with their
talk of setting the world to rights, Coddin wanting me to break the
power of the hidden hands, Fexler's ambition grander still, to turn
some non-existent wheel and return us to how things were meant to
be, to make the world once more as it was given to us.

Two Ancraths, the wise had said, two to undo all the magic, to
turn Fexler's wheel! A sour smile quirked my lips. They'd better pray,
both of them, Coddin and Fexler, the dying man and the ghost, pray
that prophecy meant nothing, for there would be just the one Ancrath
in Vyene and he'd brought with him no clue as to how to repair a
broken empire, let alone a broken reality.

More rode on this matter than the power and influence of a few
sorcerers, more than the enchantments of Sageous's peers, men like

Corion and Luntar who played their games with lives. Fexler's third way rested upon the restoration of what had been normality. Michael and his brotherhood saw flesh as a disease that could be burned out, thereby ceasing the rotation of that wheel, stopping the world from cracking open. Fexler alone had entertained larger thoughts: he alone had believed we might turn back what had been done and spare mankind from a second coming of the fire that he had once brought down upon us.

In truth I took my firstborn to the place where the Builders would start their fire. If Fexler proved as deluded as Michael had suggested—if he couldn't change the nature of existence—Vyene would burn and new suns would rise on man's last day.

We narrowed the distance to Vyene and the weather closed around us, late autumn chill, river fog refusing the sun, persistent rain, cold and sapping the spirits, making mud of the land. The countryside grew more dour with each mile that passed beneath our hooves. We found whole villages abandoned, reviving memories of Gottering and filling every treeline with threat. The guard discovered fresh graves disinterred, late crops flattened in the field, apples rotting on the bough.

Riders passed us, their horses blown and ragged, the men not much better. All of them bore tales of the Dead King's forces, of their strike through Ancrath, their advance into Gelleth, and now the threat to Attar, cutting a dark wedge through empire along the path we had taken only days before.

It might be said that destruction and disaster have always dogged my heels, but never before had that curse been so manifest. I travelled to Vyene and hell followed in my wake.

We stopped that night in the town of Allenhaure and ate at table within a great beer hall that could hold close on three hundred of the Gilden Guard. In Allenhaure at least, on the very doorstep of the empire's heartland, neither winter nor the Dead King's blight had yet sunk their teeth. The locals brought huge haunches of roast meat on wooden platters, lamb in a crust of garlic, herb, and hazelnut, beef unadorned and bleeding. Beer too, blonde with a thick white head, in tankards built like barrels of wooden stays bound by hoops, and in glass steins for the high table. They seemed genuinely pleased to see us, a festival atmosphere throughout. I wondered though if it were merely that if they feted us the guard might choose to restock provisions at the next town.

The beer had a clean taste, sharp, and I drank too much of it, perhaps to dim the images from Chella's carriage, playing again and again through my mind, making me feel at once both sullied and hungry for more. Late on in the evening I leaned across Miana and took our son from the crib at her side.

"Don't wake him, Jorg!"

"Oh shush, I'm taking him for a walk. He'll like it." To his credit William, still looking only half-human as new babies are wont to look, lay limp in sleep while I manhandled him to my chest, and seemed impervious to disturbance of any kind. A cold tremor ran through me as I remembered Degran lying in my hands, lifeless, a ragdoll. I bit down on the memory, refusing to let it cripple me each time I held my boy. The death burned out of my touch the day I broke the siege at the Haunt.

"At least wrap him up warm, take the—"

"Shush, woman." For such a tiny thing she held an endless supply of nagging. "Be thankful I'm not leaving him on a hillside like the Spartans."

I carried him between rank upon rank of the Gilden Guard, all bent over their meat and beer, voices lifted in half a dozen songs. By the main doors, open to vent the stink and heat of the road-ripe hundreds within, I caught sight of Gorgoth, unmistakeable, just outside at the edge of the torchlight. I went out, William clutched to my chest.

"Gorgoth." A name that feels good in the mouth.

"King Jorg." He turned his cat's eyes on me, his great head turning slowly on a tree-trunk neck. He had a gravitas about him, did Gorgoth, something leonine.

"Of all the people I know." I moved to stand beside him and followed his gaze out into the night. "Of all of them, since the Nuban died—it's your friendship, your respect, I wanted. And you're the one not to give it. I didn't want it because you didn't give it—but I do want it." Perhaps the beer spoke for me, but it spoke true.

"You're drunk," he said. "You shouldn't be holding a baby."

"Answer the question."

"It wasn't a question."

"Answer it anyway," I said.

"We can never be friends, Jorg. You have crimes on your soul, blood on your hands, that only God can forgive." His voice rolled away from us, deeper and darker than the night.

"I know it." I lifted William closer to my face and breathed him in. "You and I know it. The rest of them, they somehow forget, convince themselves it can be swept away, misremembered. Only you and Katherine see the truth. And Makin, though it's Makin he can't forgive, not me."

I passed William to Gorgoth, pressing him forward until the leucrota lifted one massive three-fingered hand to receive him. He stood very still, eyes wider than wide, staring at my son, almost lost in the width of his palm.

"Men shun me—I have never held a baby," he said. "They think what corrupted me will pass to their children if I touch them."

"And will it?" I asked.

"No."

"Well then."

We stood, watching the rise and fall of a tiny chest.

"You're right not to be a friend to me," I said. "But will you be a friend to William, as you once were to Gog?" The boy would need friends. Better men than me.

The slowest nod of that great head. "You taught me that. Somehow you taught me what Gog was worth." He lifted William close to his face. "I will protect him, Jorg of Ancrath. As if he were my own."

41

Chella's story

"There's no room at the inn." Kai twisted a grin at her. Allenhaure is full. He climbed back into the carriage, slipping off muddy boots.

"Full of?"

"King Jorg's escort," Kai said.

"So have Axtis press on to the next town," Chella said.

"It's a long haul to Gauss and the guard are always treated well here. Rumbles of discontent I'm hearing, as if there's real men under all that gilding and those stern expressions."

"Not my concern. Let's be moving." Though as she spoke the words it seemed that perhaps it was her concern. She tasted it at first, a wrongness in the air. "Wait."

Kai paused, a boot half-returned to his foot. "What?"

By the pricking of my thumbs, something wicked this way comes . . . "Just wait." She held up a hand.

Wrongness. A dry sharp sense of wrong, like grit behind her eyeballs. The temperature fell, or perhaps her body just thought it did for her breath didn't steam.

"Lichkin." Kai felt it too.

"Hiding himself," she said. "Thantos."

"What does he want?" Kai's poise fell away when lichkin drew near. Keres had terrified him. Thantos was worse.

"It's a reminder," Chella said. Some part of her had been hoping the plan forgotten or changed, a large part, and growing larger as life reclaimed her. She cursed Jorg Ancrath and steeled herself to this new task.

"Go into town, get a cart, and have it loaded with ale casks. We'll camp in the fields toward the river. The guard can have their revels."

Kai sniffed. "Looks like rain."

"Have them build fires. They won't notice the rain after long."

"Ale will do that for you." Kai nodded. He couldn't manage a grin though, not with death stalking so close, scraping every nerve raw.

Chella reached into the purse on her dress-belt. "Take this." She spilled four heavy pieces of gold into his hand, Brettan bars.

"What—" He nudged the small vial of black glass lying amongst the gold in his palm. From the change in his face she could tell he understood.

"Styx water. One drop per cask."

"What a thing it would be." Chella held the goblet before her, making a slow swirl of the ale, the foam all but gone, just islands in a dark and moonlit sea. "To fly."

"Yes." Kai stared into his own dark sea, his own foam scattered islands. Perhaps it reminded him of his drowned land.

A long silence. The soft rain made no sound. Far, in the distance, a muted cheer from Allenhaure, some celebration amongst Jorg's guard.

"I almost did." Kai set his silver goblet on the table between them. "Once."

"How can you almost fly?" Chella shook her head.

"How can you almost love?" He looked up at the sky, starless and bible-black. "I stood on a lip of rock, held out over the Channel Sea, where the waves pound on white cliffs. And the wind there, it blows so cold and sure, takes the heat from you, wraps your bones. I leaned out into it, nothing but the wind to hold me, and those dark waves slapping and pounding way, way below. And it filled me, like I was made of glass, or ice, or air, and the only thing in my mind was the voice of that east wind, the voice of forever calling me."

"But?"

"But I couldn't let go. If I had flown I would have flown away from everything I knew. From me." He shook his head.

"And what wouldn't we give to fly away from being us right now?" Chella flicked her goblet over and stood as the liquid spilled over the table. All across the field men of the guard lay sprawled as if in sleep, lying, some of them in their gold armour, in the muddy grass. Captain Axtis had ended on his back, half-out of his pavilion, sword in hand, eyes staring at the sky and full of rain. Out of nearly three hundred men only eleven hadn't at least sipped the Allenhaure ale. The lichkin had found those men in the dark and played his games, first making them silent with the wet tearing of flesh.

"Will Thantos be needing the others too?" Kai pushed away the white arm of a camp-girl, sodden dress, hair dark with rain, face-down in the dirt. He levered himself from his chair and stepped over her to join Chella.

She nodded. "They'll go to the woods and join the Dead King's force when he arrives."

Kai drew his cloak tight. A mist lay ankle-deep around them, rising out of nowhere as if it bled from the ground, white as milk.

"It's starting."

The sense of wrongness that had scratched at her all evening, twisting likes worms beneath the skin, now crystallized into horror. When the dead return there's a feeling of everything flowing the wrong way, as if hell itself were vomiting them out.

Axtis sat up first, before his men, before the dead whores, the boys with their serving plates and polish rags. He didn't blink. The water ran from his eyes, but he didn't blink. Wrong.

All around them men stood in their golden armour. The Styx water had left no mark upon them, save for the few who tumbled into the open fires, of course. Styx water does its work without hurry, dulling senses, bringing sleep, paralysing the voice first, then the larger muscle groups. At the last the death it offers is an agony of tortured muscles fighting and failing. Chella had enough necromancy in her fingertips to know that they had not died easy. Their pain echoed in her.

"I still don't understand," Kai said. "It won't take long before someone discovers something is wrong with them. And then all that talk of diplomacy is just noise. We'll be fortunate to escape without being beheaded then burned. That's what they do to our sort, you know? That's if you're lucky. If not, it's burning first, then behead what's left."

"The Dead King has his reasons," Chella said.

"All this to spread terror? It seems extravagant."

Chella shrugged. Better Kai not know the Dead King's reasons. She'd rather not know them herself. "We ride from here. In the saddle."

"What? Why?" The rain fell faster, harder, just to over-score his point.

"Well, you can stay in the carriage if you want." Chella wiped the water from her face and spat. "But Thantos will be in there, and lich-kin aren't the best of travelling companions."

42

Vyene is the greatest city on earth. I could be wrong, of course. It might be that in the vastness of Ling, or beyond the Sahar at the heart of Cerana, or somewhere in the dusts of the Indus there lies a more fabulous work of men. But I doubt it. The wealth of an empire has been spent in Vyene, year upon year, century upon century, exchanged for stone and skill.

"Incredible." Makin took off his helm as though it might somehow hinder his ability to absorb the glories on every side. Rike and Kent said nothing, struck dumb. Marten kept close at my side, every bit the farmer once again, as if six years of war, of leading armies to victory, had slid from him, scared away by the majesty of our surroundings.

"Lord Holland would be a peasant here," Makin said.

Few of the cities I had taken in the year following my conquest of Arrow held a single building to compare with the grand structures lining our approach to the palace. Here nobles of the old empire had built their summer homes, in all shapes and sizes, from confections in rose-marble to edifices in granite that scraped the clouds, all competing to impress the emperor, his court, and each other. My great-grandfather had been such a noble, Duke of Ancrath, holding the lands in the name of the empire and at the steward's pleasure. When the steward died and the empire fell into its pieces, Grandfather made his own crown, claimed Ancrath for himself, and called himself king.

Even in Vyene though, a nervousness ran through the streets. More than the excitement of Congression. The place held a tension, a drawn breath waiting release. Bonefires burned in alleyways and distant squares, corpses given to the flame in fear that something worse might take them. The crowds that watched our procession had a restlessness to them. A guardsman on a skittish horse lost his helm and laughter went up among the locals, but it rang too shrill, edged with hysteria.

The roads to the palace, and there are four, each lie broad enough that a man couldn't throw a spear from the gates of the residences on one side to those on the other. Our column rode at the centre, fifteen abreast and thirty deep with the carriages in the midst and the wagons to the rear. The followers and hangers-on, including Onsa's wheel-house packed with negotiable affection, had melted away in the outer reaches of the city. Captain Devers had sent out word to the effect that no undesirables should approach the Gilden Gate. I had to grin at that. I'm sure a wheel-house full of prostitutes would carry less sin through those gates than the Hundred on their best day.

I rode on, my mood growing more grim. I came to swap one crown for a different one, to exchange my throne for a less comfortable chair. Perhaps I would find Fexler Brews' third way and paper over the cracks that ran through the world. I didn't know. But I knew the Jorg who wore that new crown, who might sit upon the all-throne, would be no different. No better. No more able to tear free of his past and the hooks that sunk too deep.

The emperor's palace sits amid a square so vast that the grand houses on the far side appear tiny. The four roads converge upon the palace dome, passing through an acreage of flagstones devoid of statue, fountain, or monument. On normal days the wealthy citizens might flock in this space, spending coin at stalls and stands able to cater to their excess. Around Congression the autumn winds sweep through unhindered.

"God's whore!" Makin broke into my musings. He stood in his stirrups.

Sir Kent had himself a frown at that. Not so keen on the blaspheming since his conversion.

"Such language!" I tsked at Lord Makin. "What pray tell is amiss?"

"You could see for yourself if you weren't riding on your dignity," he said, half-smiling but still blinking in disbelief.

I sighed and stood too. In the distance, halfway to the palace, a thin line of black-cloaked soldiers stood across the breadth of West Street. Something familiar about the red-crested helms, the way the gleaming plate armour gave way to ridiculous pantaloons striped in blue and yellow.

"Well fuck me, it's the Pope." I sat back down.

"The Pope?" Rike asked, as if unfamiliar with the word.

"Yes, Brother Rike." The column began to slow. "Fat old woman, interesting hat, infallible."

We closed the distance, hooves clattering on the cobbled road. The papal guard waited, impassive, polearms with their butts to the flagstones, pennants fluttering, blades to the sky. Captain Devers brought his men to a standstill before the line. Behind the Pope's men a sedan chair rested, a huge and ornate construction closed in on all sides against the weather and prying eyes. The ten bearers stood at attention beside the carrying poles.

"Her holiness will speak with King Jorg." The centremost of the guardsmen called out the demand, perhaps the leader of the squad but marked no differently from any other.

"This will be interesting." I swung out of my saddle and walked toward the front of our column.

Miana opened the door as I passed Holland's carriage. "Make

this right, Jorg," she told me. "Next time Marten might not be there to save the day."

I turned, took her hand, and made a smile for her. "It cost me forty thousand in gold to get this meeting, I'm not going to waste it, my queen. I may be foolish on occasion, but I'm not an idiot."

"Jorg." A warning tone as her hand slipped mine.

The front ranks parted and I approached the papal guard. The man who summoned me forward now looked pointedly at Gog, scabbarded at my hip.

"Well, show me to her holiness, then. Can't wait all day, I've got business to attend to." I nodded to the great dome of the palace rising behind him.

A pause, and he turned to lead me through the line. We came to the carriage-box and three of the bearers hastened forward with chairs, two hefting a broad purple-cushioned stool, one with a simple ebony ladder-back for me.

Another bearer joined them and they stood two to either side of the door to the carriage-box. A very wide door, I noted. A fifth man scurried around to the rear and I heard the opposite door click open. I guessed he might be tasked with pushing.

The closer door opened and an acreage of purple silk, strained across wobbling flesh, began to emerge. The bearers reached in and retrieved short arms, pudgy hands overburdened with gemmed rings. They pulled. The fifth man pushed. The mountain grunted and a head appeared, bowed forward, sweat making straggles of thin dark hair across a crimson scalp. A crucifix of gold hung below the wattles and folds of her neck, a hefty thing half an inch thick, a foot in length, a ruby at the crossing point for the blood of Christ. It must have weighed more than a baby.

And out she came, the supreme pontiff, shepherdess of many sheep, a slug teased from her nest. The flowered reek of perfumes and oils couldn't hide the rankness that emerged with her.

They sat her on the stool, overflowing. The guard from the line stayed at my side. He had the look to him, pale eyes, watchful, scarred hands. I didn't let the pantaloons distract me. Watchful men are to be watched.

"Your holiness." Pius XXV if I were to call her by name.

"King Jorg. I thought you would look older." She couldn't be shy of seventy but hadn't a wrinkle on her, all stretched away by her bulk.

"All alone," I asked. "No cardinals, no bishops dancing attendance? Not so much as a priest to carry your bible?"

"My retinue are the guests of Lord Congrieve at his country estate, investigating reports of irregularities at the Sisters of Mercy, a nunnery with a chequered history." She deployed a purple kerchief to wipe spittle from the corner of her mouth. "I will rejoin them in due course, but I felt a private meeting between us would be more . . . conducive. The words we exchange here will appear on no records." She smiled. "Even for a Pope, speaking for God himself, it is no simple matter to thwart the will of the Vatican archivists. To them there are few sins greater than allowing a Pope's utterances to be lost." Another smile and the folding of many chins.

I pursed my lips. "So, to what do I owe this pleasure?"

"Shall I have Tobias bring wine? You look thirsty, Jorg."

"No."

She paused for the pleasantry or explanation. I offered none.

"You're building a cathedral in Hodd Town." Dark eyes watched me, currants sunk in the pale pudding of her face.

"News travels fast."

"You're not the only one that speaks to *Deus in machina*, Jorg."

The Builder-ghosts spoke to her—Fexler had told me as much. He'd told me that they steered the church against magic in all its flavours, as much to blind the priests to their own potential for wielding the power of the masses as to have them quell its use by others. Any kind of faith stacked up behind a creed or title could amplify the will of the relevant figurehead to a frightening degree. It pleased me to see her hamstrung by what she thought of as secret and sacred knowledge.

"Why build the cathedral now?" she asked.

"The cathedral has been under construction for twenty years and more," I said. "My entire life."

"But soon it will be finished, and people will expect me to come to bless it before the first mass." She shifted her bulk on the stool. "I heard this news on my tour of Scorron, and came here to speak with you. You must know why."

"You feel safer here," I said.

"I am the Vicar of Christ, I walk in safety anywhere in Christendom!" Anger in her tone now, but more bluster than true indignation.

"Walk?"

She let that pass, cold eyes on me. "I will hear your confession, Jorg. And offer forgiveness to the penitent."

"*I* will confess to *you*?" I rolled my head, vertebrae popping in my neck. "Me to you?"

Her guardsman took half a step closer. I wondered what other roles he held. Executioner? Assassin? Perhaps he trained with the white-skinned dream-smith who visited the Haunt on Vatican business.

"You sent an assassin after my wife and unborn child." In some inner darkness cold winds stirred and the ember of an old rage glowed once more.

"We walk in a vale of tears, Jorg, the only matter of consequence is how we place our steps."

"What does that mean?" Was I supposed to nod wisely? To assume her wisdom surpassed the need for meaning?

"Your father's funeral will be held soon, no doubt. To have the Pope herself usher him into paradise at the ceremony would do your standing at Congression untold good. Not to mention the small matter of papal sanction on the inheritance."

"He's truly dead?" I saw his face, without emotion gazing over his court. He would look no different, laid in the tomb. No less human.

"You didn't know?" She raised a heavy brow.

"I knew." I saw him at the battlement on the highest tower, sunset lighting him in crimson and shadow, hair streaming in the wind. I saw him with Mother, laughing, too far away to hear.

"Four days. That's how long Ancrath's defences held without him. The Dead King's creatures are on the march now." She watched me for some reaction. "Hard upon your heels."

"And how will you stop them, Holiness?" The dead wouldn't seek out and lay siege to castles, they wouldn't claim lands, levy taxes. The Dead King wouldn't rule, only ruin.

"We will pray." She shifted her bulk. "These are the end of days, my son. All we can do is pray."

"Your son?" I tilted my head, seeing the pale-eyed killer beside me without looking. Road-eyes, that's called. Seeing without looking. I drew the deepest breath and that hidden ember grew white-hot.

Tobias moved his right foot, just a fraction. He knew. Pius would depend only on the best. She thought her guards a mere formality. Like so many before her, despite the evidence writ plain in the trail of bodies behind me, she thought to bind me with nothing more than convention. Tobias, though, he knew my heart, shared my instinct.

"You're not my mother, old woman."

Fat people are hard to kill with your bare hands. They carry their own padded armour. I tried to throttle Fat Burlow a time or two, even Rike found that a challenge. Tobias would let his polearm fall in the moment he moved to act, a prop, nothing more, another piece of papal foolishness, convention. He would go for his knife, hidden somewhere. And I for mine, no time for swords. And for all of Brother Grumlow's teachings, I would be in a chair with my back to him, he would be standing, and I'd die before the fat bitch got her squeal out, before I so much as scratched her.

"Play nice, boy." She didn't stir to anger. You don't win the cardinals over with roaring. The thickest skin, patience, time, inexorable pressure, these will move even the most weighty backside into the papal throne if the owner is sufficiently shrewd.

I blinked. "Did they not tell you about me? Was Murillo not enough of a hint?" Quick hands, that's what a knife fight is all about. But quick hands are wasted if you're hunting your weapon while the other man's fingers are wrapped around his. Don't waste your speed at the start of the first move. All that does is advertise that it *is* a move. "You sent an assassin to kill—"

"A king rules by the will of his people." Just a hint of irritation now. "The people look to Roma for their eternal salvation. You're old enough to know where your interests lie. And those of your son. The cathedral—"

I leaned forward in my seat, unhurried, the intent listener, then reached out, slow enough, but sure: hesitation is the killer. Then fast. Ripping the crucifix from about her neck. I threw it, hard as hard, tearing it through a flat arc and releasing it to fly straight and true. Tobias caught it. A neat catch between the eyes, one soft, heavy arm of the cross punching through his forehead so that the whole thing hung there as he toppled. Now my knife. *To everything there is a season, a time to every purpose under heaven.* Memories of Bishop Murillo's priests sprang up as I dragged the blade through the folds of fat about Pius's neck. "A time to die."

Pius hit the ground first, then Tobias, then the polearm. Then for the longest time those of us not on the ground dying just stood there looking at each other.

43

"Captain Devers, I believe I'm about to be attacked on your watch!"
I hollered it at him, thinking it best to pre-empt the matter rather
than bring it up as forty or more papal guards started trying to
perforate me.

I saw motion among the gold helms back by our carriage. It would
take a moment or three for Devers to come to grips with the situation.

"Oh come on, I just killed the fecking Pope. You *are* going to
attack me, aren't you?" I drew Gog and smiled invitingly at the nearest guards. Pantaloons or not, they would prove deadly enough. Mul-
tiple polearms against a single sword in open space is not a contest. I
started to back around the sedan chair. The bearers scattered. Not
pious men it seemed.

Still half-dazed the five guards closest to me levelled their weapons. All along the line the polearms fell in a wave, aiming at me.

"That man is under my protection!" Devers found his voice and
urged his stallion forward.

Somehow that galvanized the Pope's men and they surged forward, screaming incoherent rage. Even the bearers thought to join in,
reaching for me with over-long, over-muscled arms, though you'd
have thought they'd be grateful not to have to carry her any more.

The Gilden Guard rushed in from behind, and I played "find the

Jorg," skipping in and out of the sedan chair, threading my way through the bearers, whilst we had ourselves a good old-fashioned slaughter.

It ended too soon. Polearms outreach swords, but if they're pointed the wrong way the fight will be a short one. They'd been pointed at me. They should have watched the guard.

Gog caught in a man's spine and had to be hauled out with both hands on the hilt and a foot to the fellow's chest. Fortunately he was the last of the bearers. I got the blade free, turning just in time for Makin to grab me by the breastplate and slam me into the Pope's chair.

"What the hell are you doing?"

Devers came up beside him, sword dripping. "You killed the Pope!" As if I hadn't noticed.

"She killed herself when she went after my son." I lay back against the sedan's wooden wall, relaxing in Makin's grip.

"You killed the Pope," Devers said again, staring down at the blood-soaked mess of her, an armless bearer sprawled across her holy legs.

"What you need to do, Captain Devers, is have your men load her carcass into this handy box behind me. And whilst they're doing that, and carting all the other bodies away, you need to get the Lord Commander of the Guard out here.

"I suspect that when Lord Commander Hemmet considers the fire that will spread from the flame I set burning here, he will wish that it never happened. He will wish that the Gilden Guard had not slaughtered the Pope's personal detachment of papal soldiers. And he will be very interested to hear that there are no surviving witnesses from Rome. Anything that happens without witnesses never really happened at all.

"In three days I expect to be crowned emperor and those who have failed to support me will live to regret their lack of discernment. But not for very long.

"If it turns out that I am not crowned then I'll be too busy to let it worry me overmuch—I'll be raising a nine-nation army to march on Roma so that I can burn that den of corruption to the ground. So all in all, if your Lord Commander wants to avoid rivers of blood and making a personal enemy of the next emperor, for the sake of a *Pope* . . . he will say that Pius and her guards fell foul of a lichkin. Ship her remains back to Vatican City and be done with it. I can even suggest a replacement . . ."

Makin let go, allowing me to slide a couple of inches down the wall of the sedan chair, from tiptoes to heel and toe. I hadn't realized I was nearly off the ground. "It will never work. You can't hush up something like this."

"Look around you, Makin." I swept an arm. "It's a wasteland. Anyone who counts is in the palace, and none of them will be looking out, I can tell you that for fact. And their servants will be hard at work way over there." I waved to the distant mansions. "And the good folk of Vyene are hiding in their homes. To some degree because they're not invited to the party. But mostly because the Gilden Guard are deployed to escort duties leaving no one to protect them, and the dead are on the move."

"It doesn't matter. Someone will know. Someone will talk. There'll be rumours—"

"Rumours are fine. Rumours just put an edge on things—add some weight to what I have to say. Accusations . . . not so good. Charges? Then it's time to march on Roma. And don't forget, your average Gilden Guard affords the church far less respect than they do the women in Onsa's wheel-house."

That gave him pause. The guard really did despise anything that smacked of Roma's influence in the empire's business. To have the Pope herself in Vyene itself, waylaying members of the Hundred under guard escort, must have burned them no end.

"It can't work." Makin shook his head.

"Either way, the bitch is dead." I shrugged him off. "Devers!" I clicked my fingers in front of his face. "Wake up, man! Can you remember what I've said? The Lord Commander—cover-up or bloodbath. Yes? Sort it out or so help me I'll ride to Roma with her head on my spear."

Captain Devers gave the nod of a man not convinced he isn't dreaming. I walked past him, stepping around the corpses. It's never a good idea to step over a fallen man. You might get a knife between the legs.

"I'll be in the palace if I'm wanted."

Rike and Marten stood cleaning their swords. Kent's axe hung loose in his grip, still crimson. He looked lost.

"If God talks to anyone, Kent, it's not that evil old woman back there. That faith you've found—you didn't find it in church, now did you? You found it in pain and blood. Whatever reached out to touch you, it wasn't a priest in robes."

"The holy spirit found me, Jorg. Christ Jesu, risen, led me out of darkness and cooled my burns." No "king" today, no "sire."

I don't respect many men and Kent was never sharp enough of wit, never wise enough, never virtuous enough to inspire me. And his new credo, since the fire, seemed borrowed, other men's dogma worn as a shield. But I respected his instincts as a killer and I liked the honesty of the man. And who was I to judge? I'd fucked a necromancer and killed a Pope within the space of a week.

"I need to trust you, Kent." I spread my arms. "I need some of that faith. So listen to that spirit. Listen hard. And if I need to die for my crimes—be the one to strike me down."

The cold wind blew between us. And I discovered I meant every word. I dared him, as I dared the storm long ago. Strike me down. I saw Gretcha slide from my blade, faint surprise in her eyes, and crumple to a small heap, bones and skin in a little girl's clothes.

"If someone had done this for me when I was a child it would have saved everyone a lot of trouble." I'd said it to her. I said it to the storm on a wild night atop the Tall Castle. I said it to Red Kent, his hands white on that Norse axe of his. "Do it!"

Kent dropped the axe. Shook his head. "We're in this to the end, Jorg."

*   *   *

I came back to the carriage. Miana, with babe in arms, Katherine, Gomst, and Osser were all outside, huddled in furs and cloaks against the wind's icy fingers. They watched my approach through the guard as if the stench of my misdeed had already reached them, a cold mix of horror and disgust upon those pale faces.

"Jorg? We heard fighting . . . there's blood on you." Miana stepped toward me.

"I made it right, my lady. As you asked me to."

"You killed her." Katherine spoke the words not in accusation but to hear them out loud, to see if they could be true.

"She died. The how of it is a matter for discussion, for theological debate. And what of it? Has the hand of Roma supported the people of this empire or choked them? And hasn't that grip grown tighter over the years that Pius spent spreading across the papal throne? The time has come for fresh blood, I say, for someone who actually believes in God to wear the silliest hat in Christendom."

I looped an arm around Bishop Gomst's shoulders. "Time for someone who doesn't want to be pope to be pope. What do you say, Father?"

He looked up at me. I hadn't realized how short he was, bent prematurely under years and cares, or perhaps how tall I'd grown. "You really killed her?"

I made a smile though it tasted bitter and said, "Forgive me, Father, for I have sinned."

And old Gomsty, though he was stiff from the carriage, and sore in heart, bowed his head to hear my confession.

44

Five years earlier

"Vyene is the greatest city on earth." The guardsman sniffed again and wrinkled his nose. I probably did stink. It had been a long journey from the coast of Liba. "We don't let just anyone in."

The greatness or otherwise of the city was still up for debate. So far I'd ridden through a sprawl of industry and town houses, taverns and markets, strung out for miles along the Danoob. None of it particularly great or grand, but certainly well-to-do. The real Vyene lay hidden behind the high walls that had once enclosed the whole city. And the guard before me had his doubts about whether such a road-stained youth had any right seeing it.

"I expect you let travellers in if they have coin to spend." I opened my hand to reveal five battered coppers from as many nations. A tilt of my palm had them slipping, and he caught them as they fell.

"Don't break any laws, or expect to get broken yourself." And he stepped aside.

I led my horse on through. Ten or more guards were performing the same sort of quality control on other hopefuls, most of the exchanges punctuated with loud and prolonged haggling.

"Get along." I tugged on the reins. The mare—Hosana the seller had called her—ambled along. It's not until you've ridden a camel, then a sway-backed mare, that you start to realize how very much you miss your own horse. Brath had always been a temporary replacement for Gerrod, but now I found myself hoping Yusuf lived up to his promise and had arranged for him to be taken back to Castle Morrow.

A heavy shower began to rattle down around me as I set off into the old city of Vyene, water vomiting in torrents from high gutters. Summer had started to head south. In the cold bays of the jarls winter would be honing his weapons, putting an edge on the north wind and preparing his advance.

Hosana and I found shelter from the downpour in the stables of the first inn we reached. That at least saved the bother of selecting a place to stay. I passed her reins to a lad with straw in his hair, and set off into the ale-room to secure a bed upstairs and a tub to wash off some of the road. "She'll be dry before she reaches the stalls or I'll want to know why." I flicked him a coin.

The ale-room stank of hops and sweat. A dozen travellers dotted among the tables and chairs, perhaps a few day-drinkers among them. I caught the inn-keep's arm as he passed with a plate of steaming meat and gravy. I couldn't tell you what meat, gristle in the main, and sinews, but it made my stomach growl.

"I'll have a room. Send up a plate of that if you can find any more dogs. An ale too."

He nodded. "Take Seven. End of the hall. Throw Elbert out, he don't pay no-how."

And so I ended up in Seven on straw pallet, crawling no doubt, with the patter and drip of the rain outside and Elbert's moaning from the other side of the door as he picked up whatever came loose when he hit the wall. Eat, drink, shit, sleep. In the morning I'd clean up and spend a little gold to dress something closer to my part. It would take more than velvets and suede to get me into the palace though. Nobody there would believe King Jorg of Renar had come alone to the Gilden Gates, without herald or retinue.

The cut on my cheekbone still ached. A careless moment in Mazeno Port, drunken sailor with a knife. With my head down on the straw I could hear the bloodsuckers moving, tiny dry feet tickling over the bedding. The ceiling boards held my attention, eyes searching the patterns for meaning, until sleep took me.

The comfort of shaving with your knife is in the knowing that it is honed to perfection. Aside from that it's a chore and leaves you scratchy however sharp the blade. I went down to break fast with a brick of the local dark bread and a flagon of small beer. Outside, the street lay bright but the sunshine lied and the air carried the scent of frost.

I walked on further into the great city, leaving Hosana stabled at the inn. The Olidan Arms to give it its full title—I'd not noted it in the downpour that drove me there. Named not for Father of course but for one of the more famous stewards who kept Vyene in the name of Emperor Callin in the years he spent on campaign to expand our borders east.

Beggar children followed me, though I hardly looked moneyed. Even here in the richest of cities. Little blond children, remote descendants of past emperors' by-blows quite possibly, starving in the streets.

I pressed on into more exclusive neighbourhoods where town-laws chased away the urchins and gave me looks that said they'd do as much for me if I were a touch less scary. By two turns and a bridge, past ever more impressive homes, I came to one of the four great roads that lead into the heart of Vyene: West Street. Here, still a mile from the palace, trading houses lined the margins. Not market stalls, or merchant shacks, but grand houses of stone, slate-tiled, opening to the road with wares set out for display and rooms within for negotiating the sale.

I came to one such house, a tailor's, with the proprietor's name laid out upon a board fully ten yards long between the first- and second-storey windows. "Jameous of the House Revel," no allusion to his trade, not even a pair of cloth shears marked out. Except for a man going toward the rear door with two bolts of taffeta over his shoulders, and another coming out the front with a fancy house-cloak on some kind of hanger, I wouldn't have known what business oc-curred there. Unlike the leatherworkers next door, and the silver-smiths further along, Jameous had his shutters folded against the chill, or perhaps just against curious eyes. There is, after all, nothing like a sense of exclusivity to draw in foolish money. And yes, I too was drawn in, though I would claim it was my need that drew me. The need to adopt the same plumage as the local strutting cocks so I might start to play the role of king once more.

The door, a heavy oak affair, had closed behind the man leaving with his cloak, or rather with his master's cloak since he wore servant garb, albeit of finer cut and better repair than my own garments. I walked up and gave a rap.

The door opened a hand's breadth. "This is the House of Revel." The creature addressing me appeared to straddle both genders, doe-eyed, fine-boned, and soft-voiced, but with close-cropped hair and flat in the chest. A hand moved to close the door, as if simply identifying the place should be enough to see me on my way.

I put my foot in the door. "I know that. It's written in letters larger than your head just above us."

"Oh," said the woman. I'd decided on woman. "Who told you that?"

I gave the door a shove and walked on in.

A well-appointed room, stuffed chairs that you could drown in, a single soft, thick rug covering the floor from wall to wall, crystal lanterns burning smokeless oils. A large man, balding, tending to fat, stood with his arms raised whilst a second man moved around him wielding a measure tape. A third fellow stood with a ledger, noting vital statistics. All of them looked my way.

The measuring man straightened up. "And who might this be, Kevin?"

Kevin picked himself off the rug. "Sir, I'm sorry, sir—this . . . gentleman—"

"I forced an entry, shall we say?" I shone them my most winning smile. "I need some suitable clothing, and in a hurry."

"Suitable for what? Labouring?" the big man scoffed. Kevin covered his mouth to hide a smirk. "Get on with it, Jameous, throw him out and let's have this finished. I'm to be at Lord Kellermin's within the hour."

I resolved to be at least half-civilized. I was after all in the empire's capital city, a place where one's deeds are apt to resonate, where one's words can spread. I fished out a gold coin and played it from finger to finger over the back of each knuckle. "There's no need or possibility of throwing me out. I merely require clothing. Perhaps something Lord Kellermin might approve of."

"Get him out. The villain's mad, crawling, and Lord knows who he's just robbed to get that coin." Red patches appeared high on the beefy fellow's cheeks.

"Of course, Councilman Hetmon." A quick bow to the councilman and Jameous clapped his hands, a summoning if ever I saw one. He turned back to me. "We're very choosy about our clientele, young man, and I can assure you that a full set of clothes suitable for Lord Kellermin's receptions would cost rather more than a ducet in any event."

The coin flickered, gold across knuckles. In Hodd Town I could empty a tailor's with a single uncut ducet.

A pair of men emerged from the back of the shop, journeymen tailors by the looks of them, in neat black tunics. One held crimping shears, the other a yard rule. I took a deep breath, the kind we pretend will calm us down. Quality costs. Manners cost nothing.

"Will this suffice?" I drew out a handful of gold: ten, maybe fifteen coins. There's a weight to that many gold pieces that lets you know what you're holding is worth something.

"Call the town-law on this one, he's clearly murdered someone of consequence, or left them bleeding in an alley." Councilman Hetmon took half a step my way before realizing there was no one ready to hold him back.

Calm.

I took another of those deep breaths. The two tailors, with the shears and the rule, advanced, each trying to be the slower one, neither keen to arrive first.

Since Hetmon's half-step did little to close the gap between us I closed it myself. Be calm, I told myself. Four quick strides and I had him by belt and shoulder. A hefty man but I managed to propel him with enough speed that he put a Hetmon-shaped hole through the shutters. I turned to find the shorter of the two journeymen swinging his rule my way. I let it break across the breastplate beneath my cloak. Behind me the remainder of the shuttering came free and fell with a crash. It turns out I don't listen to good advice even when I'm the one offering it.

"The choosing of good clientele is of course a priority," I told Jameous. "But since you appear to have no other calls on your time, perhaps you can schedule me in for an immediate fitting?"

The master tailor backed away, glancing at the hanging fragments of shutter. The journeyman with the shears promptly dropped them; the other seemed fixated by the splintered end of his broken rule.

"Clothes!" I clapped to summon a little attention, but Jameous kept glancing to the road.

I took a look myself, wondering if the town-law had turned up to lend the councilman a hand and try my patience. In place of the padded armour and iron-banded clubs of the town-law rank upon rank of bearded Norsemen marched past, the weak sun glinting on ring-mail, garish colours on their wide, round shields, helms set with ceremonial horns to either side. I made it to the window in time to see the centre of the parade approaching. Four figures on horseback, the warriors ahead of them encircled by the coils of serpent horns.

"Damn me!" I stepped out through the splintered wood. Councilman Hetmon crawled away at a good lick, but I'd lost interest in him, and indeed in all my sartorial ambitions. "Sindri!" Riding high on that white gelding of his, a robe of white fur, hair now unbraided and confined instead by a gold band, but Sindri even so.

"SINDRI!" I bellowed it at him. Just in time as the two warriors marching before his horse winded their serpents and drowned out all other noise.

For a moment it seemed he hadn't heard, and then he turned his horse, shouldering through the ranks, setting the marchers in disarray.

"—ell are you *doing* here?" His words reached me as the howl of the serpent horns died away.

"I've come to see my throne." My cheeks ached with a smile that hadn't needed me to put it there. It felt good to see a familiar face.

"You look like hell." He swung down from the saddle, furs swishing, some kind of arctic fox by the look of them. "I took you for a Saracen at first. A sell-sword, and not one finding much luck."

I glanced down at myself. "Heh. Well, I guess I picked up a few things in Afrique. A pretty good tan for one." I set my dark wrist to his pale one.

"Afrique? Are you never still?" He glanced back at the column halted in the street. "Anyhow, you must come with us. You can ride beside Elin. You remember my sister Elin?"

Oh I did. Visit us in winter, she had said. "My horse is back at the inn," I told him. "And where are you bound? And for what? Has it grown too cold in the north?"

"Getting married." He grinned. "Walk with me, if it's not beneath a king's dignity."

"Dignity?" I matched his grin and flicked a splinter from my shoulder.

Sindri rejoined his column on foot and I took the place of the warrior beside him. "My lady." I nodded up at Elin, pale in black velvets, white-blond hair cascading behind her.

"You've not met my uncle Thorgard, and Norv the Raw, our bannerman from Hake Vale?" Sindri indicated the other riders, older men, grim, helmed, scarred.

I smacked a fist to my breastplate and inclined my head, remembering the low opinion such men held of the courtesies traded in Vyene. "And your father?"

"His duties keep him in Maladon. Dead things rising from the barrowlands. Also his health is—"

"A chill, nothing more." Duke Maladon's brother leaned across his nephew.

The column restarted with a blast of serpent horns. We marched on into the silence left in their wake. "Married?" I asked. "To a southerner?"

"A lass from the Hagenfast, good Viking stock. One of Father's alliances, but she's a pretty thing. A hellcat in the furs."

Elin snorted on the other side of him.

"So you've all trooped down to Vyene . . . ?"

Sindri reached up and flicked one of the bull's horns on his helm. "We're traditionalists. Frozen in our ways. We've barely let go of the old gods three thousand years after the Christ came. In the north any marriage of great consequence must be witnessed by the emperor, and that means coming to court. Even if there's no emperor. Or steward. So here we are."

"Well, it's good to see you." And I meant it.

45

Five years earlier

I came to the Gilden Gate dressed in Sindri's spare cloak and tunic, with boots from one or other of his warriors, my rank recognized by the Gilden Guard on Sindri's vouching. The Gate lay deep inside the palace, not an entrance but a rite of passage. I had always imagined the Gate would tower, stand wide enough for a coach and horses, require ten men to open.

"That's it?"

"Yes." Hemmet, Lord Commander of the Gilden Guard, didn't elaborate. He must have met this reaction dozens of times.

We stood, Sindri, his inner party, Hemmet and I, in an ante-chamber the size of Father's throne room and appointed with more grandeur and more taste than anything most of the Hundred could aspire to. And in the expanse of the west wall, set with the busts of emperors past, each in white marble deep in its niche to watch the ages, stood the Gilden Gate. A modest entrance in which an ancient wooden archway stood unsupported. Oak perhaps, black with age, any carving smoothed away by the passage of years.

"Why?" I asked.

Hemmet turned his gaze on me, very blue, crinkles at the corners. He scratched at the white stubble on his chin. "Go through." He gestured with his staff of office, a rod of steel and gold, ending in a strange crest of red velvet tongues.

I shrugged and walked toward the arch, no taller than nine foot or so, a little narrower. Nothing until the last two steps. One more and the raw agony of my burn woke again in old scar tissue all across the left side of my face. At the same time the sharp and critical pain of Father's knife thrust pierced my chest once more, spreading through my veins like acid. And the thorn-patterned box at my hip grew so heavy it made me stagger, dragging me down. I managed to reel back, a hand clasped over my burn scar, cursing and spitting.

"Nothing tainted may pass," Hemmet said. He tucked the rod of office into his belt. "When the Hundred meet no magics can be taken within, no mind-sworn can enter to sway men's loyalties, none tainted with ungodly powers can enter to threaten their fellow rulers with more than men should possess. Any influences exerted on a person will be wiped away should they be able to pass through the gate."

I straightened, the pain fading as quickly as it had come. "You might have warned me." I wiped spittle and blood from the corner of my mouth.

Hemmet shrugged. "I didn't know you were tainted." A big man, solid in his years. The golden half-plate he wore hardly weighed on him. A stunning piece of work, lobstered over the shoulders and around the back of his neck where it rose to a helm that bore more than the suggestion of a crown.

"You try it," I told him.

He walked on in, turned and spread his hands. You could see he cared little for the Hundred, whether they call themselves king, or duke, or lord. There were many of the hundred, more names than most men could summon to mind, and but a single Lord Commander of the Gilden Guard. Hemmet.

"So I'm to be left out here?" I tried not to make it sound like whining.

"Captain Kosson will show you in through one of the side passages." Hemmet smiled. "It's only at Congression that you will be excluded, or should you seek to petition the emperor when the throne is occupied again."

And so I took the longer route into the emperor's throne room. Whilst Sindri, Elin, and the other untainted nobles were led in through the Gilden Gate, poor Jorgy had to slink in around the back like a servant. Kosson led me through long dark corridors holding a lantern to light the way.

"Most palaces can afford better lighting." It seemed a far cry from Ibn Fayed's grand home.

"Most palaces are inhabited by royals," Kosson replied without looking back. "Nobody lives here save a few servants to keep the dust stirred up. The guard come in and out during the years between Congressions, but we're soldiers, we don't need oil lamps in every niche. Shadows don't scare the guard."

I was about to say that perhaps they should, but something took the words away. "There aren't any niches." No place for lamp, lantern, or even torch, nowhere to display statuary, baubles, or any form of wealth as nobles are wont to show.

Kosson stopped and looked up. His gaze led me to a small glass circle set flush with the white stone of the ceiling. "A Builder light," he said.

I saw them now, every few yards.

"They don't work though." A shrug and he carried on walking, swinging shadows around us.

"This is a Builder hall? But—" It hardly seemed possible. "It's so . . . graceful. The dome, the archways and antechambers . . ."

"Not everything they made was ugly. This was a place of power. Some kind of legislature. They built it grand."

"I learn something new every day," I said. "You think they might have had souls after all then, these Builders?" I only half-joked.

"If it's learning you're after, I'll show you something most visitors don't get to see." Kosson made a sharp left into a smaller corridor and then another left.

"That is . . . unusual." I came to a halt at his shoulder.

A man stood with his back to us. He looked to be running but hadn't a twitch of motion in him, as if someone had taken the trouble to dress a very well-executed statue in a one-piece beige tunic and trews, belted at the waist. In one hand a long rod, almost like a broom but topped with a mass of red strips, oddly familiar, in the other a strange cup, extremely thin-walled, half-crushed in his grip, a dark liquid spilling from it, going nowhere. It set me in mind of blood droplets exploding from a broken skull, hanging in the air forever. It put me in mind of Fexler.

"So you've got yourself a Builder in stasis." I looked around for some kind of projector like the one that had frozen time around Fexler. The section of corridor looked identical to the rest.

Kosson threw me a hurt look, for a moment a child with his enthusiasm dashed. "Yes, but see *who* we have here!"

We edged around the invisible glass surrounding the man. That was how it felt. Slick glass, cold to touch, the edge of time where hours and minutes die to nothing.

"See?" Kosson pointed to a white rectangle attached to the man's chest, to the left. It looked to be a piece of plasteek and bore the legend "CUSTODIAN" in black. "That means he's the guardian, the protector. The guard archivists have books that tell the meanings of ancient words."

"He looks soft to me." Weak, white, fear in his eyes.

"The strength of the Builders was never in their arms. That's what the Lord Commander says. I agree with you myself, he's no warrior. The Lord Commander tracks his ancestry back to the first custodian. This man. He's the family's patron saint."

And in that moment I understood why the man's broom-thing seemed familiar. "That staff of office Hemmet's got. It's copied from this, isn't it? Shorter, prettier, but this?"

Kosson nodded.

"Patron saint, you say?" I sucked my teeth trying to figure that one through. "You're telling me Roma canonized a Builder?"

"You'll have to ask the Lord Commander that one." Kosson shook his head. "Come on." And he led back the way we'd come.

We were reunited before the throne, a plain wooden chair, high-backed and sturdy, ancient work, crudely fashioned. Here and there gleaming bolt heads drew the eye, on the armrests, the front legs, the sides, smoothed flat to the wood. Legend had it that kings among the Builders had sat in this same seat and the same secret fire that ran through their machines had run through their veins. It had been shipped in across a great ocean long ago.

"Will you have me keep my distance? Stand over here? Unclean as I am." I paused some yards back.

Sindri grinned and waved me forward. Elin intercepted me as I approached, lifting her fingers to touch my scarring. "The North knows how you came by your wounds, King Jorg, and they are no taint."

The throne stood on a dais of two high steps. The throne hall itself reached to the great dome covering the whole palace complex, and lay in a great circle surrounded by many chambers.

"The wedding ceremony will be conducted here before the throne with an honour watch of one hundred and fifty guard, the troops assigned to escorting each of your fathers to Congression," Lord Commander Hemmet told Sindri.

"A priest of Roma speaking the words within the Gilden Gate," I said. "That must grate, Lord Commander?" Whatever the disrespect the guard showed to the Hundred it paled next to that reserved for the Pope and her underlings, be it cardinal or choirboy.

"Never that, Jorg. The emperors maintained a personal priest swearing no allegiance to Roma. Such clerics are still available from a church within the palace. The Pope holds no sway within these walls, her corruption of the faith doesn't touch the guard, we keep to older ways. I doubt me that the Gate would allow any priest with Roma's stink to pass."

"Well and good," I said. "I hold to older ways myself." And I stepped closer to Elin. She smelled good, of woman and of horse, neck slender, eyes wicked. I nodded for Hemmet to continue his show and tell. Not that he was waiting for my permission.

"At Congression the Hundred break into their bickering groups and secret themselves in the preparation halls." Lord Commander Hemmet swung an arm to encompass all the side chambers. "Lord Sindri and Lady Freya may take a chamber each to house their respective wedding parties."

"Can they choose which?" I asked.

"Your pardon, King Jorg?" He had a way of speaking that made "king" seem a very small word.

"Can they have any of the chambers they wish? There must be thirty or more."

"Twenty-seven, and yes, they can have any of them." He nodded.

"Well, let's go exploring then," Elin said, and took my hand, leading me off toward a distant archway.

I heard Sindri snort behind me. "Come Uncle, Norv."

"And I'm supposed to know what to look for?" I heard the uncle growl behind us. "It's just a damn room."

We had a fair walk to the first chamber. The emperor's throne room would fit within Ibn Fayed's but with not much space to spare, and I judged it more ancient, turned to this purpose at a time when the empire was still in bud.

We halted before double oak doors inlaid with ironwood, the marquetry depicting two battling eagles facing off across the dividing line. Elin's hand felt cool in mine. She nearly matched me in height, the whiteness of her making something alien yet intriguing. She pushed a door and led me in.

The room beyond lay cavernous and dark, lit in patches by light from small windows in the ceiling, glazed using lost skills or stolen glass.

"There's nothing to see," I said. "And besides, it's just a room, what's to choose?"

"And there's me thinking this was your idea in the first place," Elin said, moving by me, pulling me into the shadows. Something in the way she brushed past lit a fire.

I had been thinking to send Sindri and his party off questing after a suitable room to claim, hopefully with the Lord Commander in tow, leaving me to poke around the empire throne in a moment of privacy. Instead we'd left Hemmet back by the throne and I was wasting my time with—

"We won't have long." Elin snaked her arms around me, strong and slender fingers kneading into the muscles along my spine.

"I don't want Sindri to—" I started.

She kissed me, challenging, hungry. Then, pulling away, "Oh shush, he knows me." She shrugged off her velvet cloak.

"I need to get to the—"

"I know what you need, my king." She drew her tunic overhead, black as moleskin, a fluid motion leaving her naked save for skirts. Skin like milk, showing only the faintest pink at the tips of full and heavy breasts.

It was true. She did know what I needed.

46

Five years earlier

"Who the hell are you?" I pushed myself from Elin and left her leaning back against the wall, still patting down her skirts.

"A man who sees the future." The intruder, a priest by the look of his robes, watched us with milky eyes. For the sake of Elin's honour I hoped he saw as little as the cataracts suggested.

"So you already know I'm just about to repeat my question?" I said.

"I am Father Merrin, priest of the Free Church of Adam."

"You're to marry my brother to his Hagenfast wife," Elin said, pulling on her top, remarkably unashamed of herself, rather pleased if anything.

"Yes," Father Merrin said.

Something niggled at me, something familiar about a man looking into the years to come. I scratched my head as if that would aid matters. It didn't.

"Can we help you?" I kept an eye out for Sindri and his uncle appearing at the door. They'd kept busy touring the other rooms. Elin said Sindri knew her mind. I'd hoped he approved—she had said he would. I did stop Ferrakind stirring their volcanoes up, after all. "Is there something you need?" I asked.

"I don't think so," Father Merrin said. The lamplight from the main hall glistened off his baldness and made something comic of his ears, too big, like those of all old men. "I came to help you instead, King Jorg."

"How so?" Something about the man tickled at me. I doubted that he would be walking through the Gilden Gate to conduct the ceremony. He'd choose a different entrance. It seemed unlikely the Gate would let him through any more than it would admit me.

"You're wanting to search beneath the throne, Jorg. Something to do with a ring you're carrying. But you can't see how to do it. Hemmet isn't going to allow you on the dais. You've thought about distractions you could make. Each plan more wild and less promising than the last. You even thought of causing some scandal with my lady here and trying to achieve your goal in the uproar."

"All true," I said. Elin punched me in the shoulder. Hard. "And why do you want to help me do that? What's going to happen when I use the ring?"

Father Merrin shrugged. It made him look young, just a boy wearing all those creases. "I don't see so much with these blind eyes, only a glimpse or two. All I know is that somehow it will make the Lord Commander owe you a favour."

"And why is that good for you?" I asked.

"That too is dim and far away," he said. "But Lord Commander Hemmet's support, the surety that his favour builds, will tip you in some decision made years from now. And that decision will help the Free Church, and what helps the Free Church weakens Roma and helps the people."

"Helps the people?" I drew the view-ring from inside the jerkin Sindri had gifted me and spun it before Elin's eyes. "Oh well. If I really must."

I motioned for the priest to lead on. "Lead on," I said, remembering he was blind.

Sindri, his uncle and bannerman, had rejoined the Lord Commander and Captain Kosson before the throne.

Sindri called out to us as we approached. "Did you find us a good room, Jorg?"

"Well, I liked it." We both grinned, naughty boys in the schoolroom. Neither of us married quite yet—growing up could wait awhile.

"Lord Commander," Father Merrin said, his voice carrying the sing-song of prayer. "It is necessary that the throne be set aside for a short while."

Hemmet scowled, as if the thought of it being touched, let alone moved, distressed him. "You're sure, Father? Is it one of your visions?"

Father Merrin nodded. Bald-headed, skinny in his robes, big ears like handles, I found it hard to take him seriously, but he held sway with the Lord Commander. Hemmet clapped his hands and four guards came trotting in from a distant entrance.

"Move the throne . . . there." He watched them take hold of it. "Be careful. Show respect."

"And the rug," Father Merrin said.

The Lord Commander raised his brows still further at that, but waved his men on. Two of them rolled back the heavy weave, a work of intricate patterns picked in silk, thick, and glistening with iridescence like a butterfly wing.

A copper plate, round, a hand span across, lay set into the floor at the point where the throne sat. I stepped forward to climb the dais. All about me the guards straightened, stiffened, ready to intervene.

"Allow this, Hemmet," Father Merrin said without heat.

The Lord Commander drew a great breath and sighed it out. He waved me on with a dismissive gesture as Merrin had known he would. The future-sworn must be hell to live with.

I kept the view-ring hidden in my hand and knelt beside the metal plate. No handle or hinge, no keyhole. I recalled the door at the mathema tower and just held the ring against the copper, dead centre under my palm. A moment of warmth and a Builder-ghost sprang up above me. I snatched my hand back. Drawn in pale shades as all the others, this ghost seemed familiar. Not Fexler, or Michael, but . . .

"Custodian!" Lord Commander Hemmet fell to his knees. The guards around him followed his lead.

The Custodian stood wordless for a moment. He flickered, frowned, slid back a foot from the copper disk, maybe two. A faint buzz of vibration from the ring and there stood Fexler. The ghosts locked eyes, furrowed brows in concentration or fury, locked hands . . . and vanished.

"Extraordinary!" Lord Commander Hemmet pressed the heels of his hands to his eyes. "What happened? There were two saints? Were they fight—"

All the lights came on. Every Builder light woke at the same moment so that the dome above our head sparkled like starry heavens. The light dazzled so that you had to squint against it, and made the flames of the oil lamps invisible as if we stood outside in high summer.

"The lights . . ." said Norv the Raw, as if we might not have noticed.

Before any further statements of the obvious could be made doors of gleaming steel started to slide down from recesses above every entrance save the Gilden Gate. The action accompanied by a squealing noise that set my teeth on edge, the sound of nails down Lundist's chalkboard.

"The doors . . ." said Norv. I resisted the temptation to beat him around the head.

It took maybe a count of ten for the doors to seal themselves, metal to stone, and without pause they began to retreat at the same rate. Guards came pouring through as the doors lifted, summoned by the squeal of the mechanism. For some minutes men of the guard rushed this way and that, set on diverse missions by the Lord Commander to establish that no attack was taking place, to see what other changes may have been wrought, to calm the servants, to set at ease the minds of other guard units, and the like.

All that frenzy came to a dead halt when they brought the Custodian in, the real man whose data-ghost we'd seen in the moment before Fexler wrestled him away again. He came in escorted by four men of the guard, with more crowding behind, discipline lost, curious children trailing a stranger in the market. Fexler had broken the Custodian's stasis.

"Well, there's a thing," I said. To Sindri's party the Builder was a stranger in strange clothes carrying a stick crested with a mass of short red ribbons. They would have to be sharp to recognize him from the brief look at his ghost on the dais. To the guards, however, a legend walked among them. To Lord Commander Hemmet a saint approached, his revered ancestor and a part of the foundation of his authority. Hemmet raised a hand and the chatter died. "Welcome, Custodian! Welcome!" A broad grin on his face.

The Custodian looked bewildered and perhaps fearful, but he had been asleep for a thousand years I supposed, so I allowed him that.

A pause, and then he spoke. But what language I couldn't say. A harsh tongue, guttural, it seemed to sit on the edge of understanding. I caught one word that sounded like "alert": he said it more than once.

"Perhaps he speaks another language," I said. "I read that there were many tongues among the Builders, almost as many across the empire as there are kingdoms. And even if he speaks the empire tongue it may be that it has changed over the course of centuries. Things move on, nothing stands still, words least of all."

Hemmet scowled at me but the anger didn't last, a cloud across the sun. "You did this, you woke him up, brought the light back to the palace. And I won't forget it, King Jorg." He set a hand to the Builder's shoulder, then moved beside him, the arm around him, protective. "I will speak with the Custodian in private. Captain Kosson, afford our guests all possible courtesy and escort them from the palace when their needs have been met."

And Hemmet left us, taking his saint with him.

I bent and scooped up the view-ring. "Well, Father Merrin, you were right. Hemmet loves me now." I frowned. "I thought someone once told me . . . I thought I heard that you couldn't tell a man his future because telling him changes it."

Merrin smiled and turned those milky eyes on me. "It depends on the future, Jorg, and how much you tell them. My own visions are so hazy that there's little detail to relate."

"So what else can you tell me about my future, Father?" I stepped closer so what sight remained to him might capture me.

"You don't want to know, Jorg," he said. "The future is a dark place. We all die there."

"Tell me anyway."

And, perhaps because he knew I would wear him down—*that* future being plain to both of us—he answered, "You will kill and kill again, do the darkest deeds, betray those you should love, destroy your brother, and lead ruin to us all."

"So, no real change then?" I ignored the look on Elin's face, on Sindri's. Disappointment put an edge on my tongue. I had thought I might grow, might be better, might be more. "Tell me, Father." And here I used "Father" as though I meant it. "Why doesn't every man of consequence find himself a future-sworn seer and plan a path to glory?"

A stillness came over the man. The type of regret that cannot be manufactured. He spoke with a gentle, self-deprecating humour but I knew he spoke true. "To look into what will be isn't unlike self-abuse. To watch yourself march through possibilities, to follow the truth through all those twists and turns. Just a little might stunt your growth." I thought of Jane, tiny and older than Gorgoth. "Or make you go blind." His cataracts seemed opalescent in the Builder light.

"And if you look too far, if you look to see what waits for us all at the end . . ."

"Tell me."

Father Merrin shook his head. "It burns."

And for an instant I glimpsed a skinless hand holding a copper box.

47

With the Pope's corpse lying out amid the slaughter, we advanced on the emperor's palace, a vast dome fashioned from thousands of huge sandstone blocks, fitted one to another without mortar and only gravity to hold them in place. A hundred guards from my retinue remained to stand watch over the dead whilst Captain Devers pondered his options.

"It's big." Makin's eloquence, vanished at the city gates, had yet to return.

"What it would be to have ridden here at the head of an army. To have a hundred thousand spears at my back. To just take it rather than to seek approval."

None of them answered: there was only the cold tugging of the wind and the clatter of hooves on stone.

On that long slow ride across Vyene's great square my father's death at last caught up with me. It had been given out in dribs and drabs. A ghost displayed by the lichkin, a dream of the Tall Castle invaded, the commiserations of a cleric. Nothing as solid or as sudden as seeing him fall, looking down upon his corpse. Nothing so final or so damning as striking the blow to end him, wiping at the blood on my hands as if it might never come off.

I felt . . . hollow. His death had struck me as a hammer strikes a bell, and I rang with it, a broken tone speaking of broken days.

"Nothing can be made right, Brother Makin."

Makin looked across. Said nothing. The wisest words.

I could have fixed my hands around that old man's throat. Choked and watched the light die from his eyes. Shouted my complaints, railed against old injustice. And it would have rung me just as hollow. Nothing would be right of it.

I ran a fingertip across the hand that held the reins, down to the scars across my wrist. "I could take the all-throne. The priests would write my name for the ages. But what the thorns wrote here—that's my story—what was taken, what can't be changed."

Makin frowned, and still he had no answer. What answer is there?

My name for the ages? *What ages?* Marco Onstantos Evenaline of the House Gold had been a test, not the start, not the beginning. A test to learn from. For years Michael and those of his order had been positioning their weapons. The fires of the Builders, the poisons and the plagues. And here we were, the new men, born from ashes and cracking the world open as we played with our magic, with the toys Fexler's kind had left us. Crack it but a little further and it would tip Michael's hand: the ghosts of our past would rise again, bearing a final solution to all problems. And what followed me? What dogged my heels? An army of the dead, a wedge of necromancy driven after me and aimed at Vyene. A wedge big enough to split us all open. No wonder Father Merrin was blind. Our future was too bright for him. Rain fell, a cold autumn drizzle, lacking challenge. It filled my eyes. I had let the thorns hold me; taken what they offered, and lost the first of my brothers. Flesh of my flesh, his care the first duty I had set upon myself. I betrayed him and left him to die alone. And though there was no price I'd not pay to undo that wrong, even an emperor hadn't the coin to set it right.

The palace dome, once so distant, engulfed us in its shadow. I shook off those memories, left mother, father, brother behind me in the rain.

Around the dome's perimeter a dozen and more low entrances, slots high enough for a man on horseback, wide enough for thirty. The guards stationed themselves there as each of the Hundred arrived, their escorts breaking off to occupy the halls behind those slots. If any enemy threatened—me perhaps with my hundred thousand spears—they would sally forth to defend Congression.

Marten tapped my shoulder and pointed off west. A column of smoke rose, slanting with the wind, black smoke.

"There are a lot of chimneys in Vyene," I said.

Marten swung his arm to a second column, further off, rising to join the louring cloud. I wondered if there were dead gathering at the city gates already, fresh-woken perhaps ahead of the Dead King's advance. Even the swiftest of his main force must be a day or more away. And yet an uncommon pall of smoke hung above those distant roofs. Were the outer parts of the city aflame?

"Maybe somebody has beaten me to it and come with an army," I said.

The guard stations around the palace are filled in order, the furthest from the grand entrance first. Our hundreds filed into the closest to the royal gates. It might be that the Drowned Isles delegation behind us would be the last of all the Hundred to arrive. Some have it that to be first through the Gilden Gate at Congression is to win the favour of dead emperors. The more practical suggest that it gives additional days in which to sway your fellow rulers and strengthen your faction. I say it just gives them time to grow heartily sick of the sight of you. On my previous attendance I had had to wait outside the throne room, too tainted to be admitted, and the only glimpse the Hundred had of me was of the occasional dire looks I slotted in at them through the Gilden Gate.

We dismounted. Osser Gant emerged from the carriage, then Gomst and Katherine climbed down, and Miana with William wrapped in furs against the wind. Dwarfed by the cavernous mouth of the Royal Gate we marched inside, just an honour guard of ten men in gold to guide us through. Captain Allan led them, Devers having remained outside to keep the Pope's carcass under consideration.

The ceremonial gates stood open, monstrous things of age-blackened timbers bound with brass. It would take a hundred men to close them—if the hinges had been kept oiled. We passed through and walked the Hall of Emperors where each man stood remembered in stone, fathers, sons, and grandfathers, usurpers, bastards-reclaimed-to-greatness, murderers, and warlords, peace-makers, empire-builders, scientists, scholars, mad-men, and degenerates, all rendered as heroes, armoured, clutching the symbols of their rule. Builder-lights, a hundred bright spots on the ceiling, leading into the distance, made each statue an island in its own pool of illumination.

"And you want to stand at the end of this line?" Katherine spoke at my side. I hadn't heard her draw close.

"Orrin of Arrow wanted to," I said. "Is my ambition less worthy?"

She didn't need to answer that.

"Perhaps the empire requires me. Maybe I'm the only man who can save it from drowning in horror, or from burning on the bonfire of its past. Did you ever think of that? Set a thief to catch a thief, I said that to you once. Now I say set a murderer to stop black murder. Fight a fire with fire."

"That's not your reason," she said.

"No."

And we came to the end of the statues, past Emperor Adam the Third, past Honorous in his steward's chair, serious, watching infinity. Up ahead an antechamber with more guards and, by the look of it, other travellers.

"Your weapons will be taken from you and stored in safe keeping with the utmost respect." Captain Allan's glance fell to Gog at my side then made a nervous flicker toward Rike. "You will be subject to various searches, necessary for entry into the throne room during Congress. If you don't return through the Gilden Gate before the final vote then the searches will not need to be repeated. You will of course appreciate that these precautions ensure your safety as well as the safety of the other delegates."

"Would you feel safe, unarmed, next to Rike here?" I nodded Allan in Rike's direction.

"Y-your weapons will—"

"Yes, we understand." I stared past him. "By God, is that? Is that? Taproot! Get over here, you old trickster!"

And breaking away from the party ahead came Dr. Taproot, his quick, erratic walk unmistakable, arms flying up, broad grin on a narrow face. "Watch me! If it isn't King Jorg himself! Lord of nine nations! My condolences on your father, dear boy."

"Your condo—"

"I assumed you would have wanted to kill him yourself, but time has its own way with us, we burn in time's fire. Look at me." Hands flitted to his temples. "Going grey. Ashes, I tell you. Burning in time's fire. Watch me."

"I am watching you, old man."

"Old? I'll show you old! I'll—"

"And why is it that you're here, good doctor?" I asked.

"Is the circus in town?" Rike loomed over us, huge and hopeful. We both ignored him.

"It's Congression, Jorg. Every fourth year a man who knows things finds himself in great demand. Yes he does. Lucrative demand. Watch me! I'm paid to whisper. Whisper this duke likes boys, that lord has a sister married there, this king thinks his line sprung from Adam the First. Little golden whispers for eager ears. Watch me! If only it could be that way each year, all year."

"You'd grow bored without your circus, Taproot. Bored men wither and die. Fuel for the fire."

"Still, it's nice to be wanted, even now and again. Nice to be in the know." His hands shaped abstracts, as if he could sketch his knowledge in the air.

I reached out, quick—you have to be quick with Taproot—and caught his shoulder. "Let's see just how much you know, shall we?"

Taproot met my gaze, still for once, not a tremble in him.

"Be my advisor. One of father's delegates had an accident. You can replace him."

A fat man in slashed velvets, black with crimson lining, approached us, his gold chain swinging to match his hurry. "Taproot! What's the meaning of this?"

"This man wishes to acquire my services, Duke Bonne." Taproot didn't look away. Quick, dark eyes he had, as if they were too busy for colour, drinking in the world.

"He may wish all he likes." Duke Bonne cradled his stomach. A short man but shrewd if looks could be believed. "What's his name, what's your advice? Earn your keep, man. Let him see what he's missed out on."

Makin and Marten came to stand at my shoulder now. Rike off to one side. The rest of my party watching beside the steward's statue.

"His name is King Honorous Jorg Renar, King of Ancrath, King of Gelleth, King of the Highlands, of Kennick, Arrow, Belpan, Conaught, Normardy, and Orlanth. You should know that he is not a good man, but neither is he a man that can be turned, and should all hell wash against these walls, as I believe it might very well do, and sooner than any of us desire, King Jorg will stand against that tide.

"My advice to you, Duke Bonne, is to put yourself in his service as I am about to do. If any man is capable of releasing the lion of empire to roar once more, it is the man you see before you."

I grinned at the "lion of empire." Taproot hadn't forgotten his tawny bag of bones and fleas that I let loose from its cage.

And so we let our blades be taken. They took the view-ring too, my daggers, a bodkin in my hair, a garrotte in my sleeve. Miana's

iron-wood rod they tried to take but I clicked my fingers and Father
Gomst—Bishop Gomst—came forward with the heavy tome I had
entrusted to him in Holland's carriage. We perused *Ecthelion's Record of
Court Judgments, Adam II and Artur IV, Year of Empire 340-346* together,
Gate Captain Helstrom and I, with Dr. Taproot all eyes at my shoul-
der. And after a modicum of sharp debate I won the day—I could, as
Lord of Orlanth, carry my rod of office (wooden) wheresoever I damn
well pleased! By imperial order.

The Duke of Bonne harrumphed and snorted and favoured me
with dark looks, but he waited for our party so I sent Makin his way
with a nod and a wink, knowing there aren't many who won't fall to
his charms.

And within the hour we were once again before the Gilden Gate,
the ancient frame of wood that had kept me from my rightful place
at the last Congression. My taint of course was burned out of me at
the breaking of the siege at the Haunt. Even so, I didn't relish
approaching that gateway. A hand that's been scorched won't want to
return to the iron, even when every sense but memory is telling you
the heat has gone from it.

"After you, my dear." And I ushered Miana through with the
baby. It turned out that another ruling, recorded by the dutiful Ecthelion in YE 345, provided that although children were not permitted
to be designated as advisors they may be brought to Congression if
accompanied by both parents. Handy things, books. And by-laws. If
applied selectively.

"I'd advise against it, advisor," I said as Katherine moved to follow my wife.

"And when did I start taking your advice, Jorg?" Katherine turned
those eyes on me, and that foolish notion I might be a better man,
that I could change, swept over me once again.

"The gate will reject you, lady. And its rejections are not gentle."
No rejection is gentle.

She frowned. "Why?"

"My father didn't know you as well as I do, as well as the gate will know you should you try to pass. You're dream-sworn. Tainted. It will reject you and it will hurt." I tapped my temples.

"I— I should try." She believed me. I don't think I'd ever lied to her.

"Don't," I said.

And she moved away, shaking her head in confusion.

"Rike," I said, and one after the other the brothers entered Congression. Marten, Sir Kent, Osser, and Gomst followed. Lord Makin with Duke Bonne.

Katherine sat on a marble bench, hands folded in her dark skirts, watching the last of us, Gorgoth, Taproot, and me.

"I don't know what will happen," I told the leucrota. "The gate might reject you, it might not. If it does, then you'll be in good company." I nodded toward Katherine.

Gorgoth flexed his massive shoulders, muscle heaped beneath red hide. He bowed his head and moved forward. As he reached the gate arch he slowed, as if stepping into the teeth of a gale. He moved one step at a time, gathering himself before each. The effort trembled across him. I thought he must fail but he kept on. The strain drew a groan from him, very deep. He moved into the arch. I could imagine the set of his face from the taut line of his shoulders. And as he stepped through the Gilden Gate it creaked and flexed, resisting him but in the end admitting his right. He slumped when he crossed into the throne hall, almost falling.

"I should try." Katherine stood, uncertain.

"Gorgoth has dipped his toes in the river. You swim in it." I shook my head.

Over her shoulder I saw three figures entering the far end of the antechamber, preceded by a pair of guards. They drew the eye, this trio. Three more different delegates it would be hard to imagine. I kept my gaze on them and let it turn Katherine.

"The Queen of Red, Luntar of Thar, and the Silent Sister."

Taproot whispered it from behind me, using my body to shield himself from their view. Katherine drew a sharp breath.

Luntar and the sister flanked the Queen of Red, a tall woman, raw-boned but handsome once. She had maybe fifty years on her, more perhaps. Time had scorched rather than withered, her skin tight across sharp cheeks, hair of the darkest red scraped back beneath diamond clasps.

"King Jorg!" she hailed me still twenty yards away, a fierce grin on her. The black swirl of her skirts flashed gem-light as she strode toward us, her collar rose behind her, whalebone spars fanning out a crimson crest that spread above her head.

I waited without comment. Luntar I had met but held no recollection of. He boxed my memories in the cinders of Thar. Next to the queen's splendour he looked dour in a grey tunic and white cloak, but few would remark on his clothing: his burns demanded the eye. I imagined that Leesha might have looked this way before the hurts done to her in the Iberico Hills closed over with ugly scar. Luntar's wounds lay wet. Thin burn-skins parted with each movement to reveal the rawness beneath.

"The Silent Sister is the one," Taproot hissed. "Watch her! She slips the mind."

And true enough, I had forgotten her already, as if it had been just the two of them, Luntar and his queen, approaching. With an effort, the kind you use when confronting an unpleasant duty, I forced myself to see her. An old woman, truly old, like the wood of the Gilden Gate, a grey cloak rippling around her, almost fog, the cowl hiding most of her face: just wrinkles and a gleam of eyes, one pearly blind.

"King Jorg," the Queen of Red said once more as she stood before me, my equal in height. She rolled my name on her tongue— unsettling. "And a princess I'm thinking. A Teuton from the look of her." She glanced at the Silent Sister, the briefest flicker. "But her name can't be taken. Mind-sworn? A dream-smith perhaps."

"Katherine Ap Scorron," Katherine said. "My father is Isen Ap Scorron, Lord of the Eisenschloß."

"And Dr. Taproot. Why are you cowering back there, Elias? Is that any way to greet an old friend?"

"Elias?" I stepped aside to expose Taproot.

"Alica." Taproot made a deep bow.

"Had you been hoping to slip through the gate without seeing me, Elias?" The queen smiled at his discomfort.

"Why no, I . . ." Taproot lost for words. That was a new one.

"And you'll be staying outside with us, Katherine dear." The queen left Taproot searching for his reply. "With the 'tainted' as the Lord Commander likes to call us."

I caught myself thinking "us" was the two of them, slipping into the conviction then jerking back as you do when sleep is trying to snare you. Focusing on the Silent Sister was hard, but I fixed my eyes on her and set a wall about my thoughts, remembering Corion and the power of his will.

"I've heard of you, Sister," I told her. "Sageous spoke of you. Corion and Chella knew of you. Jane too. All of them wondering when you would show your hand. Are you showing it now perhaps?"

No reply, just a small, tight smile on those dry old lips.

"I guess the clue is in the name?"

Again the smile. Those eyes had a draw on them, like a rip-tide. "Keep at it old woman and I'll let you pull me in—then we'll see what happens, won't we?"

She didn't like that. Looked away sharpish, smile gone.

"And Luntar. I don't remember you. And that seems to me to be your fault, no? Perhaps you did me a favour with your little box, perhaps you didn't. I'm not decided yet."

His face cracked as he opened his mouth to speak, clear fluid leaking over burn-skin. The echoes of old agony rang in my cheek, just as the Gilden Gate had woken them years ago when I first tried it. The fire still scared me, no two ways about that.

"Would you like to remember me, Jorg?" Luntar asked.

I really didn't want to. Would I like to burn again? "Yes," I said.

"Take my hand." He held it out, wet and weeping.

I had to bite down, to swallow back bile, but I met his grip, closed my fingers around the hurt of his, felt the broken skin shift.

And there it was, a glittering string of recollection, the madness, the long journey tied to Brath's saddle, raving whilst Makin led us south into the scarred land they call Thar.

Schnick. I'm staring at a box, a copper box, thorn-patterned. It has just closed and the hand that closed it is burned.

"What?" I say. Not the most intelligent query but it seems to cover all bases.

"My name is Luntar. You've been sick." A smack of lips after each word.

I lift my head from the box, my hair falls to either side and I see him, a horror of a man, a mass of open sores so dense that it is one sore.

"How do you stand the pain?" I ask.

"It's just pain." He shrugs. His white cloak, smeared with dust, sticks to him as though he is wet beneath it.

"Who are you?" I ask, although he has said his name.

"A man who sees the future."

"I knew a girl like that once," I say, glancing around for my brothers. There's only dust and sand.

"Jane," he says. "She didn't see far. Her own light blinded her. To see in the dark you need to be dark."

"And how far can you see?" I ask.

"All the way," he says. "Until we meet again. Years off. That's all that ever stops me. When I see myself on the path ahead."

"What's in the box?" Something about that box makes it seem more important than all the years ahead.

"A bad deed you did," he says.

"I've done lots of bad things."

"This one is worse," he says. "At least in your eyes. And it's mixed with Sageous's

venom. It needs to ferment in there awhile, lose a little of its sting, before it's safe to come out."

"Safe?"

"Safer," he says.

"So tell me about the future," I say.

"Well, here's the thing." He smacks those burned lips, strings of melted flesh between them. "Telling someone about their future can change their future."

"Can?"

"Choose a number between one and ten," he says.

"You know what I'll choose?"

"Yes," he says.

"But you can't prove it."

"Today I can, but not always. You're going to choose three. Go on, choose."

"Three," I say, and smile.

I take the box from him. It's much heavier than I thought it would be.

"You put my memory in here?"

"Yes," he says. Patient. Like Tutor Lundist.

"And you see my future all the way until we meet again in many years time?"

"Six years."

"But if you tell me then it won't be my future any more, and if you tell me that new future, that too will change?" I ask.

"Yes."

"So tell me anyway. Then take that memory too. And when we meet, give it back. And then I'll know that the man who stands before me truly can see across the years."

"An interesting suggestion, Jorg," he says.

"You knew I was going to suggest it, didn't you?"

"Yes."

"But if you'd told me then I might not have."

"Yes."

"And what did you see yourself saying to the suggestion?"

"Yes."

So I nod. And he tells me. Everything that would happen. All of it.

* * *

"Jorg?" Katherine pulled at my shoulder. "Jorg!"

I looked down at my empty hand, wet, pieces of burned skin adhering to mine. Lifting my gaze I met Luntar's stare. "You were right," I said. "About all of it." Even Chella. I had laughed at that and cursed him for a liar.

"So now you know a man who sees the future," he said.

48

"So now you know a man who sees the future," Luntar said.

"A man who looked too far and got burned," I said.

"Yes."

"And how do we stop that future in which we all burn?" I asked.

"It's unlikely that we can," Luntar said. "But if it can be done, then this is the best chance we have." He handed me a folded piece of parchment, stained by the wetness of his fingers. "Four words. Don't read them until the right moment."

"And how will I know what the right moment is?"

"You just will."

"Because you've seen it," I said.

"Even so."

"And does it work?" I asked.

A quick shake. "Try anyway," he said. "Not every ending can be seen."

The Queen of Red watched on, with Katherine and the Silent Sister, all three of them studying me as if I were some puzzle that might be solved. Luntar cocked his head at the trio. "What do you think, Jorg? Have we the crone, mother, and maiden? The triple-goddess of old walking amongst us?"

And for a moment it did seem that they could be three generations of the same woman. Katherine had the queen's strength in her face, the sister's knowing in her eyes.

"Best be about it, boy," the queen said. "Time's a-wasting."

And so I stepped in to kiss Katherine, bold as men are when the sands are running out. And she stopped me with her hand upon my chest. "Do it right, Jorg," she said. And I walked for the first time through the Gilden Gate.

The emperor's throne room, whilst not crowded, was certainly occupied. Close on a hundred and fifty lords of empire and their diverse advisors circulated around the throne dais. The throne seemed to float above them, a gaunt thing of bare wood, waiting for a victim.

I stood for a moment, watching. Parties broke off to occupy side chambers, others emerged in agreement or further entrenched in opposition, guards looked on from their stations about the hall's edge, and around it all the hubbub of talking and more talking.

"You there!" A tall man little older than me broke from his gathering just a few paces from the Gilden Gate. He had been holding forth to a group of a dozen or so, waving his arms as he spoke, glittering in gem-sewn velvet.

"What?" I answered him in kind, and for a moment he gaped, taken aback. He'd clearly marked me for a copper-crown, wandering in unaccompanied with my single vote. I hadn't the years to be mistaken for an advisor.

"How do you stand on the Mortrain question?" He had red and beefy cheeks, reminding me of Cousin Marclos.

"It's not something I've given any thought to." The men behind him had enough similarity in style and colouring that they might all hail from the same region. Somewhere east, to look at them. Somewhere where the Mortrain question might be significant politics.

"Well, you need to give it some thought." He jabbed his finger at my chest.

Before it stubbed against the polished steel of my breastplate I took hold of it. "Why would you do that?" I asked as he gasped. "Why would you hand me a lever to your pain?" I walked forward, bending the finger down, and he backed before me, into the crowd of his supporters, crying out, bowing low to lessen the sharp angle at which I held the digit.

Amid the group of eastern nobles, men from the steppes in their conical crowns or brightly embroidered hats, I applied more pressure and set the man on his knees. "Your name?" I asked.

"Moljon, of Honeere." He hissed it through his teeth.

"Jorg, of the west." I had too many kingdoms to rattle off for his benefit. "And you made two mistakes, Moljon. Firstly you gave me your finger. Worse than that, though. When it was taken you let it be used against you, let it be used to separate you from your pride. Don't compound your errors, man. The finger was lost from the moment I took it. You should have surged forward and let it break, a small sacrifice to regain the upper hand and knock me on my arse." I looked around the gathered kings of the east. "It would be a mistake to put your faith in this one. He hasn't the strength that's needed."

I broke Moljon's finger. A sharp crack. And set off to find my party.

"I see you've met Czar Moljon. Recently inherited, riding his father's reputation." Dr. Taproot moved beside me and guided me to Makin and the rest.

"Jorg!" Makin clapped a hand on my shoulder. "I was just telling Duke Bonne that you'd be the man to intercede on his behalf with his neighbours to the north. Cousins of our good friend Duke Alaric."

I nodded and smiled, aware that in my scarred face my wolf's grin might seem more fierce than friendly.

"And where's Miana?" I asked. "And my son?"

"She's set off to find her father, sire. Sir Kent went with her. Gorgoth too, though he went sniffing for trolls," Marten said.

"Trolls?" I turned to Taproot.

"It is reported that the last emperor had an elite guard, a guard within the guard if you like. The description I have read of them is 'not men.'" He put the matter aside with a shrug, a gesture as eloquent as the rest of his body language.

"Tell me how we stand, Taproot," I said.

"Watch me!" And he laid it out for me in charcoal upon a scrap of parchment. "You have nine votes. Duke Alaric has two, and is like to swing two more, along with Gothman of the Hagenfast—his wife carries some influence there, I believe."

"Elin." I smiled, softer now.

"Your grandfather carries two votes, Miana's father another, and between them Earl Hansa and the Lord of Wennith are like to draw three more behind them. Watch me!"

"I was just—"

"Ibn Fayed commands five votes. And that makes our tally—"

"Twenty-five," I said. "Not half of what I need."

"Twenty-six if Makin works his magic with Duke Bonne." Taproot marked Bonne down beside the caliph's votes. "It speaks volumes for you that your support hails from the raw north to the deserts of Afrique. A man who can sway such disparate votes clearly has something to offer. The Hundred look at men like Moljon with a tight bloc of neighbouring states to back his play and all they see is special interest—a threat. When they look at a man who calls on favour from caliphs out of the hot sands and norse dukes in their mead halls—they might start to think they see an emperor." Taproot sketched the crown above my head. "And consider, you need fifty-one votes only if all votes are cast."

"Interesting," I said. "Get yourself and Makin amongst the Hundred and see who might be swayed, who our enemies are, and who heads any factions that might compete with ours. When a faction is broken it's often the case that the pieces may be swept up easily." A bit of wisdom from the road. Kill the head and the body is yours.

"Set Miana and Osser to it as well. And Gomst. Use Gomst on the pious ones."

Taproot nodded. He started to go but I caught his wrist. "Oh and, Doctor, there may be a rumour circulating to the effect that the Pope has been killed. Be sure to say I had nothing to do with it. And if there isn't such a rumour—start one."

Taproot raised both brows at that, but nodded again and went on his way.

"Jorg!" Lord Commander Hemmet surged through the Hundred as if they were sheep and he the shepherd. "Jorg Ancrath!" Behind him the Custodian hurried in his wake, lips scarred and pressed tight. The story had it that he had emerged tongue-less from his centuries' sleep. My guess is that when the Lord Commander finally unpicked the tangle of old-speech he found himself not liking what the Custodian had to say.

"Lord Commander," I said. He had a face like thunder, suppressed energies sparking off him.

"Jorg!" He clasped both hands to my shoulders. Once upon a time he would have got a face full of my forehead for such a move, but life at court had taken that edge off. "Jorg!" he repeated my name again as if somehow not believing it, and drew me close, so our bowed heads all but met, voice lowered. "You killed the Pope? You really did it?"

"I damn well hope so," I said. "If she lived through that she's made of sterner stuff than I am."

A gale of laughter broke from him, drawing stares all across the hall. Then forcing himself to whisper, "You really did it? You really did it! Damn me. Damn me but that took some stones."

I shrugged. "Killing old women is easy. But if I don't walk out of Congression as emperor then I may only live a short while in which to regret the decision. There were, however, no witnesses other than my people and the Gilden Guard, and these are dangerous times. Even a Pope may meet a terrible end on the road these days." When you need something covered up in Vyene it's good to have the Lord Commander's favour.

Hemmet grinned, a fierce thing. "Yes." Then a frown. "More dangerous than ever I had thought. The dead are at our gates. Through them, even." He let me go. "It's not a matter to trouble Congression though. Their numbers are too few to reach the palace. We'll be riding them down within the hour."

And with that he was gone, the Custodian trailing after him like a whipped cur.

49

Chella's story

The towns and villages along the Danoob grew close together as Chella's column approached Vyene. Soon they would join into one unbroken sprawl, washing up against the walls of the imperial city.

"Stop!"

It irked that she had to shout her commands but the necromancy still festering in her had retreated too far for the dead to respond directly to her desire.

The cavalry came to an untidy halt. The horses didn't take well to dead riders, even if they were the same riders they had carried on the previous night and for weeks before that. Some had refused, screaming and bucking when their dead owners tried to reclaim them. Chella had thought to cut their throats, but Kai convinced her to turn the animals free and send the spare riders back to join the Dead King's advance.

"Why have we stopped?" Kai leaned in toward her, guiding his horse with both knees.

"I need to ask Thantos a question," she said.

There's a slope down toward evil, a gentle gradient that can be ignored at each step, unfelt. It's not until you look back, see the distant heights where you once lived, that you understand your journey. Chella looked up from her depths in sudden epiphany. Such moments had punctuated her life, her half-life, drawn out over a hundred years and more. Not once had they given her more than brief pause. Not once had she stepped back.

"Come," she told him, a touch of tenderness in her voice. It should have been enough to set him running.

They went together. Kai not wanting to, but pushing down his fear.

Chella set her hand to the carriage door. The metal handle made her skin dry, made it old. She pulled it open.

"Now?" she asked, speaking into the empty horror of the carriage.

And by way of answer a grey contagion flowed out. Kai screamed as it wrapped him. For an instant Chella glimpsed the lichkin, its slim bones insinuating themselves into Kai's flesh, through clothing, past armour. It took a while. Too long. Ages. Kai's choking screams drowned out all other sounds, his flesh writhing to accommodate its new occupant, until finally his jaw snapped shut and left her ears ringing.

Thantos turned Kai's head to look at Chella, bones grating. He didn't speak. The lichkin stood beyond words. Nothing that interested them could fit within such mean packages.

"He'll last. He's strong," Chella said.

Thantos climbed back into the carriage. Even drugged, the team drawing the carriage were skittish. Two had died and been replaced. There was no possibility that a horse would bear him to the palace, not even now he was clothed in flesh.

"Can you hear me in there, Kai?" Something in the eyes said he might be listening now that his screams were silent screams. "Did you never wonder that we came with five votes but only two delegates? Could not the Dead King spare three more necromancers, or cleaner men bound to his cause? We came in a pair. One host, and one to guard the host, ready to move against him if he should anticipate his fate." Secrets are best kept behind a single pair of lips.

Thantos reached out and closed the door, an awkward motion within his stolen flesh.

"But you never did anticipate." Chella spoke the words to the closed door and shook her head. "You should have learned to fly," she spat. To fault him made it easier.

Above the outlying spread of Vyenese houses, neat little homes with wooden shingles and log piles stacked to the eaves against the coming of winter, came the stink of burning. In many places hearth-smoke rose white from stone chimneys, but in others the smoke lifted in black and angry clouds. Horror stalked the streets, rose earth-covered from family graves, crept in from field and forest. The Dead King's tide swept in from the west, true enough, from the Drowned Isles, through Ancrath and Gelleth, through Attar, Charland and the Reichs, but it also rose from the very ground, as if a dark ocean waited below the soil, fathoms deep, and now swelled from the depths at the Dead King's call, lifting the fallen from their tombs.

At Vyene's gates guard units in their golds thundered past in both directions. News came from west to east. Reinforcements, regular army units from Conquence in the main, made the march east to west. More Gilden Guard manned the gate than would be necessary even at Congression. Additional troops lined the walls, archers with an even mix of longbow and crossbow. They'd clearly had little experience if they thought arrows would stop the dead.

"Hurry through, madam, you're the last and we're to seal the gates." The gate captain waved the column on, with no concern for any report from the captains of the escort, no demand that they explain their thinned number or ragged formation. Not even the lack of followers sparked his interest: perhaps he thought they had sought shelter along the way or hurried to arrive ahead of the guard.

Thantos's carriage rumbled through without remark, though the men closest to it paled, despair soaking into them through their skins.

On through the broad streets of Vyene, onto the wideness of West Street beneath the Western Arch. The grandeur on all sides worked its own magic on Chella. For all her long life she had seen nothing close. Hers were the graveyards and the mire, the bones of forgotten men and the tombs erected to their memory. In the face of such works of men as these she knew herself dirty and small, a bone-picker, a thing of nightmare and of the dark.

"The Dead King will make a necropolis here." It made her feel better to speak the words. Not that she wanted to live always amongst the returned—with life pulsing through her the thought made her stomach roil—but the sheer wonder of Vyene insulted her existence in ways beyond explanation and she would rather see it dust than endure the judgment of its empty windows.

Another contingent of guards passed them as they neared the end of West Street where it opened onto a vast square. Several hundred men, a thousand maybe, riding hard, with the Lord Commander at their head. The Dead King had mentioned Lord Commander Hemmet, spoken of the cloak and staff that would mark him out. A man to watch.

Riding to the palace it seemed that the dome would never grow closer, that its size went from incredible to impossible as they advanced. At one point, perhaps halfway between the distant mansions and the greatness of the palace, the flagstones lay stained with blood. Some effort had been taken to clean the area but the smell of slaughter is hard to disguise. A pulse of dark joy broke from the carriage, brief and then gone, but enough to set the horses pitching and jumping in fear. These deaths pleased the lichkin. A potential foe erased. The wind still carried fortune with it from the west.

Chella's troop closed on their station, the last to be filled, just to the left of the Empire Gate. They turned from their allotted path only at the final moment, and rode at a walk into the grand entrance before the gate. The thin gold line of duty-guards fell into disarray, confused at their comrades from the road dismounting in the grand entrance. Before they had much to say about it the lichkin stepped from his carriage and all the men's attention became drawn to him as a man will stare at the bloody stump where his thumb was before he cut it off.

50

"This has to be fast."

"It's been a hundred and twenty-eight years so far, King Jorg," Taproot said. "And we've not come close to selecting an emperor. Whatever this Congression throws up, fast is the one thing you can count on it not being."

"We've no time. Can't you feel it?" It beat in me like a drum, the threat, the danger, drawing closer.

Taproot offered only wide eyes and blank incomprehension. "The guard surround us . . ."

"It has to be done fast." I ran my eye over the throng, the high and the mighty. "Who leads the biggest faction?"

"I would say you do," Taproot said. "Watch me." An afterthought.

"Well, that's good. And then?"

"Czar Moljon, the Queen of Red, and Costos of the Port Kingdoms. Your father also commanded considerable support."

I spotted my grandfather amongst the crowd, Miana at his side. "Moljon is broken—his followers will be looking for new alliances. The queen is outside . . . Costos it is then. Point him out for me."

For some reason I had expected a peacock but Costos stood taller than me, with a warrior's build, clad neck to toe in burnished steel mail, enamelled across the breastplate with a sunburst behind a black ship, the detail exquisite.

"Are there laws about approaching the throne?" I asked.

"What? Yes—no, I don't think so. Any fool knows not to." Taproot's unease lived in his fingertips, pulling at hair, buttons, ties.

I walked over to the dais, slow enough, with Taproot flustering behind. Up the steps in two skips and I stood before the throne. "I hope you can hear me, Fexler. I want to know if you can work the doors and the lights for me. If you can't, well, I've no idea what the point of my last visit was." I spoke in a low voice that might be mistaken for a prayer.

For a moment the illumination grew around me, just a fraction and just for a heartbeat, as if far above me the ceiling lights aimed at the throne shone a little brighter. It called to mind the time beneath my grandfather's castle when Fexler had moved me along his path with failing glow-bulbs. I'm sure Fexler had more important reasons four years before for needing to be brought here, physically, rather than swimming through his hidden ocean. Maybe I helped him past walls I couldn't see. And perhaps we owed the fact that Vyene was not yet poisoned dust to his residence—but whatever his motivation it was lights and doors that mattered to me most in this moment.

"And will you hear me wherever I speak?" Again the glow.

"You, boy!" Costos striding my way, bristling, indignant, and gleaming.

"Boy?" I had hoped it would be him. It fell to Costos to rebuke me now. The pecking order among royals is as strict as that among chickens.

"This boy has twenty-six votes behind him, Costos Portico. Perhaps you would do better to call me King Jorg and see what inducements might persuade me to make you emperor."

That made Costos look again, and hard. Outrage at my trampling of convention warred with his lust for those twenty-six votes. He approached the foot of the dais. I knew what picture that put in the minds of the Hundred. Costos at my feet. A supplicant.

"We should speak, King Jorg." He lowered his voice to a deep whisper. "But not where idle ears might hear us. The Roman room should afford us some privacy. Come with whichever of your bannermen will show their hands."

I nodded, liege to subject, and waited for him to move away before stepping down from the dais.

"A tricksy one is Costos, watch me!" Taproot at my shoulder once again. "Violent temper, won the Port Kingdom tourney three years in a row when he was young. He was a third son and not expecting to inherit. Watch his second, King Peren of Ugal, a shrewd negotiator and cold as ice. The short man with the scar, there! See him?"

Costos moved around the hall, touching a man here, a man there, assembling his entourage. Too slow for my liking. Beyond him, Gorgoth towered above the crowd, ignoring everyone, head cocked as if listening.

"Which is the Roman room?" Taproot nodded to one of the doorways, suppressing a smile. It was the chamber Elin once showed me. She might well be in there now, showing it to her husband. Was there nothing the good doctor didn't know?

I counted fifteen men into the Roman room, Costos the last to enter.

"I should gather your supporters," Taproot prompted. It would take more than his word to bring my disparate collection of nobles before Costos.

"I'll go alone." I left him standing.

The Hundred watched me go, some puzzled, some curious, some with the name "Pius" on their lips.

I halted in the doorway. Costos's supporters stood before me in a loose arc, confident, knowing exactly how these matters worked.

"You've come alone?" Costos made his displeasure clear and loud.

"I felt it best," I said. "Close the door." And a hand span behind me the steel door slid down without a sound.

It took several seconds for any of them to find their voice. "What's the meaning of this?" King Peren of Ugal recovered first, shock still muting the others.

"You wanted privacy? No?" I walked toward them. Several backed away, without knowing why—the instinct that removes the sheep from the wolf's path.

"But how . . . ?" Costos waved a meaty fist at the sheet of steel behind me.

I let the Orlanth rod of office slide from my sleeve, catching it around the end before it escaped me. In the same motion I swung at Costos. To say his head exploded would be no exaggeration. I have seen close up, frozen in time, the damage that a bullet does in passing through a man's skull. In the bright arc of blood behind the sweep of my rod the same pieces glistened. I had killed King Peren before the first drop of Costos's blood hit the floor.

Two more men went down with cracked heads before the others scattered out of reach. Old men both, and slow. I had started with Costos as the greatest danger, but others amongst the eleven remaining had their health about them, and many of the Hundred have taken what they hold by strength of arm.

"This is madness!"

"He's crazed."

"Pull together. He's trapped in here with us." This from Onnal, one of Costos's advisors and a warrior born.

So much in life is a matter of perspective. "I rather think you're trapped in here with me," I told them.

Tutor Lundist taught me to fight with a stick. He had several good arguments for pursuing the study. Firstly there are many times when you may find yourself without a sword, but a good stick is rarely hard to find. Secondly he proved to be extraordinarily good at it. I don't normally ascribe the old man base motives, but everyone likes to show off, and how many people who've known me awhile wouldn't relish giving me a good beating with a piece of timber?

"The last and main reason," he had said, "is to instil discipline. Your sword lessons may come to that in time, but for now I see few signs. To be a Ling stick-fighter requires a harmony of mind and body."

I lay back at the side of the Lectern Courtyard, finding my breath and nursing my bruises. "Who taught you, Tutor? How did you get to be so good?"

"Again!" And he advanced, his ash rod a blur in the air.

I rolled one way then the other, failing to avoid either blow. "Ow!" Tried to block and got my fingers mashed. "Ouch!" Tried to rise and found the blunt end of his stick below my Adam's apple.

"I learned from masters in Ling, in the court where my father tutored princelings. My brother Luntar and I trained together for many years. These are the teachings of Lee, saved from before the Thousand Suns in vaults beneath Pekin City.

I took the stance, folded the iron-wood rod beneath my elbow, and beckoned Onnal forward, just a flexing of the fingers, as Lundist had beckoned me so many times.

51

Chella's story

Thantos walked Kai's body away from the newly dead guards between the empire gates. It seemed foolishness to Chella to have built such gates and to have them stand open. If they were not closed now when were they ever closed?

The corpses began to stand, awkward, jerky, drawn by invisible strings, occupied now by only the basest instincts of the men who owned them, housing only their sins. The lichkin spent his power with reckless disregard, but the Dead King had commanded it and so it would be.

"Hold the gate," Chella said, her voice soft.

Thantos turned to stare, his gaze like the touch of sudden grief, of inconsolable, intolerable loss. The creature made her feel that she had lost her child just by looking at her. What would it be to have it riding within your flesh?

Kai collapsed as Thantos flowed out, released in a single breath, red-tinged. Within an instant the lichkin was everywhere, insinuated into the shadows of the grand entrance, haunting the empty spaces. It would take the bravest of men to walk in from the failing light of day outside. It would take more than bravery for them to walk out again. At least alive.

Chella removed the thong from around her neck. The black vial depending from it had hung above her heart half the journey, nestled spider-like through long hours on the road, bounced there when Jorg of Ancrath had her. She hurried to Kai's side and dribbled the contents into his mouth while he retched and stared unseeing. The vial held ichor from a lead-lined tomb. An agent of the Dead King had ridden hard to bring it to her on the road catching up with the column somewhere close to Tyrol. Three horses died under the man between Crath City and Tyrol. He didn't tell her which tomb had been desecrated. But Chella knew.

"You should have learned to fly. You could have taken that pretty nothing with you, Kai." She spat the words and tried to hate him.

The Dead King's brew worked fast. Kai stopped choking. Knowing came back into his eyes. The thing that had last looked at Chella out of Artur Elgin now watched her from inside Kai. Though he might seize almost any corpse, the Dead King could not exercise his full might through them. It took time for him to settle into a dead man and strengthen him sufficiently to be a conduit for the terrors at his command. A necromancer, however, suitably prepared, provided a more robust host. And the contents of the vial accelerated the process beyond measure.

"This is the palace?" He sat up.

When you're among lichkin you can imagine nothing worse. The Dead King is worse. Chella tried to speak but words wouldn't come from her dry mouth.

The Dead King ignored her silence. Instead he flexed Kai's limbs, clenched his fingers into fists, and drew his face into a death's head grin. "This is good. Very good." He got to his feet. "I'm here in my power. Death in life." Again the smile, a sudden and unholy joy behind it. "More! More than my power!" His voice hardly raised but it hurt her ears even so. "I am remade. I have my foundation once again. I am more."

All around her the dead quickened. The guards' still hearts beat with swift corruption, no longer the shambling things they had been when first returned but darker, stronger makings like the quick dead of the Cantanlona swamp. Her work of months there accomplished here in seconds by her master's will.

For a moment the Dead King's exultation rang through her. The power bleeding off him thrilled and terrified. But the joy ran from him quicker than it came, leaving only grim purpose.

"Lead on." The Dead King stood. "They're all inside I take it?"

Chella nodded. The horror hung around him, a sense of hurt and loss, betrayal of all things precious. She had never seen him commit an atrocity, never heard of any deed more wicked than the destruction of those who opposed him, and yet she knew without question he was the worst of them.

"Now." The word hurt her. She obeyed without hesitation this time, leading through the vast and open gates, the Dead King behind her, and over two hundred dead men in their golden armour, bright-eyed and quick with the Dead King's hunger.

"It's time," the Dead King said through Kai's mouth. "To visit Congression. Kill the head and the body is ours. Mine."

52

"Open the door."

I stepped through quick as quick. "Close it." And the steel slammed down behind me.

The rulers of many nations crowded around me. I had found a replacement for my blooded cloak, cleaned the iron-wood rod and hidden it up the length of my sleeve, wrist to shoulder. I stood ready to answer their questions.

"Where is Costos Portico?"

"What happened in there?"

"How are the doors working?"

Dozens more, all together, in shades from angry through indignant and down into fearful.

"Lights on me." And high above us the constellation of Builder-lights grew dim, save for a tight and brilliant grouping that lit the space about me.

That shut them up.

I walked toward the middle of the chamber and the light followed me, the point of illumination moving across ceiling and floor. In the shadows before the dais Gorgoth crouched, fingers to the stone flagstones. Two quick bounds took me up the dais steps and I sat upon the throne, letting the rod of office slip free and setting it across my lap.

It was the sitting down that broke the spell. An angry clamour rose among them. These were, after all, rulers of nations.

"Costos is dead," I said and the Hundred fell silent to hear me. "His vote passes to his advisors. His advisors are dead. His banner-men also."

"Murderer!" Czar Moljon, still clutching his broken finger.

"Many times over," I agreed. "But the events in the Roman room are a mystery that none of you observed, that passed unseen by the guard. There will of course be an inquiry, I may be charged, an imperial court may be convened. These however are matters for another day. This is Congression, gentlemen, and we have matters of state to decide."

"How dare you sit in Adam's chair?" A white-haired king from the east.

"No law denies me," I said. "And I was tired. In any event it was Honorous's chair last and if any wish to dispute my occupancy they may approach to discuss the matter." I set one hand upon the iron-wood rod. "Seating arrangements do not make emperors, gentlemen. That's what we're here to vote upon."

I beckoned Taproot to me and leaned back in the throne, as uncomfortable a chair as I'd ever sat upon. Taproot climbed the steps quick enough, coming from the shadows into the light. I motioned him closer still.

"You've found out who my friends are and who my enemies are?" I asked.

"Jorg! You've given me no time. I've hardly started to mingle. I—" The silk of his doublet flapped around him.

"But you have, haven't you? You knew already."

"I know some of them, watch me!" He nodded, a sharp grin, quick then gone. No one is immune to flattery.

"Then get out there and have Makin, Marten, Kent, and Rike stand close to four of them who wish me ill. Gorgoth too, if he will. Tell him everyone is going to die if I don't get to be emperor. Those words."

"Everyone? The whole of Congression? Jorg! Excess is no—"

"Everyone everywhere," I said. "Just tell him."

"Everywhere?" His hands fell still for a moment.

"The lights will go off in a short while. Tell my brothers to be ready. When the light returns those men need to be dead. Have another set of names ready and then another. If I have to I will vote myself emperor."

And Taproot left the dais faster than he came.

"You're listening to me, aren't you, Fexler?"

No reply.

"The Dead King is coming." I didn't know how I knew, but I knew. "And he'll bring the world to ruin. Starting here." I turned the rod over in my hands. Over and over. "And to stop him—that would take such a force, such an act of magic, of will, that it would spin that wheel of yours and set the world cracking apart . . . and if that happens . . . Michael gets his way and you machines burn us all."

A faint pulse in the light.

"I would be right to guess that somewhere beneath me is an enormous bomb, would I?"

Again, the quiver in the light.

I leaned back into my uncomfortable throne and twirled the iron-wood like a baton. Likely I would be the shortest-reigning emperor in history. Out amongst the Hundred, Miana watched me. The man beside her, portly with grey sideburns and my son in his arms, was my father-in-law, Lord of Wennith. He didn't seem to be the man he was six years ago, but then who among us is?

A lord of middling years in brown suede and gold chains had been trying to catch my eye at the foot of the dais, and now moved on through coughing to raising his hand.

"Yes, Lord . . . ?"

"Antas of Andaluth." His realm bordered Orlanth to the south. "I have matters to discuss, King Jorg. The rights to the River Parl . . ."

"Would that secure your support, Lord Antas?"

"Well, I hesitate to put it so bluntly . . ."

"The rights to the Cathun River purchased absolution for the death of my mother, and of my brother, William. Did you know that, Lord Antas?"

"Why, no . . ."

"Do you not think some things are beyond purchase, Antas? Vote for me if you believe the empire needs me on the throne. The fate of a hundred nations shouldn't tip on river rights, horse trading, and back scratching."

He frowned at that. Red Kent stood behind him and just a little to the left. I guessed that Antas's support had never been going to be mine however many rivers we agreed over.

"Lights out," I said, and the throne room plunged into darkness.

I made a slow count to ten beneath the uproar. "Lights on!"

Antas sprawled at the base of the dais, neck broken. Kent had already moved on.

I stood up from the throne and the lights shone more brightly so I felt their heat upon me. It had to be now.

"Men of empire!" I raised my voice to reach the edges of the great hall, so even the Silent Sister, the Queen of the Red and Katherine could hear beyond the Gilden Gate.

All of them stopped to watch me, even with the murdered lying at their feet.

"Men of empire. A better man than I would have won your support with the goodness of his deeds, the clarity of his vision, the truth of his words. But that better man is not here. That better man would fail before the dark tide that rushes toward us. Orrin of Arrow was the better man and yet he didn't survive even to ask your support.

"Dark times call for dark choices. Choose me."

I walked the perimeter of the dais in measured steps, staring out across the shadowed heads of state. "There is an enemy at our gates. Even now. As we spend our words here, the Lord Commander spends the blood of better men to hold his city. This holy city at the heart of our broken empire. This holy city *is* the heart of our empire. And if you men, you servants of that empire, do not remake the ancient pact, if you do not set upon this throne a single man to carry the responsibility for all our peoples, then that heart will be cut out.

"You can feel it, can you not, my lords? It doesn't take the taint that the Gilden Gate keeps out for you to sense what approaches. It has festered in your kingdoms. The dead rising, the old laws being undone, magics spilling and spreading like contagion. Certainty has left us: the days smell of wrong.

"Do this now. Do it as one. For the man upon this throne will have to face what comes. And if there is no emperor there will be no one to stand against the tide. And tell me, in your heart of hearts, do you truly want to be that man?"

"Melodrama! How can you listen to this?" Czar Moljon, perhaps emboldened by his pain. "Besides, no vote will be cast for two days yet."

"Taproot." I waved him forward.

"The Congression must vote on its final day in a private ballot, but any candidate may force an early and open vote at any time, on the understanding that failure to win such a vote disbars them from future office." Taproot's hands made as to close a weighty tome, though he spoke from memory.

"Vote!" I said and the lights came up.

"The vote of Morrow for my grandson." My grandfather's voice rang out clear.

"And the holdings of Alba." My uncle beside him.

The women at the Gilden Gate drew away, a hurried motion.

"I stand with Jorg of Renar." Ibn Fayed raised his fist and the four Moorish warriors beside him followed his motion.

"Wennith for Jorg." Miana's father.

"And the north!" Sindri, somewhere behind me. "Maladon, Charland, Hagenfast."

"We stand with the burned king." White-haired twins, jarls from the ice-wastes in black furs and steel.

Gilden Guard appeared at the gate, a crowd of them. They advanced, and as each man passed through he collapsed, boneless. The clatter made the Hundred turn.

Perhaps half a dozen guards lay motionless on our side of the gate having made it no more than a yard or so within. Scores more stood almost as still, filling the antechamber beyond.

We all felt *him* approach. How could you not?

"Conaught for Jorg."

"Kennick for Jorg."

My advisors cast their allotted votes, from Arrow to Orlanth. Others followed, a sense of urgency on them now, as if we each heard *his* footsteps beneath the announcing.

And there he stood, framed in the Gilden Gate, a creature that wore Kai Summerson's skin and bones. I hoped Katherine had run and run fast.

"Hello." He smiled. Both the word and the smile unnatural things, dragged from somewhere a man would never want to look.

The Dead King approached the Gilden Gate, hands raised, palms out. It seemed he encountered a sheet of glass, for he stopped, fingers flat against the obstruction. He craned Kai's neck to one side, peering at us all as though we were rats in a trap.

"A clever gate," he said. "But it's only made of wood."

He stepped back and his dead guards approached with poleaxes to destroy the frame of the gate within the arch.

"Red March for Jorg." A stout grey woman bearing the vote for the Queen of Red's hereditary seat.

"The Thurtans for Jorg." The man buried in a horsehair robe, an iron crown on his brow.

And more, and still more.

"How do we stand, Taproot?" I asked.

"Thirty-seven out of the forty required."

Pieces of the Gilden Gate fell splintered to the ground. The Dead King's presence reached in and men fell to their knees in despair.

Even now more than half the votes held back, bound by years of prejudice and wrangling, Congression was a marketplace, to actually put an emperor on the throne, to end their own supremacy in those hundred kingdoms . . . many would rather die. But there are good deaths and there are bad deaths. The Dead King offered only the worse kind.

"Attar for Jorg."

"Conquence for Jorg." Hemmet's brother, giving away the Lord Commander's supremacy in Vyene.

The remains of the gate fell in.

"Scorron for Jorg." A stern old man, watching me with dislike.

I returned to the throne.

"Men of empire does Congression find me worthy?"

The "aye" that rang around the hall held more of desperation than enthusiasm, but it was sufficient. I sat emperor in Vyene, Lord of the Hundred—the Broken Empire remade.

Taproot came to my side, bowing close as the Dead King entered through the Gilden Arch, his troops behind him.

"Well done," I said to Taproot. "I didn't think we were anywhere near thirty-seven when I asked."

"Numbers never lie, my emperor." Taproot shook his head. "Only men."

The Hundred fell back before the Dead King, no man prepared to hold his ground.

"It does seem to have been a hollow victory, my emperor. Was it so important that you be confirmed to the throne before we all die?"

"We'll find out, shall we?" I stood once more, glad to be out of that seat. "I don't suppose you can seal the arch, Fexler?"

No response, just the continued flow of dead men into the throne room. The archway had always had the look of a later addition, something cut by masons with more poetry in their fingers.

The Dead King approached the dais, somehow a dark figure despite the sky-blue of Summerson's cloak. Behind him a golden wedge of the emperor's guard. My guard—Chella in their midst. And I stood my ground, upon the dais, before the throne, with the Hundred aligned behind me in their own wedge. Gorgoth joined me on the dais at my left shoulder, Makin at my right, Kent behind him, Marten behind Gorgoth, not a weapon between them. Sindri mounted the first step, Uncle Robert taking the same place on the far side. The guard who had watched over our Congression, a dozen men in total, stood with the Hundred, all save one who'd contrived to break his neck in the confusion and donate his sword to Rike.

I spared a glance for the men at my shoulders. I'd called them brothers on the road many a time, stood with them in the face of danger, shared meat and mead. A brotherhood of the road, sure enough, but a mean thing, men to die with rather than for. But in this place, before this enemy, who brought with him the certainty and song of death, who breathed a fear far worse than any I had felt upon the lichway when the ghosts came many years before, in this place it seemed that the men who stood with me were true brothers.

"Hello, Jorg." The Dead King looked up at me from the base of the dais.

His regard remained the same no matter whose eyes he watched me from. Somehow familiar, overburdened with accusation, a cold inspection that woke in me every sorrow I had known.

"Why are you here?" I asked.

"The same reason as you." He never looked away. "Because others said that I may not."

"*I* say that you may not," I told him.

"Will you stop me? Brother Jorg?" His tone light but with the most bitter undercurrent, as if the "brother" burned his tongue.

"Yes." Just the nearness of him took the strength from my arms. He carried death, bled it from every pore, his existence an insult to all things living.

"And how will you do that, Jorg?" He climbed the first step of the dais.

I swung at him by way of an answer, iron-wood blurring through the air. Stick met flesh with a wet thump. The Dead King closed Kai's hand about it, twisted the rod from my hand and smashed it into splinters on the edge of the second step.

"How will you stop me, Brother?" He climbed the second step. "You've no power. Nothing. An empty vessel. What little magic you ever held has long gone."

We stood face to face, close enough to reach out for each other's necks, though I knew how that would end.

"And what magic do you bring, I wonder?"

For he carried something more complex than necromancy, more than horror and the crude animation of dead flesh. The despair, the longing, and the loss that threatened to drown us all, that made the kings of nations cower and pale, that wasn't a weapon, not something made for us, but just an echo of what rang through him.

"Only truth, Brother Jorg," he said.

And with those words the bitter play of my life rose around me, Mother's music wrapping it but played too loud, a jarring discord of sour notes. I saw the moments strung out across years, cruelty, cowardice, vicious pride, a failure at every turn to be the man I could have been, a path through days littered with the wreckage of lives I lacked the courage to protect or repair.

"I've been a bad man?" I struggled to keep the weakness from my voice. "The king of dead things has waded through blood to tell me I have fallen short of sainthood? I thought you came here for battle? Put a sword in my hand and dance with me? Do—"

"You've been a coward, you failed at every turn to protect those you love." All his words fell like judgments, the weight of them crushing, though I sought to shrug them off with denial.

"You came for the empire throne, so why this obsession with my failings? If you think me weak, if you want the throne . . . try to take it."

"I came for you, Brother Jorg," he said. "For your family."

"Try." The word burned my throat, forced past a snarl. The bond to your child can form in an instant or grow by stealth, hook by hook, until you could no more stand aside than let go your skin. In that moment I knew I loved my son. That my father's strength had passed me by, and that I not only lacked the singularity of will to hold the empire throne but that I would die in the useless defence of a squalling infant too young to know I existed, rather than run to father more another day.

Without command, without battle cry, almost without sound the dead guard advanced, quick and open-handed, tearing the helms from their heads so that we could see the hunger in them.

Of the men at my shoulder only Gorgoth dropped back, retreating from the dais. If pressed to pick the man to run it would have been Makin or Kent. They had seen the quick dead in the Cantan-lona Marsh and knew the horror of them, the awful strength, the way they fought on though cut almost to offal.

"Run," the Dead King said. "I'll let you go. Just leave the child to me. Leave this little Wennith whore of yours."

The dead surged and Makin, Kent, and Marten went to meet them, passing to either side of the Dead King and me. Just moments left to us and I held nothing. Lights and doors. Empty hands. A few guards, finding their courage, sallied from the side entrances to attack their dead comrades. The first of the living fell to the dead with dismaying swiftness.

Something exploded from the floor around the dais. Somethings. In half a dozen places the flagstones shattered into sharp chunks and red blurs tore through the remains while they still hung in the air. It took long moments even to focus on the creatures as they ripped into the Dead King's troops. Trolls, but red of hide, akin to Gorgoth rather than their cousins beneath Halradra, and of larger build. The first of them picked up an armoured man and threw him over the heads of the legion behind to strike the wall above the Gilden Arch. Claws scythed through the next man's neck, mail links sheared away.

Descendants of the emperor's bodyguard, defending the throne. Six of them, terrible but too few.

I saw Kent snatch the sword of a fallen man just before another bore him to the ground. The dead swept round us, making the dais an island, cutting into the Hundred behind us.

"Run!" the Dead King said again. "They'll let you go."

"No."

"No? But isn't that what you're good at, Brother? Jorg? Aren't you well-versed in leaving the child to die while you run off to hide? Perhaps you could find another bush to cower in?"

"What— Who are you?" I stared into Kai Summerson's eyes, trying to see past them.

"You've left mother and son to die before, Jorg, slip away again. I won't tell." Acid on every word as though I'd done him some deep and personal hurt.

Somehow I had my hands on his throat, though I knew he didn't need to draw breath, though I knew he could snap my arms. "You know nothing of them, nothing!" I spun him around and he offered no resistance.

Over his shoulder Gorgoth, up against the wall, some small figure behind him, something dark in one hand, clutched against his chest. Two of the six trolls fought around him, an extravagance of violence, impossible speed, strength, skill, against impossible odds. Limbs, guts, armour, flying in crimson arcs, and still the dead rushed on. Gorgoth bent over his tiny burden, shielding it from the dead with his own body, crouching lower, lower, lost in the melee. Miana's white face now seen above his shoulder.

The Dead King smiled at me, a broken, ugly grin, my hands pale beneath his chin, the briar scars livid on wrist and forearm. The pain of those hooks burned again, and though a stone roof arched unbroken overhead it seemed that storm winds howled around me, that the rain lashed cold from black skies.

"In the end," I said, "there's no magic, only will."

I struck at the Dead King, focusing upon him every piece of my desire to see his destruction. I have lived a life driven by desire, the desire for revenge, for glory, to have what is denied me, a simple directive, pure and edged like a weapon. And such desire, such concentrated wanting, is the foundation of all magic—so the Builder told me.

Through narrowed slits I saw the Dead King's eyes grow wide, as if I really were choking him.

"You failed against Corion, Luntar dipped into your mind at will, even Sageous played you." He coughed the words past my hands, still twisting that smile. "And you think you can stop *me?*"

I could have told him I was older now. I could have said that I hadn't stood between those men and my son. But instead I answered, "Practised spells laid out in books work better than something laid out new. The runes and sigils used for centuries serve better than yesterday's invention. They're channels where men's will has cut paths through what is real. I'll beat you because a million stand behind me now. Because my desire to win now runs in the oldest channels." I told him because there's a power in the telling of a truth, and because reason has a keen edge.

"Belief? You've found God now?" He laughed, untroubled by the seal around his throat. "The will of the faithful won't serve you just because you killed the Pope, Jorg. It doesn't quite work like that."

"People can believe in other things, dead man," I told him. Screaming all around us, red hands clawing, rich men dying.

"There's nothing—"

"Empire," I said. "A million souls scattered across a vast and broken empire, praying for peace, praying for the day a new emperor will sit upon the throne. And it's me."

I struck again. Emperor in the heart of empire, unbroken. And the Dead King staggered, weakened, trapped in flesh.

"I came for revenge," the Dead King said, though I'd no idea what revenge he spoke of. "To show you what I'd made of myself after you abandoned me. And look what I have wrought!" Careless of my grip he spread his hands wide, to encompass the golden horde seething around us. "I brought you the kingdom of the dead. Let me join with you, Brother. Let me lead our armies, and I will take the empire out past all boundaries, in this world and in the next, and make it whole, entire, and ours. Set aside these friends, this unchosen wife—" He glanced toward Miana.

I struck then with every fibre of my will. I struck with the strength of empire, with the strength of a million, in that holy place, the very heart of empire, where the might and majesty of emperors past and the faith of generations had scored the paths of my power into the fabric of reality. A wind howled around us, cold and swirling, Kai Summerson fighting for release, deep within his own body, for whilst the holy may fail in any moment, the damned may in any moment reach for redemption. The gale spoke and the Dead King fought back.

My will met that of the Dead King, neither of us with the slightest give in us. The vast and sleeping mind of empire behind me, lost hopes, broken dreams, all pushing, all pressing. The deadlands behind him, the desolation of lives ended, the need, the thirst to return. Impossible pressures built, and built, and built again. I felt the wheel turn, the fabric of everything and everytime start to tear. And in that instant I knew who stood before me.

In that second Kai Summerson learned to fly. He took the Dead King's feet from the ground and the wind scoured the empty inches beneath them. A small victory but one that held my enemy prone.

One hard, cold instant and I knew who hung in my grasp, and even then, with William weak before me, vulnerable, open, even knowing that I traced my father's path almost to the letter . . . I stabbed him.

I let slip a hand from his throat, took Kai's knife from his belt, and drove it deep into his heart, the metal grating across ribs.

A single disbelieving laugh burst crimson from his lips, and then he fell, as if the knife had cut all his strings.

I released him and he fell, arms flailing, blood flooding from his chest. He fell and it took an age. My own brother. William, who I had failed in the thorns. Who I failed now. Whose death had cracked my life. Thorns held me once more. I couldn't catch him as he dropped. Kai's corpse hit the floor with the sound of ending, William already gone from him, back into the deadlands from where he had watched me for so many years, from so many dead eyes.

Luntar's paper fluttered from my sleeve. I picked it up as the dead guards toppled, in scores, then hundreds, all around the room.

"You can save him." Four words. The future-sworn see less than they think. I had stabbed my brother.

"I don't understand." Makin shouldered a corpse off him, rivulets of dark blood across half his face in three parallel lines. He spoke into the speechless moment. "How did you kill him?"

"I watched him die." I muttered the words. "I stayed hidden and let them kill him."

Makin half-climbed, half-crawled, to me.

"What?" He set a hand to my wrist, stilling the tremble in the dripping dagger. I let the blade fall.

"I didn't kill him. He was already dead. He died eleven years ago."

Marten came from behind, shoulder laid open to the bone, an ear missing. He took the paper from me, awkward in trembling fingers. "Save who?"

"My brother, William. The Dead King. Always quicker, more clever, stronger-willed. And yet it never occurred to me that death wouldn't be able to hold him."

"Death isn't what it used to be." Perhaps the wisest words ever to come from Red Kent's lips. He lay dying among the dead, among the foe he had laid low, so torn there could be only minutes left to him. Makin went to his side.

"Miana!" As I shouted it I knew a hint of the pain I would feel were she not to answer. Fewer than half the Hundred still survived, many fewer. I saw no sign of Sindri, of my grandfather or uncle. Ibn Fayed I saw. At least I saw his head.

"Here." And I found her, almost pinned to the wall behind Gorgoth's bulk. The red trolls lay broken in the carnage. Gorgoth unfolded, dripping and ripped. In one hand he held my son against his chest.

Something struck through me, seeing my child, there in that moment. Something sharper than edges. A certainty. The knowing that my father had failed to mould me in his image. I loved that baby, small and bloodied and ugly as he was. The denial had run from me. And with that knowing came another: the certainty that I could only ever hurt him. That the taint of my father would drip from my fingers unbidden and make another monster of my son.

I staggered back and fell into my throne. An autumn leaf swirled around my feet, brought in with the dead. A single maple leaf, scarlet with the season's sin. A sign. In that moment I knew myself too full of poison to do anything but drop. The fall had come for me. With numb fingers I undid the straps on my breastplate.

"Still . . ." Marten shook his head and crouched beside Kai. "A child. A boy. What was he? Ten?"

"Seven."

"A boy of seven. Lost in the deadlands. Fought his way out? Became king?" With each question he shook his head. I could see the possibilities bubbling inside him.

You can save him. Luntar's words. A man who saw the future.

"I'll bet he gave them hell." A grim smile tugged at me. I wondered if that same angel, the one that came to me past death's doorstep, had visited little William. I wondered what short shrift he gave her. "I'll bet he took the hardest path." Like the Conaught spear, William would have hauled himself deeper, aimed for the heart of darkness, found the lichkin. The rest lay beyond my imagining.

Kai sprawled, shattered and empty, William gone, the dead fallen, only Chella standing amid the gleam of their armour. My enemies defeated, and yet the sorrow remained, keener, more true, more clean, for I had always owned it. It echoed back to the thorns, the tone of a bell resounding through the years. We're fashioned by our sorrows— not by joy—they are the undercurrent, the refrain. Joy is fleeting.

"I let the thorns hold me, and a crack has run through all my days, deeper than the feelings it divides." The calligraphy of those scars lay writ across me still, white upon my flesh. "To everything there is a season." I spoke Ecclesiasticus. "A time to be born. A time to die."

"He will return: you can't destroy him." Chella from the heaped corpses, her former troops. She sounded neither happy nor sad. More lost.

"I don't want to destroy him," I said. "He's my brother. It was given to me to save him." I knew what to do. I had always known. I set a hand to the throne. "I hadn't known how bitter-sweet this would taste." Across the hall my son cried in his mother's arms, both of them beautiful. My brother would always return and my boy would never be safe, for our pain had become a wheel and the world lay broken. My brother, my son, my fault.

A tear made its slow passage across my cheek.

I stood somehow, though the strength had gone from me. And joined Makin, standing above him as he knelt with Kent. Marten at my shoulder. Rike came across, bloodied but whole, a gold chain decorated in diamonds and gore hanging from one fist, almost an afterthought.

"I don't want to destroy him," I said. "I want to save him. I should have saved him back when the thorns held me. Nothing has been right since then." Fear shook me, sudden, fierce, fear of what I had to do, fear that I hadn't the courage.

"No." Marten behind me. Marten would always be the first to understand. Marten who failed his son, who let his boy die. There are no rights and wrongs in such matters. Only wrongs. "Don't." The word choked him.

"Death isn't—" And Red Kent died amid the circle of his brothers who did love him each in our way. "Isn't what it was," I finished for him.

Chella stepped closer. No one moved to stop her. "He's gone where you can't follow, Jorg."

"You can't." Marten's voice thick with knowing.

"Even now they tell me 'can't,' Makin," I said, half in sadness, half in the joy of ending. The bitter and the sweet. "They tell me 'no' and think there must be something I won't sacrifice to get what I want." What I need.

Makin looked up at that, confused but understanding we none of us were speaking of Kent. He struggled to rise and that's when I hit him. A man like Makin you have to catch off-balance. I struck him hard enough to break my hand, and did. He fell boneless, one arm flopping out almost to Chella's feet.

"What?" Rike took his gaze from Brother Kent, amazed.

"He would have tried to stop me. Tell him he's to be steward. An order, not a choice." I cradled my hand, let the pain sharpen away sorrow. "He would have tried to stop me. Even with his little girl gone all these years, he wouldn't understand. Not Makin."

"Fuck Makin. I don't understand." Rike bristled, the sword in his fist still dripping.

Movement at the Gilden Arch. Katherine, a sword clutched across her, unsteady.

"Rike, glorious Rike! I knew I kept you around for a reason, Brother." I pulled the breastplate from me and opened my arms. "Do it."

"What?" He stared as though I were mad.

"I need to follow him, Rike. I need to find my brother."

"I—"

"Kill me. You've threatened it often enough. Now I'm asking."

Rike just stared, eyes wide and bright. Behind him Katherine had started to run toward us, shouting, begging me to stop or urging me on—I couldn't tell.

"I'm your fecking emperor. I command you."

"I—" And the big idiot looked at his sword as if it were a foreign thing. "No." And dropped it.

And that's when Chella stabbed me. My brother's knife, taken from his corpse, stuck near enough into the wound that father gave me. She went one better though, and twisted the blade. Our final kiss.

"Go to hell, Jorg Ancrath." The last words I ever heard.

53

On the road my brothers spoke of death many a time. The stranger who walked with us. But more than they talked of death they talked of dying, and often the business of avoiding it. Brother Burlow would speak of the light. The light that came to a man lying in his blood, when more of it lay out than in.

"I've heard men say it starts so faint, like a dawn, Brothers. And you look and you find yourself in the tunnel that's your life, that you've walked in darkness all your years."

Burlow was a reader, you understand. It doesn't pay to trust a lettered man on the road, Brothers, their heads are full of other men's ideas.

"But don't look into that light," he said. "For sweet as it might be, there's no coming back from there, and it will draw you in, yes it will. I've sat by too many men, laid broken on the verge, and heard them whisper about that light through dry lips. They none of them walked the road again."

At least that's how Fat Burlow had it. And maybe his light was sweet, Brothers. But I've looked into that light and it comes at first as a cold star in the dark of night. Closer and more close it draws, or you are drawn—these things are equal in a place without time—and you come to know it for what it is. A white hunger, Brothers, the incinerating incandescence of the furnace mouth, ready to consume you utterly.

That light took me in and it spat me out, far from the world.

I thought I knew death. I thought it dry. But the death I fell into was an ocean, cold and infinite and the colour of forever. And I hung there, without time, or up, or down. Waiting, always waiting, for an angel.

This death fell wet upon me.

I spat the water from a dry mouth. A cry escaped me and the pain came again, too deep to be endured. Lightning flashed and the thorns and coils of the briar made sharp black shapes against the sky. The rain lashed cold, and I hung in its embrace, unable to fall.

"The thorns." My senses had left me for a moment.

A second crack of lightning, across the rolling thunder of the previous stroke. The carriage lay beside the road, figures moving all about it.

"I'm in the thorns."

"You never left them, Jorg," she said.

She stood beside me, my angel, she of warmth and light and possibilities.

"I don't understand." The pain still lanced me, my flesh tenting crimson around a hundred barbs, but with her beside me it was only pain.

"You understand." Her voice nothing but love.

"My life was a dream?"

"All lives are dreams, Jorg."

"Was—was none of it real? I've been hanging in the thorns all my life?"

"All dreams are real, Jorg. Even this one."

"What—" My arm twitched and red agony flooded me. I found my breath again. "What do you want of me?"

"I want to save you," she said. "Come." And she offered me her hand. A hand in which colour moved like the faintly shadowed skin on molten silver. To take that hand would end all pain. She offered me salvation. Maybe that was all salvation had ever been. An open hand waiting to be taken.

"I bet my brother told you to go to hell," I said.

Lightning struck once more and there was no angel, just a Renar soldier carrying William by the ankles like a hunter's kill. Carrying him toward that milestone, carrying him to dash his head open.

Nature shaped the claw to trap, and the tooth to kill, but the thorn . . . the thorn's only purpose is to hurt. The thorns of the hook-briar are like to find the bone. They do not come out easy. If you make a stone of your mind, if you thrash and tear, if you break and pull and bite, if you do these things you will leave the briar for it cannot hold a man who does not wish to be held. You will escape. Not all of you, but enough to crawl. And crawling, I left the briar. And reached my brother.

We died together. As we always should have.

A cold stone hall. Echoing. The ceiling black with smoke. Whimpers of pain. Not human pain, but familiar nonetheless.

"One more," Father said. "He has a leg left to stand on, does he not, Sir Reilly?"

And for once Sir Reilly would not answer his king.

"One more, Jorg."

I looked at Justice, broken and licking the tears and snot from my hand. "No."

And with that Father took the torch and tossed it into the cart.

I rolled back from the sudden bloom of flame. Whatever my heart told me to do, my body remembered the lesson of the poker and would not let me stay. The howling from the cart made all that had gone before seem as nothing. I call it howling but it was screaming. Man, dog, horse. With enough hurt we all sound the same.

I looked into the flame and found it that same incinerating incandescence which had waited for me at the end of my tunnel, blind, white hunger, blind, white pain. Flesh knows what it wants and will refuse the fire whatever you have to say about the matter.

But sometimes flesh must be told.

"I."

I couldn't do it, Brothers.

"Can't."

Have you ever dared a jump, perhaps from some untold height into clear waters and found that at the very edge you simply cannot? Have you hung from four fingers above an empty span of yards, hung by three fingers and by two, and known in that moment that you can't drop? While any grip remains, your flesh will save itself in the face of all odds.

The heat of that fire. The fierceness of the blaze. And Justice twisting in its heart, screaming. I couldn't do it.

I could not.

And then I could. I leapt. I let myself drop. I held my dog. I burned.

A dark sky, a tugging wind. It could be anywhere or any when, and yet I knew I had never been here.

"You found me, then?"

William, seven years to him, golden curls, soft child's flesh, Justice curled at his feet. The old hound lifted his head at the scent of me, his tail beating once, twice against the ground. "Down, boy." William set his hand between those long ears.

"I found you." We shared a smile.

"I can't get in." He waved at the golden gates towering behind us.

I walked across and set a hand to them. The warmth filled me with promises. I pulled away.

"Heaven is over-rated, Will."

He shrugged and patted our dog.

"Besides," I said. "It's not real. It's a thing we've made. A thing that men have built without knowing it, a place made out of expectation and hope."

"It's not real?" He blinked at that.

"No. Nor the angel. Not a lie, but not real either. A dream dreamt by good men, if you like."

"So what is death, really?" he asked. "I think I have a right to know. I've been dead for years. And here you are, five minutes in, knowing it all. What is real if it's not this?"

I had to grin at that. The older brother all over.

"I don't know what real really is," I said. "But it's deeper than this." I waved at the golden gates. "Fundamental. Pure. And it's what we need. And if there's a heaven it's better than this and requires no gates. Shall we find out?"

"Why?" Will lay back, still scratching between Justice's ears.

"Did you see your nephew?" I asked.

Will nodded, hiding a shy smile.

"If we don't do this, he's going to burn. Him and everyone else. And it will get pretty crowded around here. So help me find it." No half measures. No compromise. Save them all, or none.

"Find what?"

"A wheel. That's how Fexler thought of it. And expectations seem to matter here."

"Oh, that?" Will hid a yawn and pointed.

The wheel stood on a hilltop, black against a mauve sky, horizontal on a raised shaft that sunk down into the stone. We walked across to it. The sky lightening above us, fractures spreading across it through which a whiter light bled.

From the hilltop we could look down over the dry lands, sloping away into darkness.

"I'm sorry I left you, Will."

"You didn't leave me, Brother," he said, shaking away some fragment of a dream.

I put both hands to the wheel, cold steel, gleaming. Builder-made. Builder-steel. "We need to turn this back and lock it off. It will take both of us to do it." I hoped I had the strength. My arms looked strong, smooth and corded with muscle. For some reason that smoothness surprised me, as if there should be something written there, old scars perhaps. Had there been scars once? But that was the past and I had let it go. It had let me go. "We need to turn it."

"If anyone knows how to push, it's us." Will set his hands to the steel. "Can this save them?"

"I think so. I think it can save them all. All the children. Even the dead ones. Even Marten's son, Gog, Degran, Makin's daughter, let loose from the dreams of men and given over to whatever was made for them.

"At the very least the Builders' machines won't scorch everyone we ever knew from the face of the Earth."

"Sounds good enough."

And so we strained to turn the wheel.

There was no wheel of course, no golden gates, no hill, no dry lands. Just two brothers trying to right a wrong.

54

And we must assume I succeeded. We are, after all, still here. I'm writing this journal, rather than being poisoned dust blowing on a sterile wind. And the magic that joined us at the last, that let me see beyond death with his eyes, that magic is ended. All magic is ended, cut off at the source, the wheel turned, the old reality from which we strayed so long, restored again.

I set the words here in Afrique-ink, dark as the secrets they ground up to make it. My hand traces its path across the whiteness of the page and the black trail of my days can be followed. Followed from the day I shook that snow globe, and understood that sometimes the only change to matter must be worked from without. Followed from that day to this day—this day that woke with the morning sun over Vyene, with the blue Danoob flowing silent and swift through the heart of the Unbroken Empire.

Little Will runs into the room. He comes often now, though his mother tells him not to.

"Jorg!" he says, and I appear.

"Yes."

"You're not my daddy. Marten says so."

"I'm a memory of him. And men are made of memories, Will." It's the best I have to tell him.

"Uncle Rike says you're a ghost."

"Uncle Rike is something that fell from a horse's backside, crudely fashioned into the shape of an ugly man," I say.

Will giggles at that. Then serious, "But you're white like a ghost. Nana Wennith says you can see through ghosts and I can see—"

"Yes, my emperor," I say. "I am a ghost. A data-ghost, an extrapolation, a compilation. A billion moments captured. Your father lived much of his life in a building made a thousand years ago."

"The Tall Castle." He smiles. "I've been there!"

"A building with many ancient eyes and many ancient ears. And in later life he carried a special ring. He watched through it, and it watched him. A man . . . a ghost, called Fexler, needed to understand your father, needed to know if he could be trusted to save the world."

"He wanted to know if he was good enough," Will says.

I hesitate and hide my smile. "He wanted to know if Jorg was the right man. So he did what machines do when they have a complicated question to answer. He built a model. And that model is me."

"I wish I had my real father," Will says. He is only six. Tact may yet arrive.

"I wish you did too, Will," I say. "I'm only an echo and I feel only an echo of the love he would have had for you. But it's a very loud echo."

He smiles and I know then that not all magic is gone from the world. The kind that burns—that has gone. Men will no longer fly, or cheat death of its due. But a deeper, older, and more subtle enchantment persists. The kind that both breaks and mends hearts and has always run through the marrow of the world. The good kind.

Will grins again and runs out of the room. Small boys have little patience. I watch the doorway through which he ran, and wonder what might come through it next. I could predict, of course. I could build a model. But where would the fun be in that now?

One thing I do know is that it won't be Jorg of Ancrath who walks in through that doorway. Men are supposed to be scared of ghosts, not ghosts of men. A man may fear his own shadow, but here is a pale shadow that fears the man who cast him. Jorg of Ancrath will not return though. The magic has been shut off, enchantment has run from the world. Death is, once again, what it was.

I watch the door but no one comes. I make Miana sad. She spends her time watching the young emperor grow. Katherine thinks me a nothing, just numbers trying to count themselves, trying to measure a man who was beyond measures, perhaps beyond her dreams even. I watch the door then give up. Fexler will watch it for me. He watches them all.

Instead I sink down into the deep and endless seas of the Builders. Wheels within wheels, worlds within worlds, possibilities without end.

All of us have our lives. All of us our moment, or day, or year. And Jorg of Ancrath assuredly had his, and it has been my place to tell it.

He has gone beyond me now though, and I have no more to say. Perhaps somewhere Jorg and his brother have found the real heaven and are busy giving them hell. It pleases me to think so.

But the story is done.

Finis

AN AFTERTHOUGHT

If you've got this far, then you will have read three books and several hundred thousand words on the life and times of Jorg Ancrath. It will now be apparent that you're not going to be reading any more—and you might, with some justification, wonder why I have chosen to shoot what could well have been a cash cow squarely between the eyes.

The easiest and best answer is that the story demanded it. I acknowledge that I could have told the story to go jump off a bridge and turned events in a direction that allowed me to produce a book four, a book five, six, etc. In years to come when I'm eating cat food cold from the tin, I may wish that I had. The truth is, though, that I wanted you to part company with Jorg on a high. I would rather readers finish book three wanting more than wander away after book six feeling they have had more than enough. There is a tendency for characters who march on past their sell-by date to become caricatures of themselves—to tread the same ground, growing more stale with each step. I hope Jorg avoided that fate and that together we've built something of worth.

I also very much hope you'll buy my next book!